"I'd kiss you good night, but we have an audience."

Glancing over her shoulder toward the house, she caught just a glimpse of Ben's mother before the blinds at the living room window settled. Looking back at Ben, Avi smiled. "Kiss me anyway."

He closed the last of the distance between them, lowering his mouth to hers, giving her a sweet, gentle, tender kiss that set her blood on fire. It was impressive and surprising and just a bit scary, considering she'd had tons of kisses that led to passionate nights but none of them had evoked as strong a response in her.

When he lifted his head, her fingers curled, wanting to wrap around the back of his neck and pull him down again. Her heart skipped a beat or two, and something deep inside her felt deprived...

Acclaim for the Tallgrass Novels

A Love to Call Her Own

"Deeply satisfying...Pappano's characters are achingly real and flawed, and readers will commiserate with and root for the couple...This deeply moving tale will remind everyone who reads it of the great sacrifices made by those who serve and the families they leave behind."
—*Publishers Weekly* (**starred review**)

"A solid, tender plot, well-developed, vulnerable characters and smart, modern banter are the highlights of this heartwarming story."
—*RT Book Reviews*

A Man to Hold On To

"4 1/2 stars! Through her beautiful storytelling, Pappano deftly expresses the emotions that come with love and loss. The genuine love that grows between Therese and Keegan melts the heart. Pappano's latest packs a powerful punch."
—*RT Book Reviews*

"A powerful and welcome return to Tallgrass...Pappano excels at depicting deep emotion...including plenty of humor."
—*Publishers Weekly* (**starred review**)

A Hero to Come Home To

"Pappano shines in this poignant tale of love, loss, and learning to love again...[She] creates achingly real characters whose struggles will bring readers to tears."
—*Publishers Weekly* (starred review)

"Pappano's latest is a touching story about loss, love, and acceptance. Tender to the core, her story is filled with heartwarming characters who you can't help but fall in love with, and she tells their stories candidly and poignantly. The ending will simply melt your heart."
—*RT Book Reviews*

"A wonderful romance with real-life, real-time issues... [Pappano] writes with substance and does an excellent job of bringing the characters to life."
—*HarlequinJunkie.com*

"Poignant and engaging...Authentic details of army life and battle experience will glue readers to the page."
—*Library Journal*

ALSO BY MARILYN PAPPANO

A Promise
of Forever

by

Marilyn Pappano

FOREVER

NEW YORK   BOSTON

Forever
Hachette Book Group
1290 Avenue of the Americas
New York, NY 10104

www.HachetteBookGroup.com

Printed in the United States of America

First Edition: June 2015
10 9 8 7 6 5 4 3 2 1

OPM

Forever is an imprint of Grand Central Publishing.
The Forever name and logo are trademarks of Hachette Book Group, Inc.

The Hachette Speakers Bureau provides a wide range of authors for speaking events. To find out more, go to www.hachettespeakersbureau.com or call (866) 376-6591.

The publisher is not responsible for websites (or their content) that are not owned by the publisher.

For everyone who serves, whether in uniform or not, who sacrifices years of your life or hours of your time, who fights in a hostile land or keeps the home fires burning. For everyone who feels that rush of pride upon seeing our flag, that rush of gratitude upon seeing a member of our Armed Forces, and that rush of sorrow upon hearing of yet another American casualty, and for every one of you who prays *God bless America*, thank you.

History defines strong as having great physical power, as having moral or intellectual power, as striking or superior of its kind. But with all due respect to Webster, there's strong, and then there's Army Strong.

—U.S. Army

Courage is being afraid but going on anyhow.

—Dan Rather

A Promise
of Forever

Chapter 1

Fifteen minutes after retrieving her luggage from Tulsa International Airport, Avi Grant still sat in her rental car, doors locked, windows up, keys in her hand, the temperature inside climbing. Sweat broke out on her face and hands, inside her uniform and boots, and her stomach churned so wildly that a lesser woman would lean out an open door and heave her guts onto the sizzling pavement.

She breathed deeply, head back, and focused. She could do this. An image flashed into her mind: the colonel, her mentor. Another image: Frankie, from Massachusetts, loved baseball. Another: Camarena, married with two kids. Rebecca, who'd shared her quarters and tastes in music and chocolate. Ian, organizer of soccer games with plans to be a priest. Chatham, who joined the Army to escape his overbearing parents. Miller, whose wife got pregnant every time he finished a rotation. Chandra, who'd never met a man as good as her dog.

The sweat rolled, picking up tears at the corners of her eyes and continuing down her cheeks. Finally Avi swiped her sleeve across her face, then inserted the key in the ignition. She started the engine, rolled down the windows, and turned the AC to arctic blast. It took a moment longer to back out of the space and wend her way through the parking lot to the exit.

When the plane landed, she had looked out, thinking she could have been in any medium-size airport in any medium-size city, except for that clear blue Oklahoma sky. She swore its colors, in all its moods, weren't used in any other sky; she could recognize it with half a glance. The clarity today meant there was no ozone alert. The streaky clouds moving from east to west testified to the winds up high, but down here on earth, not so much as a breath of a breeze was blowing.

She had been back in the States ten days—not long enough to fully adjust to flying, driving, being alone. She followed road signs to I-244, vaguely taking note of the changes along the way. The freeways were wider, the overpasses still bumpy, the drive-in theater on the north side of the road a welcome replacement for the historic one that had burned down a few years earlier.

There were shortcuts she could have taken to get to her destination quicker, but she was in no rush. Her parents were out of town and wouldn't be back for a week. Mom had accused her of knowing that when she scheduled this trip, and Avi had lied and said of course not; would she do that? Then Mom had apologized, and Dad had taken the phone and said, "Of course you'd do that." She'd taken four weeks, her leave for an entire year. Was it too much to want the first week of it to herself?

Dad had been relieved that she wanted time alone. A thirty-five-year anniversary cruise wasn't the sort of thing you wanted to cancel at the last minute.

She circled around downtown Tulsa, then took 412 toward Sand Springs. It seemed everywhere she looked, she saw signs for Indian casinos. She'd taken enough gambles with her life. She had no interest in doing so with her money.

Though somebody has to win, a voice whispered. *Why shouldn't it be you?*

She recognized the voice as belonging to Ian of the soccer and priesthood. He'd had a great poker face, lying to them all even as he lay dying. *Don't worry. I'm gonna be okay.*

She squinted her eyes tightly and told herself it was because of the powerful August sun starting its afternoon slide. As she turned north again, she blinked away the few drops of moisture that spilled from her eyes.

As soon as she left town behind, the scenery gave way from houses to hills, rocks, and weaving roads. The trees were green, like much of the grass, but the dustiness that covered them spoke of a dry hot summer, as if Oklahoma had any other kind. She hoped there'd been enough rain the past few months to put on a lovely show in the fall.

The farther north she drove, the fewer trees, more grass dotted with small patches of wildflowers and occasional houses. Cattle and horses lazed in the sun; dogs dozed on porches. A squirrel darted across the road in front of her, chittering as if chastising her for disrupting his day.

This was real life out here: farmers, ranchers, housewives, commuters to jobs in the city. Normal life. What was her real life? Her time in Afghanistan was over for the moment, though the Army made no promises. She'd thought she'd seen the last of the desert four times before. She'd spent a lot of years in remote provinces that most Americans had never heard of until some of their fellow citizens died there. Even then, it was a million miles away. Nothing for most people to worry about. It didn't touch them, safe at home.

And people like Avi couldn't get away from it.

When mechanical horses' heads, pumping oil in small fields, began making more frequent appearances along with real-life horses' and cattle's and kids' heads, she drew a deep breath. Her destination, Tallgrass, had been founded over a hundred years ago to support the oil and ranching industries in the area. Growing up in Tulsa, she'd visited GrandMir and Popi in the town a hundred times, but she remembered few details about it.

On the other hand, she'd never forgotten a thing about GrandMir and Popi: their house, their business, her cooking, the strays Popi collected, their church, their neighbors, and how happy they were. She'd imagined the same kind of life for herself one day.

Until she'd met a handsome Army officer, tall and forbidding in his dress uniform but quick to break into a grin that made a ten-year-old girl feel like the most important thing in his world. The day she'd met then-Major George Sanderson, she'd changed her mind about being a professional traveler, a zoologist, and Speaker of the House when she grew up—any job with the word *speaker* in its title had sounded good to her—and decided to join the Army instead.

She'd done it, too, enlisting during her senior year in high school. She'd even gotten her dream duty assignment: serving under Colonel Sanderson on this last go-round in Afghanistan.

Where three months ago she had watched him die.

A green-and-white sign stated that she was entering Tallgrass city limits, and she gratefully refocused on her surroundings. Nothing looked familiar, with most of the buildings on this southern approach fewer than ten years old, while her last visit had been fifteen years ago for Grandmir's funeral. She hadn't expected to remember any of it, though. While waiting for her flight in Houston that morning, she had called up a map on the Internet and committed the directions to her parents' house and their nursery to memory.

Once she'd passed the nondescript buildings a person could find on the outskirts of any town, she had to admit that downtown Tallgrass could charm a person if she was in the mood. The buildings were constructed of brick faded to a rosy hue or of sandstone, its drab earth tones reminding her of the desert. None stood taller than three stories, hugging the ground, a smaller target for the nonstop winds that swept across the plains.

Avi made a right turn onto Main Street and drove 1.4 miles to Grant Plant Farm. For a moment, she was seven again, coming to work with GrandMir and Popi, running barefoot through the nursery, hair in pigtails, denim overalls just like Popi's, hearing his great big belly laugh and GrandMir shaking her head, saying, *Honestly, Ernest...*

They were gone now, buried side by side in the cemetery outside the little country church they'd attended all their lives.

Avi was only thirty. Too young to have lost so many people.

We're not lost, Avery, Popi would have said. *We've just gone home.*

With a deep breath, she shut off the engine and climbed out. Gravel crunched beneath her boots as she passed through the scant shade offered by the board sign that had stood there longer than she'd been alive. To the music of chimes and water tinkling in the distance, she walked inside the open-walled structure and removed her sunglasses, breathing deeply the scent of damp earth.

She'd lived in the dirt, worked in it, had it blown by fierce desert winds into places it shouldn't have gone, but she hadn't taken off her shoes and dug in it for pleasure since the last summer she'd spent here fifteen years ago. God, she'd missed it.

Customers stood in line at both registers, and water dripped from the irrigation system. Mom had said she would leave the keys with Linda, one of their longtime employees, and Avi looked around until she found her, white-haired, tanned skin, unsteady hands culling plants past their prime from a display.

"Linda? Hi. I'm—"

A brown gaze studied her an instant, then the wrinkled face relaxed and a welcoming smile softened it. "I know who you are, Avery Grant. You're the spittin' image of your grandma Mirabelle when she was your age."

The compliment pleased Avi, though she knew her

regular-average features didn't begin to compete with GrandMir's beauty. She smiled, *I'm flattered* on the tip of her tongue, but the woman didn't pause more than a few seconds.

"So you're finally home safe and sound. Though I guess this isn't really home since your mama and daddy moved here after you joined the Army. Still, it must be glorious to be back in Oklahoma. I bet some part of you started pining for this place five minutes after you left."

Not exactly. Avi had been living her dream, following in George's footsteps, busting her butt to get through Basic, going to Signal school, finding her stride in Army life. It hadn't been until her second deployment, maybe her third, when she'd found herself dreaming of plains, hills, and forests, oil wells and cowboys and Indians, tornados and droughts and floods, blistering summers, bone-chilling winters, sadly short autumns, and the most incredible spring season anywhere.

Linda had continued talking, her familiar accent soothing with the backdrop of water and sweet-scented flowers, but she interrupted herself as Avi tuned back in. "Here I am, chattering away, and I know you must be tired from your travels. Let me get the keys for you, and you can go home and get some rest. It's such a shame that Beth and Neil's cruise happened to be this week, but I know they're excited about getting back to see you."

Avi followed her to the office, tiny and crammed to bustin', Popi used to say. She remained outside and watched while Linda sorted through a desk that should have collapsed under the weight of the mess it held, coming up with a key ring. She handed it over with a triumphant gesture. "Here you go. Now, if you need anything, you call me, okay? I'm sure your mom left notes for you all over the place, telling you everything you could possibly want to know, but we're here if you have any questions at all."

"Thank you." Avi pocketed the keys and turned toward the nearest exit, but Linda stopped her with a hand on her arm.

"Thank you for your service, Avery."

Emotions rippled through her—gratitude, discomfort, sadness, guilt—but she managed a wobbly smile. "You're welcome."

A sweet smile tripled the wrinkles on Linda's face. "No, honey. *You're* welcome. Welcome home."

*   *   *

Smoke billowed up from the grill, carrying with it the amazing aroma of roasted chicken. The wind blew it toward the house on the west, then did a one-eighty and sent it rushing into the yard on the east, carrying its flavors long after the gray wisps had dissipated.

Ben Noble had a warm, sunny day, a garlic flavored chicken on the grill, a sweaty pitcher of tea within arm's reach, and a fresh supply of ice in the cooler beside him. What more could a man ask for?

Maybe someone besides his mother to share it with?

His gaze shifted to the house sitting small and tidy at the far side of the yard. It was Lucy Hart's house, occupied by Lucy—who liked him a lot—and Norton, her mutt, who didn't. Ben liked Lucy a lot, too, enough to date her for a month or so at the beginning of the summer.

Enough to agree with her, no matter how painfully, when she'd pointed out that as far as relationships went, they were great friends.

He had plenty of friends. He hadn't been looking for another—for anything at all, in fact—when he'd met her, but it hadn't taken long for ideas to pop into his head: a girlfriend, a woman to settle down with, to have kids and a future with. But Lucy had been right. They were very good friends, but it didn't go beyond that. There was no spark, no anticipation, no promise.

No magic, she'd said forlornly.

He really wished he could have been the one to give her back the magic her husband's death had taken.

Behind him the kitchen door closed, and his mother's voice filtered across the patio. "I'm leaving for the store now. Anything you want?"

He turned to face Patricia, wearing a skirt in light blue, a shirt that picked up the color in its floral pattern, and sandals, makeup on and her hair styled expensively casual. She always looked her best, even if her only destination was Walmart. It was one of the things, she said, that her late husband George had loved about her.

Funny. Her total lack of concern with her appearance— wild hair, flowy clothes, overload of shiny jewelry, and bare feet—had been one of the things Ben had loved about her back before she'd abandoned him and his sisters, along with his father, for George.

After two decades, he could hardly bear to hear the man's name or see the uniforms that were common in Tallgrass with an Army post in town.

His fingers tightened around his iced tea glass. "No, thanks. I'm good."

"The chicken will be fine on the grill if you want to go inside where it's cooler."

"Okay." He would go in in a while, but at the moment he was too comfortable to get up.

"All right then." Her smile wavered before regaining strength, a little gaily false now. "I'll be back soon."

She still hadn't quite figured out how to say good-bye, whether it was for an hour or until his next visit to Tallgrass. Neither had he. Twenty years of virtually no contact made that sort of thing hard to peg. He wished he could put all the blame on her—after all, she was the adult, the parent—but he was an adult now, too. What had happened in the past belonged in the past...but damned if that wasn't easier said than done. He would like to think he was mature enough to silence the fifteen-year-old boy who'd mourned his mother's disappearance and his father's death a few years later, but didn't everyone's childhood shape them into the person they were?

Not wanting to explore either his childhood or the person he'd become, he topped off the ice in his glass. The cooler was foam, cheap, meant for a summer's use, then disposal, but the scoop on top of the bag inside was sterling, engraved with an elaborate S. There was probably a matching bucket in the house, probably a wedding gift for Patricia and George. *Nice things are meant to be used,* she would say.

In the silence, a chime sounded distantly. Ben's first visit to the house had been immediately following George's death, when the doorbell had rung so often that he'd heard it in his dreams. He could ignore it now, but even as the thought formed, he was rising from the chair, heading inside.

The bell rang again before he reached the hallway, its tones fading as he opened the door. The woman standing on the porch looked...not surprised, exactly, but caught off guard, something that he would imagine didn't happen very often. She struck him as the essence of a long, hot summer, with a loose pink dress, a few strands of silky black hair escaping the braid that kept it off her neck, and flip-flops that showed off her slender feet and hot-pink nails. She was pretty and tanned and dark-eyed, and she looked as if she'd rather be anyplace else in the world than here.

"Is Mrs. Sanderson here?" Her voice was husky, a local drawl underlying influences picked up outside the state.

"Not at the moment." He hesitated, thought of his mother's welcoming manner versus his lack thereof, then went on. "I'm Ben, her son. Would you like to come in and wait for her? She should be back any time now."

Offering his name didn't earn him the same courtesy. She tucked a strand of hair into her braid, and it fell out again the instant her fingers moved away. Without much more than a few movements, he could see she was going to say no, that she would come back later. But even as her mouth opened to form the words, her gaze caught on something in the window, and she didn't say anything at all.

Ben didn't need to see to know she was looking at Patricia's Gold Star flag, a small banner presented to the parent or spouse of a service member killed during service. Lucy had a Gold Star flag. So did all her friends.

"I'm sorry. You didn't know about the colonel's death?"

She swallowed hard. "I knew. I just hadn't seen..."

Neither had Ben, beyond images in the media, until Patricia had received this one. It was a simple flag: a red border surrounding white, a gold star, gold fringe across the bottom, two small gold tassels at the top. And yet its narrow borders encompassed so much: Remembrance. Pride. Honor. Sacrifice. Acknowledgment. Heartbreak. Loss. The giving up of dreams.

Patricia felt all those things for the stepfather Ben had never known. He'd met George only three times, following his, Brianne's, and Sara's graduations from high school. How much could you learn about a man at lunch while he waited for a flight back to Germany? That he had a strong handshake. That he didn't assume marrying their mother made him part of their family. That he didn't expect a generous graduation gift to make up for Patricia's absences, though he gave it anyway.

The woman in front of him apparently *had* known the colonel, because she was controlling more grief than the three Nobles had scrounged up together. Ben stepped back and opened the door wider. "Come on in. I'm supposed to be keeping an eye on the grill until Patricia gets back."

She hesitated a moment then, with a deep breath, walked through the door and waited quietly. He locked up before leading the way back to the kitchen and gesturing out a large window. "Is it too hot for you outside?"

She shook her head, and he thought maybe the heat would restore a little color to her suddenly pale face.

He took a tall glass from a cabinet, then they walked out to the patio. She chose a seat halfway between him and the grill. He handed her tea before settling back into his own chair.

She breathed deeply, then murmured, "Smells good."

"No credit of mine. My mother's the grill master around here."

"I have a grill at home, but I can never get the igniter to work, and I'm not about to stick a match in there."

"Where's home?"

She hesitated before answering. "It's Georgia now. Augusta. I just moved there."

"And your name?"

Her fingers tapped against her glass. "Avi Grant." She said it with a soft *ah* at the beginning.

"Avi. That's different."

"It's not bad if you're an Israeli football player." She managed a bit of a smile, emphasizing how delicately pretty she was.

"I'm going to take a shot and say you've never been an Israeli football player."

"What gave it away?" she asked with another faint smile.

"Maybe the hot pink on your toes."

"Aw, you don't know what they're hiding inside those soccer shoes."

Definitely an Oklahoma girl who'd been away long enough to mute her accent, not get rid of it entirely. "You just visiting in Tallgrass?"

"Yes. I got in this afternoon. Spending some time with my mom and dad."

And yet one of the first things she did was drop in on someone else's mother. What kind of connection did she and Patricia have? Patricia had practically adopted Lucy and her neighbor, Joe Cadore, as if they were her own. Maybe Avi was another friend who'd made it easier for Patricia to do without her birth-given kids.

The thought stirred the old ache deep inside at how easily she'd left them. How she'd just turned off her need for them until she'd found herself alone again and grieving. They'd grieved more than half their lives for *her*, while she'd found other people to take their place.

That's not fair, Lucy sometimes told him when his resentment spilled out.

Kids didn't have to be fair when their families were ripped apart through no fault of theirs.

"Do you live here?" Avi asked.

His eye twitched as he forced the familiar emotions back into their dark corner. "No. Tulsa."

"What do you do there?"

"I'm a surgeon."

She raised her right hand, letting it swing loose at the wrist, and said, "Hey, Doc, it hurts when I do this."

"So don't do it." His smile was reluctant but formed anyway. Why not? His issues were with Patricia, not Avi Grant. "That joke's been around longer than you and me both."

"Good things last."

This time he flat-out laughed. "You may be one of three people in the world who think it's a good one." Joe Cadore would likely be one of the remaining two, since he seemed to like anything that set Ben on edge.

"Maybe your sense of humor needs a little nip-tuck work. Or maybe mine needs a little refinement." She took a long drink of tea, and he watched. On second inspection, she wasn't small and fragile-looking; in fact, she was close to his own height, with an air of substance about her. But in a way that had nothing to do with physicality, she *did* seem fragile. Even when she'd smiled, the look in her eyes was tinged with loss. Because of George?

"So what took you from Tallgrass to Augusta?"

Her gaze went a bit vague. "I've never actually lived here. My parents inherited my grandparents' business when I was in high school. They paid people to run it for them, then as soon as I graduated and took off, they retired and started their second careers."

Ben noticed that she'd neglected to answer his question, but the sound of tires in the driveway made him let it pass. Avi heard it a beat later, sitting impossibly straight in her chair, head erect, hands knotted tightly in her lap. Not quite the response he would have expected for a woman waiting to greet a friend.

Patricia came into sight around the corner of the house, her purse over one shoulder and a couple of recyclable shopping bags in hand. "I'm back, Ben. I'll get the tomatoes in the salad and put the bread in the oven, and we'll be ready to eat in…" Her gaze slid from him to the visitor, her head tilting quizzically to one side.

Curiously, Ben stood to watch them. After a moment, Avi rose, too, the movement clumsy. She shifted her feet a few times, then swiped her palms down her skirt to dry them.

Shopping bags crinkled as they slid from Patricia's boneless fingers to the stone, and her purse followed. She took a few steps, then pressed her hands to her cheeks, eyes bright and teary, a cry slipping from her. She moved a few steps closer, caught Avi's hands, and held her at arm's length for inspection. "Oh, Avi, you're home!"

"For a while."

"And safe?"

"Safe and whole." Avi looked as if she might dissolve into tears, asking in a tiny voice "Are you angry?"

Ben retreated to pick up the bags his mother had dropped. Close proximity to weeping women who weren't his patients made the back of his neck itch. Them, he knew how to console and reassure. His sisters, Brianne and Sara, too. He'd gotten enough experience with that when he'd finished Patricia's job of raising them. Outside of those females, though, he didn't have a clue and didn't want one.

But he didn't go inside and give them privacy. He might not like tears, but when he told his sisters about this, they would beat him senseless if he couldn't finish the story.

Patricia let go of Avi's hands to hold her shoulders. "Why would I be angry with you?"

"I made you a promise, and I broke it."

Patricia's expression went blank for a moment, then her eyes widened, and she pulled Avi into her hug. "Honey, just making the promise was enough! No one could have possibly kept it. All you can do is your best, and if the worst happens, it's not your fault, because you tried. Oh, Avi, sweetie, I could never be angry with you, never, ever."

Discomfort crept along Ben's spine, making him turn and carry the bags inside. So Avi thought she had disappointed Patricia. He'd witnessed his mother giving the same sort of reassurance to his sisters a few months ago, taking their comforting over George's death and giving it back with soft words and softer hugs that they always, always held a place in her heart. She would have included Ben, too, but at the time he wasn't sure he wanted that place. He still wasn't.

He could be friendly with her. He could spend time with her. He could tell her all the things about his life that she'd missed because she'd run off—and in twenty years, she'd missed a lot. But to this day he wasn't sure if he wanted to be her son again, if he wanted her for a mother again. Friendship of a sort might be all he could handle.

At the island, he set the bags down and unloaded the last-minute groceries. A bottle of Head Country barbecue sauce had been the only thing on her list when she left. There could be no grilled meats in her house, she'd decreed, without the made-in-Oklahoma sauce. Besides a giant bottle of that, she'd picked up sweet onions, late Porter peaches, a large green box of imperfectly shaped tomatoes, a carton of vanilla Braum's ice cream, and a loaf of take-and-bake bread.

In little more than an hour, she'd hit Walmart, a farm stand, Braum's, and CaraCakes Bakery. His sisters, who knew a lot about shopping as an extreme sport, would be impressed.

Ben put the ice cream away, read the instructions on the bread, and slid it into the oven, removed the salad bowl from the refrigerator, washed his hands and the tomatoes, and began dicing them. The deep ripe red of their thick skins took him back to sunny days in Patricia's garden, sitting with her and his sisters on cool damp dirt, picking tomatoes and passing around the salt shaker. They ate them straight from the vine until their mouths hurt, until Patricia laughed and said, *Don't eat too many. There's peaches for dessert.*

And he, Brianne, and Sara had insisted: *We always have room for peaches.*

As he slipped a large bite of tomato into his mouth, she came inside, closing the door just loudly enough to chase away his memory in the old garden twenty-five years away. Seeing the tomatoes, she smiled. "Don't eat so many you can't stuff in a peach or two."

Some part of him was grateful that she remembered those afternoons. Some part just felt antsy as he dried his fingers, scraped the diced tomatoes into the salad, then left the cutting board and knife in the sink. Patricia joined him there, gazing out the window to where Avi stood, hands on hips, staring at a bed filled with red, white, and blue flowers. She looked...lost.

"Her mother didn't hint that she'd be home this soon. She looks so good. Don't you think she looks good?"

He shrugged and admitted, "She looks good."

Patricia looked at Avi again, then back at him, worry in the lines that wrinkled her forehead. "Do you really think so? I'm wondering if she's not too thin, maybe just a little too pale. Do you think she's a little thin?"

Ben gazed at Avi again. She was on the slim side, but she also had some impressive triceps and biceps. He'd bet the abdomen covered by the pink dress was perfectly sculpted, and her quadriceps and hamstrings made her legs damn interesting to look at. Girly dress, soft warm skin, powerful legs..."She looks fine."

"Yes," Patricia said absently, sounding less than convinced. After a moment, her mouth tightened and she refocused on the meal, gathering dishes, pushing a tray across for him to carry. He followed her outside, the fragrances of fresh-baked bread and spicy barbecue sauce drifting back to him.

As soon as they'd set down their loads, she smiled, extending one hand to him, one to Avi. "I want to formally introduce you two. My favorite son and orthopedic surgeon, Dr. Ben Noble, and my second-favorite soldier in the whole world, Sergeant First Class Avi Grant. Our very own hero come home from the war."

Sergeant First Class. Deep down, something inside Ben twinged, turning sour. Avi was in the Army.

Wasn't that a kick in the gut?

Chapter 2

Sometimes it seemed karma didn't care what a person was doing, how it was going, or how hard she was trying. It just smacked her anyway.

That was how Lucy Hart was feeling Saturday evening. Heaving a great big pity-party sigh, she gave the pan on the stove another stir before checking the thermometer attached to its side. The pecan pralines were almost ready to scoop onto wax-paper-lined pans, where they would harden into luscious, sweet, melt-in-your-mouth miracles of fat-creating incredibleness that she should never again let cross her lips.

Thursday she'd had her annual checkup, and the doctor brought up the dreaded subject: losing weight, following it with a comment about her blood sugar and her blood pressure. Her blood pressure, she'd wanted to point out, had been fine until he'd mentioned her weight. She'd given up regular pop. She hadn't made fudge since May. She walked twice a day most days, no matter how hot and humid it got. She'd eaten broccoli without cheese sauce or ranch dressing, for God's sake, and lost *seventeen pounds*, and all he'd been interested in was the twenty still left.

Twenty plus twenty, honesty forced her to admit.

But that wasn't why she was making candy. Neither was the fact that the nurse had called yesterday to report that her blood sugar and cholesterol were high, or that this morning she'd picked up her brand-new prescriptions—her first in seven years. It wasn't even the fact that it was Saturday night and she was home alone. Or that, the summer's short interlude with Ben Noble aside, she might never have another date again.

Certainly not with this big ol' sorry case of whatever was wearing her down. She felt prickly. Edgy. Like her body couldn't quite contain all the electricity and anxiety popping through it. It wasn't PMS. She was safe from that for another two weeks. It was...

Unable to put a name to it, she gave it voice. "Aarrgh!" For good measure, she stomped her foot, too, but it didn't make her feel better. She just wanted to explode into a million little pieces, tiny jiggly bits of pure energy that would bounce and roll around before slowly coming back together into human form. Maybe twenty pounds' worth of them would get lost in the process, lowering her blood pressure and cholesterol and blood sugar and making her feel less...more...

She knew exactly how she wanted to feel: smarter, stronger, more capable. Thinner, prettier, more involved with life, with people, with everything. Less emotional, more hopeful, more confident, not scared, not living life on the sidelines. She wanted to feel the way she had seven years ago before Mike died on her, the coward, and shook up her entire life.

Burnt sugar registered with her brain an instant before her nose. Giving a yelp that would do her dog Norton proud, she yanked the pan off the burner, then scowled at its contents. Nana had taught her early that there were two burnt foods that couldn't be salvaged no matter what: beans and sugar.

She set the pan in the sink to cool, then looked around at the mess that filled the counters. She could stay, clean, probably burn something else, and end up eating everything in total self-pity. Instead, she took a dog cookie from its jar. "Come on, Norton. Time for you to go into the bedroom a while." Following the big dog down the hall, she dug her cell phone from her pocket and punched in her best friend's number. "It's me," she said before Marti had a chance to finish *hello*. "My stove betrayed me. Let's go have a treat somewhere."

She didn't ask if Marti had plans. Marti was even more of a stay-at-home girl than Lucy was. She was happy with life at Casa Levin: regular contact with the Tuesday Night Margarita Club, occasional calls and visits with her family, and all the hours she wanted to devote to her job, her hobbies, or anything else that caught her interest. Marti wasn't looking for love or marriage or anything that resembled a commitment. She wouldn't even consider a pet.

Lucy wished she was happy with *her* life the way it was, and truthfully, for the most part, she was. But Lord, she was tired of being alone at night. And being fat. And not doing things she wanted to do because she was fat. And lonely, despite the best bunch of family and friends a woman could wish for.

She was immeasurably lonely for Mike and snuggling and kisses and sweaty sex and love and happily-ever-after.

"Where do you want to go?"

Images of their usual treat spots filled Lucy's head—Braum's for ice cream, CaraCakes for two-bite cheese-cakes, Serena's Sweets for pie, Java Dave's for dessert disguised as coffee—but her mouth didn't even water. Heavens, she had a whole counter full of brownies, fudge, oatmeal cookies, and peanut brittle that she would pack up and deliver to her neighbor in the morning. Joe Cadore was the high school football coach; his metabolism could handle the calories way better than hers.

"How about we meet at QT and get a drink, then go to City Park?"

Marti did everything with elegance and sophistication, and that included her snort. "You want to go to the park in three-digit heat and...what? Watch me spontaneously combust?"

"I'll bring you peanut brittle," Lucy coaxed in a singsong voice. She shooed at Norton as he jumped onto the middle of the bed with the cookie—he usually waited until the door was closed behind her before doing that—but he closed his eyes and pretended not to notice. It wasn't worth spiking her blood pressure, so she retrieved the yellow rubber ducky from his bed and laid it beside his head. His eyes opened to thin slits, and he sneakily swiped it in closer with his giant paw, beneath his chin, before feigning sleep.

"Is it the airy kind that doesn't get stuck in your teeth?"

"Do I make any other kind?"

Balancing her cell precariously, Lucy did her hair in a ponytail, then kicked off her flip-flops for a pair of walking shoes as worn as Norton's ducky. She'd put a lot of hard miles on them since she'd bought them in June.

Marti gave in as Lucy had known she would. "All right. You want me to stop by and pick you up?"

"Nope. I'm gonna walk."

"It's a hundred-and-crap out there, Lulu."

"Joe and I have been walking all summer. I'm not gonna melt."

"No, you'll dehydrate, and there'll be nothing left but a pile of clothes and those nasty shoes and your friends gathered around, saying 'We loved her well.'" A soft, sighing sound came over the phone, as if Marti were fanning herself. "All right. I'll be at the QT closest to City Park in ten minutes. No, better make it fifteen. I've got to find something appropriate to wear. And don't forget my peanut brittle."

"Thanks, Marti." Lucy hung up, left Norton on the bed with the door closed, and returned to the kitchen to bag a generous portion of peanut brittle. Before summer, she wouldn't have dreamed of walking to the store—before she'd met Ben, before she'd fallen head over heels in lust and begun yet another diet-and-exercise program. Now she didn't think twice about it. She put necessities into a bright orange sling backpack, grabbed a bottle of water, and headed out the back door.

She glanced at Joe's house as she headed east. A lamp was on in the living room, but his car was gone from the driveway. School had started last week, so he could be at some function there. Football, it seemed, never ended, so his absence could have something to do with that. He could be out partying with his friends or even on a date. He was way too gorgeous to not be in a serious relationship, but every time she tried to fix him up with someone, he insisted he could find his own women.

He was clueless in a really cute, overgrown boy sort of way.

By the time she reached QuikTrip, she was sweating—not a good look on her—and beads of it were running everywhere, not just down her spine. She spotted Marti's BMW parked in the corner, engine running, windows up, and AC blasting. After tossing her empty water bottle in the trash, she tapped on the driver's window, and Marti shut off the motor and got out.

"See," Lucy said in greeting. "You had something appropriate for sweltering needlessly in the park."

Marti glanced at her own outfit—cotton shorts, pressed and creased; sleeveless top in cool jersey, and adorable sandals with just enough of a heel to make her look inches taller than she already was.

When Lucy wore heels, she looked 5'3"-and-chunky-in-heels.

"I swear to you, the temperature went *up* one degree on the drive over. I'm going inside and standing in the freezer compartment." Marti beeped the key fob, and with a bird trill the doors locked.

Lucy's key fob sounded like a strangled toad's last breath. It didn't always lock the doors, either.

The QT was busy inside and out, lines at the gas pumps, the pop dispensers, and the registers. Marti headed straight for the frozen French vanilla cappuccino machine while Lucy took a bottle of lime-flavored water from a refrigerated case and got a giant cup of crushed ice to go with it. They met at the register, where Marti grinned. "Look at you, ignoring yucky pop and buying good-for-you water. I'm so proud of you."

Lucy gave the clerk her debit card. "Water's good. Almond milk's fine. Iced tea is great. But sometimes I dream of giant vats of ice-cold pop and a straw a mile long. Of everything I've had to give up, I think I miss it most."

Despite her sweaty state, Marti hugged her. "It's worth it, though, isn't it? You're healthier and happier and skinnier."

"Tell that to the doctor who poked me and said, 'You could stand to lose a few pounds.'"

"Did you tell him you already lost more than fifteen pounds?"

"Yeah, he wasn't impressed."

"Then did you tell him to keep his opinions to himself?"

Lucy pushed the door open and held it for Marti plus an incoming soldier, who nodded politely and said, "Thank you, ma'am." Young men were always calling her *ma'am*, when she was only thirty-four, for heaven's sake. She had years to go before becoming a *ma'am*.

Outside, it was her turn to give Marti a look. "Well, he *is* a doctor, and I *did* go to him for a checkup. That's pretty much the same as asking for his opinion."

Marti waved her free hand as if such minor details didn't matter. Of course, she'd never been in anything other than perfect health. Not one of her body's systems would dare misbehave, and if one did, the doctor would tell her in the kindest, gentlest way. She did *not* like hearing bad news.

Though she and Lucy had heard the worst news possible within minutes of each other over six years ago, when their husbands had been killed in the same combat incident in Iraq. For both of them it still ranked as the worst time of their lives.

As they continued their lazy stroll along patched and crooked sidewalks, Marti asked, "What's got you blue and making candy tonight?"

"Nothing, really."

"Is it Ben?"

"Nah. We're where we should be." *Friends, no more.*

"Are you ready to meet the next guy?"

"Nah. It would be nice if it would happen sooner rather than later, but no rush."

"Are you—" Marti's voice bobbled, and she sternly cleared her throat. Most times she liked to pretend she was on the practical, non-dreamy side of the fence, squarely opposite Lucy, but Lucy knew better. A wide pink streak of romance wove its way through Marti's soul, rooted the day she'd met Joshua, blossoming throughout their marriage, tattered and faded since his death, but still there, waiting. "Are you missing the magic?"

Lucy's smile was bittersweet. Neither of them was mathematically inclined, but there were some equations that needed no explaining. Joshua + Marti or Mike + Lucy = Magic. "Every time Mike looked at me, I felt like a princess at a ball, beautiful and beloved by my charming prince in combat boots," she said on a sigh. "Mike *got* me, you know, the way women dream about. He loved me, imperfections and all, and I loved him back the same way and more. It really was magic."

"I know, LucyLu." Marti's voice bobbled again. "You two were blessed. So were Joshua and I."

Restless energy bounced and rolled inside her, feeding the self-pity that was slowly consuming her. "So much loss...so much change...It isn't fair, Marti."

Marti slid her arm around Lucy's shoulder and gave her a hug. "No," she agreed, her words muffled by Lucy's hair. "It's damned unfair."

*   *   *

Avi admired the tenacity of Oklahoma natives, who didn't let a little thing like life-withering, bone-drying heat keep them from doing what they wanted and enjoying it. Though the sweat had stopped trickling down her spine to be absorbed instead by the thin cotton of her dress, though her hair was damp and stuck to her head in places where it had worked free of the braid, she couldn't imagine a better welcome home than eating dinner in an elegant outdoor setting. Feeling the breeze cool her skin, listening to the tinkle of wind chimes, smelling the fragrance of flowers—it all gave her a sense of ease, something she'd been missing for far too long.

She breathed deeply, then slowly let the air out in a long, thin sigh. She and Patricia hadn't had more than a few minutes to talk privately, but that little bit had gone a long way to soothing her conscience. They would visit longer, Patricia had whispered, when her son went back to Tulsa. *Dinner tomorrow evening?* she'd asked, and Avi had nodded, the lump in her throat too big to speak over.

Now Patricia was inside, dishing up dessert, and Avi and Ben sat silently in comfortable chairs, each holding a half-finished glass of wine. The chairs they'd moved to after the meal had sinfully thick cushions and were gathered around a black steel fire pit. The stone border edging it allowed it to do double duty as a table. It would be a wonderful place to sit in November, when winter's chill was finally settling in, or in March, when they couldn't stand another evening cooped up inside waiting for spring.

Spring in Oklahoma was a glorious thing.

Across the table, Ben shifted, drawing her attention that way. He was something of a surprise. She'd known Patricia had children from her first marriage. She'd seen pictures of them as kids and at their high school graduations. But she'd never given them much thought. For reasons she'd never asked about as a kid and never thought about as an adult, she'd known Patricia rarely saw them.

If she'd ever imagined what Ben would be like, it wouldn't have been close to reality. There wasn't a bit of resemblance between him and Patricia. Where she was average height, slim, with light brown hair and blue eyes, he was a classic cliché: tall, dark, and handsome. Black hair, dark eyes, with the strong features of one of Oklahoma's Indian tribes. Nice hands, skillful enough to become a surgeon; long legs; lean body.

She spent her life surrounded by lean bodies. She wasn't easily swayed by a fine physical specimen. If she was with her best friends right now, one of them would say *But there's something about* this *body*, and everyone would laugh, because the sheer number of times they'd heard the comment made it more than mere words. It imbued the words with the full power of countless memories of unforgettable good times. Avi knew she'd been lucky to have so many good times.

But her friends weren't here. Rosemary was stationed in Germany, spending every available free moment studying the architecture of the castles, or so she said. The others agreed that she was really fulfilling her princess fantasy. Jolie had gotten out of the Army and returned to Shreveport, where she shared her quarters with three kids and dealt with an ex-husband who acted like one. Kerry was in South Korea for her second time—or was it third? She freely admitted it was the food that kept drawing her back.

And Paulette was in Arlington.

Deliberately Avi refocused her thoughts. The friends she'd lost were never far from her mind, but the opportunity to relax and enjoy the presence of a totally hot guy hadn't come along often in the last few years.

"What do you do in the Army?" Ben asked, apparently tiring of the silence about the same time she did.

"Signal," she replied, then explained, "Communications. I'll be an instructor at the signal school at Fort Gordon when my leave's over."

"When will that be?"

"Four weeks. Mom and Dad have always come to visit me since I joined the Army, but it was time for me to see Oklahoma again." And to talk to Patricia face-to-face.

He propped one foot on the table. Like her, he wore flip-flops, though his probably cost more than her entire flip-flop wardrobe, and it was an extensive collection, one she'd started years ago. "Any brothers or sisters?"

"Nope. I'm a happy only." She'd liked having her parents' attention to herself, being the sole grandchild-light of GrandMir and Popi's lives. "You have sisters?"

"Two sisters, one brother-in-law, a niece, and two

nephews." His smile was thin. "Except for assorted aunts, uncles, and cousins, that's the extent of the Noble family."

And Patricia. She wanted him to include Patricia. She was his mother, after all, and she was alone and grieving and needed someone to love.

"You've got us Grants outnumbered more than two to one. My parents are only children, too." She'd noticed a dozen times through the meal that his ring finger was bare: no wedding band, no paler skin to indicate that one had ever been there. It had been a long time since she'd noticed such a thing. A long time since she'd sat opposite a gorgeous guy and wondered about his availability. It was a warm, shivery feeling in itself, and the ordinariness of it made it twice as nice. "No wife?"

"No. My sisters say I'm married to my job."

"Is that enough?"

His gaze darkened and shifted to stare off across the yard. Was he seeing the house on the other side, she wondered, or looking into the past? At someone who'd broken his heart? "Until recently it was." After a moment, he looked at her again. "You ever been married?"

"No. I always figured there was time for that and kids and college later." Images flashed through her mind, and the corners of her mouth pulled down. "I was wrong. Time is more precious than I realized."

The words came out quietly, more regretful than she'd intended. She was grateful when the back door opened and Patricia's cheery voice said, "Dessert! The best part of the meal."

Ben rose to help her with the tray she carried, setting it on the table. The three dishes were filled with pound cake, vanilla-bean-flecked ice cream, and a mix of mashed and sliced ripe peaches that practically drew a moan from Avi. Oh, she'd missed fresh Oklahoma peaches!

"Can I get you some more wine, Avi?" Patricia asked, holding up the bottle from the dining table.

"No, thank you."

"I won't ask Ben. Even when he's not on call, he doesn't drink enough to get a hummingbird tipsy, in case he's got to go in and assist in an emergency." Patricia chose the chair to Avi's left, handed her a dessert dish, then took her own and sank back. "I've got a son who's a surgeon, a daughter who's an oil leasing whiz, and one who's raising the three most perfect kids you ever saw. Just how blessed am I?"

There was that Oklahoma spirit again. Looking for the good in the worst of times. Avi intended to renew hers while she was home, to recover that indomitability, that glass-half-full optimism that made Oklahomans special. She had relied on a sense of fatalism to get through the last five years. *What will be, will be. If it's my time to die, I'll die. If it's my day to stick my hand inside my buddy's chest and try to keep him from bleeding out but he does anyway, it's meant to be.*

She and fatalism weren't a good match.

"This is delicious, Patricia," she said, her *yumms* implied in her voice.

"Isn't the cake lovely? My dear neighbor, Lucy, baked it. She lives right across the yard there. She's talked a time or two about opening her own restaurant or dessert shop. There's a part of me that wants her to jump right into it and a part that really would prefer to keep all the excess goodies flowing in our direction."

"How is Lucy?" That came from Ben, intent on his

dessert and asking the question as if it were an afterthought. Which, of course, made Avi think it wasn't an afterthought at all. That answered her question about whether he'd been staring at the house a few moments earlier. Did it also answer her question about a broken heart?

"She's fine. I guess you didn't have time to visit her this morning, what with Saturday clinic and all. Ben's practice is so busy that they have to schedule clinics on Saturdays twice a month to get caught up on all their patients." Patricia further explained, "Lucy and I are members of the Tuesday Night Margarita Club. Out of tragedy comes joy, they say, and the margarita sisters have provided me with a lot of joy."

Ben gazed at the house across the yard again, just for a moment, before explaining to Avi, "They're also called the Fort Murphy Widows Club."

Avi caught herself from recoiling. She'd heard of such groups, but she'd never imagined anyone she knew actually claiming membership in one. Sure, in the beginning a person needed a support group, but after a while, wasn't that just refusing to let go of the past and face the future?

What do you know, Avery? You're great at facing the future, but letting go isn't one of your talents. You just drag all your sorrows right along with you.

But she couldn't forget. The people she'd known, the things they'd done...they should be remembered forever and ever, amen.

The conversation turned lighter, tales about Patricia's grandchildren, comments about great restaurants Avi had to try while she was in town, Patricia relating her conversation with Avi's mother when she found out she would miss the first week of Avi's visit.

"I said, 'Why, of course she wouldn't schedule her first visit in a decade to coincide with your cruise. You know the Army. It's just how things happen.'" Patricia laughed, easing the worry lines that seemed to have taken up permanent residence, then gave Avi a mock-stern gaze. "Don't you ever let her know that's exactly what you did. Your mama's never been gone from home a month, much less twelve years like you. She doesn't understand how much a person can need time alone, especially when that person is her baby girl."

"I'll make it up to her, I promise." Avi set her empty dish down, her stomach filled with sweet, cold summery goodness. "Let me help you with the cleanup, then I'd better head back to the house. It's been a long day."

Patricia fluttered her hands in a brush-off gesture. "Forget about the cleanup. Ben stopped making that offer when he found out I was coming along behind him redoing everything."

"Is it my fault you're compulsive about your dishes?" he asked, one brow raised.

"I'm just a little compulsive," she teased. As she stood, a frown furrowed her brows. "Avi, I didn't see any car out front besides Ben's. How did you get here?"

"I walked. It's not that far."

"Oh, sweetie, Ben will take you home. You don't mind, do you, Ben? It's not far, but with the sun going down and her being new in town…"

Avi smiled, all too able to imagine the same arguments in her mother's voice. Forget that Avi was a soldier, that she'd done five combat tours, that Tallgrass was about as safe as a place could be. She was Beth's little girl, and she still needed protecting.

"Of course I don't mind," Ben said.

Patricia embraced Avi again, holding her tight enough to make her feel like a little kid, safe in her mother's arms. "It's so good to see you. I've prayed every day."

"Me, too." Even when she'd wondered if God was listening. That hadn't stopped her, though. Every day, whether full of faith or running on empty, she'd said her prayers. After all, what if she'd been too cynical to offer up prayers for their safety and one of her comrades had died that day? It wasn't a risk she had been willing to take.

With another squeeze, Patricia released her, then began gathering dishes. Ben gestured toward the driveway, and they headed that way. They walked in silence until they reached the street, where he stopped.

"My car's there." He gestured to a sporty car out front that cost more than she'd made her last year in the desert. "You want a ride or do you prefer to walk?"

She considered it a moment. She had a weakness for powerful little cars, especially after months when her primary mode of transportation was her own two feet or an MRAP, a mine-resistant ambush protected vehicle. But right now those feet wanted to move. "I'd rather walk, if you don't mind."

He gestured in agreement, and she turned right. It was only three blocks west, then four blocks north, to the house Popi had built for GrandMir to celebrate their tenth anniversary. It was old and comfortable and had the best yard in town, and she loved it dearly.

After a half block in silence, she said, "You don't really have to see me all the way home."

He gave her a slight smile. "My father would disagree. He had very strict rules for how men treated women.

Holding a chair, opening a door, walking on the street side of the sidewalk…" His long fingers gestured toward his position on the sidewalk.

"So if a reckless driver comes along and swerves onto the sidewalk, you can push me out of the way?" She laughed. "I had to ask GrandMir about that one. I never could figure it out myself." She hesitated. "Is your father still living?"

"No." Ben's mouth tightened, then relaxed again. "But his influence lives on."

"One of the best things you can say about a parent." She hoped one day her children or grandchildren would be paying the same compliment to her.

"My dad was a good guy. He was better suited to being a father than anyone I've ever known."

Avi pulled the elastic band from her hair, gathered the hair again, then tugged it back into a neater, higher ponytail. "Is that why you haven't had kids yet? You don't want to face such high standards?"

"Nah. He taught me well. But surgery takes a lot of hours. Clinic days, OR days, call. I wanted to get established before I considered marriage or having kids, and by the time I realized that I *was* established, I was booked solid for months ahead. I don't have time to date, fall in love, be a father."

Is that enough? she'd asked, and he'd replied, *Until recently.* "You'd better make some changes then." She thought about Lucy, wondering if she was the catalyst that made him realize work wasn't enough anymore. Avi would guess they weren't still seeing each other, or surely he would have spent this evening with her instead. Had their relationship failed, and why, and when?

It was none of her business. After all, she wasn't looking for a relationship. Fun, a boyfriend to share dinners and dances and beds, a man to help ease her back into normal life...She could do full justice to a sexy, good-for-now kind of fling in the next thirty days, with no strings and no regrets.

And for a woman who had way too many regrets, that sounded pretty damn good.

* * *

After a few more blocks, they turned right. Ben had learned in the short time that Avi was a career soldier, that she didn't like the blues or jazz—his favorite kinds of music—and that her tastes in food ran to good old home-style cooking. No fusion, saffron-scented air, tiny portions artistically arranged on huge plates and kissed with multiple sauces.

"Oh, and no trendy, cool-vibe places whose names are misspelled on purpose," she added.

He laughed. "You've just described half the places I eat at."

"I am not surprised. You strike me as a trendy, cool-vibe sort of person."

"I think I've been insulted."

This time she laughed. "Oh, no, Doc. When I've insulted you, you'll know." She slid her hands into pockets that Ben hadn't realized the dress had. He found himself wishing that she slid her hand into his, so he could feel its heat and warmth and strength, so he could imagine how a real touch from her would feel. Wanting wasn't a new thing, but it had felt like it back in the early summer with

Lucy. It felt like it again now, new and filled with potential. Pretty women and potential were one of his favorite combinations.

After a moment's silence, Avi gave him a sidelong look. "How is Patricia doing, really?"

He shoved his hands in his own pockets and shrugged. He got that question from people he worked with, from friends, and he gave them a stock answer: *She's coping*. But Avi wasn't the sort to settle for stock answers, he didn't think, and she knew Patricia probably as well as he did, if not better.

"She's dealing with it. She makes an effort to put on a good face for everybody, but..." Guilt, a feeling Ben knew all too well, seeped through him. They'd come a long way in healing things between them, but there were restrictions. She rarely mentioned George because she knew she didn't have a sympathetic audience in Ben. When she slipped, all he could think about was where was this grief when his father died. Where was this love? She'd been married to Rick almost as long as George; she'd promised to love him until his death; she'd had three kids with him.

But at Rick's funeral, there had been few tears from her. She'd come out of a sense of obligation, more for the kids she'd left behind than for the man she'd once loved.

Which was something, but Ben hadn't appreciated it at the time. Wasn't sure he appreciated it yet.

"Does she see a grief counselor?"

Ben smiled faintly. "The margarita club is her grief counselor. They're good for her. They've all been where she is. They understand in ways we don't." Though he wasn't sure he should be including Avi in that *we*. She probably knew. She hadn't lost a husband, but she'd known guys like George, Lucy's husband, all the margarita sisters' husbands. She'd worked with them, joked with them, shared meals with them, gone into combat with them, and seen them every day until, suddenly, they were gone.

The thought made him look at her in a way that went beyond the beautiful-woman-great-body-pink-toenails way, even beyond the damn-she's-a-soldier. She was a soldier who'd been assigned to a war zone, who'd lived under primitive conditions with the knowledge that the enemy wanted to kill her, seeing the results of combat firsthand: the physical, the mental, the spiritual wounds. She'd lost people she loved—not just one, not just a spouse, but one after another. How hard was that on a woman's heart?

"They were together so long. It's hard to imagine that they never will be again."

Ben couldn't stop the muscles tightening in his jaw. "You met them through the Army?"

"No." Then she smiled, her face softening, her eyes brightening. "Actually, I guess I did. My father went to West Point. That's where he and George met. Dad did his obligated service, then got out, but they stayed friends. He visited us when he had a chance—spent an entire month's leave with us one time. He's the reason I joined the Army."

Ben had known George was visiting friends in Tulsa when Patricia met him. She'd told him and his sisters that much the night she'd gathered them around the kitchen table and told them she was leaving them behind and moving to another country. So those friends had been

Avi's parents. George had come to Oklahoma, charmed Patricia right out of her marriage and Avi right into his career path.

A visit Avi remembered with great affection and love, while for Ben, it had been the worst time of his life. But it was twenty years past. He was twenty years older. He could put aside the past to enjoy the present, couldn't he? Or was he as stodgy as his sisters teased?

"Why did your father get out?"

"Dad believes everyone should do at least four years of service in the military. He felt it was his duty—and his honor—but he didn't intend to make a career of it. He got selected for the academy, got an education, did his service, then came back to Oklahoma. I thought it was pretty cool that Dad had been in, and so had Popi, and when I met the colonel..."

The look on her face was nothing less than remarkable for a woman who'd experienced everything she had: pure, childhood innocence. It wasn't a girlish-crush look, but admiration. Awe.

"He was ten feet tall and could leap skyscrapers while fending off enemy hordes. I wanted to be just like him when I grew up. I wanted to wear that uniform, do all the cool-guy stuff, and inspire little kids along the way."

She had fallen under his spell as much as, maybe even more than, Patricia. Ben could honestly say he hadn't been nearly as impressed when he'd met the man. How could he have been, after three years of watching his father disappear into grief, of rebuilding the family George and his mother had devastated, of giving up most of his hopes and dreams so he could be there for the family.

It hadn't occurred to him until much later—this past

summer, in fact—that the man he'd scorned might have been worth knowing.

"This is it." Avi stopped in front of a great old house built of sandstone and wood siding painted pale yellow. Big stone columns anchored the porch, where four rockers stood in a straight line on one side of the door and a glider sat on the other. The grass was lush and green, and flowers bloomed everywhere. Lights shone through the windows to the left of the door, and barking sounded there.

"That's Sundance," Avi said. "All my life I wanted a dog, but Mom was against it. So what'd she do when I'm grown and gone? Went out and bought an Irish setter puppy for Dad for Father's Day."

Looking closer, Ben spotted a blur of mahogany-colored hair and long floppy ears. As they walked up the sidewalk to the porch, the dog disappeared, its barks coming from the area of the door, then reappeared at the window in an excited wiggle. "Don't you usually kennel puppies when you're gone for a few hours?"

"Do you." She said it as a statement, like *that's interesting* when it really wasn't, and pulled a key from her pocket as they climbed the steps. "Are you a dog person?"

He thought of Lucy's mutt, who bared his teeth every time he saw Ben, and his sister's little ball of fur that thought his own reflection was an intruder. "Not so you'd notice."

"They left Sundance with their neighbors, who must not have known what they were getting into. I hadn't even gotten my suitcase into the house when the lady marched over with the dog and a bag of food. 'Welcome home,' she said, and 'Here's your dog.' Then she practically ran back to her own house." She paused, key in the lock. "You want to meet her?"

As opposed to retracing his steps and going home to Patricia's alone, where she would spend the rest of the evening reminiscing and worrying over Avi? "Sure."

She opened the door just wide enough to reach in and grab the puppy's collar, then backed her into the hallway so Ben could follow. As soon as Ben closed the door, Avi flipped a light switch with one hand and let go of the dog with the other.

She'd said puppy, Father's Day, eight or ten weeks ago. Little and cuddly and sweet. Sundance was a puppy who looked as if she'd eaten three or four of the size Ben had envisioned. Her coloring and floppy ears and expressive eyes were beautiful. A full-grown dog who looked just like her but could actually sit still could pass as an art object in some of the pricey homes he found himself in.

The dog ran from Avi to Ben and back again, circling their feet, trying to climb their legs, barking excitedly. Her paws were as big as saucers, and her tail beat relentlessly, swiping furniture legs, people legs, and her own. When Avi scooped her into her arms, Sundance licked every part of her she could reach, though Avi avoided face kisses by tilting her head away.

"You can pet her. She won't pee on you by accident since I'm holding her."

"None of the dogs I know have accidents in the house. Every single time is on purpose." He took the few steps necessary to rest his hand on Sundance's head. Instantly her long pink tongue reached out to swipe his fingers, and she pressed her silken fur against his hand until her face was compressed like one of those wrinkled dogs he'd seen on TV.

"She lives up to her name." With hair the color of the intense molten-fire surface of the sun and her wiggly, jiggly dancing about, she was a perfect Sundance.

"My dream dog was a beagle. I loved their baying. Second choice would have been a black Lab, because who could possibly not love a black Lab? But really, I would have taken anything, even a Chihuahua. But you're a sweetie, aren't you, girl?"

Ben watched her nuzzle the dog and found himself actually contemplating jealousy for a moment. With a wry smile, he shifted his attention to the house. A yellow sticky note was stuck to the wall a few feet from him with loopy handwriting: *Don't forget to set the alarm. (Code's on the back.)* Another clung to the closet door nearby: *Sundance's toys inside. Try to teach her to pick them up, would you? (I taught you.)*

He chuckled, drawing Avi's attention. She looked at the note and rolled her eyes. "My mom is a great believer in list-making—one item at a time. I've been gathering them since I got here, and they're still everywhere. *Buy milk; you need it for your bones. Extra toilet paper in upstairs linen closet.* Where she's kept it my entire life. *Water this plant on Tuesday. Water that plant on Thursday. Run the dishwasher when it's full. No more than three treats a day.*" A rueful look came across her face. "I hope that one's meant for Sundance and not me."

Hearing her name, Sundance started wiggling even more, with purpose this time. Avi glanced down at her. "You need to go out, baby?" She put her on the floor, and the pup's nails skittered on the wood as she raced down the hall, anxious little yips echoing back to them.

Avi followed, and Ben followed her, reading more notes on the way. *How to program the thermostat* was helpfully stuck on top of said thermostat. *Best coffee: Java Dave's. Real coffee: Keurig on counter* hung between family portraits. *Clean the dryer lint trap* was stuck to a lopsided ashtray that looked handmade, circa fourth grade.

"How old does your mother think you are?" he asked as they reached the kitchen, where an entire rainbow of notes rustled in the air from the central air conditioning.

"Thirty going on thirteen and first time ever spending the night alone in the house. It's not just me. She leaves Dad notes, too, and plasters them around work. Dad told me that when she had surgery a while back, she taped a note to her breast: *Not this one. That one. Over there.*"

Ben laughed. "I've had patients who've written notes or drawn arrows on their own knees before. A friend of mine was scrubbed in to do a cesarian, and the mom had written on her abdomen, *Remember, I want to wear a bikini again.*"

"I've never had surgery"—Avi rapped her knuckles against the wood door jamb as she stepped out the back door—"but if I did, I think I'd want to make sure everything went the way it should."

"In the OR, that's the doctor's job."

"But you hear cases about doctors amputating the wrong leg or doing a hysterectomy but forgetting to take out the uterus."

Ben shuddered for her benefit. "That means you've got a bad doctor."

"Good doctors don't ever get careless?"

"Good ones aren't careless, and careless ones aren't good." He stopped at the edge of the back porch steps. Sundance was tearing around the yard with more energy than Ben possessed in his entire body.

Avi sat on the steps, her skirt gathered close to her legs, to wait for the pup to answer the call of nature. Sundance showed no such inclination. She sniffed flowers, darted off to carefully inspect the smells around a tree, stopped to give a longing look at the hammock a foot or two above her head, then ran to sample other scents elsewhere.

After a moment, Ben sat beside Avi. The steps were wide enough that he didn't crowd her, narrow enough that her cologne scented his every breath. It was hard to be certain, given the night's heat, but he was pretty sure he felt warmth radiating from her bare arms and legs. Sweet-scented warmth with just a slight undercurrent of energy that made the air between them smell...expectant.

If she felt it, she didn't show it, and he didn't take any action. Instead, they watched the dog for a while, checking her surroundings as if she'd never seen them before, then Avi sighed quietly. Contentedly. "Your mom said you're going back to Tulsa tomorrow."

He obliquely gazed at her. "Yeah, I've got clinic Monday and surgery Tuesday and Wednesday."

"Does Patricia still go to church?"

A few months ago the question would have surprised him. Church was something she'd discovered on George's watch. But he'd learned since the funeral that God, the Bible, and church had been an important part of her and George's lives. "Every Sunday."

"Do you?"

He shook his head.

"Want to have breakfast? I have a Post-it note attesting to the incredible breakfast fare at Serena's Sweets." She flashed a grin. "Mom also drew a map so tiny that I can't read it, but I can find my way back to Patricia's and you can give me directions."

He needed to relax, Lucy was always telling him. Not everything was important or life-changing. Some things were just pure fun, and he should enjoy them when he could. How pleased would she be when he told her the next time they talked that he'd taken her advice? "Sounds good. I'll see you at nine?"

Chapter 3

Calvin Sweet stopped in front of the twenty-four-hour diner and gave the area a slow, steady once-over. The diner was located in the middle of a block of businesses that kept weekly hours and weren't very prosperous. The big windows on the dry cleaners next door were too grimy to see through, and the used bookstore across the street looked like home to the world's worst book hoarder. He imagined the smells of must, dust, and yellowed paper, and his chest tightened as if to avoid breathing them in.

On the corner, a gas station advertised unleaded for $1.89 a gallon. All the glass had been broken out of its windows, and everything of value had been taken, along with everything without value. Only a lonely squeegee remained, lying on its side where a gas pump used to be.

The diner didn't look much better. He walked in the door, swamped by the aromas of coffee, fried meat, grease, and despair. Booths with vinyl benches held to-

gether by duct tape lined the wall. A row of tables that
seated four each separated the booths from the counter,
stability provided by wads of napkins stuffed under rickety legs.

The people looked pretty rickety, too. The waitress
could have been anywhere from twenty-five to fifty-five,
everything about her sad and worn down. Two men sat in
the first booth, sharing coffee without conversation, giving Calvin a glance of disinterest. The homeless man, or
the nearest thing to, at the counter took a quick look, then
guarded his dinner a little more closely. A cook, fat and
bald, chewed on a toothpick and paid Calvin no attention
at all.

That was just what he wanted.

He went to the booth in the back corner, took the bench
where he could see the door, and scanned the menu.
When the waitress approached, he asked for a ham and
egg sandwich and coffee. She didn't say a word, not to
him or the cook.

Calvin rubbed his hands over his face. It was ten
o'clock on a Saturday night, and his wandering around
Tacoma had just begun. It would be near dawn before
he'd be able to sleep, and then he'd be lucky if he managed two hours. The Department of Defense had classi-
fied systematic sleep deprivation as torture. He knew that
better than most. He wasn't sure of the last time he'd gotten a good night's rest. Maybe back in 2007?

He'd tried booze, hypnosis, guided meditation, and
none of it had helped. Neither had warm milk, melatonin,
or prayer. Sleeping pills had worked for a while, until
he'd awakened around three in the morning and didn't
have a clue in hell where he was, how he got there, or

what he'd done. He'd flushed the pills down the toilet the next day.

He sat, back rigid, gaze sweeping the dining room and the street beyond every few moments. He kept his hands flat on the table, his muscles wound so tight that his skin practically vibrated. This skin didn't fit anymore. It hadn't for a long time. Some days he thought he would get lost inside it; others he was sure it was going to split right open, unable to contain all the sorrow that was him.

Most days he wished that today would be the day. That everything inside him would swell and grow until his shell of a body could no longer hold him, that he would explode into a thousand little pieces, and that when the dust had settled, he would be gone.

No more Captain Calvin Sweet, United States Army, veteran of the unholy war on terror, the best thing Justice and Elizabeth Sweet claimed they'd ever produced, and a sorry son of a bitch. His epitaph could say *He came home but not really*.

The waitress brought him coffee, black and steaming, its pungent aroma familiar enough to wake his taste buds. He poured a little cup of cream into it, added a packet of sugar, and stirred it long enough to lessen the potential for scalding before taking a sip.

He hadn't expected a grimy little diner in the middle of a hopeless neighborhood to have the best coffee he'd ever tasted. So much for expectations.

He'd had a lot of them when he was young. He'd expected that he and J'Myel Ford would be best friends forever. He'd expected that he would make the most of his time in the Army—would live up to their motto and be all that he could be. He'd expected to fall in love and get married, to have kids who would be overjoyed when he returned home from a deployment. To retire and buy a house in Tallgrass just down the street from his parents'. To start a second career, to coach his kids' soccer and little league teams, to celebrate regularly with J'Myel for big reasons and little reasons and for none at all. Just because they were the best friends ever.

But his friendship with J'Myel had ended, for causes he'd never really understood. J'Myel had passed not long after, and Calvin . . . he had no reason to celebrate. He had no reason to live.

He just didn't know how to die.

* * *

When Avi awoke Sunday morning, it took her a moment to remember where she was. A glimpse of the stack of Post-its on the nightstand reminded her, though, and made her smile. The first had been attached to the bathroom mirror: *Don't let Sundance sleep in your bed.* The next had been on the bedroom door: *She has a bed of her own.* And the last, on the lampshade beside the bed: *I mean it, Avery. I didn't pay $40 for a bed for her so she could not use it.*

Rolling onto her side, she gave the still-snoozing puppy an ear rub. "You don't know how good you have it, pretty girl."

The dog opened one eye to look at her, closed it again, and gave the kind of nose-to-tail joint-popping stretch that Avi envied. After that, she sat up, hopped off the bed, and trotted to the door with a whine.

Avi stretched out her own kinks before opening the

door, then following Sundance down the stairs. She let her out into the backyard, padded to the refrigerator, and found nothing to tempt her. In the pantry she located a stash of granola bars neatly arranged in a cream-and-green enameled pan with a rusty and holey bottom that GrandMir had used for storage for as long as Avi could remember. It brought a rush of warmth, of sweet memories and old times.

According to the clock on the microwave, she had a half hour to feed Sundance, get dressed, and pick up Ben for breakfast. If she were a girly sort of girl, she would need every minute of that time, but even before joining the Army, she'd been nothing of the sort. Sure, she liked to look good. She did her hair, chose clothes that flattered, and counted Bobbi Brown cosmetics as necessities of life, but getting ready and out the door was, like everything else, a streamlined process for her.

She tore open the foil wrapper on the granola bar, and Sundance let out a demanding bark. Avi let her in, broke off a piece of granola bar for her, then took a big bite for herself while getting out the chow. *Don't feed Sundance people food,* the note on the storage bin read. Avi pulled it off and found a second one underneath: *Seriously. It'll just make her fat.*

"I bet she sneaks bites to you all the time," Avi said with a laugh as she scooped out the proper amount into a decorated dish. After giving the dog fresh water, she grabbed the rest of the granola bar and jogged down the hall and upstairs.

She showered, brushed her teeth, blow-dried her hair, did her makeup, and dressed in shorts, shirt, and sandals in seventeen minutes. Good time. Maybe even record-setting. She even had time to spray on perfume, make a stab at straightening the bed, and grab her cell phone.

Sundance was waiting when she reached the front hall, her big eyes hopefully shifting between the closet, where her leash and toys were kept, and Avi. "No walk this morning," Avi said, but all the dog understood was *walk*. She bounced, jumped, and did everything but claw at the door. It required careful maneuvering for Avi to slip outside without the dog, who howled mournfully when the door closed in her face.

It wasn't even nine o'clock, and it was hot and humid and promising more of both. Dew glistened on grass that somehow managed to look wet and parched at the same time. Avi empathized. There'd been times in the desert when she'd wondered how the hell she could sweat so much at the same time her throat was so bone dry that cold water seemed a distant memory.

But she was out of the desert, now and, supposedly, for good. The President had promised the withdrawal of troops, and sometimes she believed him. Now her next duty assignment was Fort Gordon, Georgia, home of Dwight D. Eisenhower Army Medical Center and Signal Corps, where she would teach younger, newer soldiers all about the cool gear they would be using for Army communications. Augusta had been her first stop back in the States, where she'd rented an apartment and accepted delivery of her household goods before coming to Oklahoma.

It took only a few minutes to drive to Patricia's house. This was the house where George and Patricia had intended to retire—close to Patricia's hometown of Tulsa, within fifteen minutes of the post, where they would get medical care and take advantage of the commissary and exchange. They'd taken extra care choosing the house, and instead of simply living there until his next orders came down, they'd made it a home.

Where she would now live alone.

Avi's heart ached as she pulled into the driveway. Patricia's car was parked ahead of her; in the detached garage beyond that, George's pride and joy, a '65 Mustang, was likely stored. He'd loved that car and had joked that Avi could have it when he died. She'd joked right back about what a great inheritance that would be, but she'd meant in thirty years or more, when the car was better suited to her child or grandchild.

Life was so damned unfair.

She shut off the engine and got out of the rental, but before she'd gone farther than the front bumper, Ben came out of the house. He wore denim shorts and a T-shirt advertising a 5K run and walk to benefit arthritis research. Neither garment clung snugly, but damn, her libido hadn't been playing tricks on her. He was still as handsome as the night before.

"Are you a runner?" she asked instead of saying hello.

His brows narrowed, then he looked down at the shirt. "Oh. Hell, no. Our practice was one of the sponsors, so we all took part. I walked. My sister ran it twice in the same time just to prove she could."

"I think I'd like her."

"I bet you would. She's nice. They both are." He opened the passenger door, scooted the seat back to make room for his long legs, then slid in. Their doors closed about the same time with equally solid thuds.

"If you don't run," she asked as she restarted the engine, "what do you do to stay in shape?"

"I work twelve to fourteen hours a day and eat out of vending machines."

She shuddered. "Do you know how much sugar, sodium, and saturated fats are in processed snack foods?"

"Nope. Ignorance is bliss." He waited until she'd backed into the street, then gestured straight ahead. "Go east to First Street, then turn right. So when we get to Serena's, are you going to order an egg-white omelet and turkey sausage?"

"Are you going to order biscuits and gravy and bacon and ham and fried eggs?" she countered. All of which sounded really good to her at the moment. Along with blueberry pancakes, pecan waffles, scrambled eggs, and maybe even toast with jam.

"Whatever I order, don't expect me to share. You can't get an egg-white omelet, then eat my biscuits and gravy."

She laughed, easing the car to a stop at Tallgrass's main north–south street, the one she'd come into town on yesterday. "Don't worry. I'll get enough food for you and me both, and I don't mind sharing."

She took the right turn he advised, then turned left on Main. Spotting the sign for Serena's, she grabbed the first parking space, across the street and in front of a small junk store. Junking had been one of GrandMir's favorite pastimes. Avi had tagged along on a hundred trips, not always of her own free will, but she'd gotten some cool vintage toys out of the treks.

There wasn't much traffic at this time on a Sunday morning. They strolled across the street to Serena's, Avi stealing glances all the way, the romantic inside her sighing when he held the restaurant door for her.

Avi was a firm believer that she could judge the quality

of a restaurant with nothing more than a deep breath, and
Serena's definitely got two thumbs up. On top of the usual
breakfast scents, she identified some of her favorite smells
in the world: sticky buns, cakes, and pies. Apple and cherry
and peach and pecan. Oh, yum.

They took a booth at the front with a lazy view of the
street. Avi gave the breakfast menu a quick skim, doc-
tored the coffee the waitress delivered, then settled her
gaze outside. The courthouse was across the street, and
shops and businesses lined both sides of the block. Nothing was open today, at least not yet. Tallgrass was one of
those lovely small towns with a still-vital downtown district. No doubt, the Army post contributed to that, but the
town was probably lively enough on its own.

"What can I get you, hon?"

She looked from the courthouse flag rippling in the
breeze to the waitress. "Two eggs over easy, toast, hash
browns, a pecan waffle, and orange juice."

Ben stared at her. "Do you know how much sugar,
sodium, and fat of every kind are in that order?"

"I do," she replied. "I'm just choosing to ignore it this
morning."

Shaking his head, he ordered the same thing, minus the
juice. In response to her look, he said, "I eat out of vending machines. You think I'm going to opt for healthy?"

Silence fell between them, letting snippets of other
diners' conversations reach them: talk about church, the
weather, the chances for the high school football team,
putting gardens to bed until next spring, planting fall
flowers or crops. *No* talk about war or death or dying.

It was a small but very sweet pleasure.

The silence went on long enough to become uncomfortable, then even longer, morphing into something worthy of laughter. "Okay," she said, surrendering first. "I'll start the conversation. Cowboy or Sooner?"

"I went to OSU, though I root for the Sooners if they're playing anyone besides OSU."

She gave him a narrow-eyed look. "Did you go to OU's medical school?"

"No. OSU-Tulsa. You?"

"I joined the Army right out of high school, but I root for the Cowboys and every team that plays against OU."

"Aw, where's your state loyalty?"

"I've got tons of state loyalty. I have defended Oklahoma from unknowing and ignorant fools on more than a few occasions, but OU is not my state. They just happen to be located here, and nothing makes me happier than when they lose a football game." She managed a superior sniff. "It doesn't surprise me at all that OU chose to name their teams after the Sooners."

There had been Boomers and Sooners in the Oklahoma land run: those who followed the law and waited for the boom of the cannons to open the run and those who cheated and sneaked in early, trying to claim the best properties before the law-abiding citizens had a chance.

"They probably thought it sounded better than 'gate-crashing cheats.'"

"I don't know. It might be hard to fit on a uniform, but I kind of like the sound of it." Avi smiled, thinking of other things she liked: the sound of his voice, the dry humor in it, the intense look in his eyes. She liked that she was sitting in a restaurant with no more to worry her mind than clogging her arteries, and she especially liked that he was sitting across from her. It made her remember that once upon a time, she'd shared meals with men, gone to movies and clubs and parties and to bed with them. Once upon a time when life was normal.

It was a lovely, lovely feeling.

* * *

"How long have you been in the Army?" Ben asked as the waitress, arms loaded with plates, headed their way.

"Twelve years."

Which made her twenty-nine, maybe thirty, years old. A nice age, given that he was approaching thirty-six. He liked women close enough to his age to have the same sorts of memories and experiences to draw on, who got the same cultural and historical references he did.

Not that he and Avi were going to have a lot of time to bond.

"Are you planning to retire?"

She nodded. "Eight more years, and I'll have decent money and excellent benefits, as long as Congress keeps their hands off of our retirement."

"What kind of benefits?"

Avi waited until the waitress laid out their plates— two each—and refilled their coffees, then returned with another orange juice. Unwrapping her silverware from the napkin, she took a bite of waffle first, then sighed happily.

"Medical benefits are the big ones. Retirees can also use the services on post—buy groceries at the commissary, shop for everything else at the exchange, use the Morale Welfare Recreation stuff, like the golf course, the pools, the picnic areas and boat rentals at Tall Grass Lake. They can fly Space A—the A stands for available—when a military plane has seats open and go just about anywhere in the world. The different services have motels or lodges where we can stay cheap, in cool places like San Diego, Key West, or Hawaii. Some people spend their retirement traveling the world at bargain rates and seeing incredible things."

"Is that what you want to do?"

A little of the animation disappeared from her expression. "I've seen a lot of the world. I might want to travel sometime, but I'm really looking forward to living in Tallgrass, seeing my parents more often, and not moving every few years. I'll have to get tired of that before I start hitting the Space A road."

Ben watched her delicate hands wield knife and fork to arrange her eggs on the hash browns, butter the toast, and slice the waffle into bite-size pieces. She drizzled them with syrup—not maple, blueberry, or any of the other specialty syrups on the table but good ol' Griffin's made-in-Oklahoma syrup. He'd done pretty much the same thing to his meal before taking a bite.

"I've never really known any soldiers," he commented after eating a little. "The two women who started the margarita club—the widows' club—one got married again in June, and the other's wedding is scheduled for after Christmas. Anyway, I met Dane and Logan at their Fourth of July cookout, and I had a patient who broke his ankle while home on leave, but other than that, you're pretty much the first."

"Since George."

He looked up to see her brows raised, her wide eyes encouraging him to say, *Oh, yeah, George. Of course.* He couldn't do it. "I never really knew George."

"Why not?" Again, her expression was so clear he could read it: A person stayed in touch with people who mattered, whether they lived in the same city or state or even on the same continent, and a mother and her adored husband mattered.

When he'd first visited Tallgrass back in May, when Lucy had coerced him into coming to be with Patricia in the days following George's death, he'd had no problem talking about how she had abandoned him, his sisters, and his father, how his dad's broken heart had led to his early death. Everything bad between them had been her fault; she'd admitted it readily; he'd never blurred the details to protect her.

Now, faced with Avi's simple question, he didn't want to talk about abandonment and betrayal or how the thousands of miles of physical distance separating Patricia from her family had been nothing compared to the emotional distance.

So instead he shrugged, and knew it came off as lame. "They were stationed so far away."

"Yeah, but no place you couldn't have easily reached for a visit."

He shrugged again. "How's your food?"

She took a bite and thoroughly chewed it while watching him. After swallowing and taking a drink of juice, she politely dabbed her mouth. "It's living up to Mom's praise." She forked up another bit of egg and potatoes and held it in midair. "George was a great guy. I'd never seen two people better suited to each other than him and Patricia. Well, except for my mom and dad. And GrandMir and Popi."

This time he couldn't keep the words from popping

out. "Funny. I always thought the same thing about my dad and Patricia."

It put a damper on the conversation, of course. Just as he didn't want to hear how happily married Patricia and George had been, Avi didn't want to think about the family they'd broken up in order to be together. She loved Patricia; clearly, she'd loved and admired George. She didn't want to tarnish their images. Ben understood that. It was the reason he'd never asked Patricia what had gone wrong between her and his dad. He wouldn't—couldn't—allow anything to tarnish Rick's image.

After a moment, she changed the subject. "What's the best thing about being an orthopedic surgeon?"

He didn't need to think about his answer. "Helping people return to a normal life without—or at least with less—pain. What's the best thing about being a soldier?"

She didn't hesitate, either. "All the cool equipment. You should see my vehicle in Afghanistan. If you've got even the tiniest bit of a tech geek hiding inside you, you'd be super impressed. It's the age of the geek, baby."

Her smile was charming. She should be required to wear it all the time. Just seeing her smile, he was pretty sure, could brighten anyone's day, regardless of how chaotic or tedious that day was.

"Do you have a subspecialty?" she asked.

"I do ankles, knees, and hips, with an occasional wrist or shoulder thrown in. Only for my regular patients and only if the injuries are minor enough. Serious ones get referred to one of our hand or shoulder guys."

The sun through the window gleamed on her hair as she ruefully shook her head. "I find it amazing that medicine has gotten to the point where a surgeon can specialize in one specific, small body part."

"And prosper." He thought of the house the clinic's top hand surgeon had just bought: big enough for the entire Noble family, a half dozen relatives, and occasional guests without sacrificing anyone's privacy.

Though Ben chose to live in a loft in downtown Tulsa, ankles, knees, and hips were pretty prosperous, too. When he eventually had a family of his own, money would never be a problem.

"Are you good at what you do?"

He took his last bite, put his fork down, and pushed the plate a few inches away. "Very." No modesty, no apologies. He was at the top of his specialty, with more prospective patients than he could possibly handle. He could do knee and hip replacements in his sleep, had a high success rate and a very low complication rate, and drew patients from all over the States as well as outside the country.

"Confidence is a good thing in a surgeon." She eyed his plate, then reached across, cut off a quarter of his waffle, and transferred it to her own plate.

"Help yourself," he said dryly, nudging his leftover packets of butter her way.

"Thanks." She flashed the smile again. "I can live on MREs—the packaged food—but I really do love carbs for breakfast." After adding the butter plus more syrup, she said, "Tell me about your sisters."

"Sara's twenty-nine, married, and has three kids. She was fortunate enough to be able to quit her job when the first one was born. Now she keeps a schedule that makes me tired—swim lessons, ballet, gymnastics, soccer, baseball, art classes, pottery lessons, church activities. It works for them, though I can't help but wonder when the kids get to just be kids." The comment surprised him as soon as it was out. He couldn't say the thought had ever actually crossed his mind, but it must have been there in his subconscious.

Avi nodded. "My mom told me when I was about seven that I could take part in two activities, no more. She grew up here in Tallgrass, and she loved telling stories about playing in the sprinklers and climbing trees and finding a shady spot to read books from the library. She and her friends used to tear around town on their bikes, take picnic lunches to City Park, and go to the movies, and she didn't want me to miss out on that same kind of freedom." She was silent for a moment, then added, "Now that I think about it, she probably didn't want to spend all that time in the car, running me here and there."

Patricia had done a lot of running around with his sisters. He hadn't been involved in activities outside school—his favorite thing had been hanging out with his buddies in the neighborhood—but both girls had. It had ended, though, when Patricia left. Until he'd gotten his driver's license, there had been no one to chauffeur them, and by the time he got the license, they'd lost interest.

"What about the other one?" Avi prompted, drawing him out of the past.

"Brianne is thirty-one. She's the runner. She works in oil, she's single, and she's the nicest woman you'll ever meet. Sara always saw herself as the protector; Bree's the peacemaker. She can't hold a grudge worth a damn."

"Can you?"

An image of Patricia flashed into his mind: on her front

porch, the first time he'd seen her since his father's funeral; she'd stepped toward him, arms open wide, and
he'd flinched. The hurt in her eyes, and the resignation...

"I've had reasonable success at it," he replied, hearing
the self-censure in his voice. After holding a grudge for
twenty years, it was hard to let go. Especially when he
wasn't sure exactly how much of it he wanted to let go
of. He'd learned to be satisfied with life without Patricia.
He'd been anything but satisfied since she'd come back
into it.

Avi polished off the last bite of waffle, eyed the remaining piece on his plate, then laid her fork on her plate
and, for good measure, tossed her paper napkin on top.

"There's still food on the table," he teased. "Are you
surrendering?"

"I am." A sly grin lit her face. "But only because I'm
taking a couple pieces of pie home with me. Do you have
any idea how long it's been since I've had a really good
meringue pie? Or even a bad one, as far as that goes."

"I take it you can't get that in an MRE."

"Sadly, no."

"Patricia makes a killer meringue pie. I'll ask her to
make you one." He hadn't thought of his mother's pies
in years. She'd baked them for special occasions and
just-because-it's-Saturday. Her lemon meringue had always been his father's birthday choice, rather than a cake,
and the pies had filled the sideboard at Thanksgiving and
Christmas, the meringue standing six inches high, swept
into curlicues, and baked golden brown. Between him
and his sisters, those delicate curlicues had never lasted to
the start of the meal.

Unlike most people Ben knew, Avi didn't demur. *Aw,*

you don't need to do that wasn't about to cross her lips. "That would be wonderful."

"What's your favorite?"

"Lemon. Banana cream. Chocolate. Any kind, really."

The waitress cleared the table and left the check. With a glance at the half dozen people waiting for a seat, Avi sighed. "What do you think? Could we auction off our table to the hungriest ones?"

He laughed. "I bet those two cowboys would pitch in at least five bucks toward our tab."

They both reached for the check at the same time, their fingers brushing, hers small and fine, his long and nowhere near as graceful. She didn't argue over the check, regretfully. He would have liked to extend the touch a moment longer, but when he tugged, she let go and smiled. "Thank you. Next time will be my treat."

Nope, he thought. Because next time would be a date, and he always paid for dates.

Chapter 4

They walked along Main Street after leaving the restaurant, Avi carrying the small white bag that held a piece of pecan pie and another of carrot cake. She glanced in store windows, and Ben pointed out a few other restaurants: CaraCakes, located down a side street; Luca's, an Italian place also on a side street; and Rosemary, a trendy little sandwich shop in an old sandstone storefront. A pale green-and-white awning shaded the south-facing building from the sun, and mismatched tables and chairs in pastel shades filled the dining room. It was charming and adorable and reminded her of nothing so much as a pile of delicately hued Easter eggs.

"The same people who own Rosemary also own Tallgrass's priciest restaurant," he said as they passed to the next business. "It's the kind you're not fond of, though they do spell the name properly. It's called Sage."

She wrinkled her nose. "The place that was here when

I was a kid was named Diner and was always busy. No fancy name needed."

"Did you spend a lot of time in Tallgrass when you were a kid?" Ben asked.

"As much as I could. I loved staying with GrandMir and Popi and going to work at the nursery."

"Where was your favorite shady spot to read?"

She smiled at the memory. "Under the weeping willow. It was my cave, my castle, my underwater kingdom." Her sigh was long and wistful. "I love that tree. When I finally get a house of my own, the first thing I'm going to do is plant one for my own kids."

Ben bent to pick up a piece of newspaper on the sidewalk, then tossed it into the garbage can a few steps ahead. "You know Tallgrass isn't the same place where your mother grew up."

With a twinge of wistfulness, she said, "I know. But it beats hell out of where I've been. There's plenty of food, running water, health care, schools. Kids don't have to worry about IEDs or missiles or gunfire. They don't go to bed wondering if they'll wake up in the morning or fear every time their parent leaves the house that they won't come back. They know they can do almost anything they want to do. They have hope and opportunity and a future to look forward to."

When Ben didn't say anything right away, she gave him a sidelong glance. His expression was thoughtful, his gaze distant. She had no clue his opinion about the war, and frankly, she didn't care a whole lot. Her conscience was clear, and, given her job, that was the most important thing to her.

After a moment, he pushed his hands into his pockets.

"It's easy to forget about the kids sometimes," he said quietly. "It's so far away. When I think of the war, I think in personal terms—Patricia's husband, Lucy's, Carly's, all the other margarita sisters. I don't consider that there are kids and families who are just trying to survive."

"It's what they do there. It's what they've done for centuries. Try to survive. We're not making it easy for them. No one ever has."

Sweat trickled down her spine, making her wiggle her shoulders to stop the tickle. Pushing the grim thoughts to the back of her mind, she forced a smile. "I don't know about you, but I think I'm melting. Want to head back to the car?"

He swiped his arm across the sheen of sweat glistening on his forehead. "Air conditioning sounds good."

Shifting her dessert bag to her other hand, she took his hand and tugged him to the curb. Sweet feelings tumbled in her stomach, pure happiness at the contact, and her palms turned damp—if that couldn't be blamed on the weather. As they waited for a car to pass, her shoulder bumped his, and a faint shiver passed through her. "How much time do you spend in Tallgrass?"

They crossed the street at a lazy pace, and on the opposite side, she released his hand. He didn't let go, though, but instead laced his fingers through hers. "How long will you be here?"

"Four weeks."

His gaze locked with hers, his eyes dark and seriously intense. "I suspect I'll be here a lot more this month than I was last month."

Another shiver went through Avi, girlish and silly and sending quivery sensations all the way to the tips of her toes. It was always nice to know that an attraction wasn't one-sided, especially with a man as sexy and likable as Ben. The length of her leave limited whatever might happen between them, but short-term relationships could be wonderful, too. She'd had some that she would remember fondly until the day she died.

They reached the rental car too soon. She was debating inviting him back to the house, debating whether it was entirely too soon to invite him to get intimate, when he spoke.

"How about giving me a tour of the town?"

Vague relief fluttered in her stomach. She had plenty of time to get to know Ben before she worried about getting naked and sweaty with him.

She beeped the door locks, then opened her door to a rush of hot Oklahoma summer air. It made her breath catch and added a new layer of perspiration to her face. "This is my first visit in fifteen years. I'm sure you know it better than I do."

"Your Tallgrass," he clarified as they both slid into their seats. "The one you remember with GrandMir and Popi."

Hearing him say their names made her smile. She loved it when a person paid attention to what she said, remembering details that meant little to him but an awful lot to her. "Okay. How about directions to Sonic first? I haven't had a cherry limeade in years."

Once they both had icy giant cherry limeades, she headed east on Main. "You've already seen their house. They owned the nursery forever. I came to work with them every day I was here. With GrandMir, that actually meant work, but Popi was always sneaking me off to have fun." The nursery didn't open until noon on Sundays, so she stopped in the shade of the sign.

"They loved growing things—flowers, vegetables, trees, kids. They wanted a half dozen kids but were only blessed with the one, so they doted on everyone else's kids, too. They taught Sunday school and gave jobs to anyone who needed one and helped put more than a few kids besides their own through college."

"They were good people," he said quietly.

Avi swallowed over the lump that had formed in her throat. "They were very good people."

"Where did your names for them come from?"

A few blinks cleared the moisture from her eyes. "They chose them. GrandMir's name was Mirabelle, and Popi's own dad was Pops, so he wanted something close but not the same." She swung the car in a wide U and turned back onto Main. "When I spent weekends with them in the spring, they gave me flowers to plant at home. I had no sense of what went together so our beds always looked like a blind person planted them. Man, some of those colors found in nature can clash."

He laughed. "So you didn't inherit the landscaping gene."

"No, but if you want someone to dig holes in the dirt, I'm your girl."

"Makes me wish I had dirt to dig in."

She gave him a look as she turned onto a side street that was a straight shot into the countryside, wondering where he lived. Not in an apartment, not even a luxury one. He seemed more settled than that, but not enough for a house. Maybe a condo that overlooked the river. More likely one in south Tulsa, near the endless restaurants and shopping. Done speculating, she asked, "Where do you live?"

"I have a loft downtown. Near the new baseball stadium. Do you like baseball?"

"Not even as much as I like soccer, which is about this much." She pressed the tip of her forefinger flat against her thumb. "That was one of my activities when I was seven. The first practice I went to, a kid kicked the ball in my face and broke my nose. I've hated it ever since."

"We grew up loving baseball. My dad played two years in college, and he intended to raise his own team, but Mom put a stop to that after spending a miserable twenty-three hours delivering Sara. It wasn't a Noble family reunion without baseball, not even at Christmas with snow on the ground."

Avi wondered if he realized he'd referred to Patricia as Mom. It was the first time she'd heard it. "Is that why you bought the loft near the baseball field?"

He grinned as they drove past the last house on the right and the road took a sharp curve through a stand of trees. "It's a great place—tall ceilings, hardwood floors, nice views, convenient to work."

"And the baseball field."

"Okay, yeah, the fact that I can walk to the games in two minutes might have influenced me a bit."

His grin was boyish and charming and made her feel younger and prettier and freer.

"I don't like baseball," she said, "but I could be persuaded to attend a game with a hot dog, a cold beer, and something fun to do afterward."

His smile was sly. "I'll check the schedule and let you know." After taking a long drink of limeade, he gestured to the farmland they were passing, broken up by occasional slashes of woods. "Did your grandparents raise their own stock for the nursery?"

"Don't I wish. I could have been driving a tractor by the time I was ten. They bought from some small producers, but most of their suppliers were big commercial farms. Nope, this is where we're headed." Flipping on the blinker, she slowed and turned into a dusty long driveway that led between two pastures to a clearing a quarter-mile back.

Though it was barely eleven thirty, Avi was surprised to see that the gravel parking lot was empty. She parked a few yards from the church sign that had stood for decades between two metal poles. Though the glass that had protected the letters lay shattered on the ground, their message was still visible: Jordan Bible Church. Sun School 9:30. Church 10:15. Sun Night: 6. Wed night: 7. Rev. Tom Brady.

Climbing out of the car, she closed the door with a thud that sounded extra hollow. "It never occurred to me that the church had closed," she murmured. "The people who came here were so dedicated."

Her gaze swept across what had once been neatly manicured yard. Now the entire area had been claimed by Johnson grass, six feet tall with stems thicker than her index finger. Popi had considered Johnson grass a scourge, but once it got its roots in, he'd said, *There's no going back. The war has begun.*

Her heart hurt as she looked at the church itself. The white paint that had once gleamed was faded and dirty. The screens over the windows were rusted, a few hanging crookedly, and only the hardiest of perennials survived in the old flower beds.

Avi walked toward the church, kicking up dust in the gravel lot with every step. When Ben joined her, she gestured toward the small, sad building. "GrandMir and Popi brought me here every Wednesday night and twice on Sundays. They opened the windows and handed out little paper fans to help keep the air stirring, and they sang and prayed like nobody's business."

They were at the sidewalk before the path became visible, four feet wide and winding through weeds tall enough to hide them both. Stumps of mowed-down stems poked through the soles of her shoes as they walked to the cemetery.

"Little country cemeteries are the best," Ben remarked quietly, his hand resting on the curved metal arch that topped the gate. "My grandparents and my father are buried in one north of Sand Springs." He swung the gate open, its squeaks sounding like feeble birds in the shady copse.

She walked through. The old brick path was mostly buried beneath leaves and dirt, but the headstones were in good shape. Someone was taking care of the fifty or so graves, even if the church had fallen into disrepair. It was harder to leave a person behind, even just his memory, than a building.

Though she hadn't been there in years, Avi found her grandparents' graves easily. Their marker was black marble, engraved with their names and birth and death dates, along with GrandMir's favorite Bible verse: *Casting all your care upon him; for he careth for you. 1 Peter 5:7* A bouquet of flowers etched into the stone at the top commemorated their love of growing things.

Ben stood quietly as she touched the rough edge of the

stone. She knew GrandMir and Popi weren't here. They were in every lovingly placed board of the house they'd shared so many years, in every bloom in their own yard and half the yards in town. Their spirit was in everyone who'd known them, especially Avi's parents, and it was in her. The better part of her.

She stayed like that a moment longer, whispering a silent message. *I miss you so much.* Calm spread through her, the same comfort she'd felt when GrandMir had tucked her into bed at night, when Popi had cuddled her during storms, the comfort that had always come from just being with them.

Smiling, she slowly got to her feet and glanced around at the other markers. Ben was right. Country cemeteries were the best.

* * *

Usually Ben ended his weekend visits to Tallgrass early Sunday evening, giving himself plenty of time to drive back to Tulsa, see about dinner, and get a full night's sleep. He didn't operate well, figuratively or literally, on less.

This Sunday he'd overstayed his usual by an hour and was reluctant to even think about leaving. *Thanks, Avi.*

A tall jar of marshmallow crème stood empty on the counter—the secret ingredient to Patricia's incredible meringue. She'd made two pies, coconut cream and lemon, pushed to the back of the counter, peaks of golden meringue swirled over the tops. He'd pinched one curl when she'd taken them from the oven, and she'd swatted his hand, an old habit come back to life.

He'd called her Mom today. Another old habit, one that had sneaked past all those years of resentment and had felt as natural as when he was a kid. But she'd been his mom then. Now...he was still working out what she was now.

"Though I know Beth and Neil hate missing even a day of Avi's leave, I'm kind of glad we've got her to ourselves for a while," Patricia said as she straightened from checking the pot roast in the oven. "She's a lovely girl, isn't she?"

"Yeah, she is." Lovely, no doubt. Girl? She'd gone to war and seen people die—strangers, enemies, friends, a man she'd loved like a father. But in spite of that, yeah, she had a girlish quality to her that, combined with her competence and courage, was damned appealing.

He really missed finding a woman appealing.

Patricia smiled at him. "You like her."

He shifted on the stool at the island, taking a drink of tea to delay. "Sure, I like her."

"I mean *like*. The way you liked Traci Monroe."

Now there was a blast from the past. He hadn't thought of Traci in years, but when he was fifteen, she'd been all he *could* think of. Blond, beautiful, with blue eyes and braces, a cheerleader and class vice-president, honor roll student and Girl Most Likely to Make Him Hyperventilate.

"Did you ever ask her out?"

"Are you kidding? I couldn't remember my own name around her. When she started dating the quarterback, I finally accepted that goddesses were out of my league." The realization had come as a relief. He'd no longer had to worry about thinking of something to say or trying to maintain eye contact.

"That is so not true," Patricia responded. "You're handsome, you've got gorgeous eyes, you're a sought-after surgeon... Traci Monroe would consider herself lucky if you looked her way twice." She smiled wistfully. "You've got your father's eyes. The first time we met, he looked at me, and I mean *really* looked, and I was a goner. On our first date, I just wanted to sit the rest of my life and stare into those eyes."

Ben shifted uncomfortably again. *What happened?* he wanted to ask. Why had she decided that she preferred staring into George's eyes? But he didn't want to know any more than he already did. Not tonight.

None too subtly he changed the subject. "Why does everyone call her Avi?"

"Because her name is Avery." Patricia shrugged at his blank look. "It's not a name I would have given an adorable little girl. It was her great-grandfather's name. As far as Avi is concerned, they should have saved it to use if they had a little boy. As far as I'm concerned, they should have said, 'We love you, Grandpa Avery, but we're not saddling our kid with your name.'" She smiled smugly. "I, on the other hand, settled for timeless names. Who could find fault with Benjamin Richard, Brianne Leigh, or Sara Anne?"

"I dated a girl in college who suggested that I go by Richard or Rich," he said dryly. "She hated Ben."

She shrugged. "What did she know? She's not around now, is she, so her opinion counts for squat."

The chime of the doorbell echoed through the house, bringing a big smile to Patricia and a twinge of something to Ben. Anticipation, he thought. Impending pleasure.

Patricia put on giant pot holders to remove the cast iron pot from the oven. "Get that, would you?"

More than happy to.

When he opened the door, Avi greeted him with a smile. She wore another summery dress, this one in pale yellow, and her hair was loose around her face, falling over her practically bare shoulders. She had on flip-flops again—standard wear for Oklahoma at least ten months of the year—and wore the strap of a giant purse over her neck and crossing her body. She held a bottle of wine in both hands.

"Hi," she greeted.

"Hi." He leaned one shoulder against the door jamb and just looked at her. His mother's words about his father—*I just wanted to sit and stare*—came to mind, though it wasn't just Avi's eyes that drew him.

After a moment, her smile broadened into a grin. "You're letting the cold air out. Were you raised in a barn?"

"Actually, I spent a fair amount of my childhood in one. My grandfather had horses, and if we were going to ride them, by God, we were going to feed them, groom them, and muck out their stalls." He backed away so she could step inside, then closed the door behind her. "Patricia's in the kitchen."

Unlike last night's dress, this one was form fitting and showed every sway of Avi's hips as she led the way down the hall. He appreciated a woman who moved like a woman, all delicate and graceful. He would bet that even at an all-out run, she never lost that grace.

Patricia greeted her with a hug, then Avi held out the wine. "I come bearing a gift from Mom's pantry. One bottle of Twisted Sisters wine from Girls Gone Wine."

"Oh, my favorite! Did Beth tell you that?"

"It was a pretty easy guess." While Patricia took the wine to the counter and rummaged through a drawer for a corkscrew, Avi slipped a pink Post-it note from her pocket and showed it to Ben. *Patricia's favorite. Do* not *listen to any stories she tells about us going there.*

"Your mom and I drove down to Beaver Lake this past winter and visited the winery," Patricia said, her back still to them, missing the grins they shared. "You should have seen us after the tasting. Good thing there was a restaurant just down the road where we could pass the time until it was safe to drive again."

"I thought you were supposed to spit out the wine at a wine tasting," Ben said as he pulled out a stool for Avi to sit on. Watching her climb onto it in that snug dress was definitely a pleasure.

"Some say you should, some say you shouldn't." Patricia got glasses from a cabinet, carried them to the island, and poured the wine, automatically stopping after only a few ounces in Ben's glass. "I say when someone's giving you free wine and it tastes this good, swallow for all you're worth."

After gently clinking glasses with them, she rested one hand on her hip. "Have you heard from your mama?"

"Not yet," Avi replied. "She left a copy of their itinerary. They were in port most of today, so I imagine she'll call tomorrow when they're back at sea."

"Doesn't a cruise sound just wonderful? Sitting by the pool all day, all the food you can eat, all the handsome waiters you can bear to look at serving you drinks..." Patricia sighed. "The margarita club goes on adventures from time to time. Maybe I can persuade them to do a short cruise."

"They'd put you all off the ship at the first port," Ben said with a snort. "For a bunch of nice normal women, you guys sure can get rowdy. People don't know whether to cheer when they see you coming or run and lock the doors to keep you out."

Patricia smiled innocently. "Life is too short and too uncertain not to enjoy it to the fullest."

"Amen," Avi said, lifting her glass for another clink with Patricia.

Ben gazed into the distance. He hadn't spent a lot of time enjoying life. He'd played mother and father both to his sisters, gone to college and studied, gone to medical school and studied, run himself ragged in his residency, and devoted himself to establishing his practice. There would always be time later for relationships, settling down, a family, and fun, he'd told himself.

But no one was guaranteed *later*. Lucy and her husband had put off having kids because there was always later. George had put off retirement and spending more time with his wife until later. Every single one of the margarita sisters and their husbands had delayed their plans until later, and later had never come.

Ben didn't want to live with a lifetime of regrets. He didn't want to look back and think if only he'd done this or if only he'd changed that. The one sure thing in life was death. A person had better grab everything else when the chance came.

And the first regret he didn't want to live with was Avi. Nothing might ever come of it. He might expect too much or not enough. He might get his heart broken. Most likely, after four weeks, they'd be lucky to ever see each other again.

But he could handle all that. He could cope with disappointment or heartbreak or whatever. Besides, he'd have one hell of a memory.

What he couldn't deal with was the regret of waiting until it was too late. He'd had a lifetime of that, and it stopped today.

* * *

The meal was over, the sun set, streetlights buzzing and drawing haloes of tiny insects to each globe. Avi wished she'd walked to the Sanderson house; after a dinner like that, she needed the exercise of walking home. The salad had been a stab at something healthy, but the rest was pure gastronomic indulgence: tender beef roast, carrots, potatoes, and onions in thick gravy, accompanied by sweet yeast dinner rolls and followed by incredible pies. She was so full she couldn't eat another bite, but just thinking of the dinner made her taste buds dance again.

They sat on the back patio, tiki torches burning near mosquito plants, the two of them doing a pretty good job of keeping the insects at bay. As if drastic swings in the weather weren't enough to keep Oklahomans on their toes, God had given them a wide variety of insects to add an extra level of endurance to being outdoors.

Patricia had made a pot of very good coffee, and Avi was on her second cup. She was half reclining on a chaise longue with super-thick cushions, her shoes kicked off, listening to the tree frogs and occasional happy shrieks from across the street. When had she ever felt so at ease with a family not her own?

Across the lawn, a back door opened and a large dog

trotted out, quickly disappearing from the bit of light provided by its porch light.

"That's Norton," Patricia said from Avi's right. "His mama, Lucy, is one of our margarita club members and a dear friend. Oh, look, Ben, I think Norton's caught your scent."

On her left, Ben mumbled something that appeared to cast aspersions on Norton's parentage. Avi chuckled as she strained to make out the dark dog in the shadows. She caught the sound of his running paws and panting a moment before he entered the circle of light around them. Skidding to a stop a few feet away, the large dog smiled at Patricia, smiled at Avi, then curled his upper lip to show his teeth, with a bit of pink tongue, to Ben. It was accompanied by a barely audible grumble in his throat.

Avi laughed. "Come here, Norton. Come on, boy." The dog trotted over for a scratch, leaning against her leg, head tilted back to give her unfettered access to his throat. "What did you do to him, Ben?"

"I never did anything. He doesn't like me."

"Norton likes everyone," Patricia disagreed. "You must have given him a reason."

Ben declared his innocence. "You sent me to their house one day to invite Lucy over for brunch. He looked at me, growled, and has been like that ever since."

"But he's such a baby," Avi cooed. "Look at this face. You must have scared him."

"Yeah, I never met a dog who was scared of me. I'm pretty sure it's the other way around." He leaned forward to set his empty coffee cup on a table, and Avi watched Norton show those teeth again with an even fainter rumble.

Norton was trying to ease all seventy pounds of himself inconspicuously into Avi's lap when the door across the yard opened again. "Norton!" Lucy yelled.

The dog hunkered lower.

"Come on, Norton, where are you?"

"He's over here, Lucy," Patricia called, waving one hand over her head to get the other woman's attention.

After grabbing a leash, the woman headed their way, disappearing into darkness as the dog had done. A widow and a dear friend, Patricia had said. Avi was expecting a woman about Patricia's age, but the woman who stepped out of the shadows and into their circle was much closer to her own age. She was pretty, with brown hair pulled back into a ponytail, a pleasant smile, and sequined flip-flops adorned with tropical flowers on her feet. Avi liked her just for those shoes.

"Hey, Patricia. Ben." Lucy nodded in his direction, and he nodded back. Next, her gaze skimmed over Norton, who was looking guilty as sin and unable to hide it, before moving on to Avi. She smiled again. "Hi."

"Hi. I take it this sweet baby is yours," Avi said as she continued to scratch Norton.

Lucy made a show of looking around. "There must be some other sweet baby around, but the stinker is mine. For six years he's never wandered off when he goes out, but for some reason he felt compelled tonight."

"Because he smelled Ben," Patricia teased. "You know he can't pass up a chance to intimidate Ben. Lucy, this is my dear friend, Avi Grant. She served with George in Afghanistan. Her parents are George's and my best friends. Avi, this is Lucy Hart."

Lucy came a few steps nearer to shake hands. "Are you out or home on leave?"

"Leave. I'm starting an instructor position at Fort Gordon, Georgia, in a month."

"You're Signal Corps?"

"Yes, ma'am."

Lucy feigned a scowl. "Just Lucy. You don't want to know what terrible threats I rain down on the heads of young soldiers who call me ma'am."

"I hear the margarita girls make tough, strong men quake in their boots."

"Some of them do. Some of us just dream about it." Lucy perched on the edge of a brick-walled flower bed, dangling the leash between her knees.

"How is Joe?" Patricia asked. Before Lucy could answer, she explained to Avi. "Joe Cadore lives next door to Lucy. He's a runner and the high school football coach, and he's a very sweet and darn good-looking guy. He's single, too, Avi. Maybe I should introduce you."

From Avi's left came a rumble reminiscent of Norton's, but this one was more human, though not by much. She glanced at Ben, whose expression was implacable, even when she gave him a covert wink. "I'm always happy to meet sweet guys."

"Good. I'll arrange that," Patricia said. "So, Lucy, how is he?"

"Busy now that school's started. The team has a scrimmage Friday evening, then their first game the week after that. Between that and his regular classes, he's pretty booked, but he still finds time to roust me out of bed at six o'clock in the morning to walk. This has been going on for nearly three months, and it's still an ungodly hour." Lucy leaned forward, gesturing to the dog to come. When he didn't move, Avi stopped scratching him, folding her hands in her lap despite the pleading look he gave her. Even so, he still made no move toward his mom.

"Ben, would you mind walking over to my house?" Lucy asked, her tone innocent and sweet.

"So your dog will chase me?" He snorted. "No, thanks. I'm not going to be bait for an oversized creature with fangs."

Lucy dangled the leash tantalizingly. "Norton, wanna go for a walk?"

The dog looked as if he was considering it, then slid into a boneless heap beside Avi's chair.

That earned a long-suffering sigh from Lucy. "Norton, wanna go see Joe?"

Bounding to his feet, he danced so happily she had trouble attaching the leash to his collar. "Nice to meet you, Avi. Patricia, Ben, y'all have a good night."

As they disappeared into the shadows again, Ben commented, "Cadore has an unnatural influence over that dog."

Avi smiled. The more she learned about Ben—intimidated by a baby like Norton and for some reason jealous of the sweet, good-looking neighbor—the more she liked him. The surgeon with a God complex was so common, it had spawned its own stereotype, but there was no God complex here. Just an incredibly sexy guy with a few flaws.

How much sexier did that make him?

Her sigh reluctant, she swung her feet to the ground. "This has been great, but I need to head home to let Sundance out. I've been lucky so far, but according to Mom's Post-its, she averages an accident every other day, so I'm probably due."

Ben stood and offered his hand, helping her up from

the low-to-the-ground chaise. Her fingers tingled, and that quivery girly feeling danced through her like smoke on the wind. It was full of potential, of possibilities, and she was full of the need for them.

Slowly he let go, then stepped around her chair and offered his hand to Patricia. She accepted it with a tiny bit of heartbreak in her smile, giving his fingers a squeeze before letting go to gather coffee cups and dessert dishes.

"I'll get those, Patricia," Avi said, but by then the older woman had collected them all.

"You're a guest. I'm chief cook and bottle washer." Patricia grinned slyly. "Though guest status ends after the second meal and you automatically become family, to be treated as such."

"Family, huh. Then I'll be over tomorrow to vacuum, dust, and mow the yard," Avi said with a laugh. "At least, those are included in the Post-its Mom left for me."

They went inside the house, where Ben headed upstairs to get his bag. While they waited, Patricia presented Avi with a pie plate holding most of the remaining pies. Avi held the ceramic dish tightly. "I know my mom raised me to say 'Oh, that's not necessary,' but I've been pie-deprived for too long. Thank you a bunch." Carefully, she leaned in to hug Patricia and remembered again the comfort she'd felt at GrandMir's and Popi's graves. Being close to someone who loved her was the best feeling in the world.

Ben's steps echoed on the stairs a moment before he joined them. His hug with Patricia was on the awkward side. Avi couldn't imagine sharing such a stilted embrace with her mother, couldn't imagine anything that could ever come between them that thoroughly. Even when she was a teenager and they'd argued, Beth had always been able to hug her right back into a good mood. Tickling and big melodramatic smooches had worked wonders back then. They probably still did.

Outside, the sounds of children playing were louder, the splashes indicating that the kids across the street were enjoying one of the last swims of the summer. Avi and Ben walked silently to her car, parked in the driveway. She nestled the pie plate into the passenger seat, tucked her purse around to hold it in place, then closed the door before turning to him.

So . . . Would he ask for her cell number? Offer his? Make firm plans to see her again before driving away?

For the first time in a long time, the answers mattered.

Linking his fingers with hers, he pulled her to the driver's side of the car, then stood, invading her personal space. She liked it.

"Do you have any plans for tomorrow night?"

Yes! "Not a single one."

He combed his fingers through his hair. "Would you like to go out to dinner?"

She wanted to blurt out the affirmative as quickly as it had echoed in her head, but he went on. "You would have to drive to Tulsa. Tuesday is surgery day, so if I come here, I can't get here before seven, and I'll have to head back before nine."

Drive to Tulsa? An hour or less. No big deal. She'd had commutes between apartments and forts that took longer, and that was just to work. An evening with Ben was such a nicer payoff. "I don't mind."

"I usually get out of clinic around six. We could meet at my house around six thirty?"

A smile spread across her face. "I can handle that."

"Good." He wasn't smiling, but his eyes showed something just as encouraging. Relief, maybe, or satisfaction. Hmm. She could show him satisfaction.

He leaned closer, just slightly, and lowered his voice. "I'd kiss you good night, but we have an audience."

Glancing over her shoulder toward the house, she caught just a glimpse of Patricia before the blinds at the living room window settled. Looking back at Ben, she smiled. "Kiss me anyway."

He closed the last of the distance between them, lowering his mouth to hers, giving her a sweet, gentle, tender kiss that set her blood on fire. It was impressive and surprising and just a bit scary, considering she'd had tons of kisses that were a whole lot more passionate and evoked a whole lot less of a response.

When he lifted his head, her fingers curled, wanting to wrap around the back of his neck and pull him down again. Her heart skipped a beat or two, and something deep inside her felt deprived.

In the dim light, Ben looked impressed and surprised and a bit scared, too. For a moment, he stared at her, all intense and searching, then he gave a rueful shake of his head. Stepping back, he asked for her cell phone, input his number, and texted it to himself to get her number. "Six thirty," he said when he handed it back, his voice rough-edged. "I'll send you the address."

"I'll be there."

Chapter 5

Ben was on his way to work Monday morning when his cell phone rang. Steering with one hand, he fished it from the pocket of his scrubs, glanced at the screen, and grinned. "Good morning, Lucy."

"Aw, with caller ID, there's no such thing as a surprise anymore."

"No, but there's still the pleasure." He glanced at the clock on the dash. "Aren't you supposed to be walking with Cadore?"

"We just finished. I'm tired, sweaty, and out of breath." She paused a moment, then ruefully said, "Isn't that a pretty picture?"

"Any picture of you is pretty." He'd thought so the moment he'd seen her, even though he'd been filled with resentment because she'd guilted him into going to Tallgrass the day after George's death. She was one of those rare people who just radiated kindness and generosity and happiness, even though, God knew, she'd had enough sorrow in her life.

"You're a flatterer, but thank you. After an hour's walk on a Monday morning, I need flattery." Her voice lightened and took on a singsong quality. "So... tell me about Avi."

He was alone in his car, but damned if he didn't feel his temperature rising. It wasn't discomfort from talking about the new woman in his life with the old one—the one he'd desperately wanted to be The One—though he'd rather pretend it was.

Nope, the rising heat was caused by the mere thought of Avi. What little touching they'd done, that little kiss they'd shared... Every time he'd kissed Lucy, he'd willed himself to feel that—that specialness, that electricity, that affection and pleasure and arousal and hunger—but he never had. Kissing Lucy had been sweet, bland, like kissing his sisters.

Kissing Avi... *damn*.

At the other end of the line, Lucy's laugh was light and happy. "Wow, she's left you speechless. I'm impressed. For what it's worth, I liked her. She's good for you."

"You could see that in the five minutes you saw her last night?"

"Yup. That's my superpower. I can tell in mere minutes whether a person is good, bad, or ugly."

"And yet you're friends with Cadore." First meetings set the tone for a relationship, they said, and his first meeting with Cadore—every meeting—hadn't gone well. It wasn't just that he'd resented Cadore's place in Patricia's life, his place in Lucy's life. There had been a definite never-gonna-be-buds vibe going on, too.

She laughed again. "He says the same thing about you. Don't worry about Patricia introducing Avi to Joe. She's really into you, too."

Ben thought so, too, especially after that kiss, but for Lucy's benefit, he snorted. "How could you tell? We didn't even speak to each other while you were there."

"Superpowers," she reminded him. "Does Patricia know?"

"Yeah, I think so." There'd been a sly, enjoying-herself-too-much sound to her voice when she'd suggested Avi should meet Cadore.

"She must be delighted. I certainly am, and I want juicy details next time we talk, got it?"

"You expect me to kiss and tell?"

"Honey, I expect you to do a whole lot more than that." With another cheerful laugh, she said, "Gotta get ready for work. Have a good day."

He was still smiling when he pulled into the parking lot and into his usual space in the far corner. Some days the only exercise he got was the hike to and from the building. After jogging up the stairs to the fourth floor, he filled an insulated mug with coffee, ripped open a granola bar from his desk drawer, took a bite, and headed for his pod of exam rooms.

He could guarantee he would be on time for appointments only twice a day: the first one in the morning and the first one after lunch. He didn't like keeping people waiting, but some patients just needed more than the allotted time. The patients weren't the only ones inconvenienced; though the clinic closed at five, he rarely got out before six, sometimes seven.

"That's why you're paid the big bucks," he murmured to himself as his medical assistant directed him into Room 1.

Tonight, he really wanted to get out by six.

He'd texted his address to Avi last night before falling into bed. *Need directions?* he'd asked.

I'll Google it, she'd replied with a smiley face.

She wouldn't find much besides directions. He didn't have an online life. What free time he had was devoted to family, friends, baseball games, and other minor things like eating and sleeping. The clinic's website gave a basic bio; the Facebook page Bree had pestered him into doing sat unupdated; he didn't even know what the latest trend since Twitter was.

He suspected Avi was more sociable than he was. If he had a few minutes today, he just might Google her. If he was lucky, he'd find some photos of her...and forget to go back to work.

"How was your weekend?" his patient asked.

It was a standard question. He had a standard answer—*Good*—which could mean anything from double-header extra-innings wins for the Drillers, a family get-together at Sara's house, or never leaving the loft the entire time. This time, though...Just thinking of Avi raised the temperature in the room, made the air heavier and thicker so that filling his lungs was impossible. He had to swallow over the lump that had formed in his throat to answer, and even then his voice was raspy. "It was good. Really good."

The morning was half gone when the nurse told him they'd squeezed in an unexpected patient, now waiting in Room 2. Hearing a familiar voice through the open door, he stuck his head in to find Sara, Matthew, and Eli sitting on the exam table while Lainie occupied the tall chair that left her feet dangling in midair.

"Uncle Ben, Uncle Ben!" the boys clamored.

"What are you guys doing here?" He slid into the chair next to six-year-old Lainie, then noticed the ice pack on her left wrist. "Uh-oh. What'd you fall off of?"

She raised big brown eyes to him, still glistening from recent tears. "A tree. But I didn't fall. My body just jumped before my brain knew."

"And your arm broke your fall?"

"Don't say broke," Sara said, sliding to her feet. "She still has the remains of the last pink cast in the closet."

He wrinkled his nose, making both boys laugh. "Doesn't it smell?"

"Now that it's aired out, it's only slightly worse than stinky cheese."

He bent close to Lainie. "Your mom's going to take you to X ray so we can get some pictures of your bones, okay?"

Her hair bounced as she nodded. "And I have to sit still, don't I? And I get to go to CherryBerry for frozen yogurt when we're done, don't I?"

"Of course you do." Ben didn't need to look at his sister for confirmation. Sara was a big believer in the reward system, for the kids and especially for herself.

"What about the boys?" Sara asked as Lainie slid to the floor and headed toward the door.

He looked at his nephews, now lying on the table, Matthew's head at one end, Eli's at the other, Eli's feet holding Matthew's legs in the air. They were both rattling some serious fake snores. "I'll be in the hall dictating. I'll keep an eye on them."

In less than ten minutes, they were back. Ben checked the X rays, then took the wrap from the splint and cast tech. "I'll take care of this one. Good news, Lainie. It's not broken. You just got a little sprain."

Lainie's eyes narrowed. "But I still get ice cream, don't I?"

"Yes, you still get ice cream," Sara said with exaggerated patience. She shooed the boys off the table, then Ben lifted Lainie to sit on it. "You went to Tallgrass this weekend, didn't you?"

"Yeah." Ben sat beside his niece, positioned her arm, and began wrapping it with an elastic bandage.

"How was Mom?"

"Fine."

"How was Lucy?"

"Fine. Her dog got out, and she wanted me to play rabbit to his greyhound."

"And you refused, didn't you? Coward. You know Norton wouldn't hurt a fly." Sara watched him a moment before giving him the kind of look that meant she was about to have a good time at his expense. Her smile was sly, her tone all fake innocence, as she asked, "Is there anything you want to tell me?"

"Nope." Heat warmed his face so he kept his head lowered as he secured the end of the wrap. Hoping to distract his sister, he smiled at Lainie. "How's that feel?"

"Funny."

"It's not too tight?"

She shrugged. What did she know about too tight? She was six. "It's just plain ol' white." Disappointment underlay her words.

"I know. We should get some green ones with purple polka dots, shouldn't we?"

"I like pink. With orange."

"I'll look into that." He helped her to the floor, then faced Sara. "You know the drill—rest, ice, elevation."

She brushed him off. "Yeah, I know. So when are you seeing her again?"

Crossing his arms, Ben leaned against the edge of the table and surrendered. "How long did Patricia wait to call you?"

"However long it took for you to lock lips with the woman and for Mom to get both Bree and me on the line." Sara grinned evilly. "I believe you were pulling away from the curb."

His flush intensified. "This isn't big news."

"Of course it is. Your love life has been in desperate need of activity."

"You talk like I never go out." Hell, she talked like he *had* a love life. "I dated Lucy for nearly a month."

"We all knew that wasn't going to last. We love Lucy, but you two didn't have any chemistry. You were clearly meant to be friends, nothing more."

He couldn't even protest her dismissal. Hadn't he thought just this morning that kissing Lucy had been totally sisterly? While there'd been nothing the least sisterly about kissing Avi.

"Back to the subject . . . When do you see her again?"

He could try to put her off, but it would be a waste of time. Both of his sisters were stubborn, but Sara was downright relentless. It was always easier to tell her what she wanted to know. "She's driving into town tonight for dinner."

Sara smiled so brightly that he couldn't help but smile back, though it was tinged with ruefulness. "Will she be staying over for breakfast?"

He rolled his eyes, then dragged his fingers through his hair. "You know, most guys get to keep their social life private until they're ready to let people know."

"Private is not a concept the Noble family knows. Aunt Rennie practically popped the question to Rowdy's girlfriend herself, and when Tommy didn't ask Suz out for a second date, Aunt Laurie did." Sara wagged her finger at him. "Consider yourself lucky that I'm talking to you and not Avi. My kids need cousins, and if we can't count on you to give them some on your own, I have to step in."

Resolutely he shook his head. "No chance of that. She doesn't live here. She's in the Army, and in a month she's moving to Georgia. She won't be back for eight more years."

The finger that had been wagging now tapped Sara's lower lip. "Hmm. That could be a problem. My kids need cousins here, not halfway across the country."

"I need CherryBerry," Lainie piped up.

"And I need to get back to work or I won't be out of here in time for dinner."

"Well, we certainly don't want you to miss your first real date in God knows how long. Even if this one does move away, you can use the practice when you try again." Grinning, Sara hustled the kids together and toward the door before turning back to give him a wicked wink. "I hope it makes up for all those nights you've sat home alone."

Ben shook his head. Too often, a shake of his head was the only response he could come up with for Sara and Bree. But as he turned away, he wondered himself.

Would Avi be staying for breakfast?

* * *

Avi was halfway out the kitchen door after lunch when the front bell pealed through the house. She commanded Sundance to sit, then strode through the house to the door, opening it to Patricia.

"Am I interrupting anything?"

With a glance at the tablet in her hand, Avi shook her head. She had plenty of time to read, not so much to spend with people she adored. "I was taking Sundance outside. Want to come sit with me while I watch her discover a new world?"

"I thought she played in the yard every day."

"She does, but apparently she forgets it as soon as she's back inside. Everything's a brand-new discovery every time she goes out."

"I feel that way sometimes."

When they reached the kitchen, Avi set the tablet aside and grabbed two bottles of water from the fridge. As soon as she opened the door, Sundance darted outside, tearing around, barking with delight at a butterfly, cautiously sniffing a tree root, stalking, and then pouncing on a flower.

Avi and Patricia took seats shaded by the house and the towering oak next to it. "You have plans today?" Patricia asked as she unscrewed the cap on her bottle.

Avi took a long drink, watching her friend try to act innocent. When she lowered the bottle, she said, "I saw you peeking out the window last night."

"Oh, good. I hate trying to get information from someone stealthily. I'm just no good at it." Patricia squeezed Avi's hand. "Where is he taking you for dinner?"

"I don't know yet. He told you?"

"No. My granddaughter fell out of a tree she wasn't supposed to be climbing and hurt her arm, and what's the use of having an orthopedic surgeon for an uncle if you can't cuddle with him while he wraps your sprained wrist?"

"Makes perfect sense to me." Avi had gone out a few times with a doctor she'd met after injuring her shoulder six or seven years ago. The cuddling had been fun.

"Ben's a good boy. I hope you two have a wonderful time, but don't feel you have to share *all* the details with me. Though I left him on his own for a long time, he's still my son." Then the teasing smile that looked so good on her came back. "Besides, Bree and Sara will share whatever they pry out of him."

Avi laughed. His sisters might be determined, but she'd bet Ben wouldn't share anything he didn't want to. "He's close to them, isn't he?"

"Very. He stepped up when I stepped out. He's their rock."

"I wish I had siblings."

Patricia grinned knowingly. "No, you don't. You liked being an only child. You told me when you were little that if your parents had other kids, you would have to share everything—holidays, grandparents, your room— and what would you get in return? Nothing."

Avi's brow wrinkled. "I think I do remember saying something like that. Maybe what I meant to say was I wish I had cousins."

"I think you wish you had more family. But when life doesn't give you enough, you just go out and find more. There doesn't have to be a blood connection. George and I always considered you a part of our family, and I always will."

Her voice broke just the tiniest bit on the last sentence,

and Avi's heart twinged. She reached across to clasp Patricia's hand and drew a breath that hurt so she could force her voice out. "I'm so sorry about George."

"I know you are, sweetie." Tears made Patricia's voice husky, and she blinked them back unashamedly. "The margarita club tell me that the time will come when I can talk about him without tears, but I don't know. It's always going to break my heart."

"Would you rather not...?"

"Oh, no! I don't want to forget a thing about him, and I don't want anyone else to, either. When he found out you were in his new command, he was delighted. Twelve years you were in the Army together, and finally you were going to be assigned to the same place. Though he was worried, too."

"He worried about all his soldiers."

"His troops were important to him," Patricia agreed. "He used to say 'They're babies, Trish. These kids should be home going out on dates, not patrols. I swear, some of them don't even shave yet.'"

"Did you remind him that he'd been that young once?"

"Yes, but he just reminded me right back that at eighteen, he'd been safe and sound at West Point."

Sundance trotted across the yard and flopped onto the grass beside them, tongue hanging out. The first few times Avi had brought her out, she'd thought that meant *Let's go in*. Now she knew the dog was just catching her breath before starting her wild run all over again.

"Did you ever wish he wasn't in the Army?"

A semi on one of the main streets blasted its horn, disrupting the quiet of the backyard. The air settled again almost immediately, still and heavy.

Patricia shook her head. "Being a soldier wasn't a job to him. It was such an ingrained part of him that not being one would have changed who he was."

"Were you scared about leaving Oklahoma to go to Germany with him?" That part—moving halfway around the world from her kids—was hard to understand. Avi fully intended to marry and have at least a couple babies before she retired, because after thirty-eight, who knew if she'd be able to? But once she had those babies, she wouldn't be leaving them for anything less than war or an extended deployment.

"I was . . . unhappy in Oklahoma. I wanted to see someplace else, do something else . . . be someone else." Her gaze distant, Patricia seemed for a moment to age before Avi's eyes. There was such regret, such sorrow, on her face.

It takes an exceptional person to reach the age of fifty without regrets, George had told Avi during one of their last conversations.

But the only way to avoid regrets is to not take chances, she'd countered, *and not taking chances is no way to live.*

The moment had been interrupted by the ground-shaking explosion of an IED just outside the base and the chaos that followed. That time they'd been fortunate; the injuries suffered by the troops in the vehicle were minor.

A few weeks after that, George had been killed.

"You're probably wondering how I could have walked away from my kids."

A flush warmed Avi's cheeks. She bent to pick up Sundance and snuggled with her to hide it. "I don't—" After a moment, she gave up the hedging and met Patricia's gaze. "It doesn't seem like you. You've always been such a mother."

"It was a mistake—not going with George, but leaving the children. I knew it at the time, but I did it anyway." She began to speak, then compressed her lips while exhaling loudly. It took another moment for the words to start. "Did your parents ever tell you that I was married to Ben's father when George and I met?"

Avi kept her brows from raising skyward through sheer will. She had never known the story behind Patricia and George's relationship. She'd just always thought theirs was a fairy-tale romance, all sweet and wonderful and perfect because it was meant to be. "No, they, uh, they didn't."

Grimness darkened Patricia's gaze. "Then let me tell you the story. It has a lot of heart, and a lot of hurt, and no one got to live the happily-ever-after. I just hope…" She gazed off over the back fence for a moment before summoning a wobbly smile. "I hope it doesn't make you love us less."

Never, Avi knew, but her chest grew tight that Patricia thought it necessary to say such a thing. Maybe this was a story Avi didn't need to know. After all, Patricia was like a second mother to her, and George…George was her mentor. She'd lived much of her life following his lead, depending on his advice, his expertise, his moral compass, his gut feelings. He was her *hero*. If he'd made a very human mistake twenty years ago, she didn't need to know. Didn't *want* to know.

Except for Ben's sake, maybe she did.

"Ben's father and I got married right out of high school. We were young and crazy in love, and we were good together for a long time. Rick was happy as a clam right there in the middle of Tulsa. He had no desire to go anywhere else, not even for a couple days, and he never understood how I could want something else. Oklahoma was the be-all, end-all of his existence."

Avi swallowed hard, swiping her palms on her shorts. So far, she could relate. GrandMir and Popi had been just like that. Their blood ran Red River red, Popi used to say. God had birthed them in Paradise, GrandMir had added. Why would they ever want to leave?

But they'd understood that Avi wanted to see the world. Just as they'd known that someday she would come back to stay—would need to, to calm that red dirt in her veins. Rick Noble, apparently, hadn't had the same understanding for Patricia.

Sundance wiggled to the ground and dashed off to sniff the tree root and pounce on the flower again. Patricia took a drink of water before wagging one finger in Avi's direction. "Now, don't you get the idea that George broke up my marriage. You know what an honorable man he was. If he'd known I had a husband and kids at home, I don't believe he ever would have agreed to a second meeting. *I* broke up the family all on my own. I doubt Rick ever forgave me, and I don't know if Ben ever will, but my girls have, and I've had a lot of long talks with God, and He has, too."

Best advice I can give you, grandgirl, Popi had told her when she started dating. *It takes two to make a relationship, and it takes two to break one.* Then, less solemnly: *However, if you do find yourself stuck with someone you can't get rid of, you come to me. I'll break him—I mean, break it off for you.*

"I don't know how much of that visit you remember," Patricia went on. "You were in school, and your parents were at work. George had all those long hours every day to fill. My kids were at school, and Rick was at work, and I had all that emptiness inside me. And George filled it so well. We both loved art and history and travel." She smiled self-deprecatingly. "Well, *he* loved travel. I loved the idea of it, since I'd never been able to do it. He was everything Rick wasn't, everything I wanted, and I fell in love with him before the first week was gone."

He'd brought her to dinner one evening, Avi recalled. The moment she'd taken her shoes off to play in the yard with Avi while the men grilled steaks and her mother finished dinner in the kitchen, Avi had fallen in love with her. Even though her smitten girl's plans had involved marrying George herself when she was all grown up, she'd decided Patricia was worthy of him in the meantime and was happy to see them looking pretty smitten themselves.

Her movements restless, Patricia stood and wandered toward the flower beds lining the fence, bending to pluck an occasional spent bud. "I could have handled things better. I should have. I wasn't some young carefree woman who could fall in love on a whim. I had a husband. Kids. Responsibility. I should have told George the day we met that I was married. I should have gone home to Rick and tried to make things better. But I couldn't."

Avi walked barefoot alongside her, savoring the heat of the sun on her shoulders and the sparkle of droplets from this morning's watering on rich petals and lush leaves and thinking that *could* and *should* were sometimes the hardest things in the world to do.

"Rick didn't know who I was anymore. Bless his heart, he was the same person in his thirties that he'd been in his teens, with just a few more creaks and aches. It had never once occurred to him that maybe I wasn't, even though I gave him clues. I wanted to take a trip. I wanted to go to college. I wanted to have an opinion that mattered. I wanted to create something. I wanted to stop feeling so stifled. But those were just words to him. They had nothing to do with his wife and the mother of his children. Why, those two jobs alone were plenty enough for any woman, especially me."

The anguish in her tone made Avi's heart ache. In all the years she'd known her, Patricia had always been a vital woman. She loved people and new places and new experiences. She'd gotten a college degree, then two more for good measure. She'd learned crafts and cooking and history and politics, and her every opinion mattered. If she hadn't taken action, the bright, vibrant woman she was would have withered into a straggly weed without enough joy to share with anyone.

"Before George left for Germany, we agreed I would stay behind, tell Rick I wanted a divorce, move out, find a lawyer, make sure the kids understood what was going on. Finally, when all that was taken care of, two or four or six months down the line, I could join him in Germany. He got on the plane that day believing that was what I was going to do. But I was weak. For the first time in my life, I had a chance to be with a man who loved not just me but the me I wanted to be. He was supportive and encouraging. He listened to me, valued my opinions, and he gave me hope." Eyes damp, Patricia smiled at Avi. "I hadn't had hope for a long time. So I went home, told

Rick and the kids, and I was on the next flight to Germany that same night.

"I do wish I had found a way to do it without breaking their hearts," she whispered. "I cried all the way. My kids, my babies..."

Not bothering to be surreptitious, she wiped at the corners of her eyes. "I was selfish. I knew what a shock it would be, what pain it would cause, and I'm still selfish today, because, Avi, I don't regret one single moment I spent with George. We were together twenty years, and it breaks my heart that we can't have twenty more. I'm so sorry for all the hurt, but I would do it again in a heartbeat. Besides giving birth to three wonderful children, I do believe that man was the reason I was put here on earth."

After those heart-wrenching words, she glanced at Avi. "Are you hating me yet?"

"How could I ever hate you, Patricia?" Avi hugged her tightly. "You and George were meant to be together. Time proved that." She just hoped she had the chance to love a man like that, and be loved in return, for herself.

*   *   *

It was ten after six when Ben took the stairs two at a time from the clinic to the parking lot. With ten minutes to get home, he'd have ten more to take a shower and change into clothes for tonight's date. He'd bet money that Avi would be on time, if not early. After all, punctuality was a big deal in the Army, wasn't it?

During his lunch break, Brianne had called to ask where he was taking Avi for dinner. When he told her he hadn't decided, she'd sighed and muttered a few less-than-complimentary words. She had suggested several places, then groaned when he told her he was thinking about tracking down the food trucks that frequented downtown Tulsa and letting Avi choose.

The last part had been true, at least. He did intend to let Avi choose. Tulsa had hundreds of restaurants, from casual to elegant dining. She was the one who'd spent most of the last year out of the country. Whatever appealed to her was fine with him.

He'd parked in the garage that opened off the alley behind his building and gone inside the lobby to pick up his mail when he stopped abruptly. Avi sat in one of the two easy chairs there, sunglasses pushed back on her head, a tablet in her hands, a smile directed his way. She stood, and as he took in the sight, his mouth went dry and a lump formed in his throat.

She wore a red tank top that clung to her body, ending about an inch before the waistband of her denim skirt started. The skin showing between the two bits of fabric was a few shades lighter than her arms and legs and tempted him to explore it, to see how soft and silky and warm it was. Then he could do the same with her long, lean legs, mostly exposed beneath the very short, snug skirt. His gaze sliding on down, he half expected heels with tiny strips of leather hugging her feet, but she wore flip-flops, dressed up with sparkling stones on the straps. With her hair pulled back in a braid and silver jewelry around her neck, on her ears, and clinking around her wrists, she looked fresh and cool and gorgeous.

And he was in scrubs stained with surprise blood splatter from an injection into a patient's knee.

"Hi."

"Hey." He stepped closer to her, catching the scent of summer—flowers, spices—drifting on the air. Leaning closer, he kissed her cheek, and something tugged down deep in his gut. "I thought you'd be early."

She smiled. "I thought you'd be late."

"Let me check my mail, then I'll be ready in ten minutes." He unlocked the small box mounted in the wall, took out a handful of envelopes, then gestured to the stairs. Her shoes made flippy noises while his heavier running shoes thudded solidly.

When they stepped inside the loft, he set the mail aside, then watched as Avi looked around. The open floor plan had appealed to him when he'd first seen the place, along with the recycled wood floors, high ceilings, and large windows. The furnishings were sparse—minimalist, the interior designer had called it. Easy to clean, he'd thought.

"I like this," Avi said. "Lots of space."

"I have to resist the temptation to fill it with stuff. You should have seen the apartment I lived in before this. Sara threatened to call that TV show for hoarders."

She crossed the old wood floor to the relatively new rug, white geometrics on a red background. The red was the only real color in the room, with a coffeemaker to match on the kitchen counter. Everything else was subdued. Calming, the designer said. Boring, Brianne said. Unimportant, he thought. As long as the furniture was comfortable, the television was visible, and the space was livable, he didn't care about the rest of it.

"Would you like a tour?"

Smiling, she dropped her bag on the couch and clasped her hands behind her back as he joined her in the center of the red rug. "This is the living room, where I watch TV and take unscheduled naps." Taking her arm, the skin as soft as he'd imagined, silky enough that he could marvel at the texture for an hour or two, he led her a dozen feet ahead. "And this is the dining room, where I eat a meal maybe once a year, but the table looks nice, doesn't it?"

Avi's eyes were lit by the smile that still curved her mouth. "Beautiful. I love oak."

He gestured to one hand. "The kitchen. Comes with a microwave and coffeemaker."

"Vital for survival," she agreed.

Still holding onto her, he stopped at the first doorway in the long hall, sliding his fingers along her arm to her shoulder. "My office. Small children and their toys have been known to get lost inside, so if you go in, you might want to leave a trail I could follow."

He walked beside her to the other doorway at the end of the hall. "And my bedroom." What would she think? That it was too minimalist? Too boring? Maybe her least favorite room of the condo? It was definitely the messiest room in the house. Did women get turned off by that stuff or—forget women—would *Avi* get turned off?

She slipped free and walked into the room. He didn't watch her but rather the reflection of her in the dresser mirror. Everything about her had a *wow* factor: the way she looked, the way she moved, the way she stood still. Her body was long, lean, nicely muscled, her clothes and flip-flops so girly, her confidence strong. Just looking at her made his chest tighten and sent heat seeping along his nerves. Sara was right that he'd spent too many nights alone. He'd figured that out for himself the first hour after he and Avi had met.

She was amazing, and he really needed to be amazed.

Her gaze swept across the unmade bed, the crumpled pillows, the piles of clothing on the chairs, the bottles of cologne lined up on the dresser. She nudged a protruding drawer shut, then turned to face him, wearing a sweet, amused, knowing, promising, sensuous smile.

How could one look say so much? He cleared his throat. "Give me ten minutes to shower, and, uh, we can, uh, go."

She strolled back, passing him in the doorway, enveloping him in a cloud of cologne and heat and need. Again, he watched her until she was out of sight in the living room, then he heaved a great sigh as he shucked off his scrubs and he went into the bathroom.

His shower was quick. There was something about knowing Avi was waiting out for him, even fully dressed, that made his muscles quiver with every touch. By the time he'd dried off and dressed, the skin all over his body tingled, and he was hotter than when he'd stood under the hot water.

Avi sat on the couch, the tablet out again, long gorgeous legs crossed, absorbed in reading. When she heard his approach, she glanced up, her gaze sliding over him, before a small smile curved her lips. Sliding the tablet into her purse, she stood and swung the strap over her shoulder.

"You look great." He liked the dresses he'd seen her wearing the two days before, very pretty and feminine and covering far more skin. This snug top and tiny skirt were pretty and feminine and damn sexy. These clothes were going to make it damn hard to concentrate through dinner...though he was pretty sure he'd have trouble concentrating if she wore burlap from neck to toe.

"Are you hungry for anything in particular?" he asked as they headed for the door.

"I would kill for a hamburger."

"When I say 'I would kill,' it's just a figure of speech. When a woman who's accustomed to carrying weapons says it..." he teased her with a grin. "Lucky for you, no deaths are necessary. Fat Guy's has great burgers, and it's just the other side of ONEOK Field. That's where the Drillers play."

At the foot of the stairs, he paused. There were two doors in the lobby, one leading out onto the street, the other into the alley. "Walk or drive?"

For answer, she turned toward the street door. The first minute or two passed in silence, until they reached the intersection. "Do anything interesting today?" he asked while they waited for the light to change.

"No, and it was incredible. I slept in, played with Sundance, visited with your—Patricia, and talked to Mom and Dad for a few minutes. They're having a fabulous time on their cruise, and Dad's threatening to sell everything and buy a boat. Mom says a boat can't have two captains and no way is she going to be first mate to his captain. You give a man a little power, and it goes to his head."

He laughed. "You don't get many days to do nothing, do you?"

"Not as many as I would like." The light changed, and they stepped off the curb. Subtly, he thought, he reached for her hand, clasping it lightly in his. In his peripheral vision, he caught the tiny, satisfied smile that curved her lips. "What about you? Did you do anything interesting today?"

"I stuck needles in some joints, decided on surgery with a half dozen patients, set a broken leg, and treated my niece's sprained wrist."

"Patricia said she had an owie."

When he'd first begun seeing Lucy, it had seemed strange to hear her talk about his mother in casual conversation. None of his friends and certainly none of the women he'd dated even knew Patricia existed, and up to that point, he and his sisters had never talked about her. Now it seemed practically normal. "Yeah, Lainie took a tumble. She's prone to that. She's more adventurous than her two brothers put together."

"Girl power," Avi said with a smirk.

"I bet you were a wild little girl."

Her slender shoulders shrugged as a grin tugged at her mouth. "I had fun. I only broke my nose, needed stitches only three times, and had only one concussion."

He was pretty sure she hadn't grown out of her tomboy ways, and yet she was still such a *girl*. In a twist on the old motto, *No pain, no gain*, his personal motto was *No pain, no pain*. But he liked the combination in her.

A lot.

When he had to release her hand at the restaurant, he missed the contact, then put it out of his mind while they ordered their meals, then found a table near the front window. As she slipped the paper from her drinking straw, he asked, "What do you plan to do after you retire?"

"That's eight years from now. Who looks that far ahead?" Immediately she answered herself. "Smart little boys who want to grow up to be a bone doctor. Good grades in high school, four years of college, four years of medical school, and...?"

"A year of surgical residency and four years in an orthopedic residency."

She folded her arms on the tabletop and leaned forward, not much, just enough to wrap them in an air of intimacy. "Actually, I plan to come back to Oklahoma, be a mom and hopefully a wife and have a second career. Being Signal, I have mad job skills, so I could do just about anything in the communications field."

"So a smart little girl grew up and said, 'My dream is to do communications in the Army'?"

"Not exactly. I didn't really think much beyond being a soldier. When you join the service, you take an aptitude test, and that was one of the available fields that sounded cool. I like to communicate, right? My mom and dad say I've communicated with the best of them since I was eight months old."

He could easily imagine that. Shy and quiet, she was not. "That was just after 9/11, wasn't it? Didn't you realize that a job like that meant a good chance of being sent to war?"

Slowly she settled back in her chair, folding her arms over her middle. "I wanted that. Don't make the mistake of thinking that only men are qualified to be in combat, that the women have to be kept safe at the rear or, better yet, back home in the States. Not every woman is cut out for combat, but neither is every man. Women can be heroes just as easily as men."

He liked the serious look in her eyes, the furrowing of her brows, the way she managed to look relaxed while tension simmered faintly around her. He liked that she was passionate about the subject, no matter that her tone was conversational, her expression still pleasant.

"But not everyone agrees with you, do they?"

"No. Life isn't easy for women in the military. A lot of men in the service are accepting. A lot are macho bigots. There's a lot of discrimination, harassment, sexual assaults, and I honestly don't know if that sort of stuff will ever go away because it's not just an Army issue. It's a social issue. But you don't make issues better by packing up your bags and going home. If women quit serving, if they say 'Okay, the bastards don't want me here so I'll go away,' we lose, the service loses, and the ignorant jerks win. That can't happen."

Abruptly an abashed look came over her face. "Sorry. I tend to get on my soapbox when the question of women in the military comes up. Simple answer to your simple question: I joined the Army to defend our country in any way I could, and if that means picking up a gun, then I'm happy to do it. I'm strong, I'm tough, I'm as good a shot as any man I know, and I'm twice as smart as most of them. I've never traded on sex to curry favor or avoid responsibility. I've earned what I've gotten."

To lighten the moment, Ben said, "You've never traded sex? Damn. And here I was hoping..."

As he'd intended, she laughed. "Gender, okay? I've never traded on gender to get anything. Trading sex is another proposition altogether... but I've got to tell you, it takes a lot more than a hamburger, unless it's the best hamburger in town."

Ben gestured to the burgers a teenage girl delivered to their table. "Let's see what you think."

Chapter 6

The sun went down, but the temperature didn't. As they strolled along the sidewalk heading back to Ben's condo, Avi remembered again why so many Oklahomans were happy to see the end of summer. The dog days, they called it: hot and muggy, occasionally still but usually with a breeze blowing off to the east, setting up perfect conditions for thunderstorms and tornados. Then, suddenly, one day it was cooler, just a few degrees, and the slide continued through fall until winter arrived sometime between October and January, and people began hoping for summer to roll around again.

"You said you went to OSU's medical school," she remarked. "So you're a doctor of osteopathy. Was that a deliberate choice?"

He nodded. "It's more fun to say than 'doctor of medicine,' don't you think? Osteopathy just kind of rolls off the tongue."

She rolled her eyes. She hadn't met a lot of doctors who had a sense of humor. Maybe it was just that most of the doctors she'd met the past few years had been assigned to combat hospitals, trying to save lives and limbs under difficult circumstances. They'd had a lot of success, but anything less than a hundred percent had been hard for some of them to take. When they'd known the soldier, it had been even harder. George's death had caused shock and sorrow that had lasted for weeks.

"OSU was my first choice because it was here in Tulsa," Ben said. "I could live at home, keep my expenses down, and keep an eye on the girls and my dad. I was in my third year when he died."

"What happened?"

His shoulders tensed, and his voice became edged with bitterness. "Heart attack. Truth was, he never got over Patricia leaving. She broke his heart. Broke him. I think he was just waiting for Sara to finish high school. He wasn't sick, wasn't having any problems. He just went to sleep one night and never woke up."

"I'm sorry." Avi believed in true love and broken hearts. She knew of too many instances, especially with an older couple, where one died and the other didn't want to live without the spouse. But Rick Noble had been a young man, and he'd been divorced ten years. That was a long time to mourn his ex-wife falling out of love with him. It was an awfully young age to give up on hope and love and the future. Hell, the war had widowed a lot of young women and some men. Just this year alone, Patricia had told her, three margarita club members had fallen in love again, one of them with a man widowed by the war himself. Giving up wasn't an option.

But, though Avi couldn't imagine it, it must have seemed the only option to Ben's father.

"What was he like?"

They reached his building, just across the street, but he kept walking, so she did, too.

"He was a good guy," he said after a while. "The oldest of three kids, close to his family, made the All-State baseball team two years running. After two years in college, he went to work out at American Airlines. He used to say he only planned to work there a year or two, but every time he got ready to quit, they'd promote him. He wound up staying more than twenty years. He took us to the Drillers games every chance he got. Sara used to tell people that we lived at the old stadium out by the fairgrounds during baseball season."

Avi smiled. Patricia had mentioned inviting the girls to lunch one weekend soon so she could meet them. She hoped it fit into their schedules because even without meeting them, she already liked them.

"He was a great dad. He had a lot of friends, but his first priority was his family. And he loved to go camping. Stick us in a tent at Keystone Lake with a baseball game on the car radio, and he was happier than any man had a right to be."

"Camping. Hm. I think I've spent way too many nights in a tent to see the allure in it," Avi teased.

Ben's smile was faint. "I have to admit, I haven't been since our last time as a family. That was probably a month or so before Patricia left." The smile faded. "She didn't like camping. But that was the only way Dad wanted to spend his time off."

So she went and made the best of it, until she was

gone. Avi was pretty sure George had never asked her to sleep in a tent, use a latrine, or cook over an open fire. For him, she would have done it, just as she'd done it for Rick all those years. For George, she might even have enjoyed it.

"I bet he was proud of you."

"Yeah. Patricia never threatened us with spankings when we misbehaved. It was always 'Wait until your father finds out,' and we stopped immediately. The idea of disappointing him was a hell of a lot scarier than anything else that could happen."

"Oh, not me. I mean, I hated disappointing my parents or GrandMir and Popi, but I was a hardheaded child, if you can believe it. I got swatted and switched so many times, it's a wonder I can walk past a tree or a bush without suffering a meltdown."

"I can believe it," he retorted. The melancholy stirred by talk of his dad disappeared, and amusement lit his eyes instead. "The surprise is that after all that discipline, you signed up for twenty more years of it."

"I had a lot of authoritarian figures when I was first in the Army, but now I *am* an authoritarian figure." She smiled smugly. "And I like it."

They walked another moment in silence before she asked, "Do you know home's back there a few blocks?"

He glanced around, then over his shoulder. "I'd race you back, but I'd have the advantage because my legs are longer than yours and you're wearing—"

Avi spun around and darted across the street, his last words—*flip-flops...hey!*—not even an echo in her head. His legs might be longer, and her shoes might be flimsier, but she was a runner and he wasn't. She was competitive as hell, plus she'd learned in Iraq and Afghanistan that when she needed to run, little things like shoes didn't matter.

She reached the lobby door a good thirty seconds ahead of him, then gave him a triumphant smile. "And Avi Grant wins by a mile!" she declared, doing a few victory twirls that left her dizzy and tumbled her into his arms. Or had it been tumbling into his arms that made her dizzy?

For a long moment, they stared at each other, mere inches separating them. Her breath caught in her chest, and every nerve ending in her body tingled. The look he gave her damn near smoldered, her heart thudded, and her knees went weak. If he didn't kiss her soon, she was going to collapse into a puddle at his feet, and if he did, she was pretty sure her hair would catch fire.

He shifted toward her a tiny bit, and she closed the distance between them, but he was the one who initiated the kiss. His hands slid from her arms, where he'd caught her to steady her, up to her shoulders, and his mouth covered hers. Arousal flowed through her, nipping and searing and making her tremble, and she was delighted to feel it. For a year, all her energy had been focused on doing her job, staying alive; for the past few months, she'd added grieving for George, along with other friends she'd lost. Now her sexual side, turned off too long, was flaring back to life with sweet, familiar need, and she couldn't think of any man she'd rather stir it—and satisfy it—besides Ben.

There was nothing sweet or gentle or tender about this kiss. It was hungry and demanding and fierce, exactly what she wanted. What she needed. Bringing her hands to his body, she tugged his shirt loose from his trousers, undid the bottom button, then the next two, and slid her hands beneath the fabric. His skin was warm, silken, taut over muscle and bone. She knew he was that same pretty brown shade all over—Patricia had mentioned that Rick was Osage—and she loved pretty brown skin.

Ben ended the kiss abruptly, dug out his keys, and unlocked the lobby door. The look on his face as fierce as his kiss had been, he took her hand and pulled her inside, up the stairs, and into his loft. As soon as the door closed behind them, he kissed her again, pinning her against the cool surface of the door, pulling the band from her hair, stabbing his fingers into it as it tumbled around her shoulders.

She was lost in the kiss, in the hunger and the been-so-long need, her mind processing feelings instead of words. At some point she realized her feet were moving, that Ben was guiding her across the room without breaking the kiss. She lost one shoe on the way, kicked off the other near the end of the couch. Her purse slid to the floor in the hall, and fingers were curling around the hem of her top by the time they reached the bed—his, hers, fumbling together, getting in each other's way trying to pull the top over her head. Finally, choking out a laugh, he pushed her hands away and whisked the top off, tossing it toward the dresser behind him.

Hoping to find herself in exactly this position, she'd chosen her prettiest lingerie: a bra that revealed more than it concealed, its color a deep, vibrant coral, its construction all satin, ribbons, and lace; and panties in the same shade that concealed just barely enough. They were gorgeous and sexy and made her forget that she spent most of her life in combat boots.

She couldn't put an entire sentence together, but somehow, despite the burning lack of oxygen in her lungs, she managed to ask "Condoms?"

"Drawer."

The zipper on her skirt made a loud, raspy noise as he opened it. An instant later, the skirt began sliding from her waist, and she gave it a shimmy to help it along. It landed on the floor with a soft rustle, and she stepped out of it, then nudged it away with her toes. His shirt came off next. She'd intended to turn her attention immediately to removing his pants, but the sight of all that smooth skin distracted her. Her hands lingered, her palms flattened against his rib cage, absorbing warmth, making tiny strokes, bringing a low growl of pleasure from him.

He made quick work of his remaining clothing before kissing along her jaw, down her throat, to the sensitive curve of her breasts. Turning so he sat on the bed, he laved the skin between her breasts while his hands stroked lightly, gently, across her middle, over her waist, gliding across her hips. Vaguely she registered the slide of her bra away from her body, the tugging sensation of her panties gliding down her legs, the tickle of his hair as he bent his head closer, the sudden jolt of a hot, wet, greedy kiss to her hip.

When she groaned, he rolled back on the bed, pulling her with him, tumbling her down onto a soft cushion of gray linens. As she clung to him, pulled him to her, greedily tried to wriggle into place beneath him, she found her voice to once more whisper, "Condoms."

He pulled away for a moment that lasted an eternity, bracing himself on one arm, reaching into the night table drawer, then came back, pressing a small plastic packet into her hand, his mouth finding hers again, his tongue plunging inside. She ripped the package open, reaching blindly, unrolling the latex sheath over his erection, then tugged at his hips, and finally, *finally,* he slid inside her, exactly where she needed him.

Exactly where she wanted him.

*   *   *

Light shone dimly down the hall from the living room, a sort of night light for grown-ups, not bright enough to intrude but enough to keep darkness at bay. Ben lay on his back, Avi at his side, her hair falling over his shoulder and arm like cool silk. Her breathing had been as slow as his to settle, their sweat gradually drying, their heart rates eventually returning to normal. Her delicate hand was splayed across his chest, a source of warmth, a reassuring touch.

Neither of them had spoken since he'd retrieved a condom from the table, except for a few breathless *Oh*s from her. Now he turned onto his side, gathering her close against him, and said, "I guess that was a damn good burger."

She laughed, the sound surprised from her but no less amused. "Well," she said, "you bought me breakfast *and* dinner. If I'd said no, you might have decided I was playing hard to get." Then she shook a finger at him. "Which, for the record, I am. I don't have sex with just any guy who asks."

"I never thought you did."

She gazed at him a moment. "What about you?"

"I don't have sex with just any guy who asks, either."

When she poked him with that pointing finger, he said, "Ow. On the other hand, I'm a guy. If a woman asks, I'm honor-bound by my gender to say yes."

Mouth pursed, she made a *pfft* sound. "Why aren't you married, Doc?"

He remembered a time when a woman saying the *m* word in any context would have stirred his self-preservation instinct. A woman saying it in bed after great sex would have freaked him out. Was it age, security, and the desire to get married that changed things? Or was it *this* woman? "Work. Twelve-hour days, surgery, Saturday clinics. No time to meet anyone."

"And yet you met me." She preened, fluttering her lashes, doing a good job of playing coy, at least until her smile destroyed the illusion.

"I'm glad I did. And for the record, I was glad before this." He gestured to the two of them and the bed. "Now I'm ecstatic."

"Wow, I don't know that I've ever made anyone ecstatic before."

Lifting his hand, he stroked through her hair, curling the strands, letting it go. "Why aren't you married?"

"War. Twelve-month tours in the desert. Frankly, if I never see desert again—any desert—I'll be ecstatic."

"Lucky for you, then, that Georgia's not desert."

"Nope. It encompasses the best of the South. Mild winters, hot summers, high humidity, biscuits as an art form, collard greens, and mustard-and-vinegar barbecue sauces."

And an Army post filled with soldiers who had interests and a career in common. Guys who'd experienced the frequent moves and appreciated the nomadic nature of the lives they'd chosen. Surely she'd find one of them suitable for marriage and fathering her kids. He hoped she did. Really. It wasn't like *he* would ever put himself in the running. His career, his life, and his home were here in Tulsa. Always had been, always would be.

He focused his thoughts on the least important part of her statement. "You like collard greens?"

Eyes narrowing, she scowled at the incredulity in his voice. "Collard greens, when prepared right, are a gift from the gods. Popi loved them, so GrandMir cooked them two or times a week when they were in season."

He feigned a shudder. "They sound nasty."

"Sound? You mean, you've never had them?" Now she was the one sounding incredulous. "What other Southern delicacies have you missed out on? Boiled peanuts? Pork cracklins?"

"You eat cracklins, then kiss me with that mouth?" He wrestled her onto her back and discovered a ticklish spot just beneath her ribs, making her laugh and shriek.

When he stopped, she gazed up at him, catching her breath. "Actually, I don't eat boiled peanuts or cracklins. The smell is just more than I can handle." Her voice trailed away with each word until it was barely a whisper at the end. Slowly she raised her hands to his face, cradling her palms to his cheeks, and pulled him low for a kiss.

That was all it took—one kiss, and the desire and the heat and the tension were instantaneous, flaming to life, building with each breath, each touch, until it exploded again through them both, leaving them lying once more in the dim light, breathing ragged, pulses pounding, bodies throbbing.

It was a long time before either of them moved or spoke.

Finally, Avi lifted her head, gathered her hair in one hand, and pushed it over her shoulder. "Are you tired?"

Sprawled facedown on the bed beside her, he opened one eye. "This is the aftermath of ecstatic," he mumbled.

She snorted. "It looks like I'm-exhausted-and-have-to-get-up-at...what time do you have to get up tomorrow?"

"Five. My first surgery is at six."

"Ouch. When's the last?"

"Five thirty. One of my regular patients dislocated her wrist so today we added her to the schedule. I should be out by seven."

"Long day. For your patients' sake, and your own, you need a good night's sleep."

"Hm." He closed his eye, then opened it again. "Can you spend the night?"

A smile lit her face. "I'd love to, but I've got a date back in Tallgrass. I fed Sundance before I left, but if she doesn't get to go out before bedtime, she and I will both be in trouble."

He turned onto his side. "Next time you should bring her." He definitely wanted a next time, and though he'd never allowed anything that walked on all fours in his apartment—besides his nephews—dog hair on his carpet and dog spores on his furniture seemed a small price to pay for Avi in his bed.

Her expression solemn, she softly said, "I'd like that." For a moment, she just continued to look at him, then suddenly she rolled out of bed and walked around to his side, beautifully, unselfconsciously naked. "But this time I have to go. The baby's probably huddled at the back door, legs crossed, watching the clock."

She found her bra, panties, and skirt on the rug beside

the bed and her top hanging from the knob of a dresser drawer, and took them into the bathroom with her. While she got dressed, he got up and stepped into his discarded trousers, then a pair of leather flip-flops.

When she came out again a few minutes later, looking as gorgeous as when she'd first arrived, she grinned. "You don't have to see me out."

"My dad would haunt me if I didn't. He had very particular ideas about the way I should treat my dates, and since I can't walk you to the door of your house, I can at least walk you to your car."

"Gee, I'm impressed. I've known a few guys who wouldn't even get out of bed to say good night." In the hallway, she stopped to pick up her purse, then her left shoe, then the right. At the doorway, she slid the sandals on, then as they walked down the stairs, she slipped her hand into his.

Her car was parked a few spaces from the door. She unlocked it, tossed her purse into the passenger seat, then faced him. "Thank you for the best time I've had in a long, long time."

"I should be thanking you. It takes two..."

"To tango?" she finished helpfully. "Is that what we're calling it?"

He wrapped his arms around her, pulling her body snug against his. "Let's just call it great fun." Bending his head, he kissed her, and she was quick to kiss him back, rising onto her toes, pressing even closer. His entire body was responding when he finished the kiss. He didn't want to. He wanted to take her straight back to the loft, straight back to bed, and forget about surgery and Sundance and everything but her.

But those weren't options in the real world, so he kissed her again, stepped back to watch her get into the car, then smiled at her. "I'll call you."

Her smile was light and seductive in spite of its innocence as she closed the door, buckled in, and started the engine. Standing on the sidewalk, he watched her back out, then drive off with a flirty wave.

It wouldn't be long, he realized, before he would be saying good-bye to her for the very last time.

* * *

Avi slept soundly, awakening Tuesday morning energized and in the best mood ever. After breakfast, she put a leash on Sundance and took the dog out for a walk through the neighborhood, passing quiet houses, greeted occasionally by other dogs barking from their backyards. The buzz of a lawnmower reminded her that her parents' yard needed a trim before they arrived home Saturday evening, which made her think of her mom, which made her wonder what Beth would think of Ben. There was no doubt in Avi's mind that her mother would like him, though she wouldn't be thrilled to know that they'd already slept together. *When I met your father,* a lot of Beth's moral tales began, a counterpart to GrandMir's *Back in my day…*

Avi looked forward to some distant day when she could turn to her grown child and say *When I met your dad…*

Sundance trotted along, happily eyeing everything as if seeing it for the first time, when a woof rumbled from the back of the house they were approaching. Sundance stopped, planting her giant paws on the grass beside the sidewalk, and stared at the mutt peering around the corner of the house. Her responding yip sounded like it came from a pint-size pooch and earned a louder rumble, then the bigger dog started toward them.

Recognizing him, Avi followed the puppy into the grass. "Hey, pretty boy, how are you today?" she crooned, and Norton picked up speed. She held Sundance's leash tightly at her side, wanting leverage to yank if the meeting didn't go well, but Norton wasn't going to be aggressive. He dropped to his back as soon as he reached her, his paws flopping in air, and gave her a giant doggy smile, tongue hanging out. Sundance sniffed him thoroughly, then sat down to scratch herself while Avi crouched to scratch him.

"Norton? Aw, jeez, Norton! I swear, I'm sending you to live with your father!"

"Come on, buddy, before you find yourself homeless." Avi stood, tugged Sundance's leash, and started to the back of the house. Norton happily trotted along beside them. They rounded the corner in time to see Lucy locking her back door, apparently on her way out to look for her dog. "It was our fault this time," Avi said as a greeting. "He wanted to meet Sundance."

Lucy's scowl morphed into a smile. "Hey, Avi. Trust me, I don't lay blame for Norton's behavior on anyone but Norton. Well, and Joe. He's way too lenient."

"The father you just threatened him with?"

"I swear, the two of them conspire to see how high they can make my blood pressure go. But," she grudgingly went on, "Joe does let him out if I'm gone from home longer than I planned, he feeds him half the time, and he takes him to the vet and plays with him a lot."

"So sending Norton to live with him would make them both happy."

Lucy nodded, then gestured to Sundance. "She's a pretty one."

"She belongs to my parents. They're on vacation, so she's keeping me company." Avi realized she was glad of that, especially with Ben gone back to Tulsa. The company was nice.

"Want to have a seat? I have a fresh pitcher of iced tea."

"Thanks." As Lucy went back inside, Avi gave the setter's leash another tug, crossed to the patio table, and sat down. Norton went with them, dropping to his belly and wiggling into the shade underneath. After a moment circling, Sundance copied his actions.

Lucy was back out in a few minutes, balancing a tray with a pitcher of tea, two tall glasses of ice, and a small dish of sweetener and sugar packets. She took the chair opposite, filled both glasses, and handed one over. "I've met your parents a time or two," she said. "They're great people."

"Yeah, they are. I'm really anxious to see them." It was true. Though she'd planned the first week of her leave to coincide with their cruise, she was really looking forward to their homecoming. For a while, she wanted nothing more important in her life than being Beth and Neil's daughter... and Ben's fling.

"Your father went to West Point with George, didn't he?"

Avi nodded. "Did you know him?"

"Yeah, but not long enough. I love Patricia, but I never wanted her to become eligible for membership in the margarita club."

"She mentioned that. It's a widows' support group?"

"It started that way, but we've become friends with a fondness for Mexican food and margaritas. The deaths of our husbands brought us together, but we share a lot more now."

Avi wasn't sure what proper manners called for, but she took a stab that Lucy, like Patricia, wanted to keep her husband's memory alive. "When did your husband die?" she asked softly.

Lucy's expression was bittersweet, heartache softened by time and made bearable by love. "Seven years ago. He was infantry. He and Marti's husband, Joshua—she's my best friend—shipped out together, died together, and came home together." She paused for a moment, gazing off—remembering, Avi was sure—then took a deep breath. "How many times were you over there?"

"Five. Two years in Iraq, three in Afghanistan."

"You're a braver woman than me. I never could have joined the Army... but I was a damn good Army wife. My only regret is that I didn't get pregnant when I had a chance."

"That would make it a little easier, wouldn't it," Avi said. To have some small piece of her husband, to see him in his child's eyes or smile.

"A few of the margarita girls have kids. Therese has three stepkids, and Ilena found out she was pregnant not long after Juan deployed. But most of us had waited, thinking we had plenty of time. And here we are."

Avi didn't want to find herself thinking *And here I am* if she got out of the Army and didn't have kids. She loved her job and was dedicated to it, but she wanted babies to love and dote on. She wanted grandbabies when she was old and gray to spoil rotten. If she didn't find the right man to do it the old-fashioned way—courting, marriage, then pregnancy—she would look at alternative methods, because she didn't intend to look back with regret.

"You're still young," she said. *I'm still young.* "There's time."

"Time's not the problem now," Lucy said ruefully. "It's finding a man and falling in love and him falling in love with me. It was so easy with Mike. We dated all through high school. Being with him was as natural as breathing. But I was younger and more carefree and much skinnier back then. Not a lot of guys see happily-ever-after when they look at fat chicks."

"Lucy, you're beautiful," Avi admonished. "And lots of guys like curves."

"Well, if you come across any around here, send them my way, will you?"

"I will."

Avi sipped her tea, brewed strong the way she liked it, then wiped the condensation on her shorts. "Do you work?"

"I'm secretary to the commanding officer of the post hospital. He's a great guy to work for, but when I started, it was supposed to be a short-term thing. It's not exactly what I wanted to do with my life."

"What do you want to do?"

Lucy laughed. "Here I am complaining about my weight, and what I'd really like to do is something that involves food. I'm a good cook if I say so myself, and I really love it. I thought about a bakery, but CaraCakes is so good. I considered a restaurant, too, but that's a big gamble, and I'd have to go in debt forever or find investors. Maybe catering..."

Avi was lucky that she'd always known what she wanted to do. After the Army, it wasn't the job that would be important, but what she would do outside of work with family and friends. "You need to explore the possibilities. When I come back here after I retire, I want to hear everyone raving about Lucy Hart's fabulous bakery/restaurant/catering business so I can say 'I *told* her to go for it.'"

"Don't set your expectations too high." Lucy refilled her glass, then a teasing smile flitted across her face. "Tell me about you and Ben."

As a delaying tactic, Avi scooted her chair to the right to take advantage of the shade there. She topped off her own iced tea, crossed her legs, and settled more comfortably. "Ben and I are friends."

The snort from Lucy was earthy and filled with disbelief. "Okay, Ben was the first guy I went out with after Mike's death—the only guy. One thing I know about him is how he looks at a woman he's just friends with, which is the way he looked at me before we dated, while we dated, and after we broke it off. Honey, that is *not* the way he looks at you. So spill, or I'll have to nag him for details. Which might be fun, because he'll get all flushed and flustered."

Avi couldn't imagine that. It might be worth staying quiet so she could watch. But the girl inside her had been wanting to talk to a girlfriend since she'd driven out of downtown Tulsa last night, wanted to giggle and gossip and be starry-eyed for a bit. First, she cautiously asked, "Did you break his heart?"

"No, and he didn't break mine, either. I adored him—still do—but we're so much better as friends. There just wasn't any sizzle between us, you know? And life's too short to settle for no sizzle." Then Lucy grinned. "I bet you two have so much sizzle, fire alarms ring."

In response, Avi sprawled back in her chair and fanned herself with one hand before laughing.

"That's cool. You'll be good for him."

The levity slipped away, and Avi bit her lower lip. "Only for a while," she murmured. "I'm heading to Georgia at the end of my leave, so we both know it's a fling."

"Why?"

Lucy looked as if she seriously meant the question, which surprised Avi. Lucy was an Army wife; she knew about training and deployments and forced separations. She'd made a lot of sacrifices for her husband's career: job security, frequent moves, long hours, low pay, distance from her family and home. She'd done it because she loved him, because she'd been young, because she was a good Army wife. But Ben...

"Can you honestly see Ben giving up his practice and moving halfway across the country? Leaving his sisters? Starting over again?" A tiny place inside her, Avi was surprised to find out, would love it if Lucy said Yeah, sure, for the right woman. But the rueful look that crossed her face had no hope in it.

"Honestly, no. Especially leaving his sisters. He's more like a father to them than a brother. Besides—" Her brow wrinkled. "You know about Patricia leaving home for George?"

Avi nodded.

"His mother abandoned the family to go off and follow George in his Army career, and Ben's still dealing with that resentment twenty years later. I don't—" Reluctance darkened Lucy's whole face. "I don't mean to be negative, but I think Ben would see it the same way—abandoning his family to follow you for your Army career. I don't see that happening."

That place inside Avi was disappointed but just a little. A temporary fling—she'd known that from the beginning, and she'd been okay with it. Was still okay with it. She wasn't going to get her heart broken because she wasn't expecting anything more. Fun and lust and, yeah, maybe even a bit of love by the time she left, but temporary. Not permanent. No chance of permanence.

"Maybe you'll decide twelve years in is long enough?" Lucy suggested. "I know once you pass ten years, common sense says stay in and get those benefits, but if something better came along..."

Avi smiled faintly. "That sounds like a compromise, only I would be the only one giving. I wouldn't ask a man to give up his career for me. Why would I give mine up for him? All I ever wanted was to be a soldier." And a mom. "Maybe when I come back in eight years, we'll both still be single and the sizzle will still be there, and who knows what could happen then?"

So much had happened in the last eight years. Truly, who could even guess at what might happen in the next eight?

Chapter 7

When Calvin Sweet was nine years old, a new girl moved in down the street. He and his best buddy, J'Myel, didn't much like girls. Girls tended to be fussy about their clothes and getting dirty and putting worms on fishing hooks, and when they got mad, they did a lot of crying and whining. He and J'Myel had figured this girl wouldn't be any different.

They were riding their bikes down the street the day after the girl moved in. She sat on the porch step, chin in her hand, and watched as they whizzed past, pedaling as hard as they could. At the end of the street—as far as their mothers let them go—they turned around and rode by her again. About the fifth pass, they'd come back to find her standing at the edge of the street. They didn't have curbs in their neighborhood. Gran said they were lucky to have pavement.

She stepped in front of them, and J'Myel braked to a

stop, his front wheel only six inches from her shin. "What do you want?" he asked sullenly.

"I was wondering—"

"We don't play with girls."

Her eyes had narrowed as she settled her hands on her hips. "It's rude to interrupt."

"Then quit talking," he'd sassed. "'Cause we don't play with girls, and we don't listen to 'em talk all the time, neither."

So quickly that neither of them was prepared for it, she grabbed the front wheel of J'Myel's bike and yanked it up in the air. Caught off-guard, he went flying backward, landing on his butt, skinning his elbow where it hit the pavement. She gave the bike a shove, letting it fall to the ground away from J'Myel, turned to Calvin, and smiled. "I was wondering where the nearest fishing hole is."

That had been the start of a long friendship with Benita Pickering.

Calvin sat on a bench in a shabby little park in Tacoma. It was tucked away at the end of a dead-end street, with three concrete picnic tables and two matching benches. There was no playground equipment to entice families with children, no shade from the hot sun, not even an outhouse-style bathroom for emergencies. The grass was only mowed when it got tall enough to leave clumps of hay everywhere, and the park was so near the railroad tracks that everything shook when a freight train rumbled through. Even teenagers looking for a place to make out or smoke a little weed took one look and found it unacceptable.

It was where Calvin spent most of his time.

When they'd gone fishing with Bennie that first day, she'd caught a catfish so big it could have taken her hand off. Impressed, J'Myel had forgiven her for knocking him off his bike. But he'd never forgotten it, never missed a chance to insist that it was only because she'd taken him by surprise.

They'd become best friends that day. She was good at everything they did, and better than them at some of it. She was as good as a boy, J'Myel said, and Calvin agreed. In high school, they'd finally noticed she wasn't a boy. And that was when the trouble started.

Calvin rubbed at the pain in his forehead. He would give his left hand for one day without thinking about J'Myel. He'd give his whole damn arm for a solid case of amnesia. He wanted to forget the last ten years of his life—everything he'd seen, everything he'd heard, everything he'd lost. Everyone he'd lost.

He knew every name. He could list them in alphabetical order, or by date of death, or location, or cause of death. He remembered their families, their plans, their hopes, their regrets. Their first days. Their last ones. Their memorial services. In his mind, he could see the iconic memorial, one for every soldier who'd died: a pair of combat boots, a rifle, a helmet, and dog tags. He could see J'Myel's dog tags.

His best friend dead. Benita widowed. And Calvin's spirit was broken, his hope lost.

"One day, God," he murmured, his voice rusty, "without thinking about him. Is that too much to ask?"

Of course, God didn't answer.

And J'Myel was still there in Calvin's mind, laughing, teasing, hating, haunting, dead.

* * *

The Three Amigos was one of Lucy's favorite places in town, and not just because she loved good Mexican food. She had great memories associated with the restaurant, from the times she and Mike had come here to all the healing, happy meals she'd shared with the margarita girls. In the summer, they claimed half of the restaurant's patio, shaded from the sun, cooled by ceiling fans and icy drinks. Lately, those drinks had been of the nonalcoholic variety out of respect for Jessy Lawrence. Jessy had been sober about three months, and Lucy prayed for her to stay that way the rest of her long, happy, healthy life.

Miriam, their usual waitress, greeted her as Lucy slid into a chair facing the parking lot. "Wow, Lucy, I don't think you've ever been the first to arrive."

"Nope. But I took a vacation today and lounged around doing nothing, so I had plenty of time to get ready."

"Oh, honey, that's no way to spend vacation days. You should go somewhere. Playa del Carmen and Cozumel are lovely places to get away."

Miriam was from Cozumel, Lucy knew, and her husband from Playa. They went back every year to visit family and to indulge in the Yucatecan cuisine they loved. "I don't swim, snorkel, scuba dive, or lie on the beach." *Or anything that requires putting on a swimsuit.* She'd turned down an invitation to accompany Joe, his brother, and the brother's girlfriend to the Virgin Islands for just that reason. Sad but true.

"There's other things to do. Tours, dining, Mayan temples, shopping."

Another waitress delivered two glasses of iced tea, and Miriam handed one to Lucy. Marti swooped in and took the second, downing half of it in one gulp before sinking into the chair across from Lucy. "Hey, LucyLu, Miriam. I've had a hard day. Keep those iced teas coming, please."

Lucy moved five tortilla chips from the basket between them and laid them on the saucer in front of her. "You work at a desk in an air-conditioned office. How hard could it have been?"

A perfectly manicured and polished nail tipped the finger Marti wagged in her direction. "Hard days are hard days no matter where they take place. It's not always fun sitting at a desk in an office. You know that."

"What would you rather do instead? Be on your feet all day? Work outside in the heat?"

Marti thoughtfully munched on a chip. "I think that I would like to try being a kept woman for a while."

It was unladylike to snort, Lucy's mom used to tell her, but she couldn't help it. "You? Let some guy support you and tell you what to do?"

"Oh, no, no. He can pay my bills and buy me things, and I'll have sex with him once in a while, but no bossing me around."

"Good luck with finding a rich man who'll agree to that."

Marti wrinkled her nose. "You're probably right. I could take a page from my mother's book and marry an old geezer who's at death's door. Then when he dies and leaves me everything, I'll be set for life."

"Except you'll spend the next fifteen years and all of his fortune in court fighting his kids' claims that you're a gold-digging witch who took advantage of poor ol' Dad."

"Well, aren't you just cheery today?"

"Lucy's always cheery," Ilena Gomez said. She set the baby carrier that was practically as big as she was in an empty chair, shucked a giant diaper bag, then sat down between her sleeping baby and Marti. "She makes me happy just looking at her."

"Thank you," Lucy said before sticking her tongue out at Marti.

"You're welcome." Ilena leaned to the right to bump shoulders with Marti. "You're not always cheerful, but you make me happy, too."

"Thank you." Marti imitated Lucy's tongue-out.

"Anyone do anything interesting today?" Ilena asked. "Anything besides changing diapers, cleaning spit-up, and soothing a cranky baby? I bet I walked twenty thousand steps today without leaving my house."

Lucy loaded one of her chips with salsa. "I met Ben's new girlfriend," she said before popping it into her mouth.

Both women raised their brows and gasped. "Really?" Marti asked.

"Tell us all about her. If we meet her, do we have to hate her?" Ilena wrinkled her nose. "Because I have to tell you, I don't do too well with hating other people."

"No, you don't have to hate her. Her name is Avi, and she's a soldier who's friends with Patricia, and she's very nice. I like her."

"You're like Ilena," Marti pointed out. "You have trouble with hating other people, too."

"I do not," Lucy argued, though it was true. "Besides, there's nothing about Avi to hate. We talked. She's sweet and funny, and Norton loves her."

"Well, there's the seal of approval," Marti scoffed. "Norton likes everyone."

"Except Ben." Ilena reached across to shoo an insect from the baby's face. She was fair-skinned with white-blond hair and blue eyes, while little John looked just like his father, Juan: dark skin, black hair, the biggest dark-est eyes Lucy had ever seen. He was the light of Ilena's life, and all the margarita sisters doted on him, too. Lucy adored him and, when she held him in her arms, she en-vied Ilena. God, what she wouldn't give to have Mike's child. It would have changed her life so completely.

"Are you guys happy doing what you do?" As soon as the question was out, Lucy blinked, surprised it had come from her. It hadn't even been in her mind…though thoughts about her own future had been niggling in the back of her mind since the visit with Avi.

"I love my job," Ilena replied. She was the glue that held together the biggest real estate office in town. She answered phones, marshaled troops, kept up their morale, and was the first face people saw when they walked through the door. She created such a great first impression that Lucy was sure that was why most of the prospects became clients.

"Paralegal wasn't on my list of dream jobs when I grew up," Marti said, "but I like it. I get to snoop around, I'm involved in cases, but I don't have to bear responsi-bility for the outcome. Why?"

Lucy shrugged. "Just wondering if I want to do some-thing else and have the courage to try it." Or if she would settle for what she had.

Now there was a depressing thought: staying exactly the way she was. For the entire rest of her life.

* * *

The beginnings of new romances were always wonderful. Avi loved finding out everything about a new person, the passion, the potential, the particularly fun sex. One day she hoped she found a man she could grow old with, but looking for that man was a great way to pass the time.

It was nearing eight o'clock, and she was wandering around Utica Square, gazing in shop windows, and watching the people who passed. Sundance walked on her leash at Avi's side, well behaved until she sniffed a tree or bench that someone else's dog had marked with its scent. Then she showed no dignity at all.

Ben had said he would call Avi as soon as he was done at the hospital, and she'd offered to bring dinner with her. Since she wasn't about to leave the dog alone in the car, not even for a quick run inside a restaurant to pick up an order, she'd had to get a little creative in order to avoid showing up with fast food. Earlier she'd talked to the hostess at P.F. Chang's, arranging for the girl to bring their to-go order outside to her.

When the phone rang, she was greeted by a low, sexy rumble of a voice. "I'm walking out of the hospital."

"Aw, you'll get there before me."

"The lobby doors lock at eight, so I'll wait there for you."

"Okay. You'll recognize me by the food I carry and the puppy attached to my wrist." After saying good-bye, she headed across the parking lot toward the restaurant while calling to tell the hostess she was on her way.

Ben didn't beat her by as much as she'd expected. He

was just taking his mail from the box when she knocked at the door. A slow, sweet smile formed as he came across to let her in. He kissed her, his hands sliding over her spine, sending little shivers of pleasure through her, spiking her temperature, filling a bit of emptiness inside her so that now everything was perfect.

Abruptly, he sucked in his breath, then backed off, scowling down. Avi followed his gaze to find that Sundance had bound herself to his legs with the leash and was now trying to bite her way free. With a laugh, she slid the leash from her wrist, then unwound them both. "I don't know what it is with you and dogs."

"Dogs and I get along fine."

"Except Norton. Sundance met him today and adored him."

He exaggerated his faux smile. "Of course she did."

Once inside his apartment, Avi unhooked the leash, and Sundance trotted off to explore. Watching Ben watch her, Avi said, "She won't mark her territory." *Please, Sundance, don't mark anything.*

Leaving her bags on the sofa—her purse and a backpack containing toiletries, a change of clothing, and a plastic dish of food for the dog—she carried their dinner to the kitchen counter and began unpacking it. She located plates and silverware and set them out, then took two bottles of water from the refrigerator. "I wasn't sure what you liked, so I got three entrees and an appetizer. Dinner and, if we have any leftovers, breakfast."

Plates loaded, they sat across from each other at the small dining table. Sundance took up a position between them, eyes alert for falling morsels. "Don't share with her," Avi warned, picturing another of her mom's notes in her mind: *Chinese food gives her gas.* And the one beside it: *Really, really bad gas.*

"Do I look like the sort of person to share my dinner with a dog?"

"You're sharing your loft with her for the night."

"Yes, but that's because it means sharing it with you, too."

She smiled brightly. "And I thank you. How did your surgeries go?"

"Great. I hung around a while after the last one. It's not the first time I've done surgery on this patient, and she's slow to wake up. I wanted to make sure she was okay."

Idly Avi wondered how many surgeons left their slow-to-wake-up patients in the hands of the hospital staff. If she was keeping score, that would be another point in Ben's favor, but she wasn't. Hell, she was charmed even by his and Norton's mutual dislike. Which reminded her. "I saw Lucy today. She told me you two used to go out. Did she break your heart?"

Noodles dangling from his fork, he considered it. "I was disappointed rather than hurt. She's nice and funny and kind of reins me in when I get too resentful about things, and I was hoping that she'd be..." He looked at her. "You know. The one. The marriage and kids and happily-ever-after one. But..."

"There was no sizzle."

He shook his head.

But they'd had affection and fondness and respect, and that could grow into sizzle, couldn't it? Avi had heard countless stories about great friends becoming lovers, becoming happily-ever-afters. But neither Ben nor Lucy seemed to think that was a possibility for them, and who was Avi to argue?

"Is it weird that we're talking about my last girlfriend who's your new friend?"

She shook her head. "Not as long as it's over between you. If you still had feelings for her—sexual, not friendly—that would be a different matter."

"So in that case, you'd be jealous," Ben teased.

She snorted rudely as he returned his attention to his food, but when she used chopsticks to dip a slice of seared ahi into a lime/soy sauce, she wondered. She wouldn't be thrilled to hear that Ben still had romantic feelings for Lucy, but she wouldn't be jealous. She just didn't do jealousy. Did she?

Apparently deciding she wasn't going to get a treat, Sundance retreated to the living room, jumped on the couch, and curled up, chin on the padded arm, watching them with soulful eyes. *No dog on the furniture,* one of her mom's notes read. *Your dad ignores me, but you don't get to.* "She'll get down if you tell her to."

Ben glanced at her as he assembled another mu shu pork pancake. "Sundance, down," he said, and the puppy obeyed, jumping to the floor, sitting, and waiting expectantly. When no further commands and no cookies were forthcoming, she jumped back up, stretched, and lay down again.

Ben gave Avi a skeptical look, and she shrugged. "I said she would get down. I didn't say she'd stay. I don't think Dad's gotten that far in his training."

"From what I've heard, it sounds like your mom's probably the one teaching her rules."

"Yeah, Dad's not really the disciplinarian sort. He gave me suggestions when I was little. Mom gave orders." Leaning back in her chair, she chided Ben's *yeah, right* look. "Hey, you had two siblings, so your chores were probably divided by three. I was an only child, so *every* night was my night to set the table, help with the dishes, and take out the trash."

"Poor baby, you had it so tough."

"I hope you're more sympathetic to your patients."

One brow raised, silently asking if she was finished eating, he took the plate she pushed his way, stacked it with his, and carried it to the sink. "Most of them. I have some who are just whiny. They don't want to go to physical therapy, they don't want surgery, they don't want any restrictions on their activities. They just want pain medication, the stronger, the better, so they don't have to actually do anything to help their condition heal."

Avi drew her feet onto the seat and wrapped her arms around her knees. "I bet you're stingy with narcotics."

"Whatever their problem is, I've seen it hundreds of times before. I know what the level of pain is and how much medication is needed to reduce it. When patients want more pills or stronger ones, I send them to our pain management specialist, who won't give them anything I won't. So they're still whiny, but they're his problem, not mine."

After putting the leftovers in the refrigerator, he came back to the table, took her hand, and pulled her from the chair. "What do you want to do? Snuggle with Sundance and see what's on TV or come back to the bedroom, snuggle with me, and forget about TV?"

Such a question didn't even deserve an answer, she decided as she began tugging him into the direction of the bedroom.

*   *   *

Ben was somewhere between semi-awake and asleep, his eyes heavy, his thoughts scattered and unformed. Soft noises sounded beside him, kind of a whimper, kind of a wail, underscored by a reassuring hum. He pushed back the sleep, forced his eyes open—one of them, at least—and saw that it was dark in the room except for the light from the living room. Something warm pressed against his back. Avi, he thought and, smiling sleepily, he reached back to pat her hip.

He found a hip, all right, but it wasn't Avi's. It was covered with silky fur, and its owner apparently appreciated the touch, because she licked his fingers with a long, raspy tongue. "No dogs on the bed," he muttered, drying his fingers on the sheet.

"The baby needs to go out." Avi's voice was the reassuring hum from a moment ago. She was moving around, no doubt putting back on the clothes he'd had such fun taking off. "I'm going to take her for a short walk."

"I'll go with you."

"You don't need to. We'll only be gone ten minutes."

"It's dark."

"We're not afraid of the dark."

"I'm sure you're not. I don't know about Sundance." He forced himself to sit up and swing his legs to the floor. Stumbling to the dresser, he took out a pair of gym shorts and a T-shirt, dressed awkwardly, and shoved his feet into sandals. A glimpse in the mirror showed his hair was standing on end, but he let it be.

He was slow to start moving. By the time he left the bedroom, Avi and Sundance were standing at the door, the puppy panting with excitement. They hustled down the stairs and out the door, where she paused long enough to stick her nose in the air and sniff, then turned left.

"Have a nice nap?"

He dragged his fingers through his hair. "Yeah. I'm always tired after a day of surgery. All those people waiting on me, staff handing instruments to me..."

"Cutting people open and seeing them bleed would wear me out."

"Aw, you've spent five years in combat zones. I don't think the sight of blood would faze you." And she'd probably seen things that would make him sick.

He wouldn't make the mistake of implying that she shouldn't stay in a job that required those sacrifices of her. Though he'd never given any real thought to the idea of women in combat, beyond their conversation the night before, the idea of *Avi* being there...that bothered him. She'd given enough of her time, taken enough risks. Surely the Army needed a Signal instructor more than they did another body to deploy.

"I've seen more blood than a legion of vampires," she said quietly. "I don't want to see one drop more, not even my own from a nick on my leg while shaving."

When Sundance tugged hard on the leash, pulling it from her hand, Ben grabbed it, then slipped the loop around his own wrist. "You lost a lot of friends," he said hesitantly.

They'd covered thirty feet before she nodded. "Too

many. People I went through basic training with, people I went through Signal school with, people I met over there and became solid friends with. And George…"

She gave him a sidelong look. "I wish you could have known him. Not as the man your mother left your father for, but just as a person. He was kind and gentle and generous. He was the only CO I ever had who was admired by officers and enlisted alike. He was fair and honest and honorable, and he treated everyone like they mattered. His troops respected him. They would have died for him."

Ben realized the muscles in his jaw had clenched, and he forcibly relaxed them. One time, exasperated with his refusal to give up the anger he bore toward Patricia and George, Lucy had smacked him hard on the arm and muttered, *Oh, for God's sake, let it go!*

He'd rubbed his arm ruefully and said with what, looking back, must have been a pretty good pout, *I don't want to let it go.*

What are you? Six? she'd asked scathingly.

Sara and Brianne had set their resentment aside and thought he should, too. They'd been younger, he told himself. They hadn't seen the full impact of Patricia's betrayal on their father. Their lives hadn't undergone as much upheaval as his had.

Maybe they were just more mature. More forgiving. Nothing could bring their dad back. Nothing could put their parents back together. Wasn't it better to have a mother than no parents at all?

"You loved him a lot," he said quietly, slowing his steps so Sundance could sniff around a tree.

"Oh, yeah. He was like an uncle, a father figure, a counselor, a mentor. I was lucky to know him."

For a moment Ben envied her. For thirty years she'd had a father and a father figure, while his father, for all practical purposes, left when Patricia did. He could have had a relationship with George if he hadn't been so stubborn and pissed off. If he or the girls had given any hint that they wanted Patricia and George in their lives, he was pretty sure their mother would have acted on it. But he hadn't, so the girls hadn't, so Patricia hadn't, and now that chance was gone forever.

"Don't you think you would have felt different if it had been *your* mother who ran off and left you and your dad for him?"

Avi slipped her hand into his. "Yeah. It would have made a big difference. But all I can say is, he was the sort of guy who would have been worth forgiving. He was that special."

Special and gone, like Ben's dad. Patricia, though, was still here.

Finally, after sniffing the tree this way and that, Sundance did her business. Avi tugged a plastic bag from her pocket and crouched to clean up.

"You know, at some point that becomes fertilizer."

"It can fertilize Mom and Dad's yard. Anywhere else, it's got to be scooped." She zipped the bag shut, jogged a few yards ahead to toss it into a garbage can, then came back and caught his arm, pulling him and Sundance into a 180-degree arc, back toward the loft.

Above them, lightning flashed, so quick that he would have blamed it on search lights or headlights if he hadn't seen the sky for the instant it lit up. Avi noticed it, too. In a none-too-bad voice, she sang, "'Ooh, and I wish it would rain down.'"

He chose a different tune for his baritone. "'Here comes the rain again.'"

"'It's raining men. Hallelujah!'"

Unable to think of any other rain song at the moment, he used a childhood rhyme instead. "Rain, rain, go away. Come again some other day."

She swatted him, pretending to be scandalized. "No born-and-bred Oklahoman ever wishes rain away."

"Nah, Mother Nature's just teasing us. She'll give us a little lightning, maybe even some thunder. She might even blow that sweet smell our way, but in the end, it's just another false promise."

Avi heaved a great sigh. "I'm walking down the street with a pessimist."

"Nope. Just someone who will believe it's going to rain when he feels it on his head." Luck chose just that moment to plop large drops on both of them. The temperature seemed to drop ten degrees in the next instant, and a breeze stirred along the street, scuffing a foam cup over to the curb. Stepping aside a few feet, Ben scooped it up to toss in the next trash can.

"I love walking in the rain," Avi said as it gathered strength, "but my mom impressed on me every time I asked for a pet that dogs stink and wet dogs stink even more. Unless you can teach the baby to stay before we go back to bed, I'd suggest we make a run for it."

"Good idea."

Sundance thought it was a good idea, too, her giant ears flopping one way, her tail wagging the other. She ran right past the door, skidded when he tugged the leash, and came back with her tongue hanging out. As soon as he opened the door, she lunged inside, yanking the leash from his hand, gave herself a mighty shake, then headed up the stairs, leash trailing behind.

Two hours later, he rolled over in his sleep and found her stretched out on his side of the bed, her head on his pillow. He pulled it so he had more of it, but she just scooted closer to reclaim her share.

With the length of Avi's body warm and soft behind him, he eyed the dog in the dim light. "Get down," he whispered.

Sundance yawned and snuggled in deeper.

"Come on. No dogs on the bed."

She gave him no response beyond a solemn blink.

He sighed, knowing when he'd lost. Reaching across Avi, he grabbed the extra pillow, folded it in half so there wasn't enough for Sundance to share, and settled in again.

"Okay, you can stay," he whispered. "But only because I like your sister."

Liked her way more than was healthy. They'd known each other a little more than seventy-two hours, and he was pretty impressed. If she was in Tallgrass to stay, if she wasn't leaving the state again in less than four weeks, he might even be thinking she could be The One.

But she was leaving, and there was no chance that she could be that one.

No damn chance at all.

*   *   *

Ben came to Tallgrass after work on Friday evening, and he and Avi went to Luca's for Italian. She'd expected the restaurant to be busy—Friday night was date night, after all—but they didn't have to wait and had their choice of courtyard tables. When she glanced around quizzically at the empty tables, their waitress smiled and said the magic words. "High school football. It's just a scrimmage, but people still want to see how the team looks."

Avi grinned at Ben as she unfolded her napkin. Teasing him about this one issue was so darn easy. "We should have gone. Maybe I finally could have met Joe."

The waitress's eyes lit up as she handed out menus. "Coach Joe is the best. He's young to be head coach—he's only thirty-one—but he knows what he's doing. The team loves him. So do their sisters, their mothers, all the women in town. He's awfully cute."

Ben scowled down at his menu, which made Avi's smile even brighter. "We've got mutual friends. I'm gonna beg for an introduction." In fact, that introduction was scheduled for the next evening. Dinner at Patricia's. Mom, Dad, and Ben, Lucy, and Joe. Oh, boy.

After giving their drink orders, she tore a roll in half and dipped one edge in the soft butter nestled into the bread basket. "Okay, Doc, so tell me what it is you don't like about Coach Joe."

"You know sometimes, how you meet someone and you just know that no matter what, you're never gonna be best buds?" He shrugged as if that was the only answer there was. "That's the way it was with Cadore when we met."

"I know. I've met people like that." She smiled but didn't let it drop. "And on top of general incompatibility between you and Joe, there were a few little things that just sealed the deal. What were they?"

Ben shifted awkwardly, scowled at the nearby fountain, then shrugged. "Okay. He's a jock, and a good one, so he's got a big ego going. He thinks football is the great-est game ever, while I see the damage that shows up later. Do you know how many of my male patients from twelve to seventy-two are there because of football? And I don't even see the concussion or brain injury patients."

"So that's one aspect. Let's see, for reason number two…He lives next door to Lucy, and they're good friends. She gets up early to walk with him every day, cooks and bakes and makes candy for him, and they more or less share ownership rights in Norton."

His gaze narrowed. "I'm not jealous of his friendship with Lucy. When we were together, Lucy was into me. Really. Seriously. And that's not ego talking. Though he was never thrilled by my friendship with her. I believe he called me Dr. Jerk when she and I were dating."

"Hm-hm. What else?" She tapped her finger thought-fully against her chin before asking in a playfully cau-tious voice, "Were you mean to Norton?"

"I've never been mean to an animal."

Though she believed wholeheartedly in the never-gonna-be-best-buds scenarios, Avi sensed there was more than that at play here, more than sports or Lucy. She thought about dropping the subject, because their time was limited and truth was sometimes painful.

Still, the question slipped out before she realized it. "Was it Patricia?"

A muscle clenched in his jaw just for an instant, his eyes turning shadowy before going blank. "What about her?"

Avi picked up a knife and spread more butter in a thin layer across her roll, then took a bite, making a *yumm* sound. Setting it down, she wiped her fingers on her nap-kin, then cautiously said, "I understand he mows her yard and fixes things around the house and does the heavy lifting and the carrying for her. She's about his mother's age, and he's about Brianne's age, and…" Their friendship sure seemed a surrogate mother/son type to her.

Ben's jaw clenched again, and a sharp tone came into his voice. "Oh, yeah, he's a big help to her. He and Lucy treat her better…It's been a few months. Let me remember how she phrased it. 'They take better care of me than my own—' That was as far as she got before she stopped herself."

"Ouch." Avi had no doubt it was true, especially at the time the conversation had taken place. Still, the bitterness in his voice showed that, months later, it still touched a nerve deep in Ben's abandoned heart. If Patricia hadn't run off, if she hadn't removed herself from their lives, she wouldn't have needed someone else's kids to be there for her because her own would have been. Was he afraid that she'd found it easy to replace him and his sisters? That she loved Joe and Lucy the way she loved her own children?

"You know," she began gently, "by all accounts, Joe's a nice guy and a good neighbor. With George deployed, Patricia needed someone like him to help out. Even if you two had been on the best of terms before George died, she couldn't have called you in Tulsa every time she needed a piece of furniture moved or a high lightbulb replaced."

He gave her a long steady look before shifting his gaze to the linen napkin, using one finger to crease the fabric against the tablecloth. After a time, he muttered, "She's not…" That was how long it took him to think better of the words and close his mouth.

"She's not his mother," Avi said softly. "He's not her

son. They know that, Ben, trust me. She loves Joe and Lucy, but not in the way she loves you and your sisters. They're friends. You're family. No one gets to take your place."

His dark eyes intense, he dropped the napkin and reached for her hand. "No one but George."

Avi shook her head. "He didn't take your place. Given the chance, he would have been the best stepfather in the history of stepfathers, but he never would have given a thought to trying to replace you three."

He considered it grimly. Was he persuaded? she wondered. After a moment, he changed the subject without giving her a hint, his mood noticeably lighter. "So your parents are coming home tomorrow."

"Yep. They'll be in around two. Your mom has invited us all over for dinner. She wants them to meet you."

"I'll be on my best behavior."

"She's also invited Lucy and Joe."

"Damn. And with your parents home and me staying at Patricia's, I can't even get a reward if I'm good." He pressed a kiss to her palm. "I'll probably need some incentive tonight to behave tomorrow."

"Won't Patricia notice if you don't come home?"

"She won't care if I wander in late, like three, four in the morning."

Avi smiled at the thought of sharing her bed with him. It was surprising how quickly she'd gotten used to that, to snuggling close and hearing his breathing, to reaching out and touching him. She would miss it when she was gone. Would miss him.

The waitress served their salads and refreshed their drinks. Picking up his fork, Ben returned to the subject. "Tell me about your parents."

She chewed a bite of crispy lettuce dressed with a vinaigrette good enough to sip from a spoon. "My mom doesn't like dogs, but Dad does, so she bought him Sundance. She does like people, which is why she worked in human resources for twenty-some years. I was eleven years old the first I heard them argue, and it scared me half to death. I'm still waiting for the second argument."

"Do they both work at the nursery?"

She nodded. "When they started, Dad couldn't tell a flower from a weed. Now he's the expert. He could have earned a horticulture degree with all the studying he's done. They're really partners there, but at home, the flower beds are Mom's domain, the yard is his, and her hands never, ever touch a power tool or garbage can."

"Hobbies?"

"Dad's is reading the newspaper—Tallgrass's, Tulsa's, whatever city catches his interest. Mom's dabbled in cross stitch, quilting, painting, redecorating, knitting, needlepoint…She said she was searching for her inner artist. In our old house, she had a craft room that was so full of unfinished projects that Dad finally insisted she couldn't start anything new until she threw out all the old stuff. She said he put his foot down so hard, he almost broke it." Avi grinned. "By the way, while looking through the current house, I went into her 'study' and found tons of projects she started while I still lived at home."

"What about you? Do you have an inner artist?"

She snorted. "I don't have a creative bone in my body."

"I don't know. Those things you were doing in bed last night…"

Heat warmed her face: guilty pleasure. She needed a sip of tea before she could speak, and she strained for nonchalance. "Besides work, what's your favorite thing to do?"

"You." She swatted his hand, and his eyes darkened as he gave the question some thought. "I'm guessing going to Drillers games doesn't count?"

She shook her head.

"Spending time with my sisters and Sara's family."

"What's your favorite holiday?"

"Christmas. The kids always make it fun—and by kids, I mean my niece and nephews *and* my sisters. What's yours?"

"It used to be Christmas, but the first one I spent in Iraq took some of the pleasure out of it. It was hard being so far away from home and missing everyone and knowing we could get shot or blown up at any minute. We celebrated, and we smiled and laughed and sang carols, and everyone who had presents opened them, but...it was tough."

"What's your favorite now?"

"Right now?" A bit of her good mood darkened. She could choose any holiday on the calendar—Presidents' Day, Labor Day. How about St. Patrick's Day? She could claim to bake a cherry pie in Lincoln's honor or declare how much she loved corned beef and green beer and keep the mood light. But her thoughts had already turned somber, and she would honor them.

"Memorial Day. I have a lot of people to remember." She looked away, settling her gaze on the fountain in the center of the courtyard. Its splash was soothing, like rain on a tin roof. Her friends who were gone didn't need soothing anymore, and there couldn't be enough soothing in the world for the people who loved them.

Ben removed the fork from her hand and wrapped his fingers around hers. She smiled thinly, though her vision had gotten blurry. Must be some of the mist from the fountain carried across on the breeze.

"Every day should be Memorial Day," he said in a low voice.

She blinked away the moisture. "It will be for me." For the rest of her life.

Chapter 8

After days of temperatures in the high nineties or low hundreds, on Saturday the thermometer didn't rise above seventy-five. Though Patricia had been planning all along on grilling dinner, late in the afternoon she decided they should make the most of the cooler weather and eat outside, too, and so Ben found himself outside getting things ready.

Lucy crossed the yard as he shook out the paisley-patterned table cloth. "I love to see a man who knows his way around setting a table." Setting her purse and the dish she carried on a chair, she helped spread out the cloth, smoothing a wrinkle from it, telling him to tug it toward him, then to his left.

"It was my job to set the table every night until Bree and Sara were old enough to be trusted with the plates. Then I did it every third night."

"And now you eat takeout."

"So do you, and you can cook."

"A man who can do surgery can make a pot roast or bake a chicken. It's just a matter of following directions." She picked up the dish and offered it to him. "Potato salad, creamy and pickley the way you like it."

"Thank you. This is to take home with me, right? I don't have to share it?"

She made a face at him before moving a stack of plates to the table. "Where's Avi?"

"She's coming with her parents." Following her with napkins and silverware, he grimaced. "Where's Joe?"

"He'll be here. I'm not his keeper, you know."

"He needs one."

Lucy bumped her hip against his. "Funny. You should hear what he says about you."

"No, thanks." He'd given a lot of thought to what Avi had said the night before and decided she was right. Cadore wasn't a threat to Ben's relationship with Patricia. Cadore could be her friend, and Lucy's friend, and probably Avi's, too. That didn't mean Ben had to be friends with him, too. Just civil. That was all he had to manage.

Lucy bumped against him again. "Why so quiet?"

"No reason."

"Worried about dinner tonight? Joe on one side, Beth and Neil Grant on the other?" Her face softened with her smile. "Or wondering what the heck you're going to do for privacy now that Avi's parents are home?"

"Grown people shouldn't have to worry about privacy," he grumbled for her benefit.

"I'd offer you my spare bedroom, but I'm not having sex, so I'm darn sure not going to listen to other people have it. Hey, if I recall correctly, Avi's dad has a pickup truck. Everyone who lives in Oklahoma should have sex at least once in a pickup truck."

He scowled at her. "Yeah, when you're sixteen."

"You're not too old and creaky, so don't pretend. Look at it this way." She held up both hands, palms facing skyward. "Sex in a pickup." Her left hand raised six inches. "No sex." Her right hand sank as low as it could go while she stood straight. "Any questions?"

"'Bout what?"

Ben and Lucy both turned to find Joe Cadore approaching, carrying a late-season watermelon under one arm and a box from CaraCakes. He'd dressed up for the event—cargo shorts instead of his usual ratty gym shorts and a T-shirt that still had its sleeves and was, as yet, unstained and unfaded. The OSU baseball cap was a given; the only time Ben had seen him without that was at George's funeral.

"Grown-up subjects," Lucy teased. "You wouldn't understand."

Cadore snorted, then gave Ben a stiff nod in place of a greeting. "I'll take these inside and say hello to Patricia."

After the door closed behind him, Ben commented, "You never have to worry about him getting old, do you? He's stuck somewhere around fifteen." Cadore had had a totally normal life growing up—both parents, siblings, doing all the normal things kids did in Alaska. He was the youngest, so he'd never had to accept a lot of responsibility for himself, much less for his brothers or sisters. Life had been easy for him.

"It's one of his charms," Lucy said with an apologetic shrug. "He's just in such a darn good mood all the time, you can't help but be happy around him. He's a nice guy, Ben. Really, it's no more complicated than that. He's lighthearted, carefree, likes everybody, and makes them smile."

Forget everybody. Ben made Avi smile, and right now that was enough for him.

The sound of an engine filtered down the driveway, followed by the slamming of doors. Ben's pulse increased by a few beats. He'd had breakfast with Avi and spent the morning with her until it was time for her to head to the airport. Her parents had left their vehicle in long-term parking, so she'd returned the rental car and caught a ride back with them, giving them a chance to catch up before dinner.

In his time with her today, the one thing they hadn't talked about was whether they were officially together or if the secret was theirs. And Lucy's, Brianne's, Sara's...

The thoughts disappeared from his mind as the Grants walked into view around the corner of the house. The older couple faded into the background as his focus zeroed in on Avi. She wore a dress in a deep orangey-red color, baring her arms and a good deal of her legs and hugging everything in between. Her flip-flops were the same shade, with a big silk flower on the strap that separated her first and second toes, and her hair hung, long and sleek, past her shoulders. She was beaming her best smile, widening it when she saw him, and she looked incredible.

The question of how to act was resolved as she walked right up to him, rose onto her toes, and brushed a kiss to his mouth. "Hi," she breathed in a low voice before grasping his hand. "Mom, Dad, I think you've met Lucy Hart."

"We have," Mrs. Grant said, giving Lucy a hug.

"How are you, li'l bit?" Mr. Grant asked.

"And this is Ben Noble."

It seemed to take forever for the Grants to look him over, then finally speak. "It's nice to meet you, Ben. We've heard a lot about you. You can call me Beth." She extended her hand and, when he took it, clasped his in both of hers. "You're not at all how I envisioned you. I guess I expected to see more of Patricia in you."

"My sisters and I look like our father's family."

With a nod, she stepped back to allow her husband to shake hands. "Ben," he said with a friendly nod. "I'm Neil."

"Sir."

"No *sir*, just Neil. What do you do, Ben?"

"I'm an orthopedic surgeon in Tulsa. The clinic's on Utica, and we practice at Hillcrest and Hillcrest South."

"Good business choice, though I don't think I could spend all that time indoors. We're thinking about putting Avi to work for us while we're here. We'd love for her to take over the nursery when we're done, though she's not encouraging us."

Avi rolled her eyes. "By the time you and Mom retire again, we'll be talking whether your grandkids want to take over the nursery. You're barely fifty-five, and you're having way too much fun to quit."

"What Neil's really saying," Beth took over, "is that if we don't convince Avi to help us out for a while, we won't see much of her for the rest of her leave. Seriously, she spent Monday, Tuesday, Wednesday, and Thursday nights in the city. When she lived there, she always wanted out of the city."

Heat warmed Avi's cheeks, and Ben's flush was about

to make him sweat, especially when Patricia and Cadore came out to join them. Ben noticed Joe didn't need an introduction.

Patricia joined their loose-knit circle, looked around at each person, then shook her head. "I told you not to embarrass the kids," she chided the Grants. "At the very least, you should have warned Avi with one of your Post-it notes the day she got here that your neighbor across the street has a better spy system in place than the FBI, CIA, and NSA combined." To Avi and Ben, she added, "They don't find it so funny when it's their whereabouts she's tracking. Nosy old woman. Story is her husband had to go all the way to Paris to get a moment of peace from her, and he liked it so much, he never came back. He sips coffee at the outdoor cafés, keeps a wary eye on Americans, and claims not to speak a word of English."

Patricia slid one arm around Avi's waist, her fingers brushing Ben's where he still touched her. "Besides, Beth, you didn't want her to be lonely while she waited for you guys to come home. Look at that face." At her prodding, Avi grinned ear to ear. "She wasn't lonely. Now, let's talk about someone who can't be embarrassed. You should have seen Joe's team on the field last night. Despite the black-flag conditions, they played an outstanding game and won by forty points."

With the focus shifting off Ben and Avi to Joe, he murmured, "Black-flag conditions? Is that a football thing?"

"Maybe. But I know for sure it's a military thing. It's based on the air temperature and the humidity. When it reaches a certain point, they declare black-flag conditions. No humps, no battalion runs, no carrying fifty-pound packs in a march. Personally, I see black flags as an invitation to a frozen margarita, a dish of salsa, and a bowl of chips with air conditioning all around."

Lucy slipped over next to Avi. "While they're grilling Joe about the game last night, why don't we start bringing the food and drinks out? Or"—she grinned at Ben— "you can answer more questions about Monday, Tuesday, Wednesday, and Thursday nights. Being parents, I'm sure they have lots more."

Avi and Ben exchanged looks, hers amused, his still a bit embarrassed, then they followed Lucy into the house.

*   *   *

Avi learned a couple of things that night: she liked Joe Cadore; she could still be mortified by her parents; Lucy was a living doll; and Ben was so cute the way he flushed. Oh, she added as she stood up to help gather dishes, if she ate much more of Patricia's cooking, she would have to buy new uniforms before beginning her teaching post. Everything the woman touched in the kitchen turned into magic, even something as simple as a salad.

The three parents talked and sipped wine at the table outside while the younger four cleaned up. Avi began rinsing dishes at the sink, then stacking them in the dishwasher, but after two saucers, Lucy said, "Don't bother, Avi."

"She'll just redo them," Ben said.

"She likes them done her way," Joe put in. "And her way changes depending on what dishes she's washing."

"Just leave them in the sink, and she'll take care of them," Lucy added.

With a shrug, Avi continued rinsing dishes but stacked

them in the second sink. She vaguely remembered Patricia commenting on the subject one evening. No point in denying her the pleasure of doing them her way.

They dried their hands, left the kitchen in better shape than they'd found it, then joined the adults outside again. No, Avi, admitted, it didn't seem funny, not counting themselves as adults. Maybe it was just that eternal-child thing—a parent's child was always his child, no matter how old—or maybe it was just because she felt happier and younger than she had in a long time. She was lucky to not be an adult at this very moment.

Lucy and Joe said their good-byes and headed toward their houses on the far side of the yard. Avi bent over her father's chair from behind. "Hey, Dad, can Ben and I borrow the truck?"

Neil twisted his head to smile up at her. "Aw, I haven't heard that in fourteen years. 'Daddy, can I borrow the car?' I heard it enough times between her sixteenth and eighteenth birthdays that it kind of drove me crazy."

"What happened then?" Patricia asked. "You bought her a car?"

"I left for basic the day after I turned eighteen." Avi hugged her father. "Then you missed having me around to ask."

"I sure did." Neil shifted position and pulled his keys from his pocket. "Where are you going?"

"Just for a drive. I want to show Ben some places from before." It wasn't a fib. She had already shown him her grandparents' house, the nursery, their church, and the cemetery where they were buried. Now she wanted to show him Tall Grass Lake, where Popi had taken her fishing and GrandMir had taught her to swim. It was beautiful, a nice drive out of town, and sure to offer plenty of privacy on a warm end-of-summer night.

She hugged her mom, then Patricia before catching Ben's hand and starting toward the driveway. Halfway there, she turned back. "How will you guys get home?"

Beth gave her dry look. "We walk three miles every day. I think we can handle seven blocks."

"If they get worn out between here and there, I'll give them a lift," Patricia said with a laugh. "Go on now. Have fun."

Ben caught up with Avi around the corner, twining his fingers with hers. "Have you been talking to Lucy?"

"What do you mean?" she asked.

He just shook his head, even though her tone was way too innocent to disguise the fact that Lucy had, indeed, suggested they should have a little fun christening Neil's pickup.

"You want to drive?" she offered as they approached the silver pickup.

"You forget the only vehicle I ever drive is my car. This thing's as big as a tank."

"Not quite. But I have experience driving tanks, too," she said with a sly smile as she beeped open the locks, then climbed into the high seat. "I had a nice time this evening."

"Me, too," he admitted.

"I even tried to dislike Joe, out of loyalty to you, but he's a nice guy. And cute. I'm surprised Patricia hasn't tried to set him up with Brianne." She darted a glance his way and smiled with satisfaction at the scowl she found endearing, at least in this regard.

"They went out a few times, but nothing came of it."

"You could have had him for a brother-in-law."

He settled for a shudder in response.

Avi laughed. Digging through her purse, she found a soft band and used it to pull her hair into a ponytail before backing out of the driveway. With the sweet scent of crape myrtle blossoms drifting on the air and the gift of mild temperatures, she wanted the windows down so they could enjoy the night without strands of hair tangling around her or blinding her.

"The worst could still happen," she teased. "I assume they still run into each other every time she visits. Maybe the time just wasn't right. Maybe in a few months or a few years—"

"Bite your tongue."

"Or you'll bite it for me?" Laughing again, she turned onto a street that, if memory served, became a dusty two lane road just outside the city limits. Soon they left the streetlights behind, and the air blowing in turned a little sweeter, a little fresher and greener. Not counting her last remote camp in Afghanistan, she'd never lived in the country, but tonight the idea was undeniably appealing. No neighbors near enough to matter, true darkness at night, trees and prairie, far more cattle per square mile than people, and privacy. She did love privacy.

But privacy—at least, her kind—should be shared. A husband, a few dogs, and a couple of kids would be a great start. Maybe six months before retirement, she could ask her parents to start looking for some property, something with water—a creek, a little bit of Tall Grass Lake shoreline. She and her husband could build a log cabin, a cottage, or a simple farmhouse with a broad porch and high ceilings and fill it with antiques like GrandMir's.

Where had all these thoughts of marriage and kids come from? Sure, it was something she'd always wanted and expected, but she hadn't fixated on it.

Until she'd met Ben.

The man least likely to ever move away with her.

"I liked your parents," he said. His right arm rested on the door, his hand dangling outside, buffeted by the wind as they drove. "I'm pretty sure I met them when George died, but I met a *lot* of people."

Avi spared him a glance. "Mom had mentioned something went wrong with the notification. What happened?"

Ben's sigh was barely audible over the road noise. "Patricia was in Walmart when one of her neighbors called on her cell and told her two officers in dress uniforms were at her door."

"Damn," Avi whispered.

"She collapsed. Jessy, one of the margarita girls, was there, and even though they'd never met, she got Patricia home, called me, and stayed with her until Lucy could get there." He sighed again before facing her. "I didn't talk to Patricia when Jessy called. I didn't plan on coming here at all. I didn't know George. Hell, I hardly knew her. She hadn't even told us they were back in Oklahoma."

There was regret for his response in his voice, but Avi couldn't hold his actions against him. After his mother had abandoned his family twenty years earlier, no one had the right to expect him to drop everything and rush to her side when suddenly she needed him.

"What changed your mind?"

"Lucy. She asked me to do it for me, not Patricia. She said if I showed compassion to Patricia, it would mean something to me later. So I came."

"You're a good son." In spite of the emotional distance between them, Avi was sure Patricia had drawn comfort from his presence.

"Eh. I'm working on that." After a moment, he glanced around. "Where are we going?"

"Tall Grass Lake," she replied even as the sign appeared in the headlights.

"Did GrandMir and Popi bring you here?"

"At least once a week. It's the kind of place every person should have in his childhood memories."

"Keystone for me," he said. "Occasionally Skiatook Lake."

She turned onto a narrow road that wound through the heavy growth of trees. If it were daylight, they'd be able to catch glimpses of the lake through the woods, but tonight she didn't see water until she pulled off into a grassy area a half mile or so from the nearest picnic and camping spaces. They had the field to themselves with no distractions but the moonlight reflecting on the still surface of the lake.

After turning around so the back of the truck faced the lake, she cut off the engine and opened the door. The grass hadn't been mowed recently and poked up, sharp and prickly, around her calves, making for careful walking in her flip-flops.

"You know it's still warm enough for copperheads," Ben warned.

She stilled an automatic shudder. She hated snakes. "I wasn't planning on a stroll in the dark," she told him over the side walls of the truck bed. Lifting her feet high, she circled to the back, lowered the tailgate, and boosted herself onto it. It wasn't nearly as much a stretch for Ben, who kicked off his sandals before bumping his bare leg against hers.

"Lucy says everyone in the state should have sex in a pickup at least once," he said dryly.

"She's right. I was seventeen the first time."

A faint, wicked smile curved his lips. "Me, too. Wonder if this will be the truck's first time."

"It will. My dad bought it brand new."

"So? Who's to say they didn't come out here for a little mom-and-pop sex?"

"Ew!" She slugged his shoulder. "I don't talk about your parents having sex. I sure don't want to talk about mine doing it."

"Hey, your dad's only twenty years older than me. I intend to be doing it in twenty years."

"Yes, but you're not my father." *Thank you, God.* Rising, she went to the tool box mounted behind the extended cab, unlocked it, and pulled out a huge zippered bag. She removed the comforter inside, gave it a good shake, then spread it across the bed liner. "Mom's emergency kit," she explained as she lowered herself to sit, then stretched out on her back. "She makes him carry a tool kit, a first aid kit, bottled water, granola bars, one of those tools that punches out windows, and a wind-up flashlight."

"A tool that punches out windows isn't much help if you have to get out of the vehicle to get it."

"I know. He's supposed to carry the kit in the floorboard behind the driver's seat, but he considers it clutter. He tells her that if he ever goes soaring off the road into water, he'll have the time and the good sense to roll his window down ASAP."

Ben lay down beside her, and she rested her head on his shoulder. She sighed happily. "I love looking at the sky at night."

"Do you know the constellations?"

"Only the Big Dipper. I was always more interested in wishing on them than learning about them." She'd made a lot of wishes, and a lot of them had come true. Granted, they'd been backed up by prayers. Whatever the star-wishing fairies couldn't take care of, God could. If He would.

"What would you wish for tonight?"

His voice was low and made her tingle in unmentionable places. She pretended to think about the question a moment before answering, "Nothing. Right this minute, I'm perfectly, totally content."

And for that very minute, it was true. But almost immediately, she felt a twinge of loss. That was the sad thing about minutes: They didn't last. Sixty seconds of wonderful, then remembering that this wasn't her regular life. In three weeks she would go to Georgia. She might come back for Thanksgiving and get to see Ben for a few days. She might join the Christmas exodus from Fort Gordon for a few more days, shared with family. He might even spend a weekend with her in Augusta. But a few days here and a few days there was no way to have a relationship. Someday she would e-mail him, and he would take two or three days to respond. He would call, and she would let it go to voice mail. He would meet someone else, someone whose roots were sunk as deep here as his own, and probably, hopefully she would meet someone else, too, and everything that was between them would end.

Except for the memories. She would have the sweetest

memories of a wonderful time with a wonderful man, and they would stay with her forever. What more could a woman wish for?

*   *   *

"You ever considered taking up running?"

Lucy wasn't at her best early in the morning, the only time the heat—and Joe—allowed her to walk any significant distance, so it took her a while Sunday morning to figure out what he meant. When it did register, she gave him the driest look she was capable of, considering that she was drenched with sweat. "Run? You mean as in jogging? Feet pounding on pavement, sending jolts of shock up through my shins and femurs and into my spine? Doing potential untold damage to my ankles and knees?"

"Burning almost twice as many calories in the same time?"

She admitted, she did like to watch people run. There was a blonde who passed her house every morning as Lucy was leaving for work—size nothing, long, lean legs, impressive muscles, ponytail bouncing, pert boobs restrained in an adorable sports bra, matched with tiny little spandex shorts that barely covered the essentials. She looked so pretty and graceful, like a gazelle.

But Lucy wasn't a size nothing. She was five foot three, and her legs were short and chubby. She had few muscles, the last time her boobs had vaguely resembled pert was about the time Mike died, and *graceful* wasn't in her vocabulary.

The burning-double-the-calories tempted her, but truthfully, she'd rather walk double the distance. She liked her ankles, shins, and knees. They did a fine job of getting her where she wanted to go. She didn't want to hurt them.

"If I tripped or fell, you would have a heck of a time getting me home."

"I'd carry you." When she snorted, he grinned that boyish grin that brightened even the most tired Lucy. "You'd be surprised how much I can lift."

No, she really wouldn't, she thought with a look his way. He was just under six feet. He ate healthy, except when she tempted him with her cooking. He worked out every day; it was part of his job, and on top of that, he honestly liked exercise. He came from an exceptional gene pool—she'd met his mom and dad when they'd visited and seen pictures of his siblings—and *muscles* was his middle name.

He was awfully darn cute, too, with that blond hair always in need of a trim, the perpetual tan, the scruffy bristle of beard on his jaw, and amazing blue-sky eyes.

Lucy had tried to set him up with several friends, but he'd shown no interest. She'd thought Ben's sister Brianne was just his type, but that hadn't gone anywhere, either, though they still ran occasional 5Ks together.

"Do you like women?" she asked as they approached the fire station that marked their turnaround point. Swiping at the sweat running down her forehead, it took a moment for her to realize that he'd stopped walking. She turned to face his scowl, and she quickly assured him. "It's okay if you don't. It doesn't make any difference to me. I'm just wondering if the people I'm setting you up with are the wrong type. You know, gender."

Joe placed his hands on his hips, drawing his

stretched-out T-shirt snug over his broad chest and flat belly. His biceps and triceps bulged, drawing her gaze downward to his fisted hands. "Yes, I like women. No, I'm not gay. No, the women you've pushed at me aren't my type. Not my *type*, Lucy. *Not* the wrong gender."

Even frowning like that, he was so darn cute. If she was a few years younger, she just might take up jogging and chase him until she caught him.

Then the sensible woman in her gave a shake of her head. What would she do with him if she caught him? Sure, he was sex-kisses-passion happily-ever-after material, but not for *her*. He was her best friend. Like a little brother without so much of the pestyness. She was like his big sister, without the great gene pool.

If she were a different person, not just a younger one, *then* she might chase him. That was what she'd meant to say. If she was the type to be drawn to a cute, funny, young football coach.

But she wasn't. She loved Joe dearly. He was the best guy friend she'd ever had besides Mike. But she was looking for someone to fall *in* love with. Someone smart and funny and sexy and sweet and grown-up and not best friend–like. Someone not Joe.

The unsensible woman in her head regretfully sighed. He *was* awfully hot damn cute.

* * *

Saturday had been the halfway mark on Avi's leave. She'd acknowledged the milestone, then chosen not to think about it anymore. The past two weeks had been the best of her life. She would let the next two weeks be good, too. Alone in Augusta would be soon enough to face the end of her romance.

On Monday, Labor Day, she slept until nine, such a luxury, then padded into the kitchen for coffee and a warm-from-the-oven cinnamon roll. She was heading for the kitchen table when her mom stuck her head in the back door. "We're out here. Come sit with us."

Obediently Avi shifted directions, climbed over Sundance, who was stretched out in front of the door, then sat down at the glass-topped table with her parents on either side. "How long have you guys been up?"

"We're always up by six," her father said without glancing up from the newspaper he was reading on his Kindle. Preferring to avoid newspapers herself, she wondered what he found so fascinating about the news in other cities, states, and countries. Did Los Angeles really have a different take on today's violence or politics from New York?

"We put in our three miles, showered, dressed, and I baked the rolls."

Dismissing her pajamas—gray Army PT shirt and black shorts—Avi took a large bite of the roll. "Mm, Mom, these aren't from a can," she said around the yeasty goodness.

"No, Lucy shared her recipe with me. Sadly, they don't last long."

"No kidding. I plan to eat at least four of them."

"I mean, they don't have preservatives in them like store-bought, so they don't stay fresh as long." Thinking that no one was watching her, Beth pinched off a bit of the roll on her own plate and dropped it to the ground. Sundance pounced on it in an instant.

Avi would have snorted if she wasn't afraid a bit of her own precious food would go down the wrong pipe.

Still acting casually, Beth smiled at her. "So tell us about you and Ben."

Avi smiled back just as casually. "I met him on my first day home, and we've been together ever since."

"What do you mean by 'together'? Dating? Building a relationship? Exploring the future? Or just having sex?"

Finally Neil looked up from the news. "My daughter doesn't have sex. She's a thirty-year-old virgin."

"Thank you for pretending to believe that, Dad."

He acknowledged her with a nod and a wink, then went back to his Kindle.

"I've seen the way you two are with each other. I don't need nosy Maureen across the street to know you're having sex." Beth shook her finger. "I was young and horny myself once."

"Ew, Mom, please. If you ever want grandchildren from me, do *not* talk to me about your own sexual experiences." She abruptly added, "Or mine. Some things just aren't meant to be shared."

Beth rolled her eyes but changed the subject at least somewhat. "You and Patricia's son, George's stepson. You hear about best friends wanting their kids to grow up and marry each other. I never gave any thought to that, especially since we'd never met Patricia's son. Besides, what if the kids divorce? Do you lose your best friend, too? But now that we've met Ben...He's a doctor. He's handsome. He's her son." She sighed wistfully. "Now I understand the appeal."

"Mom, we're just dating. No big deal." But the words sounded hollow to Avi's own ears.

Apparently, Beth heard it, too. Cradling her coffee in both hands, she studied Avi. "You know, you don't have to retire from the Army. You've already given them a lot. They don't have the right to expect anything more from you."

All gave some, the saying went, *and some gave all.* So many of Avi's friends had given all. She was grateful to be alive, to be whole and healthy and able to carry on their fight. "Mom, it's my job," she said softly.

Beth's fingers tightened, her lips thinning. "They've sent you into a war zone *five* times, Avery. You spent five years, three months, and seventeen days in places where people wanted to kill you. That's enough."

Wow. Avi licked cinnamon and sugar from her fingertips, then wiped her hands on a napkin from the stack in the center of the table. She hadn't counted it out herself. She'd just considered it *a hell of a long time.* Roughly sixty-three and a half months. Not easy for her, obviously not easy for her mom. All the packages Beth had sent her had been full of good stuff to eat, read, and make her laugh; all her e-mails and calls had been cheerful and chatty. Of course, Avi had known a mother's worry for her child never ended, but Beth hadn't let it show. Avi had thought she was being strong, like she'd always been. That she'd been around enough Army wives here in Tallgrass to absorb some of their acceptance. That she'd had faith.

Quietly, a bit of wonder in her voice, Avi said, "You're afraid for me."

With one manicured hand, Beth swiped at her eyes. "Why would I be afraid?" she chastised. "Just because I brought you into this world? Heavens, you're fearless enough for both of us."

Rising from her chair, Avi knelt and hugged her mother. "You're the one who made me that way. You let me do practically everything I wanted."

"That was on the outside." Beth hugged her back. "Inside, I was screaming *No! Stop!* Just wait until you have kids of your own. You'll see."

Avi intended to raise little soldiers, sailors, or Marines of her own. She wouldn't ask any of them to make a career of the military, but she thought everyone should serve at least one enlistment. They owed it to the country and to the people who'd served before them. She wasn't about to tell her mom that, though. If Beth had worried about her, how much more would she worry about a grandchild? Even one who didn't yet exist.

"What's on the schedule today?" she asked after taking a long sip of coffee. "I know there's the cookout at Patricia's."

"That starts at five. Us, a few neighbors, and most of her support group."

Avi grinned. "The margarita girls."

That brought her dad's attention from the paper again. "You gotta admire a group so dedicated to a drink that they name themselves after it."

"And no drink more deserving of the honor than the margarita." Avi saluted her father with her coffee mug, and he did the same. They made her mother sigh.

"Before then," Beth went on, "I've got to make a big bowl of pasta salad and a dish of sauerkraut salad."

"Ooh, that wicked good recipe you got from Linda at work?" Forget gourmet restaurants. Avi was a firm believer that nobody, no matter how many prestigious schools they'd attended and chefs they'd studied under, cooked like the average, everyday home cook. Her mom's, Patricia's, and Lucy's food could make her drool like an overeager puppy.

"I'm going to work," Neil said as he laid the Kindle down, stood, and kissed first Beth, then Avi. "They've probably missed me."

"They probably have," Beth said drily. "Tell them I'm recuperating from our vacation but I'll see them tomorrow. What are your plans, Avery?"

She watched until her dad had gone inside, whistling a low tune to himself. "Ben and I are having a picnic at the lake." They had stayed there until well after midnight Saturday night, talking, making love, and just being silent together. There had been something purely magical about being naked and intimate outside, the night air cool on their skin, the lapping of the water against the shore soothing, the peacefulness of the dark sky, the twinkling stars, the birdsong. She'd recognized whippoorwills and bobwhites and owls, and had let the others just wash over her, a melodic chorus by voices unknown.

Her soul had reveled in it.

A little of that reveling was still going on inside her, she thought, smiling secretively.

"I can help you make the salads before we go," she offered, but Beth brushed her off, making shooing motions with both hands.

"You're on vacation, babe, and I haven't set foot in a kitchen for more than a week except to bake those rolls. You go on, get your swimsuit on, and get going."

Avi walked to the door before answering. "Actually, we were planning to skinny-dip and see if we could shock the fishes."

"As long as the fish are the only ones you're shocking. If you get arrested for outraging public decency, forget my number. And take some sunblock. You want to be able to sit for the rest of your trip."

Avi was closing the door when Beth muttered to herself, "Thirty-year-old virgin. If only."

Laughing, she headed upstairs to change.

Chapter 9

A full contingent of margarita girls was lined up for introductions when Avi and Ben arrived at the cookout. The cooking was being done on Patricia's patio, with a yellow-and-white striped tent stretching across the grass from her backyard into Lucy's. Tubs filled with ice, bottles of water and beer and cans of pop stood in each of the corners, and tables and chairs took up the rest of the space.

A few hours at the lake had made Avi tired, but just the sight of the crowd reenergized her. Lucy met them a few yards away, took Avi's arm, and made the same shooing motion to Ben that Beth had done earlier. Avi was going to have to learn how to do that—not just the shooing but making the people she shooed obey.

"I tried to make them wear name tags that I could put just a few pertinent details on, but they voted me down," Lucy said with a pout that was for show. "Meeting all of us at once is a little overwhelming."

A petite redhead stepped forward and pulled a marker from Lucy's hands. "You're not writing our names on our foreheads, either."

"As if I would even try," Lucy huffed before giving Avi a *darn!* sort of look. Then, snatching the marker back, she scrawled *Lucy* on the red plastic cup she was drinking from before tossing the marker next to an ice tub, then began introductions.

There was Jessy the redhead, dating a cowboy near the grill and the one who rescued Patricia from Walmart after her notification call went south. Carly, a third-grade teacher recently wed to the soldier with the prosthetic leg. Therese, mother to three and soon to marry a medic from Fort Polk. Tall and elegant Marti, Lucy's best friend in a sea of best friends.

Ilena was the mother of a precious infant who was every bit as strong and healthy as she was waifish and thin. Bennie was a nursing student who'd made Avi laugh with the first words from her mouth. There was Leah and Kylie and Tasha and the last one, rising from a chair with some difficulty. Lucy slipped her arm around the girl's waist— out of affection or fear she would fall without support? Avi wondered—and smiled gently. "This is Fia. She's our margarita baby."

"I'm twenty-three," Fia said, then smiled shakily at Avi. "I'm not that young."

"Young is a good thing to be," Patricia said, offering Fia support from the other side. "Don't be too eager to get old like me."

"Ha! I only hope to age the way you have. You're strong and beautiful, Patricia."

"It's nice to meet you, Fia." Avi took the hand Fia

offered, careful to keep her grip gentle. The girl might be the youngest, but Avi would bet she was also the frailest. She had no excess body fat, strain had etched semi-permanent lines at the corners of her mouth and eyes, and her feet were turned inward as if holding her body in an upright position was too much for them. Avi's heart went out to her, but she tried to keep it hidden.

They talked a few minutes before Lucy pulled Avi across the lawn to the grill. There she met the men: Dane, Keegan, Dalton, and—surprise—his twin brother, Dillon. "Hmm, God was having a good day when He created the two of them, wasn't he?" Avi murmured to Lucy.

"Yumm," Lucy agreed as Joe joined them. "You should see what He did with the Cadore family. Joe's got three brothers and two sisters, and he's the runt of the bunch. They are one fine-looking family."

Avi looked to Joe expecting a complaint about the runt comment, but he shrugged. "Yeah, I'm the little one. Even my sister's an inch taller."

"But when you're gorgeous, you don't need anything more," Avi said.

"Thank you." Joe's smile was dazzling, leaving her to wonder how Lucy stayed safe from its charm. If she was Lucy, seeing him every day, she would have such a crush.

Thinking how Joe seemed to gravitate to Lucy's side, maybe he was the one with the crush.

From behind, she heard a barely audible growl an instant before Ben appeared beside her with a tall bottle of water, cap already untwisted. Teasingly she gave him a broad, innocent smile as she took the water. "All your friends seem really nice, Lucy."

"They are. They're the best."

And they were all widows. They'd all lost the husbands they'd intended to spend the rest of their lives with. Avi let her gaze slide over them again: the laughter, the smiles, the voices raised in good fun. They were a testament to resiliency, to the ability of the human spirit to suffer unspeakably and yet heal itself.

Avi might have known their husbands, might have deployed alongside them, worked alongside them, stood at attention to pay her respects when they died. She said a fervent prayer that the spouses of the soldiers who'd died on her tours had found someone like the margarita girls to help them through. In that way, these women were the luckiest in the world. They had people who'd been there, done that, and understood every heartbreaking moment of it.

Ben's mouth brushed her ear. "You okay?"

She blinked and realized her eyes had gotten damp. "I was just thinking..."

"How lucky they are?" He moved to block everyone else's view of her so she could swipe away the moisture without anyone noticing.

"Does that sound weird?"

"No. Any loss has to be easier with someone who can relate. I feel a lot of sympathy for them, but I've never been married. I know what it's like to lose a parent, but I can't imagine what losing a husband or wife is like. And after a while, after the shock is over for everyone else, they go on with their lives, and the wives feel alone. The margarita girls, though...they're not going anywhere. They'll be there tomorrow and next year and five years from now." He glanced at the women, then his gaze settled on Patricia. "Yeah," he added softly. "They're damn lucky."

* * *

Calvin's mother was fifty-one, his father fifty-four. They held jobs that required the daily use of computers. They had e-mail accounts, and his mother shopped online. But when it came to communicating with their son, his mother relied on letters, and his father relied on his mother. The letters were on thick sheets of pretty stationery, the writing a graceful swooping cursive Elizabeth Sweet had learned in grade school. They were a holdover from a time long past, one he'd developed a fine appreciation for once he'd joined the Army. He had every letter she'd ever written him, going back to his first one in basic training. Only the addresses and the colors of the stationery had changed. Pink, green, blue, peach, lavender, and now pale yellow—all the colors of the rainbow, all covered with her pretty script, all filled with words of hope and encouragement and love.

The latest had arrived in Tuesday morning's mail, bearing a stamp showing an American flag in the breeze. He'd put it in his desk drawer, then stuck it in his pocket. He knew its contents. There'd be an update on Gran, news on people he'd known in Tallgrass, maybe a few soft-hearted complaints about his dad, a comment on the weather—*Was it always so unbearable and we just didn't realize it?*—and then the question. Always the question.

When are you coming home?

He had plenty of leave available, and she probably

knew it. He had the money to travel, and she probably knew that, too. If he didn't, she and his dad would buy him a ticket. *We just want to see you, Calvin. You know I need to see you with my own two eyes.*

With the overbearing colonel he worked for gone to a meeting, Calvin refilled his coffee, grabbed a cookie the colonel's wife had baked, then sat down and slid a pocket-knife blade underneath the seal on the flap.

The yellow sheets reminded him of fresh-churned butter that his mom used to buy from an elderly rancher widow outside Tallgrass. She'd gotten milk and eggs from the old lady, too, and dewberries and blackberries and produce when the summer garden paid off. He'd never eaten as well since.

Dear Son. If she'd ever opened with Dear Calvin or Hey, Calvin, he would know for sure the world had ended. Once, when he was thirteen, he'd asked her to stop calling him *son* around his friends. Expecting a protest, he'd been surprised when a smile spread from one ear to the other. *Why, sure,* she'd said. *What would you like me to call you instead? Honey? Babe? No, I've got it: sweet baby boy of mine.*

Wisely, he'd never complained about what she called him again.

It'll be Labor Day or past by the time you read this. I don't know if it's age or if time really is passing faster. It seems just ten years ago that we brought you home from the hospital, a tiny dark-eyed creature so fragile we were afraid we would break you. Eight years ago that you brought J'Myel home, all covered in mud, and asked, 'Can

*I keep him?' Seven years since you were starting
school, four since you were graduating, two since
you said, 'Mom, I'm going to Iraq.' It's not my
life that's passed in a blur, but yours. One day
I was changing your diaper, and the next you
were climbing on that bus at Fort Murphy to start
that long trip halfway around the world. You and
J'Myel, out to save the world together.*

That day lived in such clarity in Calvin's mind. The
usual suspects: him, J'Myel, and Bennie. The grown-ups:
Calvin's parents, J'Myel's mother, Calvin's and Bennie's
grandmothers. He and J'Myel had posed for pictures,
chests puffed out, hands on hips, and J'Myel had crowed,
We're gonna save the universe!

Calvin's dad had snickered. *God help us all.*

God hadn't helped J'Myel. He hadn't helped Calvin.

*I know something is wrong, Son. Do you think it's
something we won't understand? Do you feel like
you've let us down in any way? Because that's so
far from the truth. We are so proud of you, Calvin.
So proud to have a raised a good, honorable, brave,
loving, gentle man. You are the very best of your father and me, of generations of our families. We love
you. We can help you. We need to see you.*

Love, Mama

What was the worst that could come of a visit home?
His mom and dad would look at him and see how empty
and broken he was. He might fool everyone in the Army,

but nobody fooled Elizabeth and Justice. He might run into Bennie, who probably hated him even more than J'Myel had. Hell, J'Myel was buried at Fort Murphy National Cemetery, so Calvin would probably run into his ghost everywhere.

And what was the best that could happen? He would be *home*.

He couldn't even begin to explain the incredible power of the place called home, if he could just hold himself together, if he could get there without breaking into too many shattered pieces to put back together again. *Home.* It meant so much: love. Safety. Security. Comfort. Peace.

But he couldn't go there. Couldn't survive the visit. Didn't deserve to survive it. How many of his friends would never see home again—their parents, their girls, their families, their own sweet peaceful places? J'Myel had left as much in Tallgrass as Calvin had. He could never make his mom laugh one more time, could never give his wife one more sweet kiss, could never throw a line into their favorite fishing hole.

Why should Calvin get to?

* * *

Ben had to cancel his three o'clock procedure Tuesday afternoon, thanks to the patient's mother, who fed her son a full lunch before bringing him to the hospital. The staff hadn't had time to prep the next patient yet, so he was back at the clinic, hoping to catch up on some paperwork, when the cell phone beeped in his pocket. Pulling it out, he glanced at caller ID, then answered with an automatic smile. "Hi."

"Hey, you," Avi said. "I'm just pulling into the parking lot."

She'd driven into Tulsa to make a delivery for the nursery. *Call me when you're done,* Ben had told her, *and I'll give you a key to the apartment.* Then he'd gone by a hardware store at lunch and had keys made for both the loft and the building doors. It would be the first time he'd ever given his keys to any woman besides his sisters.

"If you give me a minute, I'll come down. I'll meet you at the north entrance." After her okay, he hung up, told his medical assistant he'd be back, and headed for the lobby. After the air-conditioned chill of the office, the heat outside felt good for about half a minute, then sweat started forming along his hairline.

The big pickup sat in a no-parking zone a few yards from the door. Avi rolled the window down as he approached, her face flushed, the strands of hair that had escaped her ponytail damp and frizzing. She was sweaty and pretty and made something catch deep in his gut. It was too much to put into words, too much to face in the bright light of the day, so he settled for a single word, filled with both awe and sadness.

Damn.

"I expected you a few hours ago," he said, resting his arms on the door frame. Even through the sleeves of his white coat, he felt the sear of the hot metal.

She took a deep drink from a jumbo Sonic drink. "The customer I delivered to was seventy-six years old and determined to get the flowers in the ground before they wilted."

"So you stayed and helped her plant them."

"Actually, she sat in the shade under an oak and directed. I planted."

"You insist on providing that kind of service, your mom and dad will be shipping you off to Georgia earlier than expected."

"Hey, in exchange, I got a tour of a house in Maple Ridge and the best lemon tea ever. How's work?"

"I'm actually on schedule. I have one more surgery, and it's an easy one." Reaching into his coat pocket, he found the new keys and held them out. When she took them, his fingers curved over hers. "Be thinking about where you want to go for dinner."

"I'll cook for you." Her forehead wrinkled with exaggerated concern. "You do have dishes and pans, don't you?"

"A full set of both, smartass." Leaning through the open window, he kissed her, hesitated, feeling both the awe and the sadness again, then kissed her again. "I'll see you later."

"Every little bit of me," she murmured with a sly grin. Giving him a wave, she rolled up the window and pulled away. He watched a moment before turning back to the building, only to find three familiar dark gazes fixed on him. *Busted*, he thought, donning a casual attitude. "What are you guys doing here?"

"That was a cowboy truck," Lainie said as she leaped into his arms, not favoring her sprained wrist in the least. A testament to her determination, the elastic bandage she wore was bright purple, no doubt thanks to her mom and a bottle of fabric dye. "Is she a cowboy?"

"Nope, sweetie, she's a soldier."

Lainie's eyes widened. "Like G.I. Joe?"

"Yeah, sort of." He looked from her to his sisters, focusing on Brianne. "Why aren't you at work?"

"Because I'm on vacation. Why aren't you in surgery? Oh, yeah, 'cause you had to take a break and neck with your girlfriend." Brianne looked like him and Sara—dark hair, eyes, and skin—but was more muscular than both of them. She'd fought her weight all through school, but that war had been won after she graduated from college, when she'd discovered that working out and eating healthy were her friends. She was gorgeous and strong enough to kick ass but so sweet she never wanted to.

Sara was just as pretty and mean enough to kick ass. She saw her job as protector and took it seriously.

"Invite us inside," Sara demanded. "I'm melting."

"What brings you by on surgery day?"

"Lainie has a follow-up on her wrist with your physician's assistant."

Holding the door open, he made a sweeping gesture for them to precede him into the lobby. Sara's killer heels clicked on the tile floor, a counterpoint to the flip of Brianne's thongs and the whoosh of Ben's sneakers.

"So what was—what's her name? Avi?" Brianne considered the name. "Aunt Avi. My kids are going to like that."

"You don't have kids."

"But I intend to, once I meet the right guy to father them. Anyway, what is Avi doing in town?"

"Running an errand for her parents' nursery."

"And preparing to make a little whoopee," Sara added.

Brianne gave their sister a brows-raised look. "Sheesh, who says 'whoopee' these days?"

"Someone who has a small c-h-i-l-d who repeats everything she hears."

Still in his arms, Lainie grinned ear to ear. "C-h-i-l-d means me." Precociously, she added, "I'm l-a-i-n-i-e, too, and k-i-d-s."

"And too s-m-a-r-t for your own good," Ben said as he nuzzled her neck.

In deference to Sara's heels, they took the elevator. Stepping inside, Brianne bumped shoulders with Ben. "Are you going to run off to wherever the Army sends Avi and leave us behind like Mom did?"

Surprise tightened his gut as Sara scowled and swatted Bree. "If he did, it wouldn't be like Mom," she chastened. "He would e-mail and call and Skype us."

"Yes, but that's not the same as being in the same city and seeing each other face-to-face."

Ben gazed over their heads as the numbers lit up. Run off with Avi? He couldn't deny that a part of him wanted her around longer than her leave allowed, or that she'd become ridiculously important to him in such a short time. But run off? Leave his family? Never. Who would he be if he wasn't full-time brother and uncle to Sara, Brianne, and the kids?

"Well?" Brianne prompted, and he found both sisters watching him.

"I'm not going anywhere, guys. This thing with Avi and me…" With an awkward shrug, he said, "She's leaving in a couple weeks." He hadn't asked for an exact date yet. Part of him didn't want to know. Part of him would start counting the days, then the hours, and that would take away so much of the pleasure of being with her.

"I know she's leaving," Brianne said. "I just want to know if you're thinking about going with her."

He tried to imagine it: giving up his practice, renting or selling his loft, saying good-bye to his family, and moving halfway across the country. Not knowing his way around town, or anyone in town besides Avi. Having to build his practice again from scratch, finding new restaurants and places to shop, meeting new people, missing home.

The images just wouldn't form.

No matter how much he would miss Avi.

"No," he said shortly. "Like I said, I'm not going anywhere."

"We're all like Daddy," Sara said with a sigh that held its share of relief. "Remember when he used to say 'If God had wanted me to travel, He wouldn't have put me in Oklahoma'?"

Ben smiled faintly. His father had believed Oklahoma was the best place in the world, and Ben agreed with him. It was partly that belief that had made it so hard for Rick to understand Patricia's desire to travel. What could anyplace else have to compete?

Could a person be competition enough?

Theoretically, sure. But theoretical didn't have a lot in common with the reality of his life. His reality was here, would always be here. No matter where Avi went.

He would meet someone else. So would she. They'd both be happy.

Maybe. Conceivably. Someday.

On the fourth floor, while Sara got Lainie checked in, Brianne walked down the treatment room corridor with Ben. Working her fingers together nervously, she asked in little more than a murmur, "Ben, what if you fall in love with her?"

She'd asked him variations of the love question regarding other women, but he hadn't come close to loving anyone before Lucy so they'd been easy to brush off. Now...If he were a better liar, he'd give her a brash grin and a confident *Ain't gonna happen*. But he wasn't a good liar, and he had zero confidence of not falling in love.

"Bree, I'm really not going to move away, no more than Dad would have."

Her bottom lip poked out. "I know it's selfish of me, but I just can't bear the idea of you living anywhere else. You and Sara—you're my family. I mean, Mom, too, and all the Nobles scattered around, but you and Sara are the main ones. I know you'd visit, but seeing you three or four times a year just wouldn't cut it."

"Don't worry about it, kiddo. Listen, why don't you wait in my office? I'll tell the front desk to send Sara and Lainie back when they're checked in, and as long as I'm here, I'll do her exam."

"Okay." She turned away, then pivoted back. "Nigel's been picked up by Chicago, and he asked me to go with him."

Ben's brows arched. Nigel was her on-again, off-again boyfriend who played hockey for the Tulsa Oilers. Ben had always thought—maybe that should have been *hoped*—that all Bree and Nigel had in common was their dedication to fitness. He was no more eager to have a wandering Canadian enforcer in the family than a small-town Alaskan football coach.

You're not going? That was what he wanted to say, but he kept the words in. If she'd decided Nigel was on-again in a permanent sense, if she loved him enough to leave her home, Ben would be happy for her. He would also be damn sorry for Sara and himself.

"Are you going?"

"Nigel's great fun, but..." She shook her head. "I'd resent him for making me leave. I mean, he's got options.

He could retire. He could coach. He could put that environmental degree to work. If he really loved me, he would at least consider it."

Avi didn't have options, not at the moment. She was under contract to the United States Army and pretty much at their mercy. They could send her anywhere in the world, and all she could do was go.

From the end of the corridor, his medical assistant beckoned, mimicking a telephone receiver to her ear. "I've got to take a call, Bree. I'll see you when it's Lainie's turn."

* * *

After a shower, Avi dressed in shorts and a T-shirt, then wandered through Ben's apartment, trying to picture herself living there. The image wouldn't form. She had called home barracks, tents, and apartments the last twelve years, perfect for the temporary nature of her stays. But when she imagined settling down, really making a home, it was always a house that occupied place of pride. A place she could paint and remodel and landscape the way she wanted. A place her kids could come back to when they were grown, that they could bring their own kids to. Who ever said *Let's go over to Grandma's loft and play hide-and-seek in the street?*

If she didn't leave, if she and Ben let nature take its course, the loft wouldn't be a sticking point. He liked it, but she was pretty sure he wouldn't balk at giving it up, especially when the payoff for buying a house was kids to fill the extra bedrooms.

If she didn't leave . . . She had to, for a while, of course. She had nearly two years left on this enlistment. Until then, she was the Army's to do with as they wanted. But two years wasn't so long to ask someone to wait.

That would put her at fourteen years. Nearly three-quarters of the way to retirement. She would lose the medical care and the pension she'd spent sixty-three months in combat zones to earn. She would be giving up goals she'd had since she was ten—too young to know better then, but goals she'd still embraced when she was eighteen, twenty-four, thirty. She *wanted* this career. Wanted to serve every single day for twenty years. Wanted to stand proud at her retirement ceremony, to say with pride that she wasn't just a veteran but was U.S. Army, Retired.

Eight years was too long to ask someone to wait.

Heaving a sigh, she plopped on the couch, lay down, and propped her feet on the back cushions. Pulling out her phone, she scrolled through the contacts until she located the number she wanted. It took more than a few rings for her friend to answer, and Avi knew it was a simple reason: She was singing along with Avi's ring tone, *Born in the USA*.

"Hey, Jolie *blon*," she greeted.

"Avi! Kids, it's Avi!"

A chorus of childish *hello*s rang through the phone, as enthusiastic as if they actually knew her. Avi grinned. "Give them all hugs for me. How are you?"

"Getting by. You take it one day at a time, you know." There was a moment's silence, tinged with regret, then Jolie asked, "How are you? You're back in Oklahoma, right?"

"Yeah, for a couple more weeks." For nine more days, not counting today and the Friday when she would fly out before noon, but she pretended not to realize that.

"Going back to Fort Gordon. Man, we had some good times there."

"Didn't we?" She had met Jolie at Signal school, along with Rosemary, Kerry, and Paulette. They'd helped each other through their classes, lusted after fellow male students and every other available man around, and partied in town every chance they got. They'd been awfully young then, not one of them over twenty, not at all sure what life held for them but certain it was going to be great.

They'd had no clue Paulette would die before she reached twenty-five. Only Rosemary had been able to attend her funeral; the others had been out of the country. Avi had gone to Arlington to visit her grave between deployments. It hadn't been a very satisfactory good-bye.

"How's Mom and Dad?" Jolie asked.

"Better than ever. Are the kids okay?"

"Yeah. They're kids, you know. They see their dad every other weekend...when it doesn't interfere with his schedule. He cancelled last time for a date and the time before that for a guys' weekend in New Orleans. Like he hasn't been there a hundred times before." Jolie blew out a frustrated breath. "Sorry. My new mantra is 'Say no evil.' I won't be that parent who badmouths the ex to their kids. He's my problem, not theirs."

"I'm so sorry about the divorce." When it came to romance, all they'd ever wanted, all five of them, was someone who loved them and took that whole *'til death do us part* business seriously. Kerry had thought she'd found it, but getting served with divorce papers three days after she deployed to Anbar Province had cleared up that misconception. Rosemary thought she'd found it three, or was it four, times, but the placing of the engagement ring on her finger had been the beginning of the end every time.

Paulette hadn't had a chance, so the rest of them had celebrated wildly when Jolie fell in love with and married a handsome Cajun while she was stationed at Fort Polk. They'd had their first child, and she was pregnant with the second when Alec finally thought to inform her that he had no intention of being married to a soldier. Jolie had given up the Army, and three tumultuous years and a third child later, Alec had given up the marriage.

"Eh," Jolie said, likely accompanied by a familiar shrug. "I thought I'd found Prince Charming, and he turned out to be king of the rat bastards instead. It happens."

"If you'd known..." Avi hesitated, then asked, "Would you have married him if you'd known he was dead set on turning you into a civilian?"

After a long silence, Jolie replied, "Probably not. But I don't regret it. Yeah, I'm raising three kids pretty much alone, and I had to find a new career, but hey, I'm nothing if not adaptable. Besides, without him, I wouldn't have my babies, and they more than make up for everything else."

After a moment, Jolie asked, "Why the interest? Avery Grant, have you met someone?"

"Yeah. Just a guy. I mean, nothing's going to come of it. He lives here, his family is here, and...it's complicated."

"*Cher*, the good ones always are." Then Jolie laughed. "Sadly, so are the bad ones."

Deliberately Avi changed the subject, and they talked

for another fifteen minutes, trading stories of old friends, sharing the fun times of kids and dogs, before a piercing shriek from one of the kids called Jolie away. After promising to call again as soon as she settled in Augusta, Avi hung up, turned on the television, and curled onto her side.

She didn't watch TV very often, and she wasn't really watching it now. She didn't even bother to change the channel from the local early news show, though it caught her attention when the logo for the Tulsa Drillers went up on the screen.

". . . playing Arkansas tonight at ONEOK Field," the anchor was saying. "The game starts at seven, and we'll have the results tonight at ten."

I don't like baseball, she'd told Ben, *but I could be persuaded to attend a game with a hot dog, a cold beer, and something fun to do afterward.*

She'd said she would take care of dinner tonight. Hot dog, cold beer, done. And she already knew the something fun. All that was left was the game.

Yep, she, Avi Grant, who didn't like baseball even more than she didn't like soccer, was going to a baseball game. For a man.

Like Jolie, she was definitely adaptable.

Chapter 10

Ben walked in the door expecting the novel experience of incredible aromas coming from his kitchen, but the only unusual scent in the air was Avi's. She was coming down the hall from the bedroom, wearing a snug-fitting top and shorts that started low on her hips and ended a few amazing inches later. Her feet were shoved into flip-flops, of course, gray ones, the straps covered with silver sequins that caught the light coming in the west-facing windows. Her hair was pulled up on her head in a style so careless, it didn't deserve the name. It should have looked a mess, but it didn't. It was, in fact, incredibly sexy.

Seeing her had the impact of a fist to the gut. He had less than two weeks left, fewer than fourteen days when he could come home to her, talk to her, touch her, make love with her, spend time with her, laugh with her. Fewer than fourteen days before she broke his heart.

Don't think about it. He couldn't, or he'd find himself dwelling on it, and dwelling never did anyone any good.

"Hey, sweetie." He met her halfway, hugging her, kissing her.

"I bet you call all the women in your life that," she teased in a husky voice that warmed his blood.

"Just my niece. And my sisters on occasion." And his medical assistant. Most of his female patients. A few nurses. An OR tech or two. It wasn't that he didn't know their names. He did. It was affection, easy and familiar and comfortable. "You prefer babe?"

"My mom calls me that."

"Sugar pie honeybunch?"

She laughed, as he'd intended.

"How about gorgeous?"

She tilted her head, forehead wrinkled as if she were giving it serious consideration, then a smile spread across her face. "I like it." Sliding out of his embrace, she gave him a push toward the bedroom. "Quick, go get changed. We're going out for dinner, after all."

"Where are we going?" He pulled his scrub top off as he went and loosened the drawstring on his pants.

"You'll see when we get there."

He was fine with not knowing. He'd figured out the day after they'd met that it wasn't where they went, what they ate, or what they did that made the time together important. It was her.

Well, having great sex was pretty damn important.

He changed into cargo shorts and a T-shirt, slid his cell and wallet into his pocket, then returned to the living room, where she waited at the door. After locking up, he pocketed his keys, too, and took her hand. "Are your parents expecting you back tonight?"

"My mom just said be careful. My dad said have a good time and don't worry about waking him because he's always up by six."

They turned right when they left the building. There was a fair amount of traffic on the streets and not a single parking space to be found. Drillers' games always made his little corner of downtown busy. This would be the third game he'd missed since meeting Avi, but that was okay. The Drillers would always be there.

She wouldn't.

At the corner, she nudged him to cross the street to the left. He looked at the stadium ahead, then at her, but her bland expression gave away nothing.

"George was a big baseball fan," she remarked. "Not as much as football—he played at West Point—but he had a fine appreciation for the game. Wherever he traveled, he saw a game if he could and bought a cap. He must have had at least fifty of them."

Ben knew he'd played football. Cadore had told him. He didn't know much else about him. Where was he from? Had he been married before Patricia? What had drawn him to a military career? Had he regretted the harm they'd caused Patricia's family, and had it been worth it?

No, Ben knew the answer to that last one. He'd seen it in the way Patricia grieved for George, had heard it from people who'd known them. They hadn't broken up her family for a fling. They'd loved each other deeply, right up until his death. She still loved him, and Ben had no doubt she always would.

Somehow that made what they'd done...not okay, but better. Patricia hadn't left the family on a whim, and that mattered.

Outside the gates to the park, Avi stopped and made a *ta-da* game-show hostess gesture. "Dr. Ben Noble, it's your lucky night. Your date includes two tickets to watch the Tulsa Drillers annihilate the Arkansas Travelers at lovely ONEOK Field. You'll be provided with all the hot dogs and popcorn you can eat, along with your choice of beverage. You'll be allowed to cheer, hoot, holler, and jeer the umpire all you want, and afterward you'll be spending the night in a beautiful loft with your gorgeous and sexy girlfriend, who's been cruising the Internet on her smartphone to find new ways to be naughty, and it's all her treat. Sound good?"

Avi, who, impossible though it seemed, didn't like baseball, was taking him to a game. He laughed, opened his mouth to say *Sounds good,* and something totally different came out. "I love you."

The words hung between them in a moment of shock. Her eyes widened, and her mouth formed a soft little *O*. She looked stunned and just a little bit afraid. He was stunned, too. He hadn't meant to say it, hadn't even known it was in his head. But he wouldn't take it back. He meant it. In the end, would it change anything? Would it stop her from getting on that plane to Georgia? Would it keep them together?

No. But not every love had to be a forever sort of thing. He'd been in love before—*not like this,* a voice whispered—but it hadn't lasted, and he'd survived. He would survive this one, too.

Slowly Avi recovered, an unsteady smile curving her

lips. "Well, Doc, you sure know how to make my inner romantic tremble with pleasure. She intends to do the same for you when this game is over." With that promise, she turned and walked to the ticket booth with a bit of extra sway in her hips for his benefit.

He didn't care that she hadn't said the words back. That wasn't his reason for saying them—though damned if he knew at the moment what *was* the reason. She liked him a lot, and that was enough.

And now she knows how much you like her. As if she hadn't figured it out already.

She came back with the tickets, and they made their way inside, bought food, then found seats. As he prepared to take a bite of his hot dog, she asked, "Did you know Arkansas Traveler is a variety of tomato? GrandMir and Popi sold it at the nursery. What kind of sports team names itself after a tomato?"

"Hey, tomatoes are very important vegetables."

"Technically, they're fruit."

"Your head is just filled with trivial information, isn't it?"

She flashed him a smile. "It's good that you said trivial rather than useless. That will earn you points in bed tonight."

A few hours later, with another game in the win column for the Drillers, Ben cashed in those points. Afterward, in the cool stillness of the bedroom, with nothing between them but steady breathing, he spoke. "You met Patricia when she and George were..."

"Dating. Falling in love." Avi's hair brushed like silk across his arm as she snuggled in closer. "Yes. She was happy, Ben, in this lighthearted, beaming, it's-a-wonderful-world sort of way. Like me these last couple weeks."

He nuzzled her hair in acknowledgment but didn't stray from the subject. "Didn't she feel at least a little guilt?"

"Maybe. I don't know, Doc. I was ten years old, and all I saw was a beautiful woman and a handsome man who were totally smitten with each other."

"Smitten," he repeated, thinking of Sara's use of the word *whoopee*. "Who uses *smitten* these days?"

"I do," she replied haughtily. "It's a lovely word that says it all perfectly."

After a moment, she went on. "I'm sure she felt guilty, Ben. She loved you guys. Part of her still loved your father. Take it from me: A person can feel guilty as hell without anyone knowing it. I'm sure Patricia wished she felt that sort of passion for your father. She didn't want to break up her family, to give up having you and your sisters in her life. But what she felt for George, what he felt for her...It was beautiful. And complicated."

He and Avi were complicated, too. He didn't want to be. He wanted everything simple and straightforward: fall in love, get married, make a home, raise a family, live a long happy life. But what kind of life would he have if he got everything he wanted?

A perfect one, at the moment.

He stroked her stomach where his fingers rested, the skin soft and smooth and warm and, after their day at the lake, a deep caramelly gold. "What do you feel guilty about, gorgeous?"

She was still a long time, her breathing steady but shallow. He was starting to think he'd asked one too many personal questions when she spoke. "I don't think it's possible to be in a combat zone when someone gets killed and not feel guilty. It's just all so random. Five vehicles pass on a road, and the sixth gets blown up by an IED. A couple of people are walking across the base, and a sniper kills one of them. A mortar blows up this tent, not that one. Someone takes his buddy's place on patrol, and he's the only one who dies, when he shouldn't have even been there. It's hard not to think *Why them? Why not me? Why did I survive when the person twenty-five feet away died?*"

Ben couldn't offer any answers to her questions. He couldn't say it was because she was special; every casualty's family thought the same thing. He couldn't say she was spared because she had things to accomplish, gifts to offer; so did everyone who died. He couldn't say she survived because she was lucky, because it wasn't her time. Even if it was true, an answer that simple wouldn't offer any comfort.

All he could do was hold her a little tighter, maybe make her feel a little more secure, and know he didn't give a damn why she survived. He was just glad she did.

* * *

Thursday morning, after her parents had left for work, Avi changed into running clothes, hooked up Sundance's leash, and headed out for a jog. Theoretically, for her, Labor Day had always meant the change from summer to fall; the weather cooled, school started, football games were on the schedule; thoughts of wiener roasts tempted, with fat, charred marshmallows slowly melting off their sticks; she began anticipating Halloween, Thanksgiving, Christmas.

Three days post Labor Day, if it was cooler, she couldn't tell. So even though she'd planned a run, she was happy to keep her pace to the quickest walk Sundance would allow. Given that the puppy felt the need to sniff every tree, street sign, and fence that might conceal a dog, it was more of a snail's crawl.

As they approached Patricia's house, Avi's steps slowed. Parked in the driveway was a vehicle she'd never actually seen in person but had seen plenty of pictures of. George's '65 Mustang had been meticulously restored, down to the Rangoon Red paint job. It was the only car he had ever owned, purchased used the day he'd turned sixteen. It was his baby, and a real beauty.

"Hey, sweet girl." Patricia came down the porch steps, purse strap over one shoulder. "I was about to come by your house and bring you back here, and there you are. How lucky can I get?"

Avi let Sundance pull her off the sidewalk and across the grass. She looked a mess next to her friend. Patricia wore pale lavender pants and a perfectly matched striped blouse, with her hair styled and her makeup expertly applied. She believed in always looking her best, for herself, for George, for any soul who happened to see her.

Avi, on the other hand, wore ratty clothes, sloppy hair, and only hoped her socks and shoes matched, and she hadn't seen the point of putting on makeup to go for a run.

"You could have called, and I would have walked over. What's up?"

Patricia dug through her purse, then offered a leather key chain. The brown leather was embossed with a rear-ing mustang, and two keys dangled from it. "Welcome home. Merry Christmas. Happy birthday."

Avi accepted the keys with a frown. "I don't..."

Patricia pulled her to the Mustang. "I was there, remember, when George told you he wanted you to have the car when he was gone. I wanted to get it tuned up, checked out, washed, and waxed before I gave it to you. But here it is, in A-one condition and with a full tank of gas."

Avi stared at the immaculate interior, soft black leather and carpet, and her fingers curled over the keys as her eyes grew damp. "Oh, Patricia, I can't. You should give it to one of your own kids."

"I have three. They'd fight over it. Besides, they weren't George's kids." Patricia gently wiped away a tear sliding down Avi's cheeks. "You were the closest he ever got to a daughter, Avi. He loved you, honey, you know that. He wanted you to have it, and so do I."

Only vaguely aware that she was rubbing her fingers across the leather of the driver's seat, Avi still protested. "This car is a classic, Patricia. It's got to be worth a nice bit of money."

"I don't care about the money. I care about knowing that George's wish was carried out. Please take it, Avi, and enjoy it the way he wanted you to." A cajoling tone came into her voice. "C'mon, it's make-a-widow-happy day."

The voice saying no inside her shushed as Avi hugged Patricia tightly. "I'm honored to have it. Thank you."

Patricia patted her back. "He was honored to be part of your life, honey."

Avi surreptitiously wiped her eyes, then asked, "Can you come and take a ride with me?"

"I'd love to, but I can't. I've got a doctor's appointment."

Concern rippled through Avi. "Are you okay?"

"I couldn't be better. You met Fia Monday, didn't you?" She waited for Avi's nod. "It's actually her appointment. Her health has been declining since early this year, and she can't get a straight answer from the doctors, so Jessy and I are going with her today. Fia's so sweet and timid and exhausted these days. They find it easy to brush her off. But I'm a colonel's wife, and I don't take brush-offs well, and Jessy's a steel magnolia who will get answers if she has to go to the very top of the chain of command—and, yes, I mean the Chief of Staff of the United States Army himself."

"Fia's very lucky to have you guys on her side."

"I think so, too, but I'm biased." Patricia's smile faded. "Honestly, Avi, these girls saved my life. They're the strongest, most compassionate women I've ever known. They've cried with me and laughed with me and listened to me endlessly talk. They didn't even know me, other than Lucy, but they were there when we buried George, and they've shown me that life goes on. I'm blessed to have them, and I hope to be a blessing to them in return."

Avi hugged her again. "Well, you've certainly been a blessing to me."

"And you to me." Patricia smiled slyly. "And to my son, as well. So tell me quick before I go: Do you have a doctor's appointment of your own this evening?"

"I do."

Avi didn't know what emotion crossed her face, but Patricia cradled it in both her hands. "Love works miracles, honey. I've seen it so many times. You and Ben...just don't give up too soon." Leaning forward, she pressed a kiss to Avi's forehead. "Now I've got to rush across town to Fia's apartment. Jessy is picking us up there, and frankly, when she's in warrior woman mode, she scares me a bit. I don't want to be late. Love you, honey."

"Love you, too." Avi watched her get into her car, back out, then drive away. Slowly she turned to the Mustang, its top down ready for a drive. Preferably sans Sundance, who had a little thing about drooling with her head out the window.

She circled the car, admiring every little detail, and decided to risk letting Sundance in for the short ride home. The puppy was a perfect lady, sitting tall in the seat, ears flapping, drool not flowing. At home, she ran ahead to the front door, racing to the kitchen for a drink, while Avi headed upstairs. An hour later, showered, changed into a nice outfit that matched, with her hair neatly braided and makeup in place, she disappointed the dog by leaving without her.

There were a half dozen cars in the nursery parking lot, with another two out back beside her parents' cars. She parked next to a display of mums in vibrant fall colors, including a russet shade that made her itch for a plot of dirt. Maybe she could fill the tiny balcony of her apartment back in Augusta with giant pots of them; maybe that would be enough to satisfy the yearning.

She found her mom watering hanging baskets, and together they located her dad in the office. "What brings you by, kiddo?" he asked, looking at her over the reading glasses his computer work required.

"I want to take you and Mom to lunch."

Her parents exchanged looks. "Hmm. Wonder what prompted that," Beth said, tapping her index finger against her lips. "Couldn't be because you're going to miss dinner with us again tonight in favor of seeing Ben instead."

"Nah, can't be that," Neil agreed. "Couldn't be because she's suddenly missing us, could it?"

Beth shrugged. "Couldn't be because she has a new car she wants to show off, could it?"

Avi gave her a chastening look. "Do you and Patricia talk every single day?"

"Sometimes twice a day," Beth replied with a grin. "She told us Monday she was getting it ready for you. Isn't it gorgeous?"

Gorgeous. She could almost hear Ben's voice from last night and she blushed a little. "Absolutely. Can you guys go?"

"Sure," Neil agreed. He saved the file he was working on and closed the computer, called to Linda that they were going out for a while, then followed Avi and her mom to the Mustang. "Man, I have good memories of this car. I've got to admit, one of the first things I liked about George was the car. It was every guy's fantasy, at least every guy I knew."

"And here I thought I was your fantasy," her mom retorted before opening the passenger door and stepping into the backseat.

Avi rolled her eyes. "Please, your child is listening. Dad, you want to drive?"

He looked tempted for a moment, then shook his head. "I've driven it my share, and I'm sure you'll give me another chance."

Secretly happy he'd turned her down, Avi slid behind the wheel. "Okay, where are we going?"

"I vote for Bubba's."

Avi twisted to face Beth, surprised that her mother even knew of the place. Avi had heard of it for the first time herself Monday evening, when the margarita girls were talking about the appeal of cowboys, and it hadn't sounded like the sort of place her fifty-something mother would be the least bit interested in. "Bubba's? That's a cowboy bar, Mom."

"I have been to a few bars in my lifetime, little girl. Besides, they have the best burgers in town. They have an onion burger—the Oklahoma kind, you know, with heaps of onions mashed in with the meat while it cooks—that's incredible."

An onion burger did sound good. It had been so many years since she'd had a genuine one that it would be depressing to add them up. "All right, Bubba's it is." With a smile for the sweet rumble of the powerful engine, she pulled out of the parking lot and pointed the Mustang west.

*   *   *

Lucy had just taken her lunch bag from the shelf behind her desk when her office door swung open and three of her favorite margarita sisters sashayed inside—at least, as much as Fia was able to sashay. Pleasure warmed her from the outside in. "What are you guys doing here?"

"Little Sister had a doctor's appointment," Jessy said, "and we came to make sure it went well."

"Did it?"

"We kicked ass and took names," Jessy boasted.

"Well, Jessy did," Fia added.

Patricia stood between the two women, her arms around their waists. "Before the doctor even had a chance to dismiss Fia's complaints, Jessy informed him of our reason for being there and laid out exactly what we expected of him. He turned as pale as a ghost, bobbed his head, and swore he wouldn't give up until he finds out what's wrong."

"She was scary, Lucy," Fia said, grinning broadly. "To be so short, she makes one hell of an impression."

Jessy preened under the praise. Even being short—the same height as Lucy—she looked pretty darn impressive in white blouse, black pants, and four-inch heels. Add in the forcefulness of her personality, and Fia had the best advocate she could ask for.

Leaving her chair, Lucy circled the desk and hugged them. It came naturally with Patricia and Fia; they were used to giving and receiving hugs. Jessy had never been as touchy-feely as the rest of them, but she was getting better. "I'm proud of you all."

"Thank you. Now put that salad away"—Patricia gestured toward the small lunch cooler Lucy hadn't opened yet—"and come dine with us. We're going to Sage—my treat. Are you in?"

Sage was one of Tallgrass's newer restaurants, and one that didn't fall into Lucy's budget except maybe for a special occasion. She couldn't possibly turn down such an invitation. "Let me get my purse." She grabbed it from the lower desk drawer, stuck the salad back on the shelf, and followed the others outside. Stopping in the open door across the hallway, she said, "Hey, Jane, I'm going to lunch."

"I'll pick up your calls," the other secretary replied with a wave.

They took the elevator to the first floor, then Jessy strode ahead to the double doors. "I can walk to the car," Fia said with a bit of a grumble in her voice, but Jessy's only response was a wave over her head. There was a hint of relief in Fia's eyes. "I hate being such a burden."

"You're not a burden," Lucy and Patricia declared at the same time.

Patricia offered more reassurance while Lucy thought about how hard all this was for Fia. She was the youngest of the margarita sisters and, until recently, had been the fittest. She worked as a personal trainer, though her bad days now outnumbered the good. She'd worked out hard, not just because she had to be strong and buff for her job but because she truly loved the effort, the results, the energy invested, and the energy gained in return.

Then she'd hurt her leg. Next it was her foot. After that her arm. Fatigue became a problem. She lost weight. Sometimes she couldn't drive. Sometimes she could hardly stand. She'd had to cut back her hours at the gym and move to a first-floor apartment. She didn't have any family besides the margarita club to count on. And, until today, none of the doctors she'd seen had taken her seriously.

Lucy hoped this new doctor liked a challenge and hadn't just said what Jessy and Patricia wanted to hear.

As Jessy pulled up under the portico in Dalton's pickup truck, a smile curved Lucy's mouth. If the doctor had just been bluffing them, he was in for a very rude awakening, because he hadn't seen anything until he'd seen Jessy Lawrence with her hair on fire.

*   *   *

Ben was tired when he stepped out of the Spine and
Orthopedic Center at Hillcrest into the muggy evening.
He'd changed into shorts since Avi was picking him up to
go to dinner. He was scanning the street for her father's
pickup when a whistle sounded to his left. Sitting in the
drive was a vintage red Mustang convertible, and driving
it was—

He walked over to the car and rubbed one hand over
the polished chrome. "Nice car, gorgeous."

"Thanks, Doc. Hop in and we'll take it for a spin."

He opened the door and slid inside, settling comfortably into well-worn leather, giving the restoration an appreciative look. "I never really considered what kind of
car you would drive, but this suits you perfectly."

"I was never this imaginative. I had a Honda, a VW,
then a Nissan. When I deployed last year, I sold the car
rather than leave it in storage, so shopping for another one
was going to be first on my to-do list when I got to Fort
Gordon."

"But you came across this beauty and couldn't resist?"

She checked to make sure there was no one waiting
behind them, then turned to face him. "Actually, this
was George's. He'd said he wanted me to have it, so
Patricia has had it in the shop, getting it checked out and
ready."

"Very nice of him. And her."

"It was. Is. I was shocked. I thought she might want to
give it to you or your sisters, but…" Her shrug was accompanied by a faintly questioning look.

"Avi, it wouldn't matter even if we were his blood kids.

If he wanted the car to go to you, of course it should go to you. Like I said, it suits you perfectly."

Her grin warmed him. "What? I'm wild, racy, and fast?"

"You're a classic beauty and very cool."

"Thank you, sweetie." After their conversation about his use of the word, she'd claimed it as her own endearment for him. He liked it. "How was your day?"

"Long." He cranked his neck around, earning a few small pops. "I wish I could do OMM on myself."

She checked for traffic, then pulled out onto Utica. The breeze dropped the temperature from sultry to comfortable within a block. "That sounds naughty."

"It stands for osteopathic manipulative medicine. I can improve practically anything that ails you by adjusting various spots and/or doing muscle energy."

Stopping at a red light, she contorted herself into a grotesque position, head bent, arms flopping above her head, shoulders twisted one way, hips the other. "Can you fix this?"

Leaning across the small console, he kissed her, and she melted back into place. "You're a miracle worker," she said breathlessly. "Soon as I get something to eat, I'm taking you home and letting you show me all the OMM you know."

Home. It didn't mean anything the way she used it. It was just a substitute for *your place, your loft, your condo.* But for just an instant, it made him feel...complete.

"What are you hungry for, Doc?"

Something he didn't have in his life. Everything. But food...that was no big deal. "What did you have cravings for while you were in Afghanistan that you haven't had yet?"

"Um... Is White River still in business?"

"Could you imagine Tulsa without it?"

"I hope I never have to."

They made the drive to North Sheridan mostly in silence. With the top down on the car, the wind would have snatched away anything they might have said. But that was okay. Some moments were meant to be quiet, to be fixed in his memory so they would last a lifetime.

The restaurant didn't look like the best seafood place in Tulsa, but looks, in this case, really were deceiving. They joined the line of customers waiting to order, then found seats in a booth.

They were only a few miles from the airport. Ben watched as a big jet came in for a landing, then looked at Avi, fiddling with the paper sleeve her silverware had come in. A line from an old song popped into his head: *leaving on a jet plane*. Because he knew it wouldn't leave him alone, he asked the question those lyrics automatically prompted. "How does the car change your schedule? You'll be driving it back to Augusta, won't you?"

Her smile faded. "Yeah. I hadn't really thought about it." She set the paper down and folded her hands together. "My leave ends at midnight a week from Sunday. I was supposed to fly back the Friday before because I need to get unpacked at the apartment and get settled in and because I didn't know I was going to meet you. Now... I can leave Saturday morning and get there late Sunday afternoon." Hesitantly she said, "Or I could still leave Friday, and you could go with me and fly home Sunday evening. I could show you a little of Augusta and Fort Gordon. Kind of a road trip/vacation."

He didn't say anything right away. A road trip across the South with Avi sounded damned appealing: beautiful scenery all day, making love and sleeping all night. But it wouldn't just be making love. It would be one long drawn-out good-bye, and that was going to be hard enough as it was.

Besides, he wasn't sure he wanted to see her in her new home, that he wanted actual images to provide the background when he thought about her. Would it be easier to know her apartment was large and homey or that she slept on blue sheets or that she reported to work in a stark brick building? Did he want to know where she would go for her runs or who lived next door or where she would head for entertainment that didn't include him?

"I don't know," he said slowly. "It might be easier for us both to..." To end it quickly, like ripping off a bandage. *It's been nice, I love you, good-bye, and have a great life.*

Disappointment flashed across her face, then was immediately replaced with a smile that lacked the usual brilliance. "Yeah," she agreed without either of them putting into words exactly what they were agreeing to. "It was just a thought."

The silence this time wasn't so comfortable. By the time their food came, he was eager for the distraction. She made approving sounds over her broiled oysters and traded him for bites of his scallops and shrimp. The onion rings and coleslaw made her happy again, and by the time they left, it was as if the conversation about her leaving had never taken place.

In the parking lot, she handed him the keys. "You sure you don't want to drive?" he asked, though he was no

fool. He wasn't going to turn down the chance to drive
the car.

"I just want to kick back and enjoy the ride."

Maybe the ride could last forever.

But Ben knew better.

Chapter 11

As things stood right now, this was probably the last weekend Ben would ever spend with Avi.

The thought sobered him as he arrived in Tallgrass after work on Friday. He'd rescheduled his last couple of appointments for today, so it was barely four o'clock when he turned onto Comanche Street. In the last three months, he'd made this trip so often that it was beginning to feel like his second home. He knew Tallgrass as well as he did Tulsa—where to eat, where to shop, which places would be busiest at which times. He liked the town. If he ever left Tulsa, this was the only place he would go. Close enough to his sisters, close enough to his real home.

He parked out front, like he always did, and singled out the house key on his key ring. Patricia had offered him the key the first time he'd come, but he hadn't felt comfortable taking it. He'd found being in the house so soon after George's death, filled with all the trappings of their life together, difficult. All he'd wanted was *out*.

Patricia had accepted his refusal with grace and left the key on the dresser in the guest room that had become his regular room. *In case you change your mind.* After maybe a month, he'd begun letting himself in—her front door was always unlocked when she was expecting him—then after another month, without making a big deal of it, he'd taken the key.

Home.

When he let himself in, he called her name, and she stepped into the doorway at the end of the long hall, an apron around her waist along with a smile that instantly took him back twenty years or more. She'd been a devoted mother: running him and the girls everywhere they needed to go, volunteering at school, chaperoning field trips, cooking for bake sales and class parties. She'd sewn Halloween costumes and wardrobes for school plays, and added patches to Girl Scout and baseball and karate uniforms. Every single day when they'd come home from school, she was waiting for them, overseeing their homework, letting them help cook dinner or work in the garden or paint on some new house project. Her summers had been particularly busy between the organized activities, their dad's camping trips, and days watching the kids at one of the city's swimming pools, and she'd never complained. It had never occurred to Ben that she might even have reason to complain.

She'd been a good wife, a great mom, but somewhere along the way, that was *all* they'd let her be. She'd had little time for herself, for interests of her own, or for adult companionship that didn't involve the family.

He felt disloyal to his father for even thinking it, but no wonder she'd been infatuated with George from the start. He'd treated her like an adult, an interesting, intelligent, attractive woman. How novel that must have been to her.

"Sit down and I'll get you something to eat," she said, shooing him toward the stools at the island. "How about iced tea and an apple turnover?"

It hadn't been long since lunch, but who was he to turn down any of Patricia's desserts? "Sounds good. But I'll get it."

Three months ago she would have jumped before letting him fix something for himself. She'd felt as awkward as he had. Now she waved a hand toward a tray on the counter, then returned to the cookies she was putting on baking sheets.

"What's the plan for tonight?" he asked.

"I didn't know if you and Avi would want to do something special since she's leaving next week, but her parents and I are going tailgating before Joe's game. Lucy will be there, too, and Ilena and little John. Ilena says she's going to coach his pee-wee football team when he's older so she needs all the experience she can get."

They laughed at the idea of Ilena, whose biggest, meanest voice more than faintly resembled a mouse's squeak, coaching a rowdy football team.

"Anyway, you and Avi are welcome to join us just for dinner or to stay for the game if you want. If you don't, you can have the house all to yourself for a couple of hours, but"—she pointed the cookie scoop his way—"I don't want to know what you do."

"I'll see what she says. And if you don't know what we'd do in a house all to ourselves, you're not giving it any thought." He put a turnover, still warm, on a saucer, then carried it and his tea to the island. The first bite was amazing—flaky pastry, tender apples, and caramel—and earned her a thumbs-up while he swallowed. "She loves the car," he remarked before inhaling another bite.

"Good. George said that car helped him pick up a ton of girls, including the prettiest of all. Like I gave a darn about the car." A faint blush colored her cheeks. "Not that Avi will use it to pick up guys. Not that she needs to pick up guys. I mean—"

"It's okay. I get what you mean." Then... "She talks about him a lot."

"And you don't mind listening?"

It was hard to keep holding a grudge when someone unrelated to the divorce had nothing but good to say. "She loved him a lot."

Patricia set down the scoop and clasped her hands together. The action didn't hide their trembling. "So did I. And he loved her, too. And so do you."

He didn't say anything. She hadn't asked for confirmation. No doubt, she'd realized it before he had, and she knew the obstacles as well as he did, too. What was there for him to say?

"Oh, Ben..." Her voice was soft, the comforting, commiserating voice he'd heard in his dreams for years after she'd left. "Falling in love should be cause for celebration, not despair."

"I'm not despairing."

"Yet. I see the dread in your eyes. You know, anything

can be overcome if you try. Look at me—a little ole Oklahoma girl who'd never been anywhere, and the first time I got on a plane, I flew all the way to Germany. I cried all the way because leaving you guys had ripped my heart out, but still...I went, and except for you kids and your father, I never had a single regret."

His gut clenched into knots, he pushed away the plate with the last bit of the turnover. "I can't go to Georgia." The words sounded flat, but that didn't stop them from hurting. It didn't ease the tightness in his chest.

"Your sisters would survive."

"My practice—"

"Your patients would find a new doctor."

"Sara's kids—"

"Would be Skyping with you before you got the first box unpacked."

"It's not the same."

"Being here with your sisters and your practice and my grandbabies isn't going to be the same, either, not with Avi gone."

He knew that. Was afraid of it.

She locked gazes with him. "Ben, trust me. I know it's scary. It's a huge thing, leaving every place you know and everyone you love behind, but the payoff can be huge, too."

Too edgy to sit still, he slid to the floor and paced the length of the room. Outside the sun shone on manicured grass that stretched from Patricia's patio all the way across to Lucy's, and the flowers in the bed bloomed profusely, as if it weren't the end of summer. After looking at them for a moment, he turned back to face his mother. "I'm like Dad in that regard. I never wanted to see anyplace else. I certainly never wanted to live any-place else. The traveling I do for work, the conferences I go to, the seminars I teach, that's more than enough of elsewhere for me. I want to be in Tulsa." With the peo-ple he loved and needed.

All of them.

"More than you want to be with Avi?"

It was such a wrong answer that he didn't want to give it. Loving someone should mean more, should mean making sacrifices and compromises, but he wasn't willing to do either. God help him, it would be so much easier if he was.

"Yes," he said quietly.

Patricia studied him a long time, then turned to put the tray of cookies in the oven. "Then you'll get what you want," she said, trying to sound casual, but he still heard the faint censure in her voice. "Avi will leave next week, and you'll still be in Tulsa. Alone, but in Tulsa. Eventu-ally, you'll forget her and you'll meet someone new—at least, I hope you do. I hope you're not choosing a place over her just to end up spending the rest of your life there alone."

Swallowing hard over the lump in his throat, so did he.

* * *

"Tailgating? Oh, too cool! Do you know how long it's been since I've done that?" Avi had known her parents were going to the football game and picnicking on the asphalt—it had been their practice since she was in her teens, for her high school games, OSU's, sometimes the University of Tulsa's, and now Tallgrass's—but she hadn't expected Ben to have any interest in sharing his meal with Joe Cadore, especially on a night that would belong to Joe.

"You didn't have tailgate parties in Iraq or Afghanistan?"

"Sadly, no. About the only games we played were soccer—you know how I feel about that—and run-for-your-life, neither conducive to sitting on a lawn chair and chowing down. You should see all the stuff Mom and Dad have been getting ready. A folding table, chairs, a canopy in case it rains, a small gas grill, extra propane tanks, and so on. They even have a set of tailgate dishes and utensils, all bearing OSU's logo. I swear, I think that's why Dad bought the pickup, because there's no way it would all fit in the car."

Abruptly she laughed. "Sorry. I didn't mean to babble."

"You can babble all you want, gorgeous." Then he asked, "What about the game? Do you want to stay for that or do something else?"

She hadn't been to a football game since the last time she'd gone tailgating. Though she remembered it fondly—gorgeous fall weather, excited kids everywhere, marching bands, and just plain old fun—football was everywhere. Time alone with Ben in Tallgrass was a commodity. "Let's share the food and leave the cheering to them."

"Okay. Your parents are coming by to pick up Patricia. When do you want to pick me up?"

"You don't want to drive?"

"You don't want to show off the car a little more?"

She laughed. "You know me well. I'll see you in fifteen minutes." After his okay, she hung up and pocketed her phone. She wandered into the kitchen as her mom finished packing the cooler. "We're going to join you for dinner, but we don't plan to stay for the game."

"Aw, it should be a good one." Beth glanced around, checking for Neil, Avi assumed, then softly said, "Just between you and me, I'd be just as happy staying home and watching *Hawaii Five-0*. That Scott Caan is awfully cute, and that voice of his . . ." She shivered. "He could book me any time."

"I heard that." Neil came into the kitchen from the garage an instant after he called out. "Is that why you wanted to go to Hawaii instead of on a cruise?"

"They could have been filming while we were there." Beth bumped hips with Avi. "You're lucky. You didn't have to go halfway around the world to find your Mr. Right."

Just halfway across the country, Avi thought. And what did it matter how far she went to find him if she couldn't keep him? "Neither did you, Mom. You guys need my help loading anything?"

"No, kiddo," Neil replied. "Go on. We'll see you there."

He didn't have to tell her twice. She grabbed her purse, hugged them both, and headed out to the car. A few minutes later, she pulled into Patricia's driveway, but before she could shut off the engine, Ben came out, taking the steps two at a time.

The first thing he did upon getting in the Mustang was kiss her. The first thing she did was a full-body shiver. After the past few years, there was something incredibly lovely about getting all quivery from nothing more than a kiss. It made her feel young and happy and girly and even a little bit innocent. She would be forever grateful to Ben for that.

Tallgrass High School was located on the southwest side of town, a grand old sandstone structure built in WPA times. The stone was cut into large rectangular blocks, the doorways all double-wide, the windowsills at least a foot deep, with concrete arches and quoins. It reminded Avi of the old Central High School in downtown Tulsa, solid and substantial and her favorite building there.

The Tallgrass drum corps was gathered near the stadium, beating out a rhythm that she couldn't help but respond to. Tapping her fingers on the steering wheel, she was wondering where to park when a pair of voices called her name. It was Lucy and Ilena, standing beside their own cars on the last row in the lot. She pulled in next to them, accepted compliments, and answered questions about the car, then bent to look at the baby in Ilena's arms.

"He's so pretty," she cooed, thinking that any child of Ben's would probably bear a surface resemblance: all dark hair and skin and beautiful cocoa-brown eyes.

"You want to hold John?" Ilena offered.

"Can I?" Eagerly she took the infant from his mother, cradling him in her arms. He eyed her for a moment, so solemn, before smiling and pressing his hand against her mouth.

Who knew making a baby smile could feel so good and, at the same time, hurt her heart?

John moved as if he wanted to sit up, so she shifted him until his padded bottom was resting on her forearm. Immediately he leaned forward, mouth open, and gummed her shoulder for a minute before sitting upright and babbling at her.

She walked back and forth with him, talking softly, smiling at his own chatter. She was starting to feel the strain of his weight in her shoulders when a man popped out from behind her and swept the baby from her arms.

Joe lifted him into the air and nuzzled his belly, making smoochy sounds. John's giggles sounded so delighted that it brought everyone else's attention to them. "In another sixteen years, this guy's gonna be my starting quarterback," Joe boasted as he flew John like an airplane back into Avi's arms. "Then we're gonna get him a scholarship to OSU, then maybe play a little pro ball for a while."

"I like a man who plans ahead," Avi said, smiling at Joe while watching Ben from the corner of her eye. While a little show of jealousy might have been flattering, it was even nicer that he was confident enough to not mind.

"Remember, Coach, he's going to play baseball, too, and maybe soccer," Ilena said.

"No basketball?" Ben asked.

Ilena's grin spread wide. "Don't be silly. As short as I am, how could I ever coach basketball?"

"Ilena thinks she's an eight-hundred-pound gorilla," Lucy said to Avi in a whisper meant for everybody.

"Hey, I'm Army strong." To prove it, Ilena raised both arms and flexed in a bodybuilder's pose.

As they laughed, Avi felt another twinge. Damn, she missed her girlfriends. It had been years since they'd all actually lived in the same place, and it was a given that they never would again. With Rosemary in Germany and Kerry in Korea, even getting together for a girls' getaway would take some money and effort.

She envied Ilena and Lucy having their best friends

right there in Tallgrass, where everyone could watch John grow up. Avi had never even met Jolie's kids. The margarita girls could meet for dinner every Tuesday night and for football on Fridays and at any other time for no special reason. Avi really wanted that kind of companionship in her life again.

Her parents and Patricia arrived a few minutes later, and right behind them were two couples about their age whom Avi hadn't met yet. They were joined by Carly and Dane Clark and Therese Matheson and her two older kids, who immediately disappeared to hang out with friends.

The food was good, the company great. Joe didn't stay long; after grabbing some dinner, he left to join the team in the dressing room, to do whatever coaches did before games. Avi wished him luck before he left, and everyone else echoed it.

Grinning, she leaned against Ben where they sat on the tailgate of her dad's pickup. "You're going to have to make friends with him someday."

"Why would I want to do that?"

"When he and Lucy start dating—"

He looked at her with horror. "No way. Cadore? And Lucy? Huh-uh. Never happen."

"Are you blind? Have you not noticed the way he looks at her?"

He shook his head, clueless. "They're neighbors. Buddies. That's all."

"You might think they're just buddies. Even Lucy might think that right now, but believe me, that's not how Joe sees her." She glanced at the woman now cuddling John while his mom ate one of Patricia's outstanding pastries. "He's awfully sweet on her, and one of these days she'll notice it or he'll tell her, and they'll be together like that." She snapped her fingers. "Then, because you and Lucy are such good friends, you're going to have to accept Joe. You'll have no choice."

He shook his head again. "Lucy's too smart. Too classy. Her taste is way better than that."

"Because, after all, she dated *you*," Avi teased.

"She did, which is pretty much proof that she's too good for Cadore."

Avi laughed at his scowl. "If he makes her happy, you'll have to put up with him."

After a moment, he feigned a put-upon sigh. "*If* he makes her happy." None too subtly, he changed the subject. "I bet you never missed a football game when you were in high school."

"I was a cheerleader. I had to attend."

He gave her a sly look. "You still have your pompoms?"

She knew the pompoms were long gone, but her uniforms—every tiny skirt, matching panty, and form-fitting top—were stored somewhere in her mom's attic. "Maybe," she said slyly. "Wanna get out of here and find out?"

She jumped to the ground, and he followed. When they said their good-byes, their parents hardly blinked. Lucy and Ilena made the same smooch sounds Joe had amused John with. Avi didn't mind. She was driving off in a beautiful car to spend the rest of the evening with a gorgeous man. Life was good.

* * *

"All the time I've spent in this house the past three weeks, I haven't seen much of it." Avi drew her fingers across the well-worn finish of the heavily carved dresser. "I remember this piece. Patricia and George brought it back from Germany with them. When we visited them that summer at Fort Bragg, I thought it was so cool. I decided I'd collect antiques from exotic places, too, while I was in the Army. So far, I have a small bookcase from Italy and a couple of rugs from Iraq."

Ben lay on his back in the bed, pillows stuffed under his head, and watched her. When she'd left the bed a few minutes ago, she'd gotten her underwear on before the furniture distracted her. It was a lovely view, all soft curves and hollows and muscles.

"Then you need a few more overseas assignments." *Great suggestion. Tell her to go even farther away than she's already planning.* "Or you could just collect American antiques."

She smiled at him in the wavy glass of the mirror before picking up a picture frame. "Aw, how cute. How old were you?"

Ben raised onto one elbow as she brought the photo to the bed. "I hadn't noticed that. Jeez, I must have been about seven." He remembered the setting—a rodeo arena, a clown leaning against the fence behind him and the girls—and the clothes, if not the particular night.

He was wearing a red shirt with pearl snaps, jeans, and a pair of brown cowboy boots. On one side of him, Brianne's clothes were a match, except her shirt was pink, and on the other side, one-year-old Sara wore a white slip and bare feet. "We were at a rodeo in Pryor. Our cousin, Charlie, was a bull-rider, and I was going to grow up to be just like him. Mom always had trouble—" Realizing he'd called Patricia Mom, he lost his train of thought for a moment, then shook his head. "Sara loved to take off her clothes every chance she got. No matter what she was wearing, Patricia always made sure her underwear was pretty because at some point, that was going to be *all* she was wearing."

It felt strange calling her Mom. And a little bit good. He'd missed having a mom.

"Does she still take them off every chance? Because if she does, I know dozens of guys who would like to meet her."

"Nah. We can take her out in public and everything. Besides that, she's married, remember."

Avi returned the picture to its spot, then finished dressing before tossing his own clothes at him. "Come on, get up and show me around the house."

He didn't argue. The game would be over soon, the parents headed home. He didn't want to get caught with his girlfriend in his room by either his mother or hers.

Avi led the way downstairs, trailing her fingers along the banister. At the bottom, she turned in a slow circle as he pointed. "Living room, dining room through that doorway, you've seen the kitchen, the pantry and laundry room are off it, and George's study is here."

Of course, she chose to wander into the study. The only other time Ben had been in the room had been a day or two after George's death. Ben and Patricia had talked in there for a few minutes, one of the more awkward of their early conversations. He'd wound up leaving the house for a walk to put an end to things he didn't want to discuss.

It was a nice room, one that Ben would feel comfortable in himself if he had the sort of business that he routinely took home. The dark, solid furniture gave it a more masculine feel than the rest of the house. Military prints hung on the walls along with framed citations and commendations. George's degree from the United States Military Academy held place of honor.

As she'd done upstairs, Avi walked around the room, touching things, studying them. Upstairs, though, her mood had been light. Now sadness settled over her, heavy and sorrowful, like a deep fog floating down from the ceiling. Facing a wall that held framed citations, she sighed. "When our battalion commander in Afghanistan got orders that brought him back to the United States, it was no big deal. He was an okay guy, not particularly special but not the kind of guy that you wanted to hide an IED in his bunk. When I found out George was taking his place, I was ecstatic. I was thrilled that finally I was going to be stationed with him. Up to that point, we'd never even been in the same part of the world at the same time."

She picked up something leaning against a picture frame, rubbed her finger over it, then held it up to show him. It was metal, silver in color, about an inch and a half end to end. "Jump wings," she said. "He was Airborne infantry. That was the one piece of advice he gave me—to go to Airborne school—that I didn't take. I didn't want to jump out of airplanes." Her fingers closed over the wings, her knuckles whitening as she squeezed, then she gently set them down again.

"A couple days after he arrived, we Skyped with my parents and Patricia. My dad asked him to take care of me, and I said no, no, *I* would take care of *him*. It was the first promise I ever made that I didn't keep."

Ben went to stand behind her, wrapping his arms around her, holding her as tightly and as tenderly as she'd held the wings. "You can't blame yourself for that, Avi," he whispered. "I make that same promise to every patient and their families, but we all know that all it really means is I'll do my best. Crap happens. Things go wrong. You do your best, you pray for the best, but sometimes you get the worst, through no fault of your own. If you'd been able to save George, you would have, but it wasn't your call. You aren't in charge of life and death. That's a power beyond you."

"My head knows that." Her voice quavered, nearly breaking his heart. "My heart just hurts."

"It probably always will." Like his. He would give a lot to ease the pain thick in her voice and stark on her face. He exhaled deeply, resting his cheek against her hair. "That's the downside of loving someone. It always hurts when they're gone—and sooner or later, one way or another, they have to leave." Just as she had to leave. Not with the finality of death, thank God, but her absence was already tearing a hole in his gut that hurt like hell. "The only way it wouldn't hurt was if you hadn't loved him. Would you be willing to give that up—all the affection, all the memories—in exchange for getting rid of the pain?"

She swiped one hand across her eyes before whispering "No, not at all."

"One of the margarita girls told me that time doesn't heal your heart—"

Both Ben and Avi turned to see Patricia standing in

the doorway, clutching her keys, her purse, and a pennant in the Tallgrass High School colors to her chest. She let them slide to the floor and came farther into the room, going on in a voice clogged with tears. "But it does grow a scar over it so you can bear the sorrow. And she's right. I figure my own scar has a long way to go, but it's getting there. Think how sad life would be if you never cared enough about anyone to mourn when they passed. You love a lot of people, Avi, and you've lost a lot of them. Sometimes it seems like too much, but I know you. You wouldn't give up a single moment of wonderful to escape a lifetime of sad."

"No." Avi cleared her throat as she wiped once again at her eyes. "I wouldn't."

"You made a huge difference in George's last months, honey. He finally got the chance to be stationed with his favorite soldier in the whole world. You should have seen his excitement when he found out. And he couldn't have been any prouder of you—as a person, a woman, a soldier."

Loving Avi was something Ben and George would have had in common, besides Patricia. From all Ben had heard, George would have been a good stepfather, a great step-grandfather to Sara's kids. He sounded like a person Ben could have liked, if he'd ever given it a chance. If he'd ever grown up enough, forgiven enough, to take the chance.

Patricia studied Avi a moment, then smiled broadly through her own tears. "Come into the kitchen with me. We'll have something to eat and drink, and you can tell me all your favorite dishes for tomorrow's dinner with the girls."

*   *   *

"What's on your agenda for today?"

Lucy glanced at Joe as she kicked her shoes off, then sat back and propped her feet on the chair opposite her. They'd just finished their walk, so now it was time for breakfast on her patio: coffee with zero-calorie sweetener and nonfat powdered cream, Greek yogurt, and a handful of grapes. She let herself dream for a moment of the Krispy Kreme doughnuts he used to bring for breakfast, then thought about the four pounds she'd lost since her doctor's appointment, and the dream faded. "Cleaning," she said as she stirred the yogurt.

"Your house is clean."

"Actually, Fia's house. Even on her good days, she doesn't have the energy after work, and on bad days, it's just impossible. So Jessy's taking her out to the ranch for a bit of pampering, and I'm cleaning her apartment while she's gone."

"Doesn't she have family who can help her out?"

"Her mother was disinterested, and her father only came around when he needed money. She pretty much raised herself. But she's got all the family she needs in us." She looked at his breakfast, the same as hers but with much bigger portions, and suppressed a sigh. If she was a football coach, a trainer, and taught nutrition, would she be as lean and muscled as he was?

Maybe. But the idea of that much physical activity made her shudder.

"I'll help you," he announced.

"Help me what?" she asked absently.

"Clean Fia's place."

That brought her attention all the way back to the conversation. "You don't clean your own place."

"But that doesn't mean I don't know how." Then he scowled at her. "How do you think my house gets clean?"

She shrugged. "I don't know. I assumed your mom cleans it when she visits, or maybe one of your girlfriends, or you made it an extra-credit project for class."

He looked insulted. "My mom comes to visit *once* a year, and I would never take advantage of my students like that."

She spooned out another bite of yogurt. "You left out the girlfriends."

"When was the last time you saw a girlfriend over there?"

A long time ago, she admitted. The woman had been tall and willowy and lean, tanned, blue-eyed, and blond-haired, had dressed in adorable clothes designed for skinny bodies, and had been indecently fond of jogging and lifting weights and hitting the gym. Lucy had thought she was a perfect match for Joe, but he'd lost interest in her less than a month after they'd started dating.

"You're sure you like women," she half said, half asked.

"I'm sure." He frowned hard. "But I don't need any fix-ups. You worry about your social life, Luce, and I'll take care of mine. Now, do you want my help or not?"

"Absolutely. I will zip my lip." She went through the motions. "This is me, not saying anything else on the subject."

They ate awhile in silence. She finished the yogurt, set the spoon aside, and crumpled the cup, then picked up one fat red grape. "Brianne Noble is going to be at dinner this evening. I hear her hockey player boyfriend's transferring to another team."

Joe's brows drew down low over his eyes, and he bared his teeth at her. Lucy thought it was in her best interest to drop the subject.

When they finally began talking again, it was about the football team, the game they'd won the night before, and the preparations for their next game. Lucy didn't love football the way some women did, but she knew plenty about it. Mike had played in high school, and so had her brother; it had been on the TV in their house way too many hours for her to not learn anything. She was happy to talk about it with Joe, who gave her credit for understanding the nuances of the game. He was good that way. Even though he knew a lot about things she was totally ignorant of, he never assumed that, and he never treated her as if she was dumb, just undereducated on some subjects.

She wouldn't have heard the doorbell if Norton, snoozing under the table, hadn't suddenly alerted. Expecting Jessy, she slid to her feet and padded across the concrete to the rear door. When she got to the front door, no one was there but Fia, waiting in the passenger seat of Jessy's car. She waved, leaned across to the open driver's window, and called, "She headed around back."

"Great. Joe's back there. Prepare to wait while she drools." Lucy waved good-bye before going back out.

Sure enough, Jessy was standing near Joe's chair, her green gaze making an appreciative sweep over him. Seeing Lucy, she rested her hand on Joe's shoulder. "Hot damn, doll, how do you live with this guy next door and not melt at his feet every day?"

As Joe smiled smugly, Lucy replied, "Oh, please, don't feed his ego. It's already monster sized."

"But he's so cute, aren't you, Joe?"

"A hundred percent adorable."

Lucy feigned a scowl. "Hey, remember Dalton."

The expression that came over Jessy was a pleasure to watch. She'd always been the toughest margarita girl, strong and brash and blunt, with her sentimentality kept carefully hidden. Since falling in love with Dalton Smith, though, she was just a gooey mess at times, and Lucy loved her even more for it.

"Dalton's got my heart...but that doesn't mean I can't look." Jessy pulled the key from her shorts pocket and tossed it over. "You're a sweetheart for doing this, Lucy."

"Hey, I'm helping," Joe said.

Jessy gave him a smile and a wink. "You're always a sweetheart, Joe. This just makes you world class. Give me a call when you're done. Oh, and Fia said to tell you thank you thank you thank you." A small frown appeared. "She also told me to give you a hug and a kiss, Lucy. Joe, take care of that for me, will you?"

The look that came into Joe's eyes was enough to distract Lucy from Jessy's leaving. It was sly and scheming and—and...she didn't know what else. He wouldn't take Jessy seriously. Heavens, the last time he'd hugged Lucy, she was pretty sure it would have been more accurately described as a headlock, and he might even have rubbed his knuckles across her scalp while doing it.

As for a kiss...Aw, man, she missed kisses. In seven years, the only man who'd kissed her was Ben, and that had been disappointingly passionless. But that didn't mean she wanted Joe to kiss her. It would be like kissing her brother. Yikes, yuck, and poo.

Then she looked at him again, too darn handsome for his own good, and thought about that sly look, and the grin she loved, and everything else about him that she loved and hated and drove her crazy, and for the first time since they'd met, she'd found herself wondering the impossible.

What would it be like to get a kiss from Joe?

Chapter 12

Thunderstorms moved in Saturday evening, bringing much-needed rain that continued to fall long after the thunder and lightning faded away. It moved the family dinner inside, where Sara's kids tried to burn off the energy they would have depleted in the backyard in better weather. Avi had a great time with them, and she saw her mom watching them with longing. She was probably thinking how unfair it was that Patricia had three grandkids while she had none. *I'm gonna work on it, Mom. Soon as I get settled in Augusta. Soon as I meet the right guy.*

Soon as I get Ben out of my heart.

Good luck with that.

After dinner, the kids persuaded her father to take them out on the front porch. Seeing him through the living room windows, watching patiently while the little ones raced each other from one end of the porch to the other, she slipped out the door, dodged three giggling bullets, and sat down next to him on the old-fashioned glider.

"I see you haven't changed," she teased affectionately. "Still the life of the party."

"The way I see it, a party only needs one life, and there's at least three of them in there." He set the glider moving with the push of a foot. "I can't believe your month is nearly over."

"I've still got almost a week left."

"For your dad, that's nearly over. Time passes faster for me than it does for you." He patted her arm. "I hear you're grown up and everything, but I hate to see you drive all the way to Fort Gordon by yourself. Why don't you ask Ben to go with you, then fly back?"

She smiled despite the lump forming in her throat. "I suggested it. He didn't jump at the chance." But he hadn't turned her down. They'd left the question hanging. Maybe he would surprise her. She wasn't pinning her hopes on it, though.

"Let me know if I need to twist his arm a little."

"He's an orthopedic surgeon. He'd just untwist it."

Neil rocked the seat for a while, absently calling to four-year-old Eli when he ventured past the first two steps. After a while, he tilted his head to study her. "This visit has been good for you."

"It has," she reflected. "I should have done it years ago."

"Your mother tried to tell you."

She had. Given Beth's way, though, Avi would never go anywhere else on leave. Oklahoma had its allure, but so did the oceans, the mountains, and the cities. Still, this had been exactly what she needed this time. She was more relaxed than she'd been in years. She'd eaten better, slept better, and laughed more. It was exactly what the doctor would have ordered if she'd consulted one.

"I wish I had half their energy," Neil said with a nod toward the kids. "Am I going to get any of those while I'm young enough to enjoy them?"

"There's an awful lot to it, Dad. To start with, I have to meet a guy." Unless she and Ben had had a condom failure in the past few weeks. Wouldn't it be something to find out in two to four weeks that she was pregnant? That would cast everything in a different light. It would certainly keep Ben in her life.

Though not the way she wanted.

"You're a pretty girl. Finding a guy won't be hard. After all, all you really need is a sperm donor." Then Neil reflected on that. "Though, as your father, I'd prefer someone who makes you happy, wants to marry you, and wants to be a father."

"You and me both." She'd counseled young soldiers under her command who'd found themselves pregnant after a careless night partying, with the father in the wind. Not only were they still expected to do their jobs, the same as before, but now they'd had a tiny helpless baby to care for. The usual caretakers of new babies—grandmothers and grandfathers, aunts and cousins and friends—more often than not lived in another state, and Lord knows, affordable child care wasn't easy to find in an Army town. Working a schedule of days, along with an overnight watch, then two weeks of training out of town here, another week there, switching to a night shift…Even two parents had problems when they both wore the uniform.

"You gonna be all right at Fort Gordon?"

"Sure," she said breezily, tucking her feet beneath her, resting her arm on the back of the glider and leaning her head against her fist. "I make friends quickly."

"I mean, about Ben. Are you going to be okay without him?"

"We knew nothing would come of this from the beginning."

"It doesn't matter what you knew at the beginning. Do you think I had any clue when I first met your mom how I was going to feel about her a month later?"

Avi gazed down the porch, where the kids were now seated in a circle on the floor, Lainie talking excitedly, the two boys listening as if fascinated. It was hard to imagine a time when her father didn't love her mother. They were so perfectly suited that surely they must have been together from the beginning of time.

She sighed wistfully. "I thought it was possible we'd get too involved, but it was a risk I was willing to take. Nothing's changed, really. I came here with the intent of returning to Augusta after a month, and that's still on the schedule. I'll be fine, Dad. So will Ben."

Neil gave her a chiding look. "No offense, sweetheart, but I'm not real concerned about how he'll be doing this time next week." He let a moment or two pass quietly before saying, "Your mom was right, you know. You don't have to retire from the Army. I didn't. Your grandfather didn't."

"I know. But this is what I want to do with my life." She was as sure of it now as she'd been three weeks ago, but somewhere deep inside, it sounded just a little bit hollow. Hadn't she always wanted to get married, too, and have kids? Had the career become more important than the family? Maybe. For the moment. When she couldn't have both.

"I know it's all you ever really wanted. I just want you

to remember that getting out is always an option. Sure, you'd lose your retirement benefits, but you marry a doctor, honey, you don't have to worry about health care, and you won't need that pension."

She swatted his arm playfully. "I can't believe my father, who brought me up to be independent and to always rely on myself, is suggesting that I get married to secure a comfortable life."

Laughing, he dodged her second swat. "Hey, there are many ways of taking care of yourself. Marrying a rich man just happens to be one of them. Besides, you've got your folks to worry about. One day, your mom and I are going to reach old age. It would be easier for you to pay for our cruises, our ski chalet, our beachfront property, and our luxury lifestyle if you were married to Ben."

She couldn't help but snicker. Her parents might age, but they would never be old, and even if they were, it was a matter of pride to both of them that they'd provided well for their future. They would no more accept her support than she would take theirs. "I don't think Ben is exactly rich," she pointed out.

Her father smiled at her in that mindful way of his. "He is in the way that counts, sweetheart. He's got you." He patted her on the knee. "If you don't mind keeping an eye on the kids, I believe I'll go in and see what's for dessert."

"Eat double for me."

The door had hardly closed behind him when the younger two kids approached Avi. Matthew stayed at the other end of the porch, sprawled in a wicker chair, apparently contemplating his well-worn sneakers. "I saw you at Uncle Ben's work," Lainie said. "You're G.I. Joe."

"No, she's not," Eli disagreed.

"Yes, she is. Aren't you?"

Avi smiled. "I'm a soldier."

"See?" Lainie fisted both hands on her hips. "G.I. Joe."

Eli shook his head. "Joe's a football pwayuh and a wawn mowuh."

A lawn mower. Joe would probably get a kick out of that, Avi thought.

Swiping her hair back, Lainie climbed onto the glider. "He thinks only one person in the world can have a name." She leaned closer and confided in a loud whisper, as if it explained everything, "He's four. Are you gonna marry Uncle Ben?"

Longing surged deep inside Avi, but she ruthlessly pushed it down. "Uncle Ben and I are friends."

"You're his girlfriend," Lainie corrected, and Eli chimed in, "Girlfwiend."

"He kisses you." She made kissy sounds, and Eli giggled. "Aunt Bree says what if he goes away to live with you and we never see him again. Me and my brothers— we don't want him to go away."

Aunt Bree should check for small children who absorbed everything they heard before she spoke, Avi thought. "I don't think Uncle Ben's going anywhere."

"Aunt Bree says sometimes people do silly things. Like this." Lainie held up her arm, still encased in an elastic bandage with a vibrant tie-dye color scheme going on. "I climbed a tree."

"She falled," Eli put in.

"I didn't fall! My feet jumped, and the rest of my body had to go, too."

Avi checked the smile trying to curve her lips. "That's

happened to me before." When one part of her body committed, the rest of her just had to go along. Once her heart had gotten involved with Ben, her brain had had no say in the matter.

"What does a soldier do? Can you drive a tank? Do you have a big gun? Where's your soldier costume?"

Grateful for the change of subject, Avi answered her questions. She expected the answers to prompt further questions, but they got an interruption instead, in the form of chatty Aunt Bree.

Brianne lifted Lainie, took her seat on the glider, then settled the girl on her lap. Lainie grinned at her. "It's okay, Aunt Bree. We told her you and Mama and us don't want her to take Uncle Ben away, and she's not."

Brianne's cheeks turned pink. "We try to spell everything around her, but she's learned to sound out most of the words. Blasted phonics."

Eli patted his aunt's hands to get her attention. "Can we pway in the wain, Aunt Bwee?"

"No," she said simply. End of discussion.

Avi liked her for that alone. On one of her early visits to Tallgrass, when her grandmother had said no to something she'd wanted to do, Avi had come back with a whiny *Why not?* GrandMir told her for the first and only time that she was the adult, Avi was the child, and no meant no. Reasons didn't matter. Explanations weren't owed. At the time, Avi had thought it unfair, but she'd come to value the simplicity of it. She intended to use the same reasoning with her kids.

"You ever been married?" Brianne asked. When Avi shook her head, she replied, "Me, either. I didn't have my first date until I had graduated from college. I was the cheery fat girl who told lots of jokes and that guys didn't look twice at. Sara likes to say I was big-boned, but I had passed 'big-boned' about a hundred pounds earlier."

"That's hard to imagine." Brianne was nearly as tall as Ben, maybe six foot, and there wasn't one excess ounce on her. She was sleek and hard-muscled, a long lean body capable of working hard and efficiently, and she looked killer in her snug sapphire blue sleeveless dress. "Congratulations."

"Thanks. I had the best time at my ten-year high school reunion. All the boys who could never remember my name suddenly couldn't forget it. It was lovely."

"If I didn't have a job where I had to work out regularly, my—" Avi glanced at Lainie, seemingly oblivious to the conversation, then laid her hands over the girl's ears. "My bravo-uniform-tango-tango would need a wide load sign."

"I heard that," Lainie said.

"Yes, but did you understand it?"

The girl shook her head.

"Good." Avi offered her fist for a bump, and the girl who looked so much like Ben did it enthusiastically. She grinned wide, her deep brown eyes both intense and playful, then slid to her feet and ran off to the other end of the porch.

*   *   *

There was something disconcerting about a park after dark, when everyone had gone home and the playground equipment stood silent and empty. Or maybe the disconcerted feeling came from deep inside Ben because time was running out for him and Avi. He sat on a swing at Tallgrass's City Park, a broad swath of heavy-duty canvas secured to the metal A-frame by lengths of steel chain. The ground beneath his feet was sandy, warm, and damp, the air scented with aromas from a grill somewhere among the nearby houses.

It was Sunday evening, and he should have been home by now. Instead, he braced his feet in the soft dirt and twisted the swing so he could watch Avi beside him. Her white dress gleamed in the night, and her hair floated free behind her as she used gentle pushes to keep her own swing in motion.

Sara had liked Avi. Brianne, always a little more passionate, adored her. *You shouldn't let her go,* she'd said just before she, Sara, and the family left for Tulsa Saturday. *She's a keeper.*

He couldn't keep someone who was obligated to leave.

But he didn't have to let go. Long-distance relationships might not be ideal, but they worked for a lot of people, and he had enough money that regular trips between Tulsa and Augusta wouldn't be a strain financially.

But it wasn't the life he'd imagined for himself. What was the point of being in a relationship or a marriage when you could see each other only forty-eight hours a week? How could that work when the kids came along? He didn't want to be a part-time husband, and he damn well wouldn't be a part-time father.

Long-distance worked for a lot of people, but he was pretty sure he wasn't one of them. He wanted—needed—the people he loved close.

"What'cha thinkin'?" she asked in a singsong voice.

"Nothing."

She shook her head. "'Nothing' doesn't make your face scrunch up like that. 'Nothing' gives you kind of a blank, bland look because, well, it's nothing."

"Okay. I was thinking about you leaving and whether we could make things work with you halfway across the country."

She stopped swinging, planted her feet, and twisted to face him. Her long, slender fingers gripped the chains a little tighter than two minutes ago. "And?"

Grimly, he shook his head.

"What? You don't care enough?"

He scowled at her ridiculous question. "I care too much. I want more, Avi. I want a normal life, a wife and a home and a family, with all of us living in the same house and my wife and me sleeping in the same bed, not once every few weeks or months but every night. All the time."

She turned in a circle, winding the chain around itself. "You want me to get out of the Army." Her tone was flat, her words a foregone conclusion in her mind. And damn if she wasn't right.

"Is that so much to ask?"

She did another circle. "No, of course not. After all, you're the man and I'm the woman, so I should be the one to sacrifice." She turned once again. "Your job is *not* more important than mine, Doc. And I can only be a soldier in so many places, while you can be a doctor anywhere."

"It's not just a job. It's a career."

"So is mine." Lifting her feet into the air, she leaned back and let her head tilt, her hair flowing behind her, as the taut chain unwound itself. When it came to a stop, she stood and put her hands on her hips. "Even if I wanted to get out—which I don't—I've got nearly two years left on this enlistment. What would you suggest? That you live your life and I live mine and we visit when we can and see other people when we can't?"

At that moment, the sound of her voice made his head hurt. The question she was asking made his heart hurt. "No, Avi, I'm not suggesting—"

"You knew I was a soldier when you asked me to breakfast that Sunday. You knew that next weekend, I'd be kicking the dust of this town off my heels and heading to Georgia. Yet you still spent time with me, kissed me, made love with me—"

"I didn't intend to fall in love with you!"

She drew back, blinked, then folded her arms across her middle. He'd earned that response from enough women in his life to know that nothing good ever came from it. But, as usual, Avi proved herself different. She didn't display any anger, didn't say anything flippant or hurtful. She breathed deeply a couple of times, then lowered her arms. "I didn't intend to fall in love with you, either," she admitted. "They say the road to hell is paved with good intentions. If that's where we're headed, then it's all your fault for being so damn lovable."

He'd never felt less like laughing, not when everything inside him was tender and sore and aching, but it happened anyway. "No one, not even my mom, has ever called me lovable. Some of the nursing staff I work with think I'm cranky, even demanding."

"You? *No.*" She looked aghast, but the humor in her eyes undermined it. She offered her hand, and he took it, rising from the swing. They started a slow stroll toward the sidewalk that circled the perimeter of the park.

"I get that you always wanted to have an Army career,"

he said after a while. There was defeat in his voice. "But didn't you ever consider that something else might come along? Something maybe worth giving it up for?"

She shook her head. "Do you know how many married military members there are? I just assumed I would be one of them. Be a soldier during the day and go home and be wife and mom the rest of the time. I figured whoever I married wouldn't have a problem with the soldier part because, hey, I would already be a soldier when we met."

"I can't be the only person in the world who doesn't want that life."

"No, of course not. I've seen a lot of divorces. A lot of spouses who got tired of the hours, the deployments, the separations, the pay, the stress. But I assumed that wouldn't be *my* spouse because I am Super Soldier."

"I'm not Super Spouse." The admission pained him, like a giant hand grabbing hold of his insides and squeezing hard. He had always believed with everything in him that his father's heartbreak over the divorce had contributed to his death. He was more sure of it now than ever.

But he wasn't his dad. He wouldn't shut down over this. He might not be Army husband quality, but he was strong. He would miss Avi like hell for a while, and then he would move on. Eventually. Somehow.

"I'm sorry, Avi."

Her only response for a long time was a squeeze of his fingers. It wasn't until they'd reached the sidewalk and turned toward Main Street that she spoke. "It's all right. Neither of us is any good at compromise. That's good to know before Ben and Avi Junior come along."

Ben rubbed the knot in his gut and bleakly said, "I could have lived my whole life without knowing."

"Me, too." Then she laughed and flashed him a wicked look. "I'll ask Lucy to set you up. She's got lots of single friends."

There wasn't a single tiny place inside him that felt like teasing. He dug deep, though, for a voice that didn't sound miserable, for words that didn't plead. "You do that, I'm putting a profile for you on every online dating site I can find."

"I'll hook you up with Iron Curtain brides wanting to come to the U.S."

"I'll post your picture and write your phone number on every men's room wall in Georgia."

"I'll start a Facebook page: Find Ben Noble a Wife."

"I'll take semi-naked pictures of you, add your phone number and e-mail address, and put them on Instagram."

She stuck her tongue out at him, then said airily, "There can't be any naked pictures if I don't let you see me naked again."

"You mean, no sex this week?" He didn't need to feign the dismay in his voice. The thought was enough to scare him. Like saying good-bye to her did. Facing a future without her. Wondering how much he would lose—they would both lose—for their stubbornness.

"Only under cover of darkness. I'll dress and undress in the bathroom behind locked doors, then disrobe under the covers."

"You don't have a robe," he pointed out.

"I'll buy one."

They stopped at the next intersection to allow a car to pass. In the light from the streetlamp, she looked so damn beautiful and sweet and just the littlest bit sad. For a moment, just a moment, he wished he'd never met her, but immediately he recanted. Friday night he'd asked her, *Would you be willing to give up all the affection, all the memories, in exchange for getting rid of the pain?*

He wouldn't. Loving Avi was special. Losing her would break his heart, but the time with her was worth that. The heartbreak would eventually fade, scarred over, like his mother had said, but the memories would remain forever.

The best memories he'd ever had.

* * *

"What are you doing up so early?"

Avi lifted her cup from the coffeemaker, breathing deeply of the rich, bold aroma. She needed coffee every morning, but she absolutely could not start a Monday without it, the stronger, the better. Something had to jolt her heart and brain awake. "I thought I'd go to work with you today," she said as she turned to face her mother.

Beth blinked. "Did your father coerce you into doing this?"

"No, I haven't seen Dad yet this morning. I have experience, you know. GrandMir and Popi took me to the nursery all the time."

"I'm not worried about your experience." Beth swatted her as she passed to make her own coffee. "I'm worried about your muscles. Your dad's starting a new project today, and if you're there, he'll surely rope you into helping him."

"What kind of project?" Normally Avi didn't use cream in her coffee, but her mother bought a bottled kind that was hazelnut flavored and incredibly rich. She used it with a heavy hand, then left the bottle for Beth. After her first sip, she closed her eyes and sighed happily.

"A fountain with a multi-level retaining wall creating terraces around it."

"Sounds lovely."

"Tell me that again after you spend your day lifting rocks and hauling dirt."

"I don't mind."

Beth smiled at her. "Better you than me. I helped him build the first fountain. After that, I just flat refused. Since I passed the big five-oh, the only heavy lifting or bending I have to do is what I want." She took two bagels from a plastic bag, sliced them, and popped them into the toaster, then got a tub of cream cheese out. "Do you still like the chive flavor?"

"I do." Avi leaned against the counter, warming her hands on the coffee mug, taking an occasional heavenly sip. Since it was a Monday, and she hadn't slept well the night before, it seemed a good time to ask a cheerless question. "Mom? Are you happy here?"

Beth leaned against another section of counter. "In Tallgrass? I love it. It's home."

"You don't miss the house or your job or your friends in Tulsa?"

"The house and the job, no. Though I do wish I had a few more memories of you here. As far as my friends, I still see the ones I was really close to. They come here, I go there, or we meet in between. The ones who aren't willing to make that effort...they're missing out. And your father..."

The toaster popped up, and she fished out the bagels with her fingers, dropping them on saucers. Avi set down her coffee, smeared way too much cream cheese onto hers, then went to sit at the kitchen table.

Beth joined her a moment later. "Your dad is happier here than he ever was in Tulsa. He loves the nursery, the house, the town, the people. His job is more fun than work. He's outside all the time, digging and building and plotting. The only thing that could make him happier is to have his little girl living here." She hesitated, then added in an emotional voice, "That goes double for me. And in eight years, we plan to give you the retirement party and welcome-to-Tallgrass party to beat all parties."

Breaking her life down into eight-year segments, the wait really wasn't so long.

At the moment, it seemed like forever.

They ate their bagels and finished their coffee, then headed to Avi's car together. It was a beautiful morning, so she put the top down. Even if it was freezing, she admitted, she would have put the top down and blasted the heater on high. It was just so fun, the wind blowing through her hair, the sun beaming on her skin. It made her feel ten years younger. Freer.

At the nursery, her dad had already started work on the fountain. It was located at the entrance, visible from the street, a temptation to customers going inside, a place for disinterested spouses to rest and wait. Beth gave the pallets of stone and bags of mortar mix a shuddering look, then disappeared into the cool, sweet-scented shadows inside.

Avi saluted sharply. "Sergeant First Class Avery Grant reporting for duty, sir."

Her dad returned the salute just as sharply. "I'm glad to have the help, sweetheart."

The first step was digging the foundation for the half-circle retaining wall. Avi picked up a shovel, jabbed the point into the dirt, and pushed hard with all her weight to sink the tool. Up came a spadeful of dirt, which she tossed into a wheelbarrow.

She'd missed hard work. Her leave had become a vacation from everything—not just her job, but also her diet and physical activity. She felt this work in her shoulders, her spine, and her legs, a challenge to her fitness that felt good.

By the end of the day, she'd lost the challenge. She was exhausted. Her hands under her work gloves were tender and red. The muscles along her shoulder blades burned, and she was soaked with sweat and dirt. It was only thanks to the ball cap and sunblock her mom had provided that she hadn't burned to a crisp.

"You're a trooper," her father said, his arm around her as he surveyed their accomplishments. The footing was in place, along with most of the wall: ten feet across and two and a half feet high at the front, four at the back. The fountain would be built of the same stone, copying the curve of the wall, and flowers would fill the two levels of the wall.

"I'm a pooped trooper." She carefully worked the band out of her hair, which was soaked to the scalp, then combed her fingers through it. "Do you work like this all the time?"

"Oh, no. No, no. Your mother's wanted this fountain for a year, and I just got around to it today because I knew I could have your help if I needed it."

"And you didn't even need to ask." She exhaled heavily. "I'm going to clean up, then head to Tulsa."

"Be careful." He pressed a kiss to her forehead. "And stay the night. I don't want you driving back when you're this tired."

"I'll sleep on the couch," she said with a wicked grin, remembering his comment about his thirty-year-old virgin daughter. She waved good-bye to her mom, waiting on a customer, then walked to her car.

Sundance was at the door when she got home, dancing the dance of joy. She didn't get to spend days at the nursery yet, Beth had said, since the few times they'd tried taking her, she'd peed in the flower beds and slipped off to sit in the middle of Main Street. But Beth had hope. After all, she'd trained Avi up right, hadn't she?

Avi kicked off her shoes and socks so she wouldn't track dirt inside, then let the dog out the back door. Stepping into the laundry room, she stripped down to her underwear before guzzling a bottle of cold water while waiting for the dog to finish her business. As soon as the setter came back in, Avi headed upstairs to shower.

She looked like crap in the bathroom mirror, but she'd looked worse. Iraq and Afghanistan had some hellacious sandstorms, called *haboobs*, and she'd been caught in her share, hunkered down, every exposed part of her turning brown or red. She had coughed and sneezed dust for the next six months.

After toweling off, she dressed again in a black jersey dress and piled her hair on top of her head. She put on makeup, sprayed cologne, and fastened a silver chain around her neck, then with a yawn and a shrug of her stiffened shoulders, she lay back on the bed just for a moment to let her spine relax. Maybe Ben could do some OMM on her as soon as he got home.

When she opened her eyes again, the first thing she noticed was that the sun was low on the horizon, its rays reaching only the bottom slats of the window blinds. Blinking, she checked the bedside clock, saw that it was nearly eight o'clock, and jumped up with a gasp. She grabbed her phone and called Ben's number, wondering if her dress was too wrinkled, if she'd rubbed off her makeup, if her hair was sticking out at strange angles.

"Hey, gorgeous."

His voice made her close her eyes and draw a deep, relaxing breath. "Hey, Doc. I'm so sorry—"

"Don't worry. Your mom called and said your dad worked you like a red-headed stepson."

"That's one way of putting it."

"We decided it would be wiser to postpone tonight. She said she'll throw you out after lunch tomorrow. She also said that if you wore something really tight and short and snug to this place called TwoSteps, you could pick up an entire work crew for nothing more than the cost of a few beers."

"What?! My own mom is suggesting I pimp myself out at the sleaziest soldier bar in town?"

Ben chuckled. "I think she said it's not pimping if you don't flash anything or let them touch."

Avi opened the blinds and stretched out on the thick pad of the window seat. "My mom's gotten a little strange since I moved out."

"Maybe it comes from living so close to my mother."

"Wouldn't you hate to send them off on a road trip together? First, neither of them can read a map. Second, my mom knows how to operate a gas pump. She just refuses. She says for the prices they charge today, she should get full service. She's lucky she hasn't been stranded in the middle of nowhere. Funny thing, though, she always finds someone who will pump the gas for her."

"They both get distracted by good-looking young men," Ben added. "I don't know about yours, but mine tries to mother everyone she meets."

"Mine flirts with them. The only reason she hasn't tried it with you is because Patricia told her you were hands-off."

"Patricia went to buy ice on the Fourth of July and brought home three soldiers who didn't have any plans. They stayed for dinner, watched the fireworks, and had a great time."

Avi thought of several holidays where she'd been the one alone with nothing to do and someone had invited her to join their family or friends. It had been a life-saver. Patricia had spent so many holidays away from her family that, of course, she couldn't bear it for some-one else. "Aw, that's sweet."

"Hmm." Ben's voice vibrated over the phone. "She showed them where she lived. She gave them a tour of the house. She introduced them to all the margarita girls and pointed out Lucy's house across the yard."

Avi hoped this story didn't have a bad ending, like they came back and stole everything they could carry. "So what did they do?"

"They cleaned up the mess when the evening was over, and the next day they sent her flowers. A week later, they all chipped in and took her to dinner at Luca's." There was a tone in his voice, as if he hadn't expected that out-come.

"She obviously read them right. They were good kids,

probably missing their families, who were thrilled that
someone took the time to be so nice to them." She
stretched out her feet, and the muscles in the back of her
calves and thighs throbbed. "You've never lived out of
state, Doc. It can get awfully lonely to have no place to go
and no one special to be with. I think the military commu-
nity is more open to remedying that, maybe, than civilians
are because we've all found ourselves in that situation before."

"That's one of the benefits of not moving around. You
have a place to go and people to be with."

Snorting, she slid lower until she was lying on the window seat, her knees bent. The firm cushion felt very good
against her achy spine, but the inverted vee of her legs
wasn't doing anything to help her knees. She braced her
bare feet on the wall and vowed to not give up her work-
out again just because she was on leave. "Lots of people
never move and still have no one to do holidays with."

"That's because they're not blessed with a family like
mine."

Her smile was bittersweet. If it wasn't for his family,
she was pretty sure he could be persuaded to give Georgia
a chance. His practice was important, but his sisters and
the kids were the real reason he was so tied to Tulsa, and
it wasn't even that they truly *needed* him. They'd been
abandoned by their mother in divorce, by their father in
death, and Ben, who had been hurt the deepest, couldn't
bear to do anything remotely similar.

Of course, Avi would never wish his family away. His
devotion to them was one of the things she loved about
him. He would be even more devoted to his wife and children, and that was a special quality in a man.

"What kind of project are you helping your dad with?"

She was grateful he'd changed the subject, because all that hard work with the usual Oklahoma fall spores, molds, and pollens in the air had made her eyes watery. She described the fountain and the retaining wall/bench/flower beds. "I lifted seventeen thousand pounds of rock today."

"Uh-huh," he teased.

"I mixed twenty-nine bags of mortar. 'To the consistency of brownie batter,' Dad tells me. Do I look like a girl who makes brownie batter?"

"Huh-uh."

"Then I hauled off *three* tons of dirt one wheelbarrow at a time."

"Poor baby. I bet tomorrow you'll be wanting to see what kind of magic I can work."

Everything inside her went kind of warm and fuzzy and quivery. "I've already seen your magic, Doc. You are the magic man."

He didn't laugh, as she'd thought he might, but got very quiet and serious. "Only with you, gorgeous. Enjoy your evening with your parents, because tomorrow night's mine, okay?"

"Okay." She hesitated a moment, then blurted out, "I love you, Ben."

"I know," he said smugly. Her *grrr* made him laugh, then he went soft again. "I love you, too, gorgeous. Good night."

Chapter 13

Calvin had left his cell phone behind when he'd gone out to pick up dinner, and it was ringing when he walked back into his apartment. He dropped the thin bag on the coffee table, got a bottle of water from the kitchen, sat down on the couch, and silenced the phone without looking at it. It would ring again and again until he finally answered, and he didn't see that happening anytime soon. *Sorry, Mom, it's just not your month.*

After turning on the television, he unwrapped the sandwich he'd brought home and stared at it. Between the time he'd ordered it and the time the teenager behind the counter handed it over, his turkey and provolone with mayo on white had morphed into a ham and cheddar with mustard on wheat.

What was so damn difficult about it? Tens of thousands of people walked into delis every day, this meat on that bread with those vegetables and these dressings. Making them was a small matter of following directions.

All the kid had to do was *listen* to Calvin—just listen, that was it—and then do what he was told. A monkey could have done it. Hell, the idiot kid could have done it if he'd taken the damn earbuds out and paid attention.

Anger built inside Calvin, not the good righteous kind but the ugly, irrational sort. The kid had screwed up his order. It wasn't a big deal, but it felt like one. It felt like just one more thing in a hundred-mile string of bad things that plagued Calvin wherever he went, whatever he did. It seemed like people were just damn determined to mess with him—at work, on the street, in the damn freaking deli. Hell, even people on the phone, he added as the cell started ringing again. Grabbing it from the coffee table, he threw it the way he would have thrown a baseball, with a good wind-up, flinging it hard with a little extra oomph.

It slammed into the wall next to the door, and the next ring was a cartoonish little warble before it hit the floor and went silent. The slamming continued, though, raising the hair on Calvin's neck, until he realized someone had chosen that moment to knock at his door.

His normal response was to sit quiet, and they would go away. When he'd just destroyed a smartphone two inches from the door, anyone who continued knocking was either brave or foolish. Slowing his breathing, he took a few steps toward the door. It was probably the manager of the crappy apartments, or maybe the next-door neighbor. It couldn't be a friend. He didn't have any. Didn't want any. Would never have any again.

The knocking came again, then a voice. "Calvin? Calvin Sweet?"

The voice sounded authoritative. Maybe a police officer. Had he given anyone cause to call the cops on him?

He couldn't honestly say no. Some mornings he couldn't always remember everything that had gone on the night before. Sweat began to gather between his shoulders, rolling down his spine. He didn't want any run-ins with cops, especially white ones. It could be bad for his career, to say nothing of his life.

Two more steps brought him to the table beside the door. He didn't notice the phone, and it skittered off the toe of his shoe to hit the wall again. Stealthily, he drew open the drawer, removed the Springfield XDM, and held the .45-caliber weapon in his right hand, along his side, tilted slightly back for maximum concealment.

As another round of knocks started, he eased up to the peephole in the door. It wasn't the manager or a neighbor or a police officer standing in the light of the bare bulb overhead in the corridor. It was worse.

It was the damned chaplain.

"Calvin, it's Chaplain Reed. I know you're here," said a heavily Southern accented voice. "I saw you come in a few minutes ago. I know there's no rear exit. I saw the shadows when you checked the peephole. Can I come in and talk with you?"

If the chaplain left, it wouldn't mean Calvin's problem was solved. It just meant it would become official tomorrow. Maybe, if he cooperated right now, he could shut this down before it went anywhere.

Silently, he returned the weapon to the drawer, then opened the door. The chaplain was leaning one shoulder against the door frame, looking comfortable, like he wasn't leaving until he got what he wanted. Calvin made a gesture, then turned and went back to the sofa.

Reed came in, giving the place a quick look. It wasn't

the sort of place Elizabeth ever would have imagined her boy living in. *I've seen pigpens cleaner that this,* he could hear her saying. *What's wrong with you, son?*

Everything. Everything in his whole damn life was wrong.

The chaplain ignored the empty end of the sofa and dragged a wood chair from the dining table over to sit on. Once seated, he studied Calvin. "I got a call today. Miss Elizabeth is worried. Not answering her letters, not even picking up her calls anymore..."

"How'd she find you?"

"I'm in the phone book." He shrugged, both hands turned palm up. "Mamas have resources, Captain. They are fearsome creatures."

Fearsome. Calvin couldn't think of a better description of his mother. She was fierce and stern and demanding—even his father knew better than to cross her—but she'd shown him enough love for ten kids. She deserved better treatment than he'd given her. He just didn't know anymore how to give it to her.

He didn't know how to make himself care enough to try.

"She's worried about you, Calvin."

"She's got nothing to worry about, Chaplain."

Reed made a point of looking around the apartment, then at the broken phone. "Are you sure about that? Calvin, our troops lived better than this in the early days in Iraq. I bet none of your neighbors heard that phone break because if they've got jobs, they're the kind that keep 'em out on the streets at night. I saw your vehicle out there. All of its windows are cracked, and two of 'em are completely gone. Just living here is something to worry about. Miss Elizabeth would 'bout have a heart attack if she knew."

Of course he was right. Calvin's mother's family had never had much; neither had his dad's. But they'd been proud of what they'd had, and they took care of it. They might have been poor, but their kids, their houses, and their vehicles had been spotless and in good working order.

Seeing Calvin living like this would rouse a lot of emotions in his parents: concern, fear, and—if he had no good reason to explain it—anger and shame. *We raised you better than that,* his father had told him the one and only time he got into trouble at school. It was true; they had. But this stuff going on now...

"Is money an issue?"

Calvin shook his head. He'd built a nice savings account while he was deployed and still added to it the first and fifteenth of every month. Little of his income went for living expenses.

"No gambling? Drinking? Drugs?"

Another shake of his head. Part of him wanted to demand *Who the hell are you to be so damn nosy?* His job performance hadn't suffered. He wasn't missing work or getting arrested or out raising hell in the strip clubs. What business was it of Chaplain Reed's what he did on his time off?

But this was the Army, and everything he did was pretty much their business.

"No," he said flatly. "None of that."

Reed glanced around again. There wasn't much to see. No furniture that belonged to Calvin, no pictures on the walls, no souvenirs from his previous tours, no knickknacks, nothing personal. Just walls that might have been white twenty years ago, furniture that should have been lit on fire ten years ago, and emptiness.

"How long have you been here?"

"At JBLM? Fourteen months."

"You must have some buddies here."

Calvin shook his head. "I don't have time for that."

"What keeps you so busy?"

He didn't answer.

Reed leaned forward, his elbows on his knees. "I've been over your record, Calvin. You've been a rising star since basic. Every single evaluation report has been stellar. Despite your four rotations to the Middle East, you earned your college degree with a 3.98 grade point average. You've been an outstanding soldier, personable and well liked by everyone you worked for and everyone who worked for you. So what is this?" He indicated the apartment with another sweeping gaze.

Calvin's fingers tightened at his side. "Would it make you happier if I found a nicer place to live, Chaplain?"

"No. It would make me happy if you'd seek help for what's bothering you."

Seek help. No. No, no, and hell, no. *Seek help* meant see a doctor who would give him a referral to psychiatry. Psychiatry meant a diagnosis of posttraumatic stress disorder. Calvin was no fool. He knew that was the label they would hang on him, and that would likely mean the end of his career. It wasn't much at this point, but it was all he had, and if he lost it . . .

He stood, forcing a smile so foreign that it actually hurt. "I appreciate the visit, Chaplain, but I'm fine. I'll find a better place to live. Hell, I'll even go out to the club

for a drink. And I'll call my mama. I'm sorry she bothered you for nothing." He said the last with an inward
cringe. If Elizabeth ever suspected he'd apologized for
something she'd done, she'd stand him at attention and
chew his ass like a private.

Reed wasn't convinced by Calvin's change in attitude,
but he let him usher him to the door. There, he stopped
and fixed his gaze on him. "My office is right down the
hall from yours. Any time you want to stop by, the door's
open."

Calvin kept the smile on his face through sheer will
until the door was closed and he was leaning against
it. Heaving a sigh, he picked up his cell—busted—and
swore. Now he'd have to talk to his mother *and* find a pay
phone to do it.

Chaplain was right, he thought as he dug his keys from
his pocket. Mothers were fearsome creatures.

* * *

"Time for you to knock off, sweetheart," Beth said shortly
after noon.

"But I've still got a lot to do," Avi's father protested,
and she poked him with her elbow.

"Not you. Avi. You keep working until this project is
finished. Avi, you come with me."

Obediently Avi straightened, stripped off her gloves,
and stretched the kinks from her back. "See you later,
Dad." As she walked with her mother toward the car, she
added in a low voice, "Thanks for rescuing me. I don't
know how he works like that."

"You and me both. Keeps him in fine shape, though,

doesn't it?" Beth cast him a lascivious look over her shoulder.

Avi laughed. She didn't want to watch her parents ogle each other like teenagers, but better that than to have them hardly notice each other's existence. "Where are we going?"

"To get Sundance a sister."

After starting the engine, Avi faced her wide-eyed. "I could never have one dog, but now you're gonna have *two*?"

"Your father and I are gone all day. Sundance gets lonely."

"Yeah, I bet she gets real lonely curled up on the couch with the ceiling fan blowing on her."

"Sundance doesn't get on the furniture."

"Uh-huh," Avi said in the same skeptical tone Ben had used upon hearing of the rigors of her work the day before. Maybe it hadn't occurred to Beth: She could post her no-no notes all over the house, but unless Sundance learned to read, the pup was doing what she wanted. "Where are we getting this sister?"

"From the animal shelter. I splurged on Sundance because your father had always wanted a purebred setter, but I don't approve of buying dogs from breeders when there are so many in need of homes."

That was something new. Avi totally agreed with her, but she hadn't supposed her mother had even thought about dogs in the fifteen years before acquiring the setter.

Beth gave her directions to the shelter, located on the north edge of town. Given its purpose as a home for unwanted pets, it was a cheerful enough place. Dogs barked and played and snoozed in the outside enclosures, while cats appeared to rule the indoor office.

They were greeted by two gorgeous blondes who introduced themselves as Angela and Meredith, owners of the shelter. Angela handled the day-to-day running, and Meredith provided veterinary services in her free hours from the clinic where she worked. They talked with Beth a bit about what she wanted, then headed through a door into a large room with kennels lined in neat rows. The ones against the outside walls opened into runs. The ones without openings were home to the newer, needier dogs who were still adjusting to the change in their circumstances. They hadn't been cleared to mingle with the others, or they had behavioral issues.

Of course, the first one to tug on Avi's heart was included in that bunch. It was just some indefinable sadness in the black Lab's eyes that brought her to her knees a safe distance from the kennel's wire. "Look at this face, Mom."

Her mother looked, made an *aw* expression, then wrinkled her nose. "I really want another puppy, Av."

"Doesn't everybody? But just look at everything"— she tilted her head back to read the sign at the top of the kennel—"Sadie can teach Sundance. And look at her little white chin hairs. They're just like yours."

"Avery!" Beth exclaimed, instantly raising one hand to cover her chin as Angela and Meredith stifled their laughs. "I swear, you raise a perfectly nice child, send her out into the world, and she comes back talking about your chin hairs *in public*."

Footsteps sounded from the direction of the door going out into the runs. "I heard 'Avery' followed by a shriek and figured it had to be you." Jessy Lawrence came around a stack of cages, wearing shorts and a tank top and smelling rather like the dogs. Sweat stuck her red hair to her forehead, and water and suds spotted her clothes.

"You work here?" Avi grinned. "Lucky you."

"I am the luckiest woman in the world," Jessy agreed. She knelt beside Avi while the other three moved on to look at puppies. "You trying to persuade your mom to adopt Sadie?"

"She didn't even want to look at her."

Jessy opened the gate, hooked a lead onto the dog's collar, and drew her out to a corner of the room empty but for an old sofa and a few chairs. "A lot of people don't want to adopt an older dog. Best guess, Sadie's maybe nine, ten. People look at her and see that the best of her life is behind her. They think all that's left is for her to get sick, maybe run up a lot of bills, and die. But they're wrong."

Avi sat on the sofa. Sadie studied her a long time, standing unnaturally still, before taking a step toward her.

"She's a little timid. I think maybe she's like a lot of us. She lost the only family she knew, and now she's afraid to get close to someone new for fear they'll leave her, too." Jessy shrugged. "It can be hard trusting again. At least, it was for me."

Avi continued to watch the dog while considering what she knew about Jessy. Her husband had died a few years ago, and she'd had a tougher time than anyone realized. But just this year, she'd met and fallen in love with Dalton Smith, and she seemed not just happy but peaceful. "It was worth the effort, wasn't it?"

Jessy flashed a high-wattage smile. "Absolutely."

Sadie came still closer, until her head was bumped against Avi's leg. After sniffing her carefully all over,

Sadie lifted one foot onto the couch, then another, then levered herself up to sit next to Avi. She was warm and sweet and didn't overwhelm by springboarding off a chair, the way Sundance would have done. Avi stroked her ribs, and Sadie's legs slowly slid out from beneath her until her head rested on Avi's lap and the scratching was on her belly.

"So Sadie could have another two or three or five years in her," Avi said.

Jessy nodded. "None of us have expiration dates tattooed on. Just like you and me, she'll live the time left her, and she'll go when it's time."

"What happens if no one adopts her because she's too old?" The thought made Avi cringe inside, but it was something she needed to know.

"We're a no-kill shelter. We'll find her a foster family or keep her here. She'll be fed and petted and loved the rest of her life. It just won't be the same as having a home with a mama."

Avi gazed at the dog who trusted her enough to close her eyes with a heavy sigh. She understood Beth not wanting to fall in love with an older dog who was doomed to die in the next few years. By choosing a puppy, she was increasing her odds of more fun and a lot longer time before the inevitable heartache.

But Avi knew a lot about heartache. She knew she could survive it, for starters. Sadie could help her survive. Giving the dog a safe, happy, healthy place to spend the rest of her years would do some incredible healing for both of them.

She raised her gaze to Jessy's. "I'm moving to Georgia on Saturday, and in exchange for a hefty deposit, I can have a pet. Can I adopt her?"

Jessy studied her a long time. "I hope so. I'll put in my two cents' worth on your behalf."

And that was how, on her way to Tulsa later that afternoon, Avi stopped at the shelter to pick up a beautiful, bathed, groomed, and newly microchipped tennish-year-old best friend who loved riding shotgun in a classic red '65 Mustang convertible roaring down the road.

Oh, and Sundance got a sister, too, a cute, cuddly mixed beagle whose ears were longer than her legs, whom Beth was determined would answer to the name of Nyla. Sundance was adorable. Nyla was cute.

But Sadie ruled.

* * *

Ben let himself into the loft that evening, his mood lighter than it had been since Sunday. He'd missed sleeping with Avi Sunday night—not the sex, though that was damn good, but being able to reach out and touch her, hold her, feel her, and hear her heart beating. He'd missed it even more Monday night. Tonight, even if all they did was share space, it would be enough.

He closed the door behind him and kicked off his shoes nearby. Avi's purse was on the dining table, her flip-flops next to the sofa. She'd left a Sonic cup on the coffee table, and a dog—

He stopped abruptly. There was a dog on his couch, watching him with sleepy eyes. He/she/it was significantly bigger than Sundance, and significantly blacker, and he—it looked a lot warier. "Avi?" he called.

"Yeah?" she replied from the bedroom. The dog jumped at the sound of her voice, ran down the hall, and skidded around the corner. By the time Ben made the same trip, with a little more grace, he hoped, the dog was standing behind Avi, face pressed between her knees to peer at him. "Doc, you scared my pupper. Sadie, it's okay, baby. This is Ben. He's my sweetie, and this is his house, so suck up to him, huh? Shake hands."

Faintly trembling, the dog slithered out from behind her and offered her right paw. Ben felt foolish, but if it pleased the girl in his life, he would please the girl in her life. "Hey, Sadie," he said softly, taking her paw gently. After a moment, he slid to the floor and ran his hand along her spine, from neck to tail, giving a gentle massage along the way. She sank onto her belly in front of him, rested her chin on his foot, and lay still so he could do it again.

"How old is she?"

Avi sat down, too, the bed at her back. "Nine or ten."

"Shouldn't she be at home with the family who's raised her this long?"

"If they were decent people. One of Dalton's neighbors saw someone dump her on a country road. She chased them until she couldn't run any more. When he went looking for her, he found her exhausted by the road, so he took her to Jessy, who took her to the shelter, where most people don't want older dogs."

Something warm and sweet twinged inside Ben. "Avi Grant, of course, isn't most people."

"I couldn't walk away from that face. She's scared, she's been abandoned, and she doesn't know why. I can make her feel safe and loved again. How incredible is that?"

While they'd been talking, Sadie had been moving,

just a few inches at a time, scooting closer to them. Finally she climbed onto his lap with her back end, settled her front legs and head on Avi's, and gave a soft, shuddering sigh.

"Welcome home, Sadie," he said quietly as he slid his free arm around Avi. "You'll be the best-loved dog in the entire state of Georgia."

Avi rested her head on his shoulder. "You'll still be the best-loved doc in the state of Oklahoma." She paused, then hesitantly asked, "Have you given any more thought to driving to Augusta with us? It's okay if you don't want to. I was just…wondering."

Unable to meet her gaze, Ben shook his head. "I'm used to being the one left behind. I don't think I can be the one doing the leaving."

She wrapped her fingers around his. "It's okay. Really." But her voice sounded kind of thick, and he was afraid if he looked, there might be a sheen to her eyes. "Sadie has just discovered the joy of riding in the front seat of a convertible. I'm not sure she'd be willing to give it up for the backseat so soon."

After a moment, she sniffed. "But we don't have to talk about that. Sadie and I have much more important things on our minds, namely what's for dinner? Her tummy's been rumbling ever since we left Tallgrass. I think she'd love a Fat Guy's burger if we could find someplace decent outside to sit and eat."

"They have tables outside, though I don't know if they allow dogs. If not, we can find a place in Reconciliation Park. Let me get changed." He started to push up, but Sadie pushed down. "Sadie, let me up, sweetie."

She pushed even harder.

Grinning, Avi took pity on him. "Sadie, wanna go for a walk?"

The old girl jumped pretty agilely and trotted down the hall, then circled back to wait on Avi. "We'll meet you at the door. Bring extra money. Sadie's got an appetite."

It took Ben just a couple of minutes to change. By the time he'd shoved his feet into sandals and stuck his debit card in his pocket, Avi was wearing her shoes and Sadie had on a lime-green leash to match her collar.

"She moves pretty well," he remarked as they started along the street toward Fat Guy's. "She doesn't seem to have any problem with stiffness."

"Meredith—she's the vet at the shelter—says she's healthy. Just sad. If no one had adopted her, they would have kept her and Jessy would have loved on her every day, but that's not the same as having a home where you're special." Avi gave him a sidelong look. "You should probably consider adopting a dog. They have a lot that need homes. Or maybe even a cat."

"I have to say, adopting a pet has never crossed my mind."

"Until now." She flashed him a grin. "It's in there now, and you'll find yourself considering it after I'm gone because you'll miss me."

He didn't admit that he was considering it now, and it had nothing to do with missing her. It was what she'd said earlier. *I can make her feel safe and loved again. How incredible is that?* To have that kind of impact on someone else's life... pretty damn incredible.

And, yeah, maybe it would help him not to miss Avi so much. At least he wouldn't be totally alone.

"Why would her people just dump her?"

"Jessy says some people can't afford their pets any more, or they don't want the hassle, or maybe it was the kids' dog and the kids have grown up and moved out, or a guy moves in with his girlfriend and when they break up, he leaves his dog there and she doesn't want it." Avi shrugged. "They should be shot. The least they could have done was leave her at the shelter. She could have been hit by a car, attacked by coyotes, bitten by a copperhead…" She muttered an obscenity Ben had never heard her use before.

"How is she going to fit into your life when you move?"

"Beautifully," she said with a matching smile. "She's old enough and calm enough that she'll be fine while I'm at work. I'll walk her before and after work, and I'll get her a crate to use if she wants it, but I'm not Mom. I like the idea of snuggling with her on the sofa or in bed."

"You sound well informed."

"I've been talking to Jessy, plus while they groomed her, I was online checking out pet websites. Sadie's my firstborn. I have to take good care of her and yet spoil her, too."

Ben slid his arm around her shoulders, pulled her close, and kissed her hard. When he released her, she said, "Wow. What was that for?"

"No matter what happens, Avi, I'll always be glad I met you."

For a moment, she looked as if she wanted to speak, to give voice to the heartache that briefly appeared in her eyes, but she smiled instead and rested her head on his shoulder as they continued to walk.

Then why can't we work this out? That might not have

been what was on her mind, but it was certainly on his. He loved her. She loved him. They had the great beginnings of a perfect family, with Sadie the firstborn. Why couldn't they resolve their issues, get married, give Sadie two-legged siblings, and live happily ever after?

Because some issues were unresolvable. Because they were selfish. Unreasonable. Or maybe it was just him. He'd wanted to fall in love, and *boom*, there was Avi. He could marry her, could live the rest of his life with her. He should be putting a For Sale sign on the loft, resigning from his practice, telling Sara and Brianne and the kids *I can love you and be a part of your lives in Georgia as well as here.*

He could, should... Couldn't? Or wouldn't?

So he was selfish, unreasonable, *and* a coward. Avi deserved better.

And she would probably find it in Georgia.

* * *

After dinner at the Three Amigos with the margarita girls, Lucy went to bed with a heavy heart and woke up Wednesday morning feeling as if she couldn't breathe. Her chest was achingly tight, her skin was prickling, and she had an overwhelming urge to cry. Rolling onto her side, she turned off the alarm clock, calculated the time in California—three forty-five—and pulled the covers tighter. Across the room, Norton's rubber ducky squeaked as he got up, stretched, then trotted down the hall.

She should get up, too, brush her teeth, and get dressed. Norton liked to eat before going for a walk, and he surely needed to pee. If she didn't want to clean up his favorite indoor spot—the middle of the kitchen floor—she really should get moving.

Instead she pulled the covers over her head, hiding in the gloom but finding no comfort.

"Happy birthday, Mike," she whispered. The words felt as empty as her bed, her life, her heart. Most days she did all right. She coped. She was even happy. But then a special occasion would come along, or maybe nothing special at all, and her heart broke all over again. This was the seventh birthday Mike had missed. Seven years that he could have been living and making babies and making life better for everyone around, including—especially—her. Seven birthdays that neither she nor his mom nor his grandmother had been able to hug him, kiss him, or watch his goofy faces as he blew out the candles with all the excitement of a kid.

Norton's whine at the back door was silenced by a couple of clicks: Joe had let himself in with his key. He'd held the door for Norton, and now, she knew from experience, he was filling the dog's water bowl and dishing out his chow. He would get the leash from the hook by the front door, set out a granola bar for Lucy, and let Norton back in. Then Lucy had five minutes to put in an appearance.

She should have begged off last night. He would have asked for an explanation, but she could have given him any of a hundred excuses. She could even have pled pure laziness. She'd done it before, and he'd let her. Once.

Quiet footsteps sounded in the hall an instant before Joe rapped on the open door. "Luce? You okay?"

"Hmm."

"You'd think, dealing with teenagers every day, I'd have interpreting grunts down to a science, but I'm not sure whether that one means 'Yeah, I'm fine,' or 'Go the hell away.'"

Despite the protection of the covers, she squeezed her eyes shut. She usually planned ahead for this day. The first three years, she'd taken vacation and gone home to mourn/celebrate with family. The next two years, she'd taken the day off work and stayed in bed. Last year she had treated it as an almost normal day: She'd gone to work; she'd spent hours on the phone with her mom and Mike's; and Marti had come over that evening after work with three half gallons of ice cream and two jars of caramel topping. They'd gorged themselves, watched TV, talked, and cried.

She'd thought that had been a turning point.

She had been wrong.

Norton's ducky squeaked again, courtesy of Joe's size fourteen shoes, then landed with a thud on his bed. A moment later, the empty side of Lucy's bed sagged beneath Joe's weight. "Come on out of there, Luce." He caught a fistful of fabric and began pulling it away, slowly exposing her.

"That grunt meant 'I'm hiding in my bed under my covers and I'm not coming out until tomorrow,'" she muttered, shoving her hair back from her face.

"Okay. You're entitled." Joe folded the extra pillow in half and leaned back. "Did you tell your boss yesterday?"

Her lower lip poked out. "No. I thought…"

"I'll call. What should I say?"

She stared at the ceiling. "I don't care."

"Okay. I'll tell him that you undercooked the chicken

last night and ate it anyway, and now you have a stomach-ache and the runs."

"I would never undercook chicken!" At least, not since she was thirteen and learning to cook from her mom and Nana.

"How about you closed down Bubba's last night and sprained your ankle dancing on the bar?"

She scowled at him.

"Or you woke up with a gorgeous guy in your bed this morning and you're trying to remember how he got there?" Grinning, he waggled his brows.

"I know how he got there. I made the mistake of giving him a key."

The grin widened. "Oh, so you think I'm gorgeous."

She didn't mind stroking his ego this morning. "Every woman in town thinks you're gorgeous. Why are you in my bed?"

His expression turned somber, his blue eyes darkening with sympathy. "Because today is Mike's birthday, and you're missing him more than usual."

Huh. More often than not, Lucy thought of Joe as an overgrown kid, with all the maturity one would expect of that, but he'd remembered Mike's birthday. Even her besties didn't do that. She was surprised and touched and once again close to tears. Groping blindly, she grabbed a tissue from the box on the nightstand. "How do you know that?"

"You told me."

"When? I don't remember doing that."

"I'd just moved in a month or so before, and you went home to spend his birthday with your families."

"And you just remembered it all these years?" Six

years, he'd remembered. She was even more touched now.

"I'm not just a gorgeous face, you know."

"I know," she muttered. She punched her pillow in half, then lay on it, mimicking his position, and stared at the ceiling. "Life is so damn unfair."

"It is," he agreed. "You work hard, do your best, and sometimes you still lose. But it's always been that way, and it always will, so you still work hard, you still do your best—"

"And you still lose."

"Yeah. But sometimes you win, too. And you have the satisfaction of knowing that you didn't give up. You always, always tried."

She gave him a sidelong look. "You sound like some kind of damn coach."

His only response was a faint smile.

"I'm tired of trying, Joe. I'm tired of living alone and sleeping alone and being alone and missing Mike and not knowing if it's ever going to get better, if anything's ever going to change. I'm a widow. My friends are all widows. I'm surrounded by broken hearts, and damn it, sometimes it's just too much pain and sorrow and sadness and despair." Her eyes teared up again. "I want a do-over!"

He was silent a long time. "We don't get do-overs in real life, Luce. But we do get second chances."

He slid his hand across the covers and clasped hers, and a tingle started in her palm and danced along her nerves into her arm. It was so unexpected that she almost jerked her hand away. She almost jumped from the bed, wrapped the sheets around her—though he'd seen her in her jammies plenty of times—and made a dash to lock herself in the bathroom until he left the room, the house, preferably the whole town.

But something stopped her. The tingle. The surprise. The warmth that traveled from him into her. And a little voice deep in her brain, saying *Stay. Don't run. This is good, Lucy, and it's okay.*

It was a voice she hadn't heard in an eternity, a voice she would never forget. It was Mike's voice. And so, surprised, comforted, and curious, she stayed.

Chapter 14

Avi woke with a bad case of bed head, a furry body snuggled against her, and a case of morning breath bad enough to make her wince. The morning breath wasn't hers, she was happy to realize as Sadie yawned and sent a blast of it into her face.

Ben was rustling on the other side of the bed, smelling of shower gel and expensive cologne, pulling on clothes, and Sadie snored quietly.

"You really should shave before you go to bed, Doc," she murmured, eyes still closed, as she stroked the dog.

"You're not fooling me. I know you know that's your new roommate and not me." He leaned over to nuzzle her neck, and she bent her head to make it easier. His warm kisses made all her girl parts happy and greedy for more, but she wasn't so lucky.

When he pulled away, she rolled onto her side to face him. He was wearing faded green scrubs, his usual uniform along with a lab coat, both in the clinic and the hospital. They were a good look on him. But wasn't everything?

"You going to have a busy day?"

"They all are," he replied as he laced his running shoes. They looked like a totally different creature from her runners. Of course, she actually *ran* in hers. "Are you working at the nursery again?"

She groaned at the thought, and only part of the groan was melodrama. She might carry a fifty-pound ruck on her back at work sometimes, but the rest of her work activity hadn't prepared her for all the bending and lifting of building a fountain. She was still achy. "Unless I get a better offer," she said, giving him a hopeful look.

His answering look was sympathetic. "Sorry. My only offer would be hanging out in my office so I could sneak in to see you between patients. In fact, I've got to get moving, or I'll be late."

She sat up as he circled the bed to her side and let the sheet fall away to her waist. His gaze swept over her breasts, and his expression turned rueful. "See you this evening?"

"There's not a place you could hide where I couldn't find you." She wrapped her arms around his neck as he kissed her, sweet and tempting and possessive. Reluctantly, she let him go, pulled the sheet up, and settled back in bed to watch him leave.

Once the door closed behind him, she started petting Sadie again. "Well, baby girl, do you think we should head back to Tallgrass now or sleep a little more?"

The dog thumped her tail without opening her eyes and went back to snoring.

Sleep it was. Except now that she'd been kissed, Avi

couldn't fall back to sleep. Instead, she found herself staring out the window and counting: today, tomorrow, Friday. On Saturday, she was loading up Sadie in the Mustang, heading south to I-40, then turning east toward Georgia.

The mere thought made her heart hurt. How was she going to endure this?

She would endure it because she wasn't just Army strong, she was *woman* strong. She was committed to doing what had to be done.

And what had to be done right now was getting up, showered, and dressed. Sadie would need a walk and food, and Avi's stomach was starting to rumble.

She was maneuvering around Sadie to get to her feet when the opening of the front door stopped her. Grabbing a sheet in case it was one of Ben's sisters, she leaned to see through the doorway and down the hall. "Hey," she said with relief when he came into view. "Forget something?"

"Nope, but I've got a better offer for you now. I was two blocks down the street when the office manager called and said the building's without power. Something about the main distribution line failing. PSO's working on it, but it involves digging up part of the street, so we're taking an unscheduled holiday."

The prospect of spending an entire day with him unexpectedly thrilled her more than it should. She knew why: She was storing up hours of memories to sustain her when she was gone. "Oh, goody. I'll tell Mom that she'll have to be Dad's helper today. But first I've got to get Sadie out."

Ben looked at the dog, who hadn't roused at his return,

and his lips twitched. "Yeah, she looks like she just can't wait another second."

Avi shook her finger at him. "We don't know exactly how good her house-training is, and these are *your* wood floors and rugs. Being a girl, I suspect she'd prefer a rug, since there'd be less splash-back."

"Good point. Get in the shower, gorgeous. I'll take Sadie for a walk."

At the sound of the magic word, Sadie's ears perked, then she stood and stretched. Hopping off the bed, she trotted down the hall and barked impatiently from the door.

"I'm being summoned," Ben said. "Make it quick, and I'll take you to breakfast when we get back."

Avi was good at quick showers. By the time Ben and Sadie returned, she was dressed, her damp hair pulled back and clipped off her neck. She'd called her mom and told her she would see her the next day and set out a bowl of food on the kitchen floor next to Sadie's water dish.

Avi watched the dog eat, inhaling the food but guarding it, her gaze constantly darting to make sure no one intended to steal it. She hadn't been on her own long enough to have to scrounge for food. Had she come from a home with multiple pets, where mealtime was a free-for-all, or had food been scarce there? *Never again*, Avi vowed.

"How do you feel about a fast-food breakfast where we can eat in the car?" Ben asked, coming to stand beside her. "That way Sadie can go, too."

She slid her arm around his waist and hugged him tight. "See? You're going to be a good dog daddy." But what she was really thinking was *See why I love you?*

When Sadie was ready, they loaded up in the Mustang—

Sadie didn't mind either the doggy seat belt Avi had picked up yesterday with the rest of the dog supplies or being in the backseat—and, with Ben behind the wheel, they headed out. After breakfast at Sonic, they went for a walk along the pedestrian bridge across the Arkansas River, an old railroad bridge that connected to running trails on both sides. They drove to Whiteside Park, the neighborhood where Ben had grown up. Another drive to the Pearl District, not far from his office, and she showed him the house she'd grown up in. Then they headed west past Sand Springs before turning north toward Prue and to the small country cemetery where his father was buried, and they talked about nothing important.

It was the best day of Avi's life. Part of her wished for pictures to commemorate every moment. The larger part of her knew she would never forget.

As they walked across the cemetery, Ben pointed out various graves: his grandparents, great-grandparents, aunts, uncles, cousins, important tribal members, and old family friends. They reached his father's grave, three rows from the back, a simple marker like all the others, the stone engraved with the usual information.

"What language is this?" she asked, gesturing to his father's headstone. Most of the words were in English, but others were unfamiliar.

"Osage."

"Do you speak it?"

"No. Dad knew some, and he wanted us to learn at least the basics, but..." He shrugged as he laid his hand gently on the stone. "It didn't seem very important when we were kids. We—I wasn't concerned with little things like culture and heritage."

His tone was apologetic, but she understood too well how it had been. Life seemed so very long and so very full of chances to a teenager. In a large, global sense, of course she'd understood that kids could die, but in the sense that mattered—her own intimate world—it had never happened. *She* couldn't die. Her friends couldn't. It had been a worst-case scenario sort of thing. She was young, and life went on forever.

And then she'd found herself living the worst-case scenario, up close and damned personal.

"It's not too late," she said. "To learn the culture and heritage and language. As long as you're breathing, it's never too late."

Ben's smile was wistful. "You sure about that?"

"Scout's honor," she replied, holding three fingers in the air.

"Aw, you were never a scout, were you?"

"Okay, soldier's honor." Lowering her hand, she looked around. The cemetery was at the end of a bumpy red-dirt road, set among oaks and red cedars, surrounded by a wire fence that sagged in places. There wasn't a sign to identify it. The people with loved ones buried there were probably the only ones who remembered its existence. Shade from the trees kept the grass and weeds to a minimum, and birds in the branches provided music, the only sound to break the stillness besides the occasional rustle of the wind and a bark or two from Sadie, waiting beside the car.

"It's a lovely place," she said softly.

"It was one of my dad's favorites." After a moment, he asked, "Is that weird?"

"I don't think so. It's beautiful, quiet, peaceful. But

then, I like cemeteries." She thought of the national cemeteries, which provided the final resting places for far too many of her friends, and rephrased, "Some of them." She had one more to visit before she left: the colonel's gravesite at Fort Murphy National Cemetery. Every few days she'd thought about it, and every few days she decided there was still time. No longer true.

The mood changed by the time they walked out of that small square plot of land, both his and hers. Life was such a wonderful thing to consider. Death, not so much. And sadness... Seeing his father's grave, knowing how the last of his years had gone, must have been hard on Ben. Thinking of George, whose life had become happiest when Rick Noble's had fallen apart, made Avi blue.

She wondered if he was thinking about his father, buried there alone, without his precious Patricia there to mourn. Was he imagining his own burial, years from now, possibly alone like his father?

That wasn't going to happen. He would fall in love and get married. It was as natural as the sun rising in the east. She would be happy for him when it happened. Really. She would smile through her tears.

He took her hand, holding it tightly on the way back to the car. After helping Sadie into her backseat harness, he waited while Avi settled, closed the door, and leaned forward, forearms resting on the window. "You ever been to Mexico?"

"No."

"You want to go now? With me? Forty-eight hours from now we could be on a beach and you could be wearing the ittiest, bittiest bikini ever made."

She laughed.

Ben didn't. "Margaritas under the tropical sun with me at your side don't tempt you?"

"Sweetie, in a little more than forty-eight hours, I'll be in my new home. If you want to run away, run to Georgia with me."

A frown flitted through his eyes. "I'm talking real world."

"Georgia's not real?"

"Not for me. It's just a fantasy." With a tight smile, he circled the car and got in.

He didn't say the words, but he might as well have, because they hung in the air between them, as heavy the red dust that trailed them back to the paved road. *Fantasies don't come true.*

* * *

It was a tough couple of days. By the time Ben reached Patricia's house late Friday afternoon, he was exhausted. Thank God, his personal life didn't interfere with work, or he would have had to cancel his surgeries for yesterday and his appointments today. Luckily, he could turn off everything when he walked into the OR or an exam room. But there was no turning it off now. Avi's going-away dinner was tonight—a farewell, Patricia called it—and tomorrow morning she and Sadie would drive off.

He wasn't sure he could stand it.

The dinner was being held at the Grant house and would be just her family, Ben, and his mother. Ben would have preferred a crowd: his sisters and family, the margarita sisters and their families, Cadore's football team, all the neighbors, and every soul who had ever bought even a single flower from the nursery. A ton of people wouldn't make it any easier for him, but it would have been easier to hide.

Patricia had sent him out to the patio while she finished up in the kitchen. She was making snacks for Avi's trip—three different kinds of cookies, caramel corn, and apple tartlets—to go with the pumpkin sourdough dog cookies Lucy had baked for Sadie. Now she joined him with two glasses of wine. When he shook his head, she insisted.

"I know you're the best orthopedic surgeon in Tulsa, Ben, but if someone needs you tonight, they'll just have to settle for the second best. Drink the wine. You look like you need it."

As she sat beside him, he took a drink, then another. It was sweet, acidic, tart, and warmed him a little from the inside out.

"You've been dreading this weekend practically since Avi came home," she remarked.

"Haven't you?"

She raised her free hand and waggled it. "In the beginning, when George had to go away, I started missing him as soon as I found out he was leaving. It didn't matter whether it was six days or six months, it was awful. Finally, I learned that it was better to appreciate him while he was there and make the most of it, then deal with his leaving after he was gone. I got good at it, too. I will miss Avi, but at least I know she's out of the war zone. She's back in the States; she'll be teaching instead of getting shot at. I can go visit her, and she can come visit here." She paused, then asked, "Are you going to go visit her?"

He shook his head.

She opened her mouth, closed it, then thought better of it. "Have you really considered what you're giving up, Ben?"

This sip of wine was really more of a gulp. She was right. He did need it. Especially if they were going to have a mother–son talk about losing Avi. "We've discussed it. She doesn't want to get out of the Army, and I don't want to give up everything and move. I don't want to be an Army spouse."

"I didn't, either," Patricia declared, surprising him. Her sly look showed that she was well aware of it. "But I wanted to be George's spouse. I would have followed him anywhere, Ben. I gave up my home and my kids and everything I knew to be with him. That's how much I loved him."

He shook his head again, stubbornly. "I'm not you. Giving up everything isn't an option."

"It's the only option right now. Sweetie—" She paused, her gaze going distant for a moment. Thinking that this was the first time she'd called him by anything but his name in twenty years? Remembering that she'd called him and the girls that all the time when they were little? Was that why he'd used it with his patients from the beginning—because it reminded him of a time when life was good and he'd felt reassured and secure?

"Sweetie," she began again. "Your career is just a job. Your home is just a building. Your sisters... well, they'll always be your sisters whether you're living here or in Timbuktu—which, by the way, George and I visited and thought was quite remarkable. They'll love you, call you, and visit you so much, you'll wish you were back here so they'd leave you alone." She raised one hand to ward off protests. "Just kidding. But Sara's kids already know how to Skype. They call me at least once a week."

The idea of his mother Skyping with her grandkids made him smile faintly. When he'd gotten his first computer all his own for his last birthday before she'd left, she'd declared, *I'm a dinosaur. Technology has left me behind, and I like it that way.* He stayed informed on technological advances in the surgical field, especially in the joint replacement surgeries he did, but personally he was as much a dinosaur as she'd claimed to be then.

"It's not the same," he said, and hated the way he sounded like a cranky child.

"No, it's not. All the video chats in the world can't compete with a single hug or a kiss. But when George was in Afghanistan, I got to sit right here on my patio and see him, hear his voice, and watch him laugh. With the kids, I can get comfy in bed in my pajamas and read them stories at bedtime. I get to see and hear them say 'Sweet dreams, Grandma. I love you.'" Her eyes had watered at the mention of George and stayed damp through the rest of her words. She wiped at them without embarrassment.

"You know what else isn't going to be the same, Ben? Sleeping in that big bed of yours without Avi. You'll always have the memories, and if that's all you *get* to have, like me, like Lucy and all the others, fine. Great. Memories are precious. But if that's all you settle for because you're too afraid or stubborn to have more, they're going to be precious little comfort."

Fingers clenching around the stem of the wineglass, he scowled at her. "Exactly when did I say 'Give me advice on how to live the rest of my life'?"

She laughed, not the least bit impressed by the scowl, and squeezed his hand. "It was part of the deal, sweetie. I birthed you, and that entitles me to interfering in your life."

He would have appreciated more interference when he was sixteen, eighteen, and twenty. Maybe that was why he really didn't mind now. She was saying mostly things he'd thought, things he already knew—and she was speaking from experience. She knew what he was going through in ways no one else did.

Including him.

In an effort to lighten the mood, he referred back to a statement she'd made at the beginning. "So you think I'm the best orthopedic surgeon only in Tulsa?"

She laughed again. "In all of Oklahoma. Heck, in the entire country, if not the world. If I broke any of my creaky bones, I'd want you to be the one to fix them."

"Thank you." They toasted with their half-empty glasses, then Ben gazed across the lawn. It was neatly kept, thanks to Cadore's mowing and Patricia's gardening. She and George must have had such plans when they bought this place. No more packing boxes, sorting through the stuff they'd collected over the years. No more changing addresses or house-hunting or temporary living. This was to have been their home for the rest of their lives. Not just a house. *Home.*

And all they'd gotten was a few months living in it together before he'd deployed. Before he'd died. *You'll always have the memories, and if that's all you get to have, like me, like Lucy and all the others, fine. Great. Memories are precious.* She definitely had those. Twenty years' worth.

She should have gotten at least another twenty years' worth.

"I wish I'd known him," he said absently.

"Who?" she asked just as absently.

He was surprised he'd spoken the words aloud, but they were true. "George. I wish I'd known him."

Tears welled in her eyes. "Oh, sweetie…" Sniffling, she set her glass aside. "There's never a tissue around when I need one," she said, pushing to her feet and turning toward the door. "I'll be right back."

Ben returned to gazing across the lawn, at least, until a soft voice spoke from behind him. "That's probably the nicest thing you could have said to her."

He turned to find Avi, pretty in a pink dress with white dots, standing a few yards from the driveway. Her hair shone in the sunlight that reached it, hanging sleek past her shoulders, held back from her face by a white band with pink dots. With matching dotted flip-flops, she looked about seventeen, beautiful and innocent and sexy.

"You know what the hardest part of my job as an orthopedic doc doing total knee replacements in Oklahoma is?"

Shaking her head solemnly, she came toward him.

"Convincing my patients to give up their flip-flops."

Reaching him, she gave his feet a pointed look.

"Yes, but my patients don't know I wear them myself outside of clinic."

She bent to kiss him, just a *hey, you* sort of kiss that was sweet enough to make him ache and sad enough to break his heart. Sitting in the chair to his right, she crossed her gorgeous legs, letting one shoe dangle, and helped herself to his wineglass, holding it up to eye level.

"How much did Patricia pour for you? Thirty ccs more than what's left?"

"She filled it practically to the rim."

Avi raised her brows so her eyes opened wide with wonder. "Oh, God, don't tell me I've driven you to drink."

"I'm not the only ortho doc in Tulsa. Hell, I'm not even the only hip, knee, and ankle guy in my own office."

"Uh-huh." She handed the glass back to him, not quite understanding his point.

"I'm not on call this weekend, and if whoever is on call needs help, he can get it from someone else. I don't have to be responsible and sober twenty-four hours a day three hundred and sixty-five days a year." He always had been. Always. Not once in the years since he'd graduated medical school had he ever had one single, entire drink. Whether he was home alone, on a date, or celebrating something special, he'd never indulged in an entire drink so he could be ready *if* he was needed.

How many times in all those nights had he been needed? Maybe ten: multi-car crashes, partial amputations, one skydiving jump gone terribly wrong, a few industrial accidents. And if he hadn't gone? He'd saved some legs, but his partners could have done the same. Would have.

Patricia returned from the house, carrying an empty glass and a full bottle. "Hey, Avi, honey, take a glass, please. Fill your own and top off Ben's. He's not driving anywhere tonight, but don't let him get so hammered that all he wants to do at bedtime is go to sleep."

Avi chuckled, and Ben frowned at both women. "I'm not drunk."

"No, but you don't hold your liquor the way Avi and

I do," Patricia said with a sweet smile. "We've had a lot more practice than you."

Avi filled her own glass and topped off Ben's as instructed, just not quite as full as before. When she was done and had handed the bottle back to Patricia, she met his gaze and winked. He claimed her free hand, twined his fingers with hers, and closed his eyes, concentrating on them. Her nails were shorter than usual; she'd broken a few working on the fountain. Her skin felt a little rougher than usual, despite the gloves she'd worn, and there was a bubble of a blister on her left index finger.

This night would be the last time he held her hand like this. He wasn't going to get maudlin over it; he'd promised himself on the drive over, but wine and sympathy made maudlin way too easy a destination.

"Are your parents about ready for us?" Patricia asked.

"Dad was in the shower when I left the house, and the chicken was resting. By the way, Mom sent a message that if you want to talk to Dad, you need to do it before the seven o'clock kick-off. The Tallgrass team is playing at Stillwater, and he'll be watching it on his computer, thanks to one of his friends who mounted a video camera on an assistant coach's ball cap."

Patricia stood, anxious to get going. "Let me get the dishes I'm taking, and we can walk over now."

Ben got his first clue when she pulled a garden cart from beneath a nearby tree. He gave Avi his glass as Patricia began pulling it up the steps, and helped carry it inside while Avi balanced the wine bottle and the glasses.

"These are treats for you, Avi," Patricia said as she lifted a sturdy box into the cart.

Ben picked up the top bag, filled with bone-shape

cookies. "Look, pupper cookies. You have to sit and speak before you get one."

"Those are for Sadie, from Lucy. They're all natural. Way better than that stuff you buy at the grocery store." Patricia added a bowl of corn salad, another holding chunks of peeled, sweet cantaloupe. The aroma filled the room even with the plastic wrap stretched over the top. A pie carrier holding one of her sky-high meringue pies got place of honor, with the nearly full bottle of wine nestled beside it.

The last thing to go in was a small quilted bag. "What's that?" Ben asked.

"It's personal."

"That looks like your yellow pajamas sticking out."

"It is. Underneath are my toothbrush, tooth paste, nighttime medication, house slippers, and a dress for tomorrow. Come on, the Sanderson train is moving out." Wrapping her fingers around the cart handle, she began wheeling it through the kitchen and down the hall.

"You having a slumber party tonight, Mom?" Ben asked as he and Avi followed.

Patricia turned, caught his face in her palms, and pressed a kiss to his cheek. "You called me Mom."

His face flushed, and not because of her hands pressed to it. "I guess I did."

After wiping any trace of lipstick from his cheek, she released him. "And for that, you and Avi get free run of this house tonight. Have all the fun you want, but let her get some sleep. She's got a long way to go tomorrow. Now, help me get this cart down the front steps. You don't want to be late for Beth's famous grilled chicken, take my word for it."

* * *

Dinner was lovely: barbecued chicken with crispy skin; potato salad; corn salad; the last cherry tomatoes from Beth's garden tossed on the grill until their skins split; juicy cantaloupe Avi thought worth licking her fingers; and lemon meringue pie. She'd eaten enough to pop, but if she did, at least she would break into a million pieces surrounded by the four people she loved most in the world.

Even if one of them was attached to the computer by the plug for the headphones Beth made him wear, his cheers or groans occasionally punctuating the quiet.

"You're not disappointed we chose to have a small party, are you?" Beth sat on the arm of Avi's Adirondack chair, the vintage teal color of the wood a perfect play for her pink and white dotted theme. She needed such chairs if they would fit on her new balcony: one for her and one for Sadie. Of course if anyone decided to visit for a few days, Sadie would be happy to lie on the floor instead. Probably.

"No, Mom, this is perfect." Perfect weather, food, location, and especially people.

"Did Patricia tell you she's spending the night over here?"

"Yep."

"Does it embarrass you that your mother and your boyfriend's mother are arranging privacy so you can have sex?"

"A few weeks ago, maybe. Tonight, not at all." Avi glanced at Ben, just come out of the house, carrying a tray with cups of coffee. Behind him, Patricia carried cream, sweetener, sugar, and spoons.

"You've never taken a trip like this before," Beth said. "Two days on the road, with only Sadie for company..."

Avi smiled. She was thirty years old. She'd been driving half her life. But Beth was right. She'd flown to Fort Benning, Georgia, for basic training. She'd flown to her first duty assignment. In fact, she hadn't bought a car until Fort Hood, Texas. The longest road trip she'd made was to Fort Carson, with two other transferring soldiers along for the ride.

"If you get tired, pull over," Beth said. "Never, ever pick up hitchhikers. Don't rely on sweets to keep you going; eat healthy meals and stretch your legs when you're done. It's better to fill up the tank when you don't need to than to need it when there's no gas station around. And most important: Never pass up a bathroom break. But carry a roll of toilet paper just in case."

Ben and Patricia, who'd joined them with the coffee, burst into laughter, and so did Avi, but she pulled her mom into a fierce embrace first. "Mom, I'm not a little girl anymore. I'm the grown woman and potential mother of your grandchildren. Believe me, I can drive two days to Augusta."

Beth hugged Avi tightly, then pulled back and blinked away her tears. "Maybe I should go with you. Your dad can handle things this weekend. I can make sure you get there safely and fly back Monday."

Patricia slid her arm around Beth. "Remember the last road trip you took, honey? You missed the turn south for Dallas and were halfway to Amarillo before you realized it. And that was in Oklahoma City."

Beth feigned righteous anger. "*I* was the driver. *You* were the navigator. *You* missed those turns."

"My point exactly, which is that Avi is smart enough and capable enough to get wherever she needs to go without any help from either of us."

Ben leaned close to Avi from behind. "That was her point?"

She took a cup from him and inhaled the incredible scents of coffee, sugar, and hazelnut. "I'm an innocent bystander. This conversation has nothing to do with me."

The two women were still good-naturedly fussing when Ben slid into the chair beside Avi, another Adirondack, this one painted flamingo pink. "You need these chairs," he remarked.

"I was thinking the same thing."

"And a big veranda to put them on."

"My tiny balcony would have to do."

"Tell me about your apartment."

She sipped her coffee, then shrugged. "It's just a regular apartment. It's right off Gordon Highway, so I rented it more for its proximity to the main gate than its features. It's got one bedroom, big windows, a small kitchen, and the aforementioned smaller balcony. The complex has a gym and a pool, and there's access to a running trail. The walls are off-white, the carpet is tan, the tile is beige, and it's got zero personality."

"You and Sadie will provide the personality."

"What was she doing while you were making coffee?"

"Watching you through the window. So was Sundance. Nyla tried to brace herself on Sundance's back so she could see, but she's too short."

She smiled at the image. The dogs had bonded so well that she would take all three of them with her, given the chance, but there was no way her parents would allow that to happen. Beth, her no-dogs-not-ever mother, was as in love with Nyla as her dad was with Sundance. As Avi was with Sadie.

Their mothers pulled up chairs, and a short while later, Neil joined them. "Halftime," he said. "We're ahead by fourteen."

"Good for us," Beth said dryly.

"Good for Joe," Patricia added. "I'd love to see him become the winningest coach in Tallgrass history, but then some bigger school would hire him away."

Avi glanced at Ben, half expecting him to mutter something like *good riddance*. He didn't, though. He didn't even let his nose twitch the way he usually did. "Maybe Lucy should marry him to make sure he stays."

The other three adults turned astonished looks his way. "*Lucy?*" his mother echoed, and Neil added, "Li'l bit?"

Ben immediately threw Avi under the bus. "It was her idea. She's the one who thinks Joe has a thing for Lucy."

That earned her astonished looks, too, but after a moment's consideration, Patricia started tapping her finger thoughtfully against her chin. "Hmm. Joe and Lucy. They *are* adorable together. And they're best friends. We all know the kind of passion that can grow from that." She gave Ben a look. "At least, sometimes. When it's right."

Avi tuned out the matchmaking conversation that followed, tilted her face up to the sky, and closed her eyes. Four weeks ago tomorrow, she'd arrived in Tallgrass hoping for a little peace, for forgiveness and laughter and a few good times. She'd gotten all that and so much more. Healing. Hope. Renewal.

A broken heart was a small price to pay for all that.

Though it hadn't finished breaking yet, she reminded

herself as Ben claimed her hand. By the time it was in pieces all around her, she might be in need of more healing. But not hope. She had enough hope to share with everyone around her.

She and Ben would be all right. Not together, but all right.

It was dark, the temperature cooled to the mid-seventies, when they said their good nights. With her nightly needs in a backpack slung over one shoulder, Avi bent to give Sadie a good rub and tell her good night. The dog whimpered so loudly that Patricia hooked on her leash, gave her a hug, and said, "Miss Sadie, you have the honor of being the first four-legged creature I've allowed inside my house. Not even Sara's yippy dog is welcome, but you're much more a lady than she is."

"Because Sara's 'she' is a 'he,' " Ben murmured to Avi as she took the leash.

After hugs and kisses all around, they strolled down the steps to the sidewalk and turned south. It was a quiet walk to the Sanderson home. What was there to say? *Please change your mind. Please come with me. For the love of God, please don't break my heart.*

He hadn't wavered, not once. He wasn't leaving Tulsa, period, end of discussion. And she *had* to leave. It wasn't a choice for her.

The earliest she could get out of the Army was in two years, and if she could live without Ben for two years, if he could live without her, what was the point? But if he was still single in eight years, and so was she...

The possibility brought very little comfort.

Though Sadie had sniffed and made use of every tree, sign, and most shrubs along the way, they lingered in the yard for a few minutes while she checked out new scents, then climbed the steps and entered Patricia's house. Dim lights shone in the living room and the kitchen and at the top of the stairs. Avi unhooked the leash and hung it over the doorknob, then started upstairs. Sadie trotted at her side, and Ben brought up the rear.

Sadie sniffed the guest room, taking particular interest in the runner beside the bed. Lifting her head, she sniffed Ben's legs, then plopped down on the runner. She associated the scent of him with comfort. Silly, but it made Avi's throat tighten.

"I'm following Patricia's rule for Sara when she was little," she said in an unsteady voice as she unzipped her dress. "I'm wearing my prettiest underwear." She slipped off the dress and struck a pose, one hip jutted forward, both arms raised over her head, turning a few times to show the minuscule fronts of the hot pink confections, along with the even more minuscule backs.

"Aw, now I feel bad. You splurged on Victoria's Secret, and I just wore my Calvins," he teased, but he didn't sound as if he really meant it. That was okay. They didn't have to pretend that everything was normal when a tidal wave of blue was just waiting to crash over their heads.

"It's not what they are that matters. It what's inside them." She unhooked the bra, shimmied out of the panties, and helped him out of his Calvins. As they kissed and embraced their way to the bed, she felt like an attention-deficient kid, her hands rambling everywhere, her kisses starting one place and ending far away. She wanted to touch, taste, feel every bit of him. She wanted to close her eyes three years from now and remember the little scar on the side of his left knee or the exact angle of his arm around her when he was asleep versus when he was awake.

They made love fast and slow, sweet and demanding, and sad, so sadly. His looks seared her skin, his kisses burned the memories deeper, his caresses were enough to make her soul weep. Before, they'd made love. This time, she realized through the sorrow and the grief, they were saying good-bye. When they were done, she wanted to curl up and cry, but she didn't. Oh, she did a lot of curling, but very little crying.

She was strong. She would survive. She would stay alive. She would thrive. She whispered that to herself a few times before sleep finally came.

Chapter 15

Damp and humidity were as much a part of Washington as earthquakes were of California or tornados across the South. At his mother's insistence, Calvin had developed a tolerance for the weather wherever he went. *You're a real boy,* his mother used to tell him on the occasions he'd wanted to play video games in the house instead of go out and play. *You won't melt, shrivel up, or blow away.* Fresh air, in Elizabeth's opinion, might not cure what ailed you, but it made you feel better.

After the chaplain's visit, Calvin had called home. He'd told his parents that things were good, had relieved their worries and stirred them up at the same time, claiming that he'd been working long hours getting ready to deploy again. They hadn't wanted to hear that, and just as he'd known they would, they'd pushed it to the back of their minds. Instead Elizabeth had asked if he was eating healthy, if he'd found a church to attend, what had happened with that pretty woman he'd met a month or two ago. He lied about the eating and the church, and the pretty woman had been fiction to start with. It had made her feel better that he had a girlfriend, so he'd created one.

Now it was Friday night, late, and something about that phone call with his parents had clicked inside him. It was time. He'd been driving around Tacoma for the last hour, pretending he didn't have a destination in mind. He turned onto a narrow, rutted street that didn't appear to have a name. It dipped beneath railroad tracks, then went two blocks before abruptly ending— no curbs, no circle to turn around in. There were houses on either side, mostly boarded over. In all the time he'd been coming there, he'd never seen a sign of life. Even the rats, it appeared, had moved on to more prosperous neighborhoods.

He pulled into the poor excuse for a park, shut off the engine, and quiet fell quickly. Closing his door created a sharp report that echoed in the pines. His footsteps crunched over too-tall grass, the damp clinging to his shoes, soaking through to his socks. The dew soaked into his jeans, too, when he sat on the concrete picnic table, his back to the street, facing the railroad tracks.

He'd known this day would come, this time when he was too tired, too distressed, too weary to go on. When the last bit of hope had fled, when he'd become a danger to himself and everyone else. He hadn't lied when he told his mother they were deploying again. That was what had led him here. He couldn't go back to combat. He couldn't lose another friend. He couldn't witness another death. He was so tired of hurting, and he couldn't think of a damn thing in life that would make it stop—

the dreams, the nightmares, the voices, the blame. That would make him feel like he had a *right* to live anymore.

Nothing could make him feel better.

But one thing could stop the pain.

Dim light filtered from the nearest street lamp. The other lights were shot out, one pole bent like a vee after a crash with a vehicle. It had been like that all the months Calvin had been coming here, like no one realized. No one cared.

In the weak light, he withdrew his weapon. After so many deployments, the heavy semiautomatic sat comfortably in his hand, an extension of his arm. He'd thought ahead: It was loaded with only one bullet in case some kid found it before the authorities found him. One round to undo all the damage the countless ones fired at him in Iraq and Afghanistan had caused. It had taken him a while to realize that a bullet that missed could kill you as surely as one that hit. This one wasn't going to miss.

For the first time in months, tears filled his eyes. They were tears of relief that, finally, he was going home. He was finding a way out. He would never hurt again. He wiped them away, gripped the pistol in his right hand, and raised it to his temple. Slowly he applied pressure to the trigger, proud that his hand remained steady, and—

Something slammed into him from behind, knocking him off the picnic table where he sat. His arm thrust out to break his fall, and his elbow cracked as a solid weight landed on top of him.

"What the hell do you think you're doing?" a young male voice demanded at the same time Calvin twisted, bellowing, "Get off of me!"

The attacker lunged to his feet, grabbed the gun, and stuck it in the back waistband of his jeans. Calvin had a harder time getting up, cradling his broken arm to his ribs.

"Man, I hope your arm hurts. That's the least you ought to have when you do something stupid—and this ain't even your neighborhood. Who the hell goes to someone else's neighborhood to blow his brains out? You think we're poor so it's no big deal?"

"It's no one's damn neighborhood," Calvin muttered, trying to find a comfortable position for his arm. Through the haze of pain, he identified a teenage boy, fourteen, maybe sixteen, with black hair and dark skin and a faint accent.

"It's *my* neighborhood, dude, and you got no right." The kid crossed his arms over his chest and scowled. He was big, six feet or so, but thin, painfully so, like his bones were too big for his body.

Homeless, was Calvin's first thought, then he amended that. *Hungry.* If Calvin had it in him to care about anything, he'd feel bad for the kid. He would take him out to eat, give him whatever cash he had. But right now he cared about only one thing.

"Give me the gun," he said quietly.

The kid was cocky. "Ain't gonna happen. Why're you here? Why didn't you do this in your own part of town?"

"It's none of your business." Calvin tried to reach into his hip pocket for his wallet, but intense pain made his breath catch, made him close his eyes and sway unsteadily, reaching blindly with his good arm for the table behind to steady him. Once the pain settled into a dull throb, he tried the maneuver again with his other hand, grunting, twisting. Sticking his left hand into his right back pocket was almost more than he could manage, but at last he fished out the worn leather wallet that had been a high school graduation gift from his parents.

He tossed the wallet on the table about halfway between him and the boy. "There's money and a debit card in there. Give me the gun, and it's yours."

The ground began to vibrate beneath their feet. In another moment, the 10:15 train was going to come rumbling through here, blasting the quiet all to hell, blowing its whistle for the crossing a few miles to the north. When it was gone, Calvin knew from experience, the quiet would seem overwhelming for a few minutes.

The kid looked at the wallet, then at the oncoming train, its light cutting through the damp air like a beacon. With Calvin's luck, he would keep the gun, take the money, and run, leaving Calvin to live another day. He couldn't bear the thought.

Without conscious thought, he grabbed for the boy, catching a handful of shirt, but all the kid had to do was shove his right arm and Calvin collapsed to his knees. Spinning, the boy ran toward the tracks, scrambling up the hillside toward the right-of-way. His feet sliding in the gravel, he threw the gun.

Calvin heard the thunk of metal on metal as a boxcar with an open door passed. The kid whooped with glee, confirming that, against odds, the pistol had landed inside the car.

Calvin sank from his knees to sit on the ground, watching hopelessly as the gun, his only chance of escape this cool, damp night, rumbled on down the tracks.

The red light that had replaced the cabooses of his childhood was passing as the boy came back. He looked pleased with himself, but not exactly satisfied—like he knew that he hadn't prevented the solution to the problem. He'd just delayed it.

"Come on." Grabbing hold of Calvin's good arm, he heaved him up. "You need to go to the hospital and get your arm looked at."

"I don't care about my damn arm." Having gained his feet, Calvin shoved the kid away, dug his keys from his pocket, and took a few staggering steps toward his car. *Why, God? Why give me the courage, the hope, the relief, then stop me like this? I should be dead now. I want to be dead now.*

The kid caught up with a few light steps, snatched the keys from his hand, and grinned. "I'll drive."

* * *

If good-byes weren't one of the hardest things in the world, would hellos still be sweet?

The thought ran through Avi's mind as she drove away from her parents' house, losing sight of her mother and father, Patricia and Sundance and Nyla and Ben, after a few blocks. Her parents and Patricia had still been waving. Ben had stood to one side, hands in his pockets. She hadn't looked at him more than a second in her rearview mirror. That wasn't how she wanted to remember him.

She had one stop to make before leaving Tallgrass, one that she'd put off as long as she could. Driving east on Main, she flipped on her signal and turned through the gates of Fort Murphy National Cemetery. Her dad had given her directions to the colonel's gravesite, one of far too many recent ones in the cemetery. She parked in the shade to protect Sadie and walked to the marble stone, still looking white and fresh, not yet showing the signs of weathering.

She stood there a long time, until a chill washed over her. She hadn't needed to see the colonel's marker to bring home the fact of his death. She'd lived with that for more than three months. But, somehow, it did just that. It made her realize that she would never see him again. Ask his opinion. Listen to his advice. He wasn't just stationed at another post across the country or around the world. He wasn't just out of reach.

He was gone. And no matter how deeply her life had been touched by his—inspired, enriched by his—she had lost him. Forever.

Tears streaked down her cheeks, and she made no effort to wipe them away. She had cried over him before—good-byes had never been easy—but every time until the last, she had known she would see him again. That wasn't going to happen in this time.

From the front seat of George's car, Sadie made a low, mournful sound. *Erooo.* Avi turned to find her leaning her chin on the door frame, her big brown eyes looking puppy-dog sad. But she followed the wail with a bark. There was a time for sadness, and a time for moving on and facing new adventures, and in Sadie's opinion, that time was now.

Turning back to the marker, Avi pressed her fingertips to the stone. "Duty, honor, country," she murmured, the U.S. Military Academy motto. Straightening, she drew back her shoulders and snapped off a crisp salute.

"At ease, sir. You're now at rest."

*   *   *

Over the next week, Ben went to work, saw patients, and did surgery, but his heart wasn't in any of it. He wasn't concentrating during the day or sleeping much at night. He couldn't count how many times he reached out in bed, expecting to find Avi there, or even Sadie or Sundance, and getting a handful of cold sheet instead. Every evening when he came up the stairs to the loft, there was a moment where he'd forget, when he'd slide the key into the lock and think *I'll be glad to see Avi* before the bleak emptiness of the loft brought him back to reality.

He knew Avi had arrived safely in Augusta with Sadie. He'd been at Patricia's house that Sunday evening when Beth called to tell them that. He had hoped Avi would call him herself, and he'd prayed she wouldn't. He'd been enough of a mess. Hearing her voice again would have been that much worse.

Not hearing her voice, he'd decided, was worst of all.

Living life without her was the absolute worst of all.

And the hell of it was, he didn't have to.

Sometime before dawn Saturday morning, he'd decided he wasn't going to. The only thing keeping him from Avi was his own stubborn self, and today he was getting out of his own way.

He'd spent much of the morning on the phone: getting airline reservations, talking to the office manager about his schedule, talking to his partners about his plans. No one had been happy, except possibly the airline that had filled one more seat, but he didn't care.

After a lifetime of taking care of others, of being the responsible one, not caring was a huge relief.

Now he had to tell his sisters, say good-bye to Lainie and the boys, and call Patricia. The first two tasks would be easy—*easy* being a relative thing—since the five of them, plus Sara's husband and Brianne's new boyfriend, were gathered around the kitchen island, eating bakery treats before the Drillers double-header started at eleven.

Though he sat in the living room, not yet having brought up the subject.

"How're you doing?" Brianne dropped down on the couch beside him, bumping shoulders with him.

"I'm okay." Looking at her sweet sympathetic smile, he reconsidered his use of the word *easy*. For twenty years, they'd been more than brother and sister, more than family. She and Sara had been the two most important people in his life, the ones he loved best and worried most about. They'd been the focus of his life for so long that he'd forgotten how to focus on anyone else. Leaving them, the family he loved so damn much, would be the hardest thing he'd ever done.

For the woman he loved, God help him, even more.

"Aw, you miss Avi." Her tone was soft, full of sympathy. "You didn't know you'd miss her this much, did you?"

He smiled wryly. "Knowing it in my head and actually feeling it in my heart are totally different things."

"Yeah, you've always been a head kind of guy when it comes to women."

They sat in silence a moment, shoulder to shoulder. Ben knew he should call Sara over and tell them his decision, but before he bothered to look over his shoulder and open his mouth, Brianne spoke again.

"Remember, when we were kids, when you were planning for college in high school?"

Curious about where she was going with this, he shrugged. "Of course I remember."

"You were going to move to Stillwater, live on your own, do all the things kids on their own in college did. Then Mom left, and Dad fell apart, and you went to OSU, but you had to commute because you couldn't leave home. You couldn't leave us. And you wanted to go to medical school at Baylor, but you couldn't do that, either, for the same reasons. And after Daddy died, you had to do your residency right here in Tulsa so you could look after Sara and me."

"It was no big deal." His family had needed him. Of course they'd come first.

Brianne scowled at him. "It was a very big deal. You settled, Ben—on your school, your residency, your practice, your life. I know other clinics and hospitals have tried to lure you away with offers doubling what you're making here. But you've always settled for what was best for us instead of what you wanted."

So *that* was where she was going with it: She was weaving a little trail to Augusta. To Avi.

He hid his smile. "Yeah, I was a little disappointed that I couldn't live in Stillwater."

"Or go to Baylor for medical school."

Or apply for a residency at Massachusetts General or the Cleveland Clinic. "I'm happy with the education and training I got. After all, my reputation is good enough to get those job offers that would double my income." He didn't spend what he already made, and his roots had been planted deep in Tulsa.

But he'd realized in all those painful moments alone that a healthy tree's roots had to spread far beyond the tree itself. If they didn't grow deep and wide, the tree would never survive the first drought or strong wind. They could spread halfway across the country—halfway across the world, if needed.

"Well, you know what, Ben? Sara and me—we're all grown up. We have jobs and homes and pay our bills and everything. Truth is, we don't *need* you the way we used to."

Overhearing, Sara left the table and came to sit on the coffee table in front of them. "Way to be tactful, Bree."

Brianne's frown matched Sara's. "You try tactfully telling someone you don't need him, O master of subtlety."

Ben couldn't help smiling at her taunt. Sara and subtlety didn't belong in the same sentence. It was a fact: Their younger sister was blunt. She didn't coax or wheedle; she demanded. There was never a question of what she wanted. She made it crystal clear from the start.

"You'll always be the head of our family, Ben," Brianne went on. "The one we go to when we need help, the one we depend on to *be* there. You'll always be in charge." Then she very softly added, "But we're grown enough now that you can be in charge from a distance."

Ben angled toward her. "Just a week or two ago, you were in my office wanting me to promise that I wouldn't move away. Why the change of heart?"

"Because now I see how much you miss Avi. Besides, haven't you heard that home is where the heart is? And your heart is *not* here. If I loved Nigel— really loved him—I'd move to Chicago with him in a heartbeat. And look at Mom. She moved new places every few years, and it was okay because she was with

George, and she would have lived on Mars to be with him. Besides—" Her voice quieted to what Ben thought of as her tattling voice. "Sara said I made the biggest fuss, so I had to be the one to undo it."

"Bree!" Sara pinched Brianne's knee, making her jump and squeal.

"Ben!" Brianne shrieked, and he automatically responded, "*Sara.*"

Sara reached out to pat his knee, and he automatically moved away to avoid a pinch. She graced him with a frown, then stuck out her tongue at him. "Listen, bubba—"

Bubba. She hadn't called him that since she was still little enough to need tucking into bed at night.

"I've got to get my tribe to the game so they can get their picture taken with Hornsby. You can come, too, but I don't think even posing with a blue bull will cheer you up. Personally, I'd prefer you stay here and pack some bags because you know what? You're not gonna be happy in Tulsa without Avi, so you just gotta go where she is. And we want you to be happy. Really. You've earned it."

With a squeeze of his knee that was a little harder than strictly necessary, Sara stood, but before she could gather the others, he caught her hand, pulling her down again. He also took Brianne's hand in his. Theirs were smaller, softer, more delicate, but every bit as capable as they needed to be. Brianne was right: They *were* all grown up. Imagine that.

"You know what?" he began, his voice unsteady. "My job is just a job. I can always get another one. And the loft…it's nothing special. But the three of us—we're always going to be together no matter how far apart we are.

So I'm taking your advice. I'm going to Augusta today, and I'm going to ask Avi to marry me, and wherever the Army sends her, I'm going, too."

Their shrieks hurt his ears as they both grabbed him in a fierce hug. He held on just as tightly for a long moment before gently disentangling himself. "I'll have to come back to settle things here, and you and the kids will have to teach me how to Skype. But right now, you'd better head over to the field. You never know how much fun you might have with a blue bull."

Once Sara and Brianne had herded everyone out, he went to his bedroom, pulling a suitcase from the back of the closet, tossing clothes into it. With his cell braced between his shoulder and ear, he called Patricia. Her *hello*, cheerful and happy and light, took him back twenty-five years and made him smile, really smile, for the first time in a week.

"Remember last Friday when you said 'Drink the wine. If someone needs you tonight, they'll just have to settle for second best'?"

She chuckled. "It sounds like something I'd say."

"You know what? In my career—my *job*—second best is good enough. I might have been named the best, but there's nothing I can do that the second-best surgeon in town can't also do. And I'll always be Bree and Sara's big brother, but I can do that long distance. I can be your son long distance." His voice got a little unsteady, and he swallowed hard to steady it. "But I'm the only man who can love Avi the way she deserves to be loved, and I can't do that long distance, not and do it justice."

His mother could get weepy faster than anyone he knew. "Oh, sweetie...I'm going to miss you so much, but it'll be the best kind of missing there is. When are you leaving?"

"My flight leaves in two hours."

"Are you surprising her?"

"Yeah. It's a kind of thing that should be done in person, don't you think?"

"I do. Call me."

"I will. So often that you'll wish I was back here so I'd leave you alone."

She choked up again. "Never, Ben."

He tossed in his toothbrush, toothpaste, and razor, then zipped his bag and started toward the door. "I love you, Mom."

With that, as he'd known she would, she burst into tears.

*   *   *

Saturday afternoon in a new town, familiar though it was, was a lonely place to be. Avi stretched out on the couch with Sadie near her feet, flipping through an insane number of channels on the television to find one that she could bear to watch for more than five minutes.

Her workdays hadn't been awful. She'd kept busy from the time she reported to the office until she drove out the main gate of Fort Gordon every afternoon. She'd become friendly with some of her fellow instructors. She'd gotten familiar with her neighborhood and spent a lot of quality time with Sadie.

Today, though, with nowhere to go and nothing to do, had been brutal.

It was okay. Tomorrow would be better. Next Saturday

she would make plans to go shopping, to a movie, or out clubbing with her new friends. Next Sunday she and Sadie would go for a long drive, maybe to Clarks Hill Lake. She, Jolie, Kerry, Rosemary, and Paulette had had a lot of good times there back when they were going through Signal school.

Realizing she'd gone through all however many hundred channels, she turned off the TV, tossed the remote onto the cushions, and scanned the apartment for something to do. Sadie had fresh water. The dishes were done. She'd vacuumed and dusted that morning, scrubbed the toilet, and done a load of laundry. She'd bought groceries at the commissary last night and had enough leftovers from lunch's takeout for dinner.

Then her gaze wandered to her phone. She could call her parents, but she'd talked to them three times already this week. She could call Patricia, but it would just make her blue. She could try to catch Jolie or Rosemary or Kerry, but surely Jolie was busy with the kids on a Saturday afternoon, and she wasn't up to figuring time differences for Germany or Korea.

Truth was, there was only one person she wanted to talk to, and she shouldn't call him. Shouldn't, wouldn't, couldn't.

Sadie lowered her front feet to the floor, stretched long and hard, then hopped off the couch and trotted to the door, where she sat politely and waited.

Despite her melancholy, Avi checked her watch, then laughed. If this was a typical weekday, she would have been climbing the stairs about now, then opening the door to find her sweet girl waiting for her. Since she was already here, she decided Sadie's behavior was a quiet request for a walk. That was the first thing she did after work every day: change out of her uniform and take Sadie out.

She stood up, stuck her cell in her pocket, and got the leash. The sun was shining, the pines that lined the trail were sweet-smelling, and schedules were good for dogs, right? After tucking the last two of the cookies Lucy had made for Sadie into her pocket, Avi hooked on the leash and walked out the door.

Her second-floor apartment opened onto a small stoop shared with the apartment across from hers, then directly onto stairs that made a straight shot to the sidewalk. She was holding the leash loosely in one hand while locking the door with the other when the dog plunged forward, jerking free and racing down the stairs, the leash a bouncing lime-green blur behind her.

"Sadie!" Gripping the handrail, Avi ran after her. The dog was so well behaved that she didn't even so much as tug on the leash when they walked. Avi couldn't have been more surprised by her behavior until she raced around the corner at the foot of the steps and skidded to a faltering stop.

Sadie was sitting in the grass ten feet ahead, not just her tail but her entire body quivering. Bent over her, giving her ears a good scratch, was Ben.

Slowly he raised his gaze from the dog to her, and a look came into his eyes that was so intense, it made *her* entire body quiver. "Hey, gorgeous."

"Hey, Doc," she said, and her voice trembled on those two small syllables. "What are you doing so far from home?"

"I'm not far at all." Straightening, he closed the distance between them, standing very, very close to her, so that all she would have to do to touch him was lift her fingers a bit. "Haven't you heard that home is where the heart is?"

Her eyes grew watery with no breeze to blame it on. "What about your career?"

"It's portable. I'm guessing people injure or wear out hips, knees, and ankles here just as much as they do in Tulsa."

Her voice got softer, wobblier. "What about your loft?"

He shrugged. "I'll probably sell it. It really won't suit us once we move back to Oklahoma. We'll need a second bedroom, and a third and probably a fourth."

Marriage. Babies. Happily-ever-after. They were going to get it, after all. Every bit of it. Just the thought made her heart do a little happy dance in her chest. "What about your sisters?"

He grinned sheepishly. "They informed me today that they're all grown up and that I can boss them as well from here as there. What they didn't mention was that they can ignore me all the more easily from here than from there."

Everything inside Avi softened and melted and turned all girly and gooey. They would be all right, she'd told herself the night before leaving Tallgrass, and she'd believed it, in a long-time-comin' sort of way. In a year or two or eight.

But he'd proven her wrong. He had left everything he loved because he loved her more. They *would* be all right, starting from this very moment, forever and ever.

She lifted her fingers those few inches and touched him for the first time in more than a week. It felt sweet and wonderful, like being made whole again after losing a part of herself. Raising her other hand to cup his cheek, she grinned a million-watt grin. "I love you, Doc."

He kissed her, the kind of kiss that made her weak-kneed and easy, that stole her breath and made her nerves tingle. Then he took Sadie's leash in one hand, Avi's hand in the other, and said, "Let's walk the baby."

His smile turned wicked. "And then you can show me just how much."

Since she had her heart broken, Bennie finds solace in her friends in the Tuesday Night Margarita Club. But when she falls for Calvin, an old friend who is dealing with his own trauma from serving in Iraq and Afghanistan, Bennie discovers that love may be the only thing that can save them...

Please see the next page for a preview of

A Chance of a Lifetime.

Chapter 1

You can't go home again, someone had famously said.

Someone else had added, *But that's okay, because you can't ever really leave home in the first place.*

Calvin Sweet was home. If he tried real hard, he could close his eyes and recall every building lining the blocks, the sound of the afternoon train, the smells coming from the restaurants. He could recognize the feel of the sun on his face, the breeze blowing across his skin, the very scent of the air he breathed. It smelled of prairie and woodland and livestock and sandstone and oil and history and home.

There were times he'd wanted to be here so badly that he'd hurt with it. Times he'd thought he would never see it again. Times he'd wanted to never see it—or anything else—again. Ironically enough, it was trying to ensure that he would never come back except in a box that had brought him alive and unwell.

He didn't close his eyes. Didn't need a moment to

take it all in. Didn't want to see reminders of the streets where he'd grown up, where he'd laughed and played and lived and learned with an innocence that was difficult to remember. He just stared out the windows, letting nothing register but disquiet. Shame. Bone-deep weariness. It wasn't that he didn't want to be in Tallgrass. He didn't want to be anywhere.

"You have family in the area," the driver said, glancing his way.

It was the first time the corporal had spoken in twenty miles. He'd tried to start a couple of conversations at the airport in Tulsa and in the first half of the trip, but Calvin hadn't had anything to say. He still didn't, but he dredged up a response. "Yeah. Right here in town."

When the Army sent troops to the Warrior Transition Units, they tried to send them to the one closest to home so the family could be part of the soldier's recovery. Calvin's mama, his daddy, his grandma and aunties and uncles and cousins—they were all dedicated to being there for him. Whether he wanted them or not.

"How long you been away?"

"Eleven years." Sometimes it seemed impossible that it could have been so long. He remembered being ten and fourteen and eighteen like it was just weeks ago. Riding his bike with J'Myel and Bennie. Going fishing. Dressing up in white shirt and trousers every Sunday for church—black in winter, khaki in summer. Playing baseball and basketball. Going to the drive-in movie, graduating from grade school to middle school to high school with J'Myel and Bennie. The Three Musketeers. The Three Stooges.

The best memories of his life. He'd never thought it

possible that *All for one and one for all!* could become *two against one*, then *one and one*. J'Myel had turned against him. Had married Bennie. Had gotten his damn self killed. He hadn't spoken to Calvin three years before he died, and Bennie, forced to choose, had cut him off, too. He hadn't been invited to the wedding. Hadn't been welcome at the funeral.

With a grimace, he rubbed the ache in his forehead. Remembering hurt. If the docs could give him a magic pill that wiped his memory clean, he'd take it. All the good memories in his head weren't worth even one of the bad ones.

At the last stoplight on the way out of town, the corporal shifted into the left lane, then turned onto the road that led to the main gates of Fort Murphy. Sandstone arches stood on each side, as impressive now as they'd been when he was a little kid outside looking in. Just past the guard shack stood a statue of the post's namesake, Audie Murphy, the embodiment of two things Oklahomans valued greatly: cowboys and war heroes. Despite being scrawny black kids and not knowing a damn thing about horses, he and J'Myel had wanted to be Audie when they grew up.

At least they'd managed the war hero part, if the medals they'd been given could be believed. They'd both earned a chestful of them on their tours in Iraq and Afghanistan.

With a deep breath, he fixed his gaze outside the windows, forcing himself to concentrate on nothing that wasn't right there in front of him. They were passing a housing area now, the houses cookie cutter in size and floor plan, the lawns neatly mowed and yellowed now.

October, and already Oklahoma had had two snows, with another predicted in the next few days. Most of the trees still bore their autumn leaves, though, in vivid reds and yellows and rusts and golds, and yellow and purple pansies bloomed in the beds marking the entrances to each neighborhood.

They passed signs for the gym, the commissary, the exchange, barracks and offices and the Warrior Transition Unit. Their destination was the hospital, where he would be checked in and checked out to make sure nothing had changed since he'd left the hospital at Joint Base Lewis-McChord in Washington that morning. He tried to figure out how he felt about leaving there, about coming here—psychiatrists were big on feelings—but the truth was, he didn't care one way or the other.

His career was pretty much over. No matter how good a soldier he'd been, the Army didn't have a lot of use for a captain who'd tried to kill himself. They'd diagnosed him with posttraumatic stress disorder, the most common injury suffered by military personnel in the war on terror, and they'd started him in counseling while arranging a transfer to Fort Murphy. Soon he would be separated from the Army, but they would make a stab at putting him back together before they let him go.

But when some things were broken, they stayed broken. Nothing could change that.

Within an hour, Calvin was settled in his room. He hated the way people had looked at his medical record, hated the way they'd looked at him. *He's a nut job, a weak one. Killed the enemy in the war but couldn't even manage to kill himself. What a loser.*

More likely, those were his thoughts, not the staff's.

He sat on the bed, then slowly lay back. He could function on virtually no sleep—he'd done it too many times to count—but sometimes his body craved it. Not in the normal way, not eight or nine hours a night, but twenty-hour stretches of near unconsciousness. It was his brain's way of shutting down, he guessed, of keeping away things he couldn't deal with. He could go to sleep right now, but it wouldn't last long, because his parents were coming to see him soon, and Elizabeth Sweet wouldn't let a little thing like sleep deter her from hugging and kissing her only son.

Slowly he sat up again. His hands shook at the thought of facing his parents, and his gut tightened. Elizabeth and Justice hadn't raised a coward. They'd taught him to honor God, country, and family, to stand up for himself and others, to be strong and capable, and he'd failed. He'd tried to kill himself. He knew that sentence was repeating endlessly, disbelievingly, not just in his head but also in theirs.

He was ashamed of himself.

But he'd do it again given the chance. The only difference would be the next time he would succeed. No public park, even if he'd never once seen anyone there in all the times he'd been, and no misguided teenage punks to intervene. Diez was the name of his particular punk. After "saving" Calvin's life, he'd stolen his wallet and car and disappeared. Some people got the Good Samaritan. He got the thieving one.

Announcements sounded over the intercom, calling staff here or there, and footsteps moved quickly up and down the hall, answering call buttons, checking patients. Calvin sat in the bed and listened, hearing everything and nothing, screening out all the extraneous noises until he heard the one he was listening for: the slow, heavy tread of his father's work-booted feet. Justice had a limp—arthritis in knees punished by years laying floor tile—and the resulting imbalance in his steps was as familiar to Calvin as his father's voice.

The steps stopped outside his door. Calvin took a deep breath and imagined his parents doing the same. He slid to his feet as the door slowly swung open and his mom and dad just as slowly came inside. For a moment, they stared at him, and he stared back, until Elizabeth gave a cry and rushed across the room to wrap her arms around him.

She was shorter, rounder, and he had to duck his head to rest his cheek against her head, but he felt just as small and vulnerable as he ever had. There'd never been a thing in his life that Mom couldn't make better with a hug—until now—and that just about broke his heart.

It seemed forever before she lifted her head, released him enough to get a good look at him. Tears glistened in her eyes, and her smile wobbled as she cupped her hand to his jaw. "Oh, son, it's good to see you." Her gaze met his, darted away, then came back with a feeble attempt at humor. "Or would you prefer that I call you sweet baby boy of mine?"

He managed to phony up a smile, or at least a loosening of his facial muscles, at the memory of her response when he'd complained about being called *son* in front of his friends. "Son is fine." His voice was gravelly, his throat tight.

"You know, I can come up with something even worse." But there was no promise behind her words, none of that smart mouth that she lived up to quite nicely most of the time. She was shooting for normal, but he and she could both see there was nothing normal about this situation.

Justice stepped forward. "Move on over a bit, Lizzie. Let a man give his only boy a welcome-home hug." His voice was gravelly, too, but it always had been, rough-edged and perfect for booming out *amen*s in church or controlling small boys with no more than a sharp-edged word.

Elizabeth stepped aside, and Justice took his turn. His hug was strong and enveloping and smelled of fabric softener and the musky aftershave he'd worn longer than Calvin had been alive. It was so familiar, one of those memories that never faded, and it reminded Calvin of the person he used to be. The one he'd liked. The one who could do anything, be anything, survive anything, and prosper.

The one he would never be again.

After his dad released him, they all stared at each other again. Calvin had never seen them looking so uncomfortable, shifting their weight, wanting to smile but not sure they should or could. His fault.

The psychiatrist in Washington had tried to prepare him for this initial meeting, for the embarrassment and awkwardness and guilt and disappointment. For no one knowing what to say or how to say it. For the need to be honest and open and accepting and forgiving.

Calvin had been too lost in his misery—and too angry at Diez—to pay attention.

Should he point out the elephant sitting in the middle of the room? Just set his parents down and blurt it out?

Sorry, Mom and Dad, I tried to kill myself, but it wasn't you, it was me, all my fault. Sorry for any distress I caused. Now that we've talked about it, we don't ever need to do it again. So…how's that high school football coach working out?

And, as an aside: *Oh, yeah, that suicide thing…I'm getting help and I haven't tried anything since. We're cool, right?*

At least, until he did try again.

His throat worked hard on a swallow, his jaw muscles clenched, and his gut was tossing about like a leaf in a storm, but he managed to force air into his lungs, to force words out of his mouth. "So…it was cold outside when I got here."

"Dropped to about thirty-eight degrees," Justice answered. "Wind chill's down in the twenties. The weather guys are saying an early winter and a hard one."

"What's Gran say?"

Elizabeth's smile was shaky. "She says every winter's hard when you're seventy-six and have the arthritis in your joints."

"She wanted to come with us, but…" Justice finished with a wave of his hands. "You know Emmeline."

That Calvin did. Emmeline would have cried. Would have knelt on the cold tile and said a prayer of homecoming. Would have demanded he bend so she could give him a proper hug, and then she would have grabbed his ear in her tightest grip and asked him what in tarnation he'd been thinking. She would have reminded him of all the switchings she'd given him and would have promised to snatch his hair right out of his scalp if he even thought about such a wasteful thing again.

He loved her. He wanted to see her. But gratitude washed over him that it didn't have to be tonight.

"Your auntie Sarah was asking after you," Elizabeth said. "She and her boys are coming up from Oklahoma City for Thanksgiving. Hannah and her family's coming from Norman, and Auntie Mae said all three of her kids would be here, plus her nine grandbabies. They're all just so anxious to see you."

Calvin hoped he was keeping his face in a sort of pleasantly blank way, but a glimpse of his reflection in the window proved otherwise. He looked like his eyes might just pop out of his head. He'd known he would see family—more than he wanted and more quickly than he wanted—but Thanksgiving was less than a month away. Way too soon for a family reunion.

His mother went on, still naming names, adding the special potluck dishes various relatives were known for, throwing in a few tidbits about marriages and divorces and new babies, talking faster and cheerier until Justice laid his hand over hers just as her voice ran out of steam. "I don't think he needs to hear about all that right now. You know, it took me a long time to build up the courage"—his gaze flashed to Calvin's, then away—"to get used to your family. All those people, all that noise. Calvin's been away awhile. He might need some time to adjust to being back before you spring that three-ring circus on him."

Elizabeth's face darkened with discomfort. "Of course. I mean, it's a month away. And it'll be at Auntie Mae's house so there will be plenty of places to get away for a while. Whatever you want, son, that's what we'll do."

They chattered a few more minutes, then took their

leave, hugging Calvin again, telling him they missed him and loved him, Justice thanking God he was home. Her hand on the door frame, Elizabeth turned back. "I don't suppose...church tomorrow, family dinner after...It would just be you and me and your daddy and Gran..."

Calvin swallowed hard, looking away from the hopefulness on her face. "I, uh, don't think I can leave here yet. Being a weekend, they're a little slow getting things settled."

Disappointment shadowed her caramel eyes, but she hid it with a smile. "Of course. Maybe next time."

Calvin listened to the door close behind them, to his father's heavy tread walking away, and his mother's earlier words echoed inside his head. *Whatever you want, son, that's what we'll do.*

The problem was, what did a man do when he didn't want anything at all? How did he survive? How did he let go? Was there any conceivable destination that made the journey worthwhile? Or was he going to suffer until the day he finally died?

* * *

Lifting as many reusable shopping bags from the trunk as her two hands could carry, Benita Ford hurried along the path to the back door of the house she shared with her grandmother. Lights shone through the windows, and the central heat and air system hunkered against the house on the back side was rumbling, meaning it would be warm and cozy inside. Why in the world had she worn a dress, tights, and her new black boots to go shopping today? She'd lost contact with her toes a long time ago, and every time the prairie wind had blown, it seemed the cold had headed straight up her skirt for a *woo-hoo* of the sort she didn't need. Jeans, wool socks, leather running shoes, a long-sleeved T-shirt, a long-sleeved sweater, and the gorgeous wool coat that reached almost to her ankles—*those* were shopping clothes.

"Brr! At least I know my ice cream didn't melt on the way home." Mama Maudene Pickering was waiting in the kitchen, ready to unpack the bags while Bennie went after the rest. The old lady wore black sweatpants that puddled over her shearling-lined house shoes, along with an orange, black, and purple Halloween sweater that was scarier than much else having to do with the day.

"I don't remember ice cream being on the shopping list," Bennie teased.

Mama shook a finger at her. "You don't want to give an old woman palpitations. But if you do, be sure to ask for good-looking firemen when you call 911."

"And you do the same for me if I ever need it." Ducking her head, Bennie rushed out into the cold again. She had another six or eight bags, along with four cases of bottled water that she had to haul in or risk finding her trunk covered in icicles the next day.

By the time she made her last dash, she was finally warm, sweating inside her clothes. She took off the cardigan that was a cute match to the dress, tossed it on the back of a chair, and began helping her grandmother.

"See anyone interesting at the store?"

"Just people hoping to get home before they froze."

"You young kids. In my day, we didn't have all the nice clothes and gloves and central heat and a grocery store just down the street."

"No, you had a sandy warm beach just down the street." Mama had grown up on the barrier islands of South Carolina, soaking in lazy breezes and running barefoot in the sand and living—at least, to hear her tell it—an idyllic life. Bennie knew it hadn't been all sunshine and roses, especially after her marriage ended in divorce. Still, it had been sweet.

"It got cold there, too, missy. I remember one time it snowed twice in one month. Almost covered the ground both times." Mama burst into laughter. "I have to admit, if I'd known more about Oklahoma weather, I might have kept on traveling a little farther west. But when I got here, the sun was shining, the air was crisp and clean, and the leaves were the most wonderful shades of yellow, orange, and red. I knew this was where I wanted to be." Her brow furrowed in thought. "That was in October, too."

"And this is its evil twin, Octobrrr." Bennie emptied the last of the canvas bags, rolled each one, and stuck them inside the largest bag to return to her car in the morning. "But warm weather will be back again soon."

"Most likely. I've worn shorts in January and a sweater in June." Mama shuffled to the refrigerator, arms filled with milk and yogurt. On her way to the small pantry, Bennie opened the door for her. Grocery shopping was a regular Saturday activity for her, and October was always her overstocking time. She'd been forced to trudge to the grocery store once years ago when snow and ice had kept their neighborhood impassable for days. She had learned her lesson. If the streets froze now, they had enough food to feed themselves and the neighbors for a few weeks. If the pipes froze, there was plenty of bottled water, and if the power went off, they had a huge supply of candles and batteries for flashlights, and firewood stretched the length of the house two ricks deep.

Bennie was prepared for anything.

"—reheat the leftover pot roast," Mama was saying when Bennie stepped back into the kitchen. "Chop everything up, mix it all up with gravy, and serve it with some thick slices of fresh white bread. Hm-*hmm*, that sounds good."

"It certainly does." Bennie put away the last of the groceries, then gave her grandmother a hug. "You know, your good cooking is the reason you and I are both on the round side."

Mama snorted. "I've been a size twelve my whole grown-up life. I should know, since I'm the one cutting the size tags out of my old clothes and sewing them into my new ones." Her hearty laugh emphasized the roundness of her face, filled with lines and haloed by gray hair and as beautiful as a face could be.

Gratitude surged in Bennie, tightening her chest. Her mother might have run off before Bennie saw her fifth birthday, and her father might have died before her tenth. She might have lost her husband, J'Myel, in the war, but she'd always had her grandmother. Mama's love was boundless and forgiving and warmed a girl's heart.

"Did you get all your shopping done?" Mama asked as she pulled the leftovers from the refrigerator, then gathered a knife, cutting board, and a large cast-iron pot. Bennie had once given her a much lighter stainless pot, and Mama had proclaimed it just what she needed before putting it away and continuing to use her cast iron, even when picking up a full pan required a grunt of effort.

"I bought a few things," Bennie replied as she wiped down the oilcloth that covered the kitchen table, then began setting it for dinner.

"I finished my Christmas shopping in July."

"Braggart."

"If you'd use the Internet, you could've finished yours already, too."

Bennie rolled her eyes, careful not to let Mama see. When the neighbor kid had shown her grandmother how to get online, Bennie had thought it would be a passing curiosity. Then the first purchase had arrived and proven her wrong. Since then, the UPS and FedEx drivers had become Mama's newest BFFs.

"Aw, you know me. I like to do my shopping in person. I want to touch stuff, see it, smell it."

Mama made a dismissive gesture with the knife. "I touch it, see it, and smell it when it gets here, and if I don't like it, I send it right back for something else."

Bennie wasn't an avid shopper, not like her friend Jessy, but she enjoyed the experience, especially when the Christmas decorations were up but the holiday was still far enough off that people weren't yet frantic. It reminded her of her childhood, of trips to Tulsa for the parade, of driving around the neighborhoods looking at extravagant lighting displays and visiting Santa Claus at Utica Square.

It reminded her of different times—not better, just innocent. She hadn't known about death and loss then. Yes, her mother had abandoned her, but her father and Mama had filled that void. Back when Christmas was still magical, she hadn't known her father would die. She'd never dreamed that her two best friends in the entire world would grow so far apart. She'd certainly never guessed that she would marry one of them, then lose him before their second anniversary, or that the other wouldn't even call her to say he was sorry.

Moisture seeped into her eyes. She could handle thinking about J'Myel or Calvin one at a time, but having them both on her mind saddened her. Them losing their bond still seemed impossible, as unlikely as Bennie deciding she no longer loved Mama. It just couldn't happen.

But it had.

And she'd been oh, so sorry ever since.

Forcing the thoughts and the loss away, she poured two glasses of iced tea, heavily sweetened the way Mama had taught her to like it, then went to her room to slip out of her boots and into a disreputable pair of loafers. Her toes wiggled in relief, her arches reveling in comfort, after a whole day in the heels. She would put herself through a lot to look good in public, but at home, comfort reigned.

By the time she returned to the kitchen, sleet was spitting against the windows, not much, the sort that said Mother Nature hadn't decided whether she was just playing with them or intended to give them a storm. Every tropic-loving cell in her body hoped for the former while every realistic one prepared to accept the worst.

Mama had filled two steaming bowls with roasted beef, potatoes, carrots, and celery and placed a loaf of warm bread between them on the table. They joined hands and said grace, a short prayer that had survived at least four generations in the Pickering family, then dug into their food. It tasted even better than it had sounded.

They chatted about nothing: the weather, the gifts she'd bought for her friend Ilena's baby boy John, the

presents they would ship to family back in South
Carolina, the Halloween decorations that were waiting a
warm spell so they could spookify the house. The room
was so cozy, the food so comforting, that Bennie was
slowly being lulled into lazy, hazy contentment. Then
Mama pushed her empty bowl away, folded her arms
on the tabletop, and leaned toward Bennie. "I talked to
Emmeline just before you got back."

So much for contentment. All it took was one mention
of Calvin's family and, poof, the turmoil returned. She
tried to hide it, to act casually as she picked up her own
empty bowl and carried it, along with Mama's, to the
sink. "How is Miss Emmeline?"

Mama didn't answer but went straight to the point.
"Her grandson's back in town."

* * *

Joe Cadore stood in front of the refrigerator, bent at the
waist, searching for something worth eating for dinner,
and had no more luck than the last two times he'd looked.
There was yogurt, protein drinks, eggs, fruit, milk, and
cheese—all perfectly fine in their place, but their place
was not on a dreary, freezing Saturday night. This was a
time for comfort foods like his mom's homemade maca-
roni and cheese, or Dad's chili and jalapeño corn bread,
or Grandma's pasta Bolognese.

This was a time for his neighbor Lucy's home cooking.

He looked out the window over the kitchen sink and
watched the ice where it glistened on tree branches and
fence wires. Lucy could have plans that didn't include a
self-invited guest. She could even be on a date. Everyone

had grown so used to her single status that when she'd started dating the doctor guy from Tulsa last summer, none of them was as shocked as she was, not even Joe. Thank God, the doc had hooked up with Avi Grant and moved out of state with her last month.

Just because the doc was gone, though, didn't mean there weren't plenty of other guys out there waiting for their shot at Lucy. She'd be the type to meet cute—someone changing a flat for her, helping her out of a tough spot, or reaching for the same loaf of bread she did—and *boom*.

Joe's feet had grown cold on the wood floor, and the reflection looking back at him in the window wore a scowl. Grabbing a protein drink and an orange, he returned to the living room, sliding over the back of the couch, landing on the cushions just as his phone rang. What his nieces called his grouchy face disappeared the instant he checked Caller ID, a grin taking its place. "Hey, Luce."

"Have you had dinner yet?"

He set the fruit and drink on the coffee table. "Nope. I looked in the refrigerator three times, and there was nothing to eat in there."

"You know, there are times when protein drinks and fruit just don't make the grade."

"Yeah, I know."

She laughed, and he wondered how long ago he had decided it was the best sound in the world. Probably the first time he'd heard it. She hadn't laughed a lot in the beginning, still mourning her husband, trying to figure out how her perfect life had come to such a screeching halt. But eventually the laughs had come, and the smiles and the grins, and they'd grabbed him and hadn't let go. Three years they'd been buddies, two years best friends. This past year... well, damn if he hadn't gotten so comfortable with her that he couldn't figure out how to move to the next level.

Her voice interrupted his thoughts. ". . . beef and cabbage stew and a loaf of rustic bread still warm from the oven, if you want to join me."

His heart rate increased a few beats. He definitely wanted. But he kept his tone casual. "And all I have to do is... What? Persuade Norton to go out in the sleet and do his business?"

"You think I would bribe you with food to take care of our dog?" she asked sweetly. "Besides, you're from Alaska. This weather is supposed to be like a mild fall evening to you."

He snorted as he pulled on the socks and shoes he'd left on the floor earlier. "Ice is cold no matter where you're from, Luce. Do you need anything?"

"I'm from San Diego, land of warm sandy beaches. I always stock up for times like these. So just you and your appetite. See you in five."

He hung up, put the drink and orange back in the fridge, then headed for the back door, where his heavy coats hung on a rack. After a minute, he turned and went to his room, throwing his T-shirt toward the hamper in one corner, pulling a clean shirt from a hanger and tugging it on.

Back in the kitchen, he slid into a down jacket, a black knit cap bearing the OSU Cowboys logo, gloves, and a scarf, then ducked out the back door. The ice on his patio crunched beneath his feet, taking on a different pitch when he reached the grass separating his house from Lucy's, then another crunch across her patio. Prisms of welcoming light shone through the fixture over her door, scattered by layers of glass.

Norton's bark was just as welcoming, a loud *woof* accompanied by frantic scratching. An instant later, Lucy opened the door and Joe gratefully stepped inside.

Her house was laid out just like his, but his never felt like hers. Incredible smells filled the air, there were homey touches everywhere, and he swore the house had a personality all its own. But maybe that was because Lucy had so much personality that it spilled over, filling the space around her.

"Hey, Luce." He crouched to rub behind the dog's ears, earning a grunt and a few thumps of tail against cabinet. "You need to go out, buddy?"

Usually, any time was the right time for Norton to sniff the backyard and renew his own scents, but tonight the dog backed away from him and the doorway, not stopping until his butt hit the opposite wall. There he slid down, chin on his paws, and kept a cautious watch on both Joe and Lucy.

"You know his last encounter with ice wasn't much fun," Lucy said as she dished up two bowls of stew.

"Not for him, though, as I recall, you got a good laugh from it." It had been last winter, and Norton had gone bounding out the door, unaware of the two inches of sleet covering everything. When he'd hit it, his feet had slid out from under him and he'd sailed halfway across the yard before an oak tree stopped him. He'd struggled to his feet, peed, and inched his way back to the house, body intact, dignity totally disintegrated.

Joe stripped off his outdoor clothes, tossing them on the kitchen table, then filled two glasses from a pitcher of water with lemon slices floating in it. He carried them to the coffee table, went back for napkins and silverware and a basket filled with thick slices of sweet, yeasty bread. The crust was golden and buttery, dotted with flakes of sea salt and rubbed with roasted garlic. It was in the running for one of his favorite foods ever.

They sat on the floor between the couch and the coffee table, shoulders bumping as they settled. In all the hundreds of meals he'd eaten here, not once had they ever used the kitchen or dining table. On the couch, on the floor, outside on a pretty day...they always chose best-buds comfort over propriety. It was just one of the things he liked about Lucy.

One of too damn many.

He really had to figure out what to do about it.

Fall in Love with Forever Romance

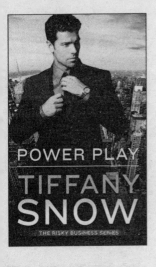

POWER PLAY
by Tiffany Snow

High-powered businessman Parker Andersen wears expensive suits like a second skin and drives a BMW. Detective Dean Ryker's uniform is leather jackets and jeans...and his ride of choice is a Harley. Sage Reese finds herself caught between two men: the one she's always wanted—and the one who makes *her* feel wanted like never before...

RIDE STEADY
by Kristen Ashley

Once upon a time, Carissa Teodoro believed in happy endings. But now she's a struggling single mom and stranded by a flat tire, until a vaguely familiar knight rides to her rescue on a ton of horsepower...Fans of Lori Foster will love the newest novel in Kristen Ashley's *New York Times* bestselling Chaos series!

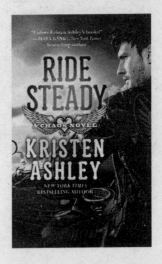

Fall in Love with Forever Romance

SUMMER AT THE SHORE
by V. K. Sykes

Morgan Merrifield sacrificed her teaching career to try to save her family's bed-and-breakfast and care for her younger sister. So she can't let herself get distracted by rugged ex–Special Forces soldier Ryan Butler. But her longtime crush soon flares into real desire—and with one irresistible kiss, she's swept away.

LAST CHANCE HERO
by Hope Ramsay

Sabina knows a lot about playing it safe. But having Ross Gardiner in town brings back the memory of one carefree summer night when she threw caution to the wind—and almost destroyed her family. Now that they are both older and wiser, will the spark still be there, even though they've both been burned?

Fall in Love with Forever Romance

A PROMISE OF FOREVER
by Marilyn Pappano

In the *New York Times* bestselling tradition of Robyn Carr comes the next book in Marilyn Pappano's Tallgrass series. When Sergeant First Class Avi Grant finally returns from Afghanistan, she rushes to comfort the widow of her commanding officer—and ends up in the arms of her handsome son, Ben Noble.